Evelyn waited a couple of minutes then crept back inside, glad to escape the keen eyes of the spectating neighbours. Ina was on her knees, picking up the remains of a shattered plate from the grubby floor. She was pale and grim-faced but sounded calm when she spoke to her daughter.

'I suppose you heard all that so there's no point in you arguing with me either, Evelyn. Tammy's moving in and that's all there is to it.' Ina looked at her daughter's tense face, sighed and hauled herself to her feet. 'Look, Hen, I know fine what you're thinking but I need his money and the weans need a strong man about to keep them in line.'

'But he's . . . he's horrible,' Evelyn stammered.

'He's a working man, just like the rest of them round here. Just like your father was!' Ina's temper flared dangerously again. 'He's no better and no worse than the rest of them, I'm lucky he'll take me and the weans on. If it works out all right we'll likely get wed. And I don't want you messing this up for me, Evelyn. Do you hear me?'

'Aye, Mam, I hear you well enough,' Evelyn said, grabbing her coat and disappearing into the early morning mist.

Anne Vivis was brought up in Fife, East Scotland, the setting for this and her previous novel, *Daughters of Strathannan*. She married a Scot and they now live in Warrington, Cheshire.

Also by Anne Vivis
and available in Mandarin

Daughters of Strathannan

ANNE VIVIS

The
Lennox Women

Mandarin

A Mandarin Paperback
THE LENNOX WOMEN

First published in Great Britain 1993
by William Heinemann Ltd
This edition published 1994
by Mandarin Paperbacks
an imprint of Reed Consumer Books Ltd
Michelin House, 81 Fulham Road, London SW3 6RB
and Auckland, Melbourne, Singapore and Toronto

Reprinted 1994

Copyright © Anne Ramage 1993
The author has asserted her moral rights

A CIP catalogue record for this title
is available from the British Library

Printed and bound in Germany by
Elsnerdruck, Berlin

To Bill
With love

Also for my parents for all their support
And to Deborah and Steven, just for being you

Is there for honest poverty
That hings his head, an' a' that?
The coward slave, we pass him by –
We dare be poor for a' that!
For a' that, an' a' that,
Our toils obsure, an' a' that,
The rank is but the guinea's stamp,
The man's the gowd for a' that!

Then let us pray that come it may, –
(As come it will for a' that) –
That Sense and Worth o'er a' the earth,
May bear the gree an a' that.
For a' that, an' a' that,
It's comin' yet for a' that,
That man to man, the world o'er
Shall brithers be for a' that!

Robert Burns

ONE

Evelyn Lennox had a crush on George Innes. Unaware that he had been singled out for her determined attentions, George's attitude was one of supreme indifference. Evelyn realised she was making little progress but, a victim of the romantic infatuation rampant among teenage girls in pursuit of their idealised male, she couldn't keep away from him. This particular afternoon found her striving to look her very best in the hope that, this time, he might notice her.

Peering into the dingy mirror which was propped precariously over the range, she brushed her thick, dark hair vigorously. Her lively brown eyes glinted back at her in anticipation. Accepting that she could do nothing more to improve her appearance without arousing her mother's ready suspicion, she tore herself away from her own reflection and pressed her nose against the sooty window pane. Clouds scudded threateningly across the heavy sky. Evelyn glared at them as if she could drive them back by the sheer force of her will. Rain would spoil everything, kill any chance she had of seeing George and then it would be next week before she got another afternoon off.

With barely concealed impatience, Evelyn waited until her mother went to take in the washing, strung on ropes between the two parallel rows of miners' cottages, then slipped out of the back door. Glancing over her shoulder to be quite sure her mother hadn't noticed her stealthy escape Evelyn picked her way through the small vegetable plots behind each tiny dwelling and made for the village centre where she met up with her three closest friends.

Lively, determined and with a surety of manner which positively demanded that less confident individuals follow her, Evelyn was the undisputed leader of their small group. When she announced that they would, yet again, walk down to the sawmill, no one had the nerve to voice any objection. Self-assured, attention-seeking and animated despite the obvious poverty of their clothes the four girls sauntered through the ugly, grey village, bright sparks of youthful vitality bringing temporary relief to their cheerless surroundings.

Evelyn led them past the austere, granite kirk with its blank, unadorned windows and locked doors, then walked a further hundred yards down the narrow country lane before taking a forbidden short cut through the grounds of the whitewashed chapel. Being all of the Presbyterian persuasion, even daring to set foot on Catholic soil felt like a sin. They kept their heads down, not even glancing up at the lovely stained-glass window, the ornate gravestones and especially not at the candle-lit figure of the Virgin Mary, set just within the open doors of the tiny church, so missing the only things of any real beauty in the whole village. A gap in the elderly fence led out on to a rough, woodland path. They scrambled through and eventually emerged on the twisting lane which led, half a mile further on, to the coast. Just past the stagnant pond, around which the village men gathered for curling contests during the winter, at the point where the salty tang of the sea began to win its battle with the heavier, cloying taste of the pits, was the sawmill, and their quarry.

If the weather was mild, and even if it was not, George Innes could usually be found here, stripped to his trim waist, feeding huge logs through the vicious saws as if they weighed nothing at all.

Evelyn and her cronies distributed themselves along the mossy wall in a well-practised pantomime of absolute indifference. Nor did George and the other young sawyers appear to notice the girls. They certainly, and mercifully, couldn't hear their high pitched giggling over the scream of the machinery.

Evelyn was alone in her admiration for George but she always made a point of being as different from everyone else as she possibly could. At five foot eight he was smaller than his workmates by a good three inches. Nor did his chest and arm muscles bulge in that blue-veined way she found so repulsive. His was more of a sinewy strength, his slender, economical body giving no more than a rippling hint of the power it concealed.

Evelyn would have been perfectly content to sit on that damp wall for hours at a time, always hoping for some small sign of interest from George, but her friends were impatient now, eager to join the other youngsters back in the village. Throwing one last coquettish look at the unappreciative object of her desires, Evelyn started for the village, her disappointment hidden under a brash show of indifference.

In less than five minutes they were back at the village centre. Craigie was a mining community. The original houses had been built by the mine owners in the last century and most were still exactly as they had been fifty years ago, lacking all modern amenities. The village was inhabited almost exclusively by colliers and their families, united by the common complaints of low pay, long hours and harsh conditions. Only half a mile inland, Craigie was a scar on the soft countryside and had nothing in common with the charming fishing villages which dotted the coast of Strathannan, attracting day trippers who would have been appalled by the stark grimness of this village and its three sisters.

The sooty, acidic stench of the pits was everywhere, in the air, in the water, polluting the breath of the miners themselves. Even after bathing at the pithead, Joe Lennox, Evelyn's father, came home with coal ingrained into the creases of his face, giving his skin the texture of an old orange over the unhealthy pallor caused by too many long hours underground.

She hated it. Feared the way he coughed coal dust from his lungs; despised the way his tall frame stooped, rounded at the shoulders after a lifetime of hewing coal in a space no bigger than a coffin; loathed the smell of his damp trousers hanging to dry in the close confines of the kitchen-cum-living-room-cum-bedroom that constituted one half of their tiny, damp dwelling; detested the blackened houses which looked as if they had been constructed from the coal dust itself and deeply resented the ugly scars the foul pits and unsightly bings made on the rolling Strathannan countryside. But no one else seemed to understand the way she felt. To her family, her friends, it was all natural, an unquestioned part of their lives. Some, like her father, even saw beauty in the grim pitheads and wonder in the machinery there.

That was why Evelyn admired George Innes so much. Last year she had overheard him telling her brother, Jackie, that he never wanted to go down a mine, that he always wanted to work in the open air, to always be able to see the sky above him. Jackie's reply had been scornful. Real men, strong men, worked in the pit. Any other way of earning a living had simply never occurred to him.

Evelyn and her friends joined a group of youngsters who habitually congregated on street corners. An hour passed in general horseplay but, as dusk fell damply, the crowd gradually dispersed. Always one of the last to leave, Evelyn made her slow way home, reluctant as ever to face her mother's persistent bad temper.

The Lennoxes lived on the very edge of Craigie in the long, dark lines, or rows, of single-storey miners' cottages, built more than a hundred years ago. They were overcrowded, unhealthy dwellings, lacking even the most basic facilities and were frequently much worse on the inside than even their mean exteriors suggested. In the half-light of evening the cottages merged into sinister shadow, relieved only by the eerie, yellow glow of dull light through narrow, sooted windows. The oppressive atmosphere was exacerbated by the fug of smoke which hung over them like a permanent, foul, reeking mist.

The knowledge that she and her family stayed in the roughest, poorest part of the village and were generally looked down on by the more fortunate residents of the new council houses, all of which boasted inside toilets and more than one bedroom, was an unending source of shame to the bright, proud child.

She trudged between the two dingy rows, trying to dodge oily puddles. Mud oozed over her stout, much-repaired shoes. The pall of smoke and dampness captured the pervasive stench of the privies, forcing it down her throat with every breath. Nowhere was it stronger than outside her own home, almost at the end of the row and sunk in a damp hollow caused by the subsidence of the ground over the mine-workings below. She reached her front door and slipped inside feeling the familiar slump in her spirits.

At the sound of the door her mother turned from the range. Even in the gloom of the poorly-lit room Evelyn knew her expression would be sour.

'About time too!' Ina Lennox greeted her only daughter. 'And where the hell do you think you've been? You know I need your help with the weans. Here,' she flung a sour cloth at Evelyn. 'Finish cleaning them up. When you've done that there's bread on the table and soup in the pot.'

Flinging her coat on to the boys' bed with all the others, Evelyn sighed and resignedly rolled back her sleeves, ready to tackle the unrewarding task of washing two of her three younger brothers. It wasn't easy. Unlike the newer houses in the village there was no running water to the rows. Every drop they used had to be collected from the communal standpipe. Consequently, in this house at least, water was used as sparingly as possible. It was, she thought glumly, a case of diluting the muck on their hands and faces and redistributing it in yet another grey layer.

The boys, five-year-old Matt and four-year-old Alec, were equally resentful and complained noisily, as they did every night.

'Can you not keep them quiet?' their father roared from the shadows of his chair where he was trying to enjoy his only smoke of the day. 'Shut your faces and hold still for your sister or I'll leather youse.'

The boys retreated into wriggling silence while Evelyn sorted out the coats and blankets which covered their mattress.

'Good lads,' their father chuckled and ruffled their hair fondly as he tucked them up. They grinned, knowing that their sins would have to be serious indeed to earn them more than a good shouting and the occasional cuff about the ear.

'Hurry and get your supper, Hen,' he smiled at Evelyn who attacked her rapidly-cooling meal ravenously.

'Get a move on, Evelyn. The wean's needing fed.' Impatient as ever, Ina whipped the bowl away before Evelyn had quite finished eating. By now the screams of the youngest Lennox had reached desperation pitch. Evelyn scooped her year-old baby brother from the floor, perched his damp backside on her knee and spooned soup ruthlessly into his gaping mouth. The child spluttered, choked, swallowed and beamed with contentment.

'Do you have to be so rough with him?' Ina snapped.

Evelyn scowled but wisely kept silent. William clapped his little hands. 'More,' he demanded.

A blast of chill air swept through the little house. Jackie, the eldest son, hurried in, tossing his coat carelessly on to the bed and getting himself into a chair at the table in one fluid movement. He greeted his family with his customary, terse grunt then stuffed bread and soup into his mouth before his father could catch the tell-tale whiff of beer on his breath.

Within an hour they were all in bed. The boys all in the kitchen on a rough, home built bed while Evelyn had the luxury of her own sleeping space, a mattress curtained off from her parents in the second room. The baby slept on the floor at his mother's side of the household's only proper bed, though, if he cried in the night, Ina always called Evelyn to see to him.

From the other side of the dividing curtain came the familiar, regular creaking of the bed, punctuated by grunts, groans and heavy breathing. Evelyn buried her face in her pillow and dragged the threadbare blankets over her head. At this rate, she thought sourly, she would soon be forced to share her own bed to make room for another baby.

The men had long gone to work when her mother roused her, well before seven the next morning. While Ina dressed, Evelyn wakened the boys and ladled out their porridge, spooning the watery, salty mess into William's eager mouth as she gulped down her own portion. That done she washed her hands and face in the dregs of water from the kettle, dragged a comb through her tangled hair and hurried out to work before her mother could find another task to delay her.

Outside, the ground was white and hard with frost. The mud had set into vicious, icy ridges which made her slip and slither as she picked her way into the village.

It was barely seven-thirty when she arrived at Craigie's only shop, her face stiff with cold, her fingers waxy-white and without feeling, her ears aching. Anxious to get every penny of value for the meagre wages she paid, Mrs McPhee immediately set Evelyn to weighing out flour, ready for the day's business. But the girl's hands were so numb that the first bag slipped from her grasp, bursting open on the floor. Mrs McPhee yelled angrily about the waste and promised to dock the value of the spilled flour from Evelyn's wages. Evelyn bridled then apologised meekly enough, careful to keep her own sharp temper well under control. She was extraordinarily lucky to have this job and knew there was no shortage of girls who would willingly step into her place if she gave the McPhees cause to dismiss her. That, Evelyn was determined, would never happen, no matter how unpleasant the older woman might be. Jobs were hard to find and most of her friends worked long hours in the textile mills in Inverannan, seven miles and an expensive bus ride away. To her mind that was little better than working in the pits.

Today was Saturday, the busiest day of the week, and the most enjoyable as the village women, their menfolks' wages snug in their purses, lingered to chat while they made their purchases.

But then, around mid-morning, quite suddenly, the shop emptied. The silence that followed was unnatural, unsettling.

'Well, I'm sure I don't know what's wrong with everyone today.' Mrs McPhee shook her grey head, perplexed by the phenomenon, then rounded on Evelyn. 'Don't you dare stand there doing nothing. Cut some cheese and then

8

get the tea and sugar weighed out. Whatever's wrong with them now they'll be back in their dozens later.'

Evelyn was glad enough to escape into the back shop where she busied herself conscientiously at the sacks, well away from the woman's scolding tongue and watchful eyes. When the bell over the shop door tinkled she looked up. Two women came in, well muffled against the cold with shawls over their coats and scarves protecting their heads.

Even in good times the life of a miner's wife was a hard one. The appalling living conditions they endured made their impoverished existence even grimmer. Faces were drawn, hands were rough and minds resigned. For many women the daily trip to the village shop was their sole source of entertainment, an opportunity to swap complaints, to sympathise over common ills and to avidly speculate about their neighbours. But these women's faces were blank and shocked-looking, their shawls pulled closely round them, their very posture speaking of some horror too great to be fully comprehended. The stifled, whispered conversation was so unlike the usual, busy chatter that it claimed Evelyn's instant attention. She felt her heart lurch into her stomach in instinctive fear and dropped the flour scoop back into the sack before going to stand silently at the counter. Six shadowed eyes flitted over her then looked away again. It was as if they were embarrassed to face her.

'What's wrong?' she asked, her voice not quite steady.

'Och, Lass . . .' Mrs Tonner, a gaunt woman of about her mother's age, glanced at her. Evelyn wasn't sure what she saw in her eyes. She hoped it wasn't pity.

'It's your father, Hen,' Mrs McPhee muttered. 'There's been an accident. At the pit . . .' The normally strident grocer's wife spoke in a whisper. This was what the whole village lived in dread of.

9

Evelyn stared, her brown eyes wide with horror, her mind reeling back to the tales her grandmother liked to tell of the last disaster, the one which had killed her grandfather and two of his brothers. She actually felt the blood drain from her face and saw the counter lurch away from her.

'Away home, Lass. Your mother'll be needing you.' Some kind soul draped Evelyn's coat about her shoulders.

'Best not keep your mother waiting, Hen. Off you go now.' Mrs McPhee shoved her between the shoulder blades.

Evelyn stumbled with the force of it then seemed to jerk to her senses. Without another word she brushed past the watching women and ran out of the shop. The village was strangely quiet. Women and children huddled in tight groups in front of their homes as if they didn't know what to do or where to go, shock stark on every face. Evelyn raced past them all, not attempting to find out more, and didn't stop until she reached the rows.

Her mother, fine hair dishevelled, coat awry, baby William wrapped in her shawl and clutched tightly to her chest, stood outside their house with their neighbour, Mrs Rankine.

'They said Daddy . . .' Evelyn panted.

Her mother nodded, her face already devoid of hope. 'And Jackie,' she whispered.

'Now, Hen, don't go getting all upset. It's much too soon for that and we still don't know exactly what's happened.' Mrs Rankine put a motherly arm round Ina's shoulders. 'All we do know is that there's been an explosion,' she explained to Evelyn, when Ina seemed unable to tell her daughter for herself.

As she spoke a thin line of women and children started to trail past, taking the shortest way out of the village to the Dene colliery. Their shoulders were hunched, their eyes blank and they walked in silence.

The baby still wrapped to her chest, Ina joined them, seeming to forget about the rest of her family. Evelyn started after her then remembered Matt and Alec. Darting into the house she grabbed their coats and wrestled her uncomprehending brothers into them. Then, a child firmly in each hand, she, too, joined the sombre procession.

Hampered by the boys it took her more than half an hour to reach the Dene where her brother and father, along with most of the village men, worked. Unusually, the colliery gates stood wide open and a large crowd had already gathered in the yard. Evelyn searched desperately for her mother and finally found her with a group of neighbours, most of whom had husbands or sons underground.

'What's happening?' she asked.

Ina didn't seem to hear her.

'We only know there was an explosion. The rescue squad has already gone down,' Mrs Rankine repeated the little she knew.

'Is Daddy one of the missing ones?'

'Aye, Lass, it looks as if he is.'

'And Jackie, too?'

Mrs Rankine nodded her greying head. Ina turned away.

'What about Mr Rankine and the boys?'

'Nae, Lass.' The stout woman smiled at the child's concern. 'They're on backshift this week. Thank God. They'll be taking their turn with the rescue, though.' The smile twisted as sudden tears sprang to her weak, blue eyes, a mixture of pity for the Lennoxes and relief that her own family were all safe.

Evelyn swallowed her own tears, knowing they were useless, and shivered. Matt started to cry. She bent to lift him up, grateful for something to take her mind off the black prospect which faced them all. Angry at being ignored Alec, too, set up a miserable wail. Mrs Rankine scooped him into her own ample bosom.

Ina stared at the pithead, oblivious to her children's needs, isolated by fear, unaware of the other women, almost as if this tragedy was hers alone. Evelyn spoke to her again but Ina stared back as if she didn't recognise her own daughter. Hurt, longing for comfort and reassurance, Evelyn clasped Matt even closer but only succeeded in making him complain.

The low, blackened buildings and the massive, looming wheels of the pithead were ominously silent and still. The crowd seemed frozen and stood now in hushed, motion-less groups. Only the crying of the children broke the cold tension.

It was more than an hour before there was a sudden hiss of steam and the gear at number one pit screamed into action. The noise seemed deafening after the heavy silence.

It was as if the world held its breath while they waited to see what the rising cage would bring. A team of hel-meted men emerged from one of the many single-storey, brick buildings, picks and shovels in their hands.

'Is there any news?' a woman pleaded, as they filed through the crowd.

The leader shook his head mutely and hurried on, urging the others quickly up the wooden steps to the waiting cages.

The crowd muttered and milled restlessly, fearful and frustrated by the lack of information.

'There's Cowan!' someone whispered. The name was instantly taken up by the crowd who pressed towards him.

The colliery manager hesitated in the doorway of his

office, seeming uncertain, but he knew he couldn't avoid them for much longer, knew he owed them this much at least. At last he shuffled forward, keeping his eyes down so that he didn't have to read the fear he knew would be mirrored in his own face.

'Can you not tell us what's going on down there, Mr Cowan?' Mrs Rankine called, lingering respect for authority moderating her tone.

'Aye! We've a right to know!' someone supported her, followed by a general roar of voices.

Cowan raised his hands, looked up at last and the crowd fell silent at once, straining to catch anything he said. 'I'll tell you what I know,' he mumbled. A hand strayed to the tight collar of his sweat-stained shirt and he made a visible effort to straighten himself, to appear detached, businesslike and in control. Whatever the outcome he knew he would be held responsible for what had happened here today, by these people at least.

'What about Arthur Cree?' a woman yelled.

'John McDowell . . . Alfie Kennedy . . . Sam McHarg?' The names, all familiar to Evelyn, seemed endless.

Ina merely stared, grey and lifeless.

'I've made a list of the missing men. If a man's name is not on this list then that man is not missing.' Cowan responded to the anger he felt rising round him. His tone was brisk now and stern, forbidding interruption. 'Do you all understand?' he demanded. 'Only the men whose names are on this list are missing.'

The crowd stilled again, edging closer to hear him more clearly.

'The rescue team has been down for nearly three hours now and more men are on their way. We are doing everything we can to get these men out safely.' He cleared his throat once before reading slowly through the list. Forty-two men and six boys.

As he finished the wheel at number two shaft, fifty yards away, ground into action with a low clank and hiss. At the same time a group of miners emerged from the stricken number one pit. It was the first rescue squad, so exhausted that they could barely make their way down the steps and through the crowd. They looked studiously ahead or at their feet, anywhere but into the anxious, waiting faces.

It was Ina who abruptly stirred and voiced what everyone else was thinking: 'Have you found anyone? Are they alive?' she demanded, her voice shrill and on the very edge of hysteria.

'Nothing.' A huge collier shook his blackened head and walked slowly on.

'Nothing!' she screamed after his drooping back. 'Go back . . . get back . . . are you too scared to help them? Is that it? Get back . . . Get back there . . .'

'Nae, Lass.' A gentle arm anchored itself firmly round her shoulders and drew her back. 'They've done their best. Let them rest.' Joe Lennox's only brother, Harry, who had himself lost a hand in this very pit, kept his good arm round Ina. 'They're all doing the best they can.'

It was already more than four hours since the explosion.

The short winter day faded into evening. The pit was illuminated in garish yellow light. The bursts of steam from the engines and the steady plume of smoke from the furnaces seemed ghostly against the dark sky. The November evening was bitterly cold.

Someone fetched tea and bread. The children, fed but cold and fretful, dozed fitfully in the arms of Mrs Rankine, Harry and Ina.

Ignored by her mother and uncle, who were both too preoccupied to spare a thought for her, Evelyn was badly frightened and chilled to the marrow. But not even for one moment did she consider going home. Not yet. Not while they still didn't know. She adored her father, the steady rock which had been the anchor of her childhood. How many times had he defended her from her mother's fierce temper, helped her with some hated chore or slipped her the odd copper from his pocket? He was her one reliable ally in a world which frequently seemed harsh and unfair. She couldn't even begin to imagine what life would be like without him. She closed her eyes, forcing her mind to see the unrelieved blackness underground, trying to will her father, and Jackie, to live, to emerge unscathed. But images of dead and dying men, all horribly maimed, forced their way into her tired brain. Her father . . . Jackie . . . it was too hideous. She couldn't let herself linger on the awful possibilities which moved closer to reality with each passing minute. Stifling a sob of rising panic she opened her gritty eyes again, yearning for a warm arm of comfort to slide round her shoulders. But it was as if she didn't exist for the other three. Slowly she moved further away from them, then crouched down in the shadowed shelter of a sooty wall, to wait.

It was eight o'clock before the first stretcher was brought up. The hushed crowd parted to let it through. The lumpy figure was shrouded in blankets. They all knew what that meant.

'Alfie Kennedy.' The name was whispered through the crowd. The new widow covered her face with her hands and wept silently as she was led away.

Three more stretchers followed. All bearing dead men. All villagers. All known to the Lennoxes. Four women and seventeen children without a husband and father to love and support them.

Then there was nothing. The crowd which had been silent while the bodies passed through, grew restless. A further hour passed before the pithead doors crashed open to reveal another team of blackened rescue workers.

Behind them Cowan, in a rough jacket, heavy trousers and helmet and as begrimed as his men, came tiredly towards the waiting relatives. He stopped in the glow of a yellow lamp, a lonely, illuminated figure, facing an accusing crowd which seemed all the more threatening because they were hidden by the shadows of evening. Harry moved forward, ready to confront the mine manager. But there was no need. Cowan knew what was expected of him.

'There is no more news,' he said, his voice hard with fatigue.

'What about the others? Where are they? What's being done?' Harry moved a step closer now, anger and impatience sharp in his voice. 'We've a right to know what's going on, Cowan.'

Cowan swayed where he stood. Behind him the other mine officials stood back a little, anonymous in the dark, forcing him to deal with this alone. He ran a hand over his face, leaving streaks in the coal dust.

'I'll tell you all I know, though God knows it's little enough,' he offered. 'There was a major explosion in number two section of the Rainbow seam. The roof is down. The dead men were on this side of the fall. The missing men were either caught under the fall itself or are trapped at the face. There is no way of knowing whether they are alive. We're trying to dig a way through and a team from Blairwood pit has gone down number two shaft to try and break through from that side. It's slow work. The roof is unstable and there's gas down there.'

If anything the silence deepened. They all knew the dangers of gas in the workings.

'We are doing everything we can.' He was almost pleading with them now, begging for their understanding. 'It may be hours yet but we are doing everything that is humanly possible to get those men out.'

No one really doubted that. The exhaustion on the faces of the rescue team spoke for itself.

'So, all we can do is wait?' Harry asked.

Cowan nodded and Harry moved aside to let the mine manager pass.

'What caused it?' an angry voice demanded, when he had almost reached the sanctuary of his own office.

'Gas, we think. But we can't be sure . . . it's too soon.' Cowan escaped, closing his door on them gratefully.

Now it started to rain. A slow, soaking, miserable drizzle. The women hunched infants closer into their wet shawls and pulled older children into the shelter of their skirts.

'Come on, Hen. Away home. I'll wait on here until we hear something more.' Harry attempted to ease Ina out of the crowd.

'NO!' she jerked away from him.

'The bairns, Hen. They shouldn't be here. They'll catch their deaths in this rain.'

Ina peered at Alec and Matt, both shivering, as if only just realising they were there. 'Take them home, Evelyn,' she ordered, hardly interested in them.

'No, Mam. I'm staying too,' the girl insisted. 'They'll be all right for a while yet.'

'I'll take them. I'm not fit to stand round here all night with my chest being what it is,' Mrs Rankine offered, coughing wheezily to emphasise her point.

Gently she loosened Ina's shawl and extracted the fretful William, wrapping him securely to her own generous bosom. The two older boys allowed themselves to be led away without protest.

'If there's no news by morning I'll fetch youse down something to eat,' she called back as she picked her way through the black puddles of the yard.

Ina ignored her, already staring back at the pithead

where the wheels were spinning again, taking fresh men below ground.

Hours passed. A little after midnight two more men were brought to the surface. Both dead. But, half an hour later two stretchers appeared. As they were carried down the steps the lights gave a glimpse of pale, coal-streaked faces. These two were alive! The women pressed closer, eager to find their loved ones. Ina forced her way to the front then drew back, her face bitter with disappointment. Neither of the two survivors were Lennoxes.

'Are there others alive down there?' Harry grabbed one of the rescuers and forced an answer.

In his blackened face the man's eyes gleamed eerily white. 'Those two were lucky,' he coughed. 'In a pocket of the fall, protected by a waggon. They were the only two there. As far as we can tell, the rest are all on the other side of the fall, at the face. We're not through yet. There's no knowing how big the fall is, but we shouldn't be long now,' he added, throwing them back some hope.

The crowd lapsed into exhausted silence. Some clung together, propping one another up. Others, like Evelyn, squatted against the dark, damp buildings. Fear and fatigue were plain in every line of each drooping body but no one slept. Evelyn shivered and leaned back against her wall watching Ina who still stood in the centre of the yard, swaying gently, never taking her eyes off the pithead, refusing to move to a more sheltered position and resolutely ignoring everyone, even her daughter. The fourteen-year-old girl had never felt more frightened, nor more alone.

Sometime before dawn the rain stopped and the temperature plummeted. The puddles turned to ice. Evelyn was numbed. Only the regular white cloud of breath from her nostrils convinced her she was still alive. Around her white frost settled on the shoulders and hair of the waiting women.

'You'll have to go now, Lass.' Harry, his moustache white with frost, turned impatiently to Ina. 'You'll freeze to death if you stand there like that.'

'No,' it was whispered but emphatic, final.

'Don't be foolish, Hen. I'll come for you as soon as . . .'

His words were cut short by an ominous, low rumbling which seemed to come from under their very feet, from the walls of the buildings, from the pithead itself.

Cowan's door burst open. The manager, flanked by half a dozen other officials, raced from the building, ignoring the crowd, and clattered up the wooden steps towards the cages. After a minute, when everyone watching seemed paralysed by fear, the crowd surged wildly forward. Voices could be heard screaming, some women sobbed, others, like Ina, seemed unnaturally calm. Activity at the pithead was frantic. Booted feet clattered over boards, orders were shouted, the wheel span, and again, then stopped. And then there were thirty long minutes of absolute silence.

At last Cowan appeared on the steps. He seemed shrunken when he faced them, clutching the rail for support, trying not to see the hope, the despair, the fear in the faces which looked up at him through the early dawn light, willing him to give them the good news they all knew was impossible now. When he was able to speak his voice was little more than a hoarse whisper. They all strained to hear his words.

'Another explosion . . . the whole working collapsed. Rescuers just broken through to the trapped men. Three injured and on their way up . . . Fire . . . No hope for the others. Two rescuers from Blairwood pit killed . . . further rescue attempts impossible at this stage.' He choked and turned back to the pithead.

Behind him a stretcher came into view, a second one close behind it. A third survivor was helped to walk unsteadily towards the steps. The crowd peered through the hoary dawn, eager hope distorting every face as they shoved forward. This was their last chance.

The stretcher cases were both unconscious, but alive. Evelyn gripped her mother's arm and felt Ina's fingers digging painfully into her wrist as they stared at the first, bloodied face.

'Davy Spowart,' Ina whispered.

'Aye,' Harry agreed. 'And the other one's Alfie Mathie.'

Evelyn hardly heard him. Her attention was on the bent miner who was managing to walk down the steps with just one man supporting him. With his darkened face, filthy trousers and coal-covered jacket he was difficult to identify but, as he passed directly under a light, she knew who it was.

'Jackie!' she screamed, tearing herself away from her mother and dashing towards him.

He faltered then stopped on the bottom step and stared at her, his face blank and traumatised.

She tried to speak but nothing came.

Ina forced her way through the crowd and shoved her daughter harshly aside. 'Thank God,' she cried, her hands going to her son's scorched face.

Jackie seemed to come to himself at his mother's touch. For a minute they faced one another, then, heedless of the coal which coated him, she drew her son to her and hugged him close as she hadn't done since he was an infant. At last he broke her grip and pushed her back a little.

'Your daddy?' she whispered, already knowing what his answer must be.

He shook his head slowly. 'No, Mam. No. None of

20

the rest of them had a chance. Father was already dead. Only seven of us survived the first blast.'

Ina pushed him away angrily then threw her head back and screamed, a long, unearthly keening sound which Evelyn was to remember for the rest of her life.

TWO

Craigie, which had lost thirty-five men and five boys in the Dene colliery disaster, emerged from its mourning to face the slightly unreal prospect of war. At Easter, Hitler invaded Czechoslovakia and, on 3rd September, Britain declared herself to be at war with Germany. Then, on 28th October 1939, a German bomber was shot down while flying over the Firth of Forth. Suddenly the war was a terrifying reality.

Engulfed by a shock wave of patriotic fever several of the younger men enlisted. Jackie chafed, anxious to join them, but he was too young. Before he reached his eighteenth birthday there was already talk of conscripting men into the pits to satisfy the urgent need for coal to fuel the war effort. So Jackie stayed at the Dene, working a seam less than a mile from the one which had entombed his father and so nearly claimed his own life.

Evelyn's attitude to the war was one of selfish resentment. Thanks to Hitler all the attractive, ambitious young men had disappeared leaving no one on whom she thought it worthwhile to exercise her considerable charms.

She was a sturdy, vivacious girl with pinkened cheeks, bright, dark eyes, strong limbs and a well-developed figure. Her hair curled attractively round a mobile face and bounced with her pert, lilting walk. The smile which brightened her expression was an earthy, frank acknowledgement of her natural assets. She glowed with health and vitality. Nothing, not even the demands of her embittered mother or her tiring job, could drain the vast energy which emanated from her. But it was the type of energy which led her to become quickly bored and restlessly impatient. Especially with the boys who did try to court her. Few had the pleasure of her company more than once. They were all miners and she despised them as one for not having the ambition to strive for something better, as she did.

Not that Evelyn had the time, or the inclination for socialising. She had lost her job in the local shop when she was forced to stay at home and care for her mother and brothers in the aftermath of her father's death. Now, with three other girls, she herded and milked the cattle on a local farm, replacing the regular labourers who were all either in the army or at the coal faces. Hard though it was, the job had been a godsend to the Lennoxes. With three growing lads to feed and clothe and only Jackie's youth's wage coming in, things had been almost impossibly difficult since Joe's death, even by Craigie's hard standard. Joe's brother, Harry, and his kind-hearted wife, Hettie, had done all they could, passing down clothes for the children and vegetables from their small plot of garden but, because of Harry's crippled arm, their own circumstances were too strained for them to give financial help, especially when Ina's reaction to their generosity was one of bitter umbrage. Knowing very well that Ina, who had defied her own family to marry Joe, had no one else to turn to, they persevered. After all, she was family and entitled to all the support they could give until she recovered from her tragic loss.

Evelyn's pay was negligible but she and the three other girls who worked at Cairns Farm were regularly and well fed by the farmer's wife who mothered them as if they were the daughters she had never had. Evelyn, who was the only one of them who didn't live in, was often given a can of fresh milk or half a dozen eggs to take home for her brothers. Ina accepted these gifts greedily but with no obvious gratitude.

Evelyn's working day was long. Always, she was up and picking her way across the fields before the sun rose. Only rarely was she home before it sank again. Even then there was still the burden of the heaviest household chores which now fell on her strong shoulders. Gone forever were those carefree evenings of hanging around on village corners with her friends. Gone, too, were the whispered secrets, the innocent flirtations and the teenage crushes. Such activities were the preoccupation of children, the prerogative of kids. These, and all other childish things, had been irretrievably lost, exchanged for the unwelcome, uneasy responsibility which had come with the premature catapulting into adulthood, caused by the death of her father.

Joe Lennox's death had left its tragic mark on every member of his shattered family. Jackie, recovering quickly from his own injuries, seemed to draw into himself, preferring the company of his peers to that of his own family. He shied away from his new position as head of the household, understanding, even without his mother's constant, bitter remarks, that he could never fill his father's place. Shamefully aware of the inadequacy of his wage he worked as many shifts as he could in an effort to deflect some of his mother's criticisms with hard cash and came home only to eat and sleep. Most of his free time was spent in the bar of the Greyhound. The younger boys, confused then hurt by their father's abrupt disappearance from their lives, took advantage of the sudden lack of discipline and their mother's apathy to run wild, secure in the knowledge that even the angry complaints of the neighbours could sting no response from her.

Sunk in a trough of depression, Ina Lennox was increasingly lethargic. She wasn't a Craigie woman but had come here from her home on the coast to marry Joe. And only Joe had made this dark, dirty village bearable. Without him to make her efforts seem worthwhile she became slovenly. The most kind hearted of women, Hettie, Ina's sister-in-law, persisted, even in the face of Ina's belligerence, to help where she could, setting a thin stew on the fire in place of the never-ending, watery soup which was all Ina could rouse herself to make, mending the boys' clothes and even washing dishes. But, at her ungrateful, abusive worst, Ina made it plain that she considered Hettie's well-intentioned help to be a gross invasion of her privacy and ordered her out of the house.

The cottage, always a nightmare to keep decently clean, became little more than a hovel to which Evelyn was too ashamed to bring her friends. The uneven floor was seldom swept, the range was dull with old grease and the two narrow windows were opaque. The resultant, perpetual gloom hid the worst of her neglect but did nothing to raise the spirits of those who were forced to live there. Ina showed no pride in her family and had little interest in anything outside her own self-pity. She spent her days in a slow, mechanical performance of the lightest, most essential household tasks and then in trance-like contemplation of the mean fire which struggled to burn in the choked grate. The results were obvious in the condition of the boys. Poorly fed on an unvarying diet of thin soup and stale bread they were gaunt and dirty with frequently upset stomachs, permanently running noses and old eyes.

At first Evelyn sympathised with her mother. Her own grief was too raw to leave room for criticism, the void in her life left by her father's death, unfillable. But, as the months and then a year passed and still Ina made no effort to rouse herself the sympathy curdled into resentment.

Looking back Evelyn could always pinpoint the precise moment when she realised just how much her mother had changed, how desperate their situation really was. It was on the night she arrived home, unexpectedly early, to find Ina lounging in the cottage's only easy chair, a cigarette dangling from lips which were still red stained from the remnants of a liberal coating of lipstick. To Evelyn's certain memory the only time her mother ever wore make-up was at Hogmany. She could recall her father saying he didn't like to see his wife 'a' paintit up'. As for smoking, only the men smoked and these days there wasn't enough money even for Jackie to have more than a couple of hand rolls a week.

'There's soup on the boil,' Ina waved in the general direction of the range.

Evelyn wondered why her mother's voice sounded so slow and lazy, almost slurred, nothing like her usual, sharp whine, but before she had time to ponder the question the door creaked open and the younger boys slipped into the house.

'Can we come in now?' Matt asked, his bare legs made even more spindly by his huge, tackety boots. Despite the cool, damp weather, he wore no jacket, only a thin, sleeveless pullover on top of a filthy shirt. His hands and legs were streaked with ingrained grime worse than any miner, his eyes shone, too brightly, from a thin, urchin-like face crowned by hair which stuck up and out in matted spikes.

'You should have been in hours ago,' Evelyn scolded. 'Get those hands washed. Your supper's ready,' she added, going to stir the ubiquitous soup pot.

The glutinous, yellow mess adhering to the side of the blackened pot and burning on the bottom, sickened her. She sniffed at it suspiciously, gagged as her stomach heaved and rounded furiously on her mother.

'This is disgusting! Could you not have made some fresh? We've been eating this muck for days. It's gone

26

bad . . . God, it smells like a midden.' She threw the ladle back into the pot and glared at her mother who simply shrugged her shoulders.

'I put a fresh onion in there this morning,' she said, eventually. 'Anyway, what's it to you? You get well enough fed up at that farm. Don't come and complain to me about the food here. I haven't got the money to feed youse like she does.' She ground out her cigarette and edged the stub under the filthy rug as she spoke.

'Aye. I get fed, but the bairns don't and they need more than this. And what about Jackie! How's he supposed to work a full shift on a dish of sour soup?'

Ina dragged herself rather unsteadily to her feet, an angry flush staining her sunken cheeks. 'When Jackie's earning a man's pay he'll get a man's meal. And you're getting above yourself, my girl. The food in this house was always good enough for you before you started working for Mrs High and Mighty up at that farm.'

'It was always fresh before,' Evelyn retaliated.

'Nobody's forcing you to eat it,' was the savage retort. 'I've not got the money to spare for the fancy food she feeds you.'

'No money for decent food!' Evelyn scoffed. 'But you've enough to throw away on make-up and cigarettes!'

She got no further. Ina's hand flew back and caught her daughter a resounding slap across the cheek. The boys looked on in awed silence.

'That'll teach you to show some respect for your mother. While you live in this house you'll mind that tongue of yours. Now, see to the boys. I'm gey tired.' With that she flounced out of the room.

Mindful of the three pairs of watchful young eyes, Evelyn bit back an angry reply and swallowed tears of humiliation which flooded her eyes. Carefully keeping her back to her brothers she busied herself with some withered potatoes.

'Fried tatties in half an hour,' she snapped. 'Now, get your clothes off until I give youse all a good wash.'

She vented her anger on the boys' filth, rubbing their hair vigorously with a bar of coarse laundry soap and rinsing them off in cold water. Thin, shivering bodies were energetically scrubbed with a rag dipped in tepid water. Their nails, knees and knuckles were still not truly clean but at least they smelt better, she thought, as she hustled them into fresh clothing.

An hour later she was tucking them into bed.

'You make sure you're all home before it gets dark the morrow,' she told them sternly.

'We came home tonight,' Matt protested, wiping his runny nose on one of the coats which covered their bed.

'Aye,' agreed Alec.

'But Mammy had a visitor and told us to get out and play.'

'What visitor?' Evelyn asked, surprised.

Matt shrugged. 'Just a man.'

'What man?' Evelyn demanded, astounded.

'Don't know. Not the same man as yesterday. A different man.'

Evelyn opened her mouth to ask another question then thought better of it. 'Anyway, she didn't mean you to stay out so late,' she said instead.

'She did so,' chimed in William, agreeing with his big brothers.

'She said we weren't to come in until we saw you coming home,' Alec explained.

'And we were only playing. Honest,' Matt added, a cheeky twinkle in his eye which was anything but reassuring.

'All right. Just make sure you stay out of trouble. I

28

don't want to hear any more complaints from the neighbours about the three of you. And no playing round the burn. Youse might fall in and drown.' She rumpled three dark and passably clean heads then planted a soft kiss on each. William's eyes were already drooping.

She sighed. God alone knew what her mother was thinking of, letting the boys run wild like this.

The next morning Evelyn woke with a sore throat and heavy head. Outside it was damp and chill. Pausing only long enough to gulp down a cup of hot tea to warm her for the long walk up to the farm she wrapped her thin coat round her and set out well before it was light.

She struggled gamely through the early morning tasks but before two hours had passed her head was thumping, her nose streaming and she felt thoroughly wretched.

'You should have had more sense than to come out feeling like that,' Mrs Cairns scolded her fondly when she handed round the morning tea. 'How will I manage up here if you give that cold of yours to the other lassies? Away home, Hen. And take these scones and the rest of this milk with you.'

Kindly but firmly she ushered Evelyn out. 'Don't worry about coming back until you feel better,' she called after her. 'We'll not go under just because you're not here for a couple of days.'

It was a long, hard walk over the fields to Craigie. The mist wafting in off the Forth settled over the rolling fields making Evelyn cough and struggle for breath as she clambered up the hill overlooking the village which sat dank and unwelcoming under an even heavier pall of smoke than usual. By the time she reached the rows she was burning with fever and aching in every limb. All she wanted to do was crawl into bed.

Gratefully she shoved the battered door open. 'It's me, Mam,' she called, then stopped, her mouth agape.

In the cottage's only decent chair sat a man and sprawled indecently across his lap was her mother. The front of her blouse was hanging open and one of the man's hands fumbled obviously inside it. The other had disappeared up her skirt. Ina's face was caked in make-up and a cigarette dangled casually from her hand. When she saw her daughter her face dropped in a way that might have been comical under different circumstances.

'Evelyn! Hen! What are you doing home at this time of the day?' she asked, squirming to disengage the man's hands then sliding awkwardly off his lap, leaving him to struggle with his trouser buttons but not before Evelyn had seen what protruded stiffly from them.

'You said we'd be alone,' he accused Ina petulantly.

'I didn't know she'd be home,' she hissed back.

Evelyn found her voice at last. 'I'm not well. Mrs Cairns sent me home.'

'You look all right to me,' was her mother's unfeeling response.

The man grunted something and hauled himself to his feet. He was small and weasel-faced, unshaven and still with the dirt of the mines ingrained in his hands and face. Even from the doorway, Evelyn could smell the animal-like stink which emanated from him. Her stomach churned.

'I'm sorry about this, Ronnie,' Ina glared at her daughter with a complete lack of sympathy. 'Come back the day after tomorrow. It'll be all right then.'

The man grunted again, tossed a handful of coins on to the table then shoved past Evelyn and out of the house.

'What was Ronnie Roberts doing here?' Evelyn demanded, slamming the door after him. She knew Ronnie, one of the village's more unsavoury characters, was married.

30

She had gone to school with one of his unfortunate daughters.

'None of your business,' Ina retorted, quickly scooping up the coins. 'If you're not well, away to your bed and get yourself better. We can't afford for you to take time off and well you know it.' She ended the conversation by retreating to the privy.

Shocked and ill Evelyn fell into bed.

Basically a healthy and resilient girl Evelyn recovered from her cold easily. As her temperature returned to normal, so too did her temper. After all, she reasoned with herself, it was three years since her father's death and her mother was entitled to have some friends of her own. And there was always the possibility that having a man friend would restore some sense of pride, give Ina a renewed interest in her home and family. Evelyn refused to allow her mind to dwell on the significance of that handful of casually-tossed coins. But her equanimity didn't last long.

It was well after nine on Friday night and pouring with rain when Evelyn arrived home, startled to find the place in complete darkness. Even the fire had been allowed to die. She shivered. There was no sign of her mother, or the boys, and Jackie would be home any minute, expecting a hot meal before he went out on the night shift. Hauling off her wet coat she raked out the choked grate and set a fresh fire, then wasted fifteen minutes encouraging the damp kindling to catch. As soon as a half-hearted flame was licking through the coal she put a pot of stovies on the hob, using the last of the potatoes and some corned beef she found at the back of the larder. It was already ten o'clock and still there was no sign of her mother or the boys. It was just possible but highly unlikely that her mother had taken the boys with her, wherever she had gone. Ina never took her family anywhere if she could avoid it. Outside it was raining even harder. Angrily she shoved on her wet coat and set off to her Uncle Harry and Aunt Hettie's cottage, at the other end of the rows.

'Sorry, Lass, they're not here. I did see your mother going past, all dressed up, just before midday I think it was,' said Hettie, who seemed to keep a mental record of the comings and goings of the whole village. 'She didn't have the laddies with her though.' She was about to close her front door on her niece but then, realising the injustice of holding the young girl responsible for her mother's faults, relented and said, 'Harry's away for a drink. He'll be back in half an hour. If you've not found them by then, come back and he'll help you look for them.'

'Thanks Aunty Hettie. I'm sure they'll turn up before then. You know what the boys are like.'

Hettie nodded. She, like everyone else in the rows, knew only too well that her nephews were the wildest, cheekiest and dirtiest children in the village. It shamed her to have them greet her in the street.

Still angry rather than truly worried, Evelyn tried all the boys' usual haunts without success. Finally, she knocked at Mrs Rankine's door.

'Ah, there you are, Hen. If you're looking for the laddies, they're here,' she said, ushering Evelyn inside.

'Thank goodness. I've been looking everywhere for them.' Evelyn sighed with relief as she followed the older woman into the house. It was identical to their own but she might have been in a different world. The Rankines were colliers too and little better off than the Lennoxes, but it was clear that this woman took great pride in her home. Although the furniture was old and well used, it was obviously cared for and the whole place gleamed. The atmosphere was homely, inviting and as different from her own drab, depressing home as it was possible to be.

Matt and Alec were sitting on the spotless linoleum which covered the floor, playing with some model cars which had once belonged to one of the Rankine boys. William was curled up in a chair and fast asleep.

'Thanks for looking after them, Mrs Rankine. Mam forgot to tell me you were having them today.'

'Your mammy doesn't know they're here, Hen. She wasn't home when the older two got in from school. William's been roaming the streets all day and he's only three years old yet. He's got a right heavy cold too. By rights he should have been tucked into a warm bed. I had to take them in . . .' she sighed. 'I don't like to criticise, Lass, but I don't know what can have got into your mother, leaving them like this.' Gently she woke William and slipped his coat on.

'Where is my mother, Mrs Rankine? Did she not tell you she was going out?'

'I haven't spoken to her for weeks, Hen.' Evelyn couldn't miss the tight curl of disapproval on the older woman's lips. 'Now, get these weans home to their beds. They've already had their supper.'

Evelyn felt her face colouring with shame. She knew all too well that the Rankines' food rations could not easily be stretched to feed three extra, hungry mouths.

'I'm sorry,' she stammered. 'I didn't know or I'd have asked Mrs Cairns to let me away early.'

'It's not your fault, Lass! The boys are your mother's responsibility, not yours and I know you do your best . . .' She left the rest unsaid.

Seething with anger Evelyn got the boys to bed just as Jackie arrived home. As usual he was not quite sober.

'Stovies! Braw!' He attacked his meal with relish. 'It's ages since Mam bothered to make anything decent.'

'She didn't bother today either. I made it,' Evelyn snapped.

'Well,' he challenged belligerently. 'What of it? Don't make an issue out of one, wee meal. You're a woman, that's what you're supposed to do, make meals, keep house, look after the family. You'd know what work was all about if you had to go down the pit like me.'

'Make meals, keep house . . . ?' she spluttered. 'As well as doing a man's job on the farm I suppose? I work as hard as you do, Jackie, and so do plenty of other women these days.'

'Don't you talk to me like that!' He was on his feet in an instant, shouting back. 'I'm the head of this house so show some respect!'

'Respect?' she scoffed. 'For you . . . fresh from the Greyhound . . . half your wages already drunk.'

A sudden racket from outside put a premature end to what threatened to be a violent argument. A woman's shrill laugh and the deeper guffaw of a man who had had much too much to drink silenced them. Furiously Jackie threw open the door giving Evelyn a glimpse of her mother, huddled into the unsavoury shelter of the privy wall, her arms tangled round a disgustingly unkempt man who was kissing and fondling her with unbridled, drunken pleasure.

Slowly realising they were being watched they reluctantly pulled apart. The man threw a drunken leer in Ina's direction then shambled off down the rows. Ina took half a second to pat her bedraggled hair and rearrange her clothing before lurching into the house.

'What are youse staring at?' she demanded, stumbling over the edge of the rug and banging into the table.

'Where the hell have you been?' Jackie bellowed. 'And who was that?'

'None of your bloody business,' his mother screamed back, slurring her words and groping her way to the bedroom.

*

34

If Evelyn thought that night was bad, what waited for her a week or so later was infinitely worse. Tired by the week's work and looking forward to a day off she let herself into the house a little after ten at night. The room was in darkness, the younger boys already fast asleep while Jackie was out somewhere. Her mother's coat, hanging behind the door and her shoes, discarded in front of the range, suggested that Ina, too, had retired for the night.

Evelyn smiled to herself, delighted at the prospect of having some time to herself. Quietly, so as not to wake the boys, she brewed some tea, drank it slowly and let herself slip into a rare state of total relaxation before creeping through to the bedroom she shared with her mother.

She stopped just inside the door, halted by a strange, musty smell that stirred vague memories of those active, noisy nights when her mother and father had indulged in personal, intimate acts within feet of the younger Evelyn's wide-awake body. Stunned, Evelyn peered into the gloom then inched towards her mother's bed. Ina's sleeping form seemed huge and lumpy but gradually became clearer and more defined as her daughter's eyes adjusted to the dark. Even after she understood that there were two bodies in the bed, Evelyn crept on, compelled to see exactly who was occupying her father's place. To her absolute disgust it was the revolting man she had glimpsed with her mother the other night. Now he slept, pressed into Ina's back, his mouth hanging open against her shoulder. Shuddering silently Evelyn backed away. She spent the night trying to sleep hunched over the kitchen table, her head cradled uncomfortably in her arms.

It was barely light and she was still dozing fitfully when the bedroom door crashed open. Clad only in his working trousers and boots, his flabby stomach hanging grossly over the top of his pants, the man stomped through the room and out to the privy.

35

'So you slept out here then?'

Evelyn span round at the sound of her mother's voice. Dressed in her best nightdress, a cigarette already hanging from her lips, Ina regarded her daughter without affection.

'I'm needing to talk to you, Evelyn,' she coughed, sinking into the opposite chair.

'About him?' Evelyn nodded balefully towards the open doorway where the man now lounged.

'His name's Tammy. Tammy McGurk and he's going to be living here from now on.'

'Living here?' Evelyn repeated incredulously.

'Aye. So you'll need to take your bed somewhere else.'

'Where?' Evelyn demanded angrily, surveying the already overcrowded kitchen.

Ina shrugged, not really caring.

'Does our Jackie know about this?' Evelyn asked, glaring at the coarse man who hawked and spat for her benefit.

Ina flushed and muttered, 'He's moved in with Hettie and Harry.'

Evelyn felt sudden envy for her brother but knew that with three little girls and a baby boy of their own there would be no room for her at her uncle and aunt's home. Nor was there space for her at the farm. 'I wish there was somewhere for me to go,' she spat angrily.

Ina laughed. 'Well there isn't. Hettie won't take you, too. It's Jackie's wage she's after. In any case, I need you to help with the boys so you'll just have to make the best of it here, won't you?'

'Are youse getting married?'

'That's none of your bloody business so don't go giving me that snotty-faced look of yours.'

Tammy McGurk lurched back into the room. 'That's enough,' he ordered, obviously fed up with their bickering. 'Get me something to eat.'

Evelyn pointedly turned her back but Ina shot to her

feet and produced bread and an enormous chunk of cheese from the furthest depths of the larder.

'Is that all I'm getting?' he snarled.

'That's all there is,' Evelyn snapped, interrupting her mother's incipient apology. 'And it's more than I get.'

The slap of his huge hand as it landed on the table jarred her into silence. Tammy McGurk's bloodshot eyes glared malevolently at her from either side of a bulbous nose. The boys, woken by the noise, sat up and watched in sleepy-eyed fascination.

'I'm the one who says what's what in this house from now on. Is that plain enough for you, Miss?' he roared. 'And I'll not take lip from the likes of you. As long as I'm paying my word's law. And that goes for the lot of you,' he added, glaring at the boys who stared back then nodded their heads in silent unison. 'That's for the house,' Tammy said, moving his great hand aside to reveal a small pile of pound notes and his book of food coupons. 'I'm away to fetch my stuff. When I get back there's to be a decent meal on the table. Understood?'

'Aye, Tammy. Thanks. There'll be a braw supper waiting for you the night.' Ina's hand closed like a vice round the money which then swiftly disappeared into the bodice of her nightgown. The door thumped as Tammy McGurk left.

Ina took herself quickly into the bedroom and slammed the door before her daughter had a chance to say anything. Evelyn slumped at the table then jumped when the outside door crashed open.

'Where's your mother, Hen?' Harry, his face flushed with anger, demanded.

'In the bedroom, Uncle Harry. I'll get her for you,' Evelyn offered, stumbling to her feet.

'Save your energy, Lass.' Ina had heard Harry's noisy entry, had even been expecting him to call on her this morning. 'If you're here to poke your nose into my business, Harry Lennox, then you'd best not waste your breath.' Ina took the initiative, and advanced on Harry with anger flashing in her eyes.

Evelyn held her breath. Harry Lennox bore a superficial resemblance to his dead brother but on a bigger, more volatile scale. He was a sterner man than her father had been, one who was guided by what he perceived as his duty, rather than by any instinctive goodness of his heart. It was duty which had brought him here in this intimidating, towering rage today. But Ina, equally furious, was more than a match for him.

'Away outside, with the boys, Lass. What I have to say to your mother is not for young ears.'

It was kindly enough said and Evelyn knew better than to disobey him. Hastily she bundled her brothers into their clothes, hacked off a hunk of bread and cheese for each child and ushered them outside. Delighted to have their freedom so early in the day the lads instantly forgot the tension inside their home and raced off to play in the grass at the end of the rows. Evelyn leaned against the wall, waiting to go back inside to wash and have a cup of tea. To her intense mortification the raised voices issuing from behind the closed door must have been audible inside a dozen neighbouring houses.

'Your behaviour is the talk of the village,' Harry roared. 'I never thought to see such shame in my own family. My own brother's wife, nothing more than a common prostitute!'

'Liar!' Ina screamed.

'Is this the way to bring up your children? Selling yourself to any man who will have you?'

'Get out of my house, Harry Lennox . . .'

'And now this! The final insult to Joe's memory. How could you?'

38

'I don't know what you're talking about,' Ina lied.

'Tammy McGurk! Tammy McGurk! That's what I'm talking about. The whole of Craigie is talking about you and Tammy McGurk.'

'Then the whole of Craigie would do well to mind its own business,' Ina retorted acidly.

'I'm warning you, Ina, if you let Tammy McGurk move in here, to live in sin with you, me and my family will never speak to you again. No decent person will want to be seen with you, or your children. For God's sake, Ina, think of them,' he bellowed.

'What right have you to come here and tell me what I can and can't do?' Ina spluttered, almost incoherent with rage. 'Think of the boys! Why the hell do you think I'm doing this? It's not for me. It's for them. Without his money they'll starve. Is that what you want?'

'You shame my brother's memory. Joe was a decent, loyal man, show some respect for him . . .'

'Don't you talk to me about Joe. He was the best there was, Harry Lennox. A better man than you'll ever be . . .'

'And this is how you honour his name . . . You're a common slut, a disgrace. Even your own son can't stand to live with you . . .'

'Get out . . . Get out.' There was the sound of breaking china as something crashed against the door. 'Get out of my house,' Ina screeched.

The door opened and Harry backed out. 'I've tried to help you, Ina. Now you can go rot in hell for all I care,' he bellowed at her as his parting shot. He was scarlet-faced and sweating when he hurried past Evelyn, ignoring her in his haste to get away.

Evelyn waited a couple of minutes then crept back inside, glad to escape the keen eyes of the spectating neighbours. Ina was on her knees, picking up the remains of a shattered plate from the grubby floor. She was pale and

39

grim-faced but sounded calm when she spoke to her daughter.

'I suppose you heard all that so there's no point in you arguing with me either, Evelyn. Tammy's moving in and that's all there is to it.' Ina looked at her daughter's tense face, sighed and hauled herself to her feet. 'Look, Hen, I know fine what you're thinking but I need his money and the weans need a strong man about to keep them in line.'

'But he's . . . he's horrible,' Evelyn stammered.

'He's a working man, just like the rest of them round here. Just like your father was!' Ina's temper flared dangerously again. 'He's no better and no worse than the rest of them. I'm lucky he'll take me and the weans on. If it works out all right we'll likely get wed. And I don't want you messing this up for me, Evelyn. Do you hear me?'

'Aye, Mam, I hear you well enough,' Evelyn said, grabbing her coat and disappearing into the early morning mist.

THREE

For all his crude manners and coarse habits, Tammy McGurk had a surprising soft spot for the boys who accepted him without the faintest sign of rebellion or resentment. Tammy was strict, never hesitating to take his belt to them if they needed it, but he was also fair and astonishingly patient. He took them for long walks to search for birds' eggs, played endless, noisy games of football and spent hours fashioning inexpert wooden forts and castles for them. Even Evelyn, who hated him implacably, had to admit that he was good for her younger brothers.

She had quickly recognised in Tammy McGurk a will as strong as her own. She loathed him with every fibre of her being, resenting him for taking her dead father's position in the household, and wasn't afraid to show it. Her open hostility soon earned her the status of unwelcome interloper in an otherwise contented family and drew nothing but criticism. Fed up with the hostility which emanated from her, Tammy wanted nothing more than to be rid of her moody, censorious presence. He accused her of laziness, selfishness, dishonesty, conceit and, worst of all, jealousy of her own mother. When all that failed to drive her away he resorted to other, even more underhand tactics.

The boys were frequently sent outside so that he and Ina could have some privacy, a commodity in short supply in the rows, but Evelyn soon understood that Tammy was actively searching for opportunities to embarrass her and it seemed that her mother was helping him. More than once she returned home, at her normal time, to find them engaged in some act of intimacy in the kitchen, where she couldn't help but come upon them as soon as she walked through the door. The growing suspicion that these incidents were planned with her humiliation specifically in mind, sickened her. The man disgusted her and, she was no longer ashamed to admit it, her mother did too.

The knowledge that Tammy took lecherous pleasure in openly ogling her own ripe body angered her but not as much as his habit of parading noisily through the kitchen, where she now slept, on his way to the privy, stark, staring naked and making absolutely no attempt to hide his private parts from her. It had got to the stage where she slept with her head smothered by the pillow. Suffocation was preferable to the risk of opening her eyes to the nauseating sight of his flaccid equipment.

Evelyn would have given five years of her life to escape but remained firmly tied to her home by the knowledge that there was simply nowhere for her to go. There was no room at the farm and her meagre wages were pounds short of what she would need to support herself independently.

One morning, about two months after Tammy had moved in, she was disturbed by his usual early-morning visit to the privy and then kept awake by the unrestrained noises which subsequently issued from the room behind her. Finally she abandoned all hope of getting back to sleep and set off for the farm a full hour earlier than normal, glad to let the early summer sunshine go some way towards restoring her spirits.

She took the road used by the miners on their way to the Dene and occasionally had their silent company for part of the way. Today she found herself being cheerfully greeted by the subject of her adolescent fantasies, George Innes. She hadn't given him a thought since the day her father died.

'Hello, George, I've not seen you for a long while,' Evelyn responded eagerly, surprised to see him in the unmistakable dress of a miner. 'I didn't know you were working in the pits.' It was disappointing to see that even George, the idol of her adolescence, had abandoned his ideals and followed all the other young men of the village down the pit.

George Innes had always liked Evelyn, fancied her really, but had been too unsure of himself to even risk talking to her in the past. A year of working in the pits and the good-natured banter that went with it had given him some confidence. 'I'd not much choice in the matter. I was conscripted. But I suppose it's better than having to join up and getting blown to bits by the Germans. So, they gave my job at the sawmill to some old man and sent me down the pit,' he said, his deep loathing of the mines clear in every angry syllable, fuelling an immediate surge of relieved admiration in Evelyn's heart. 'I've been working at Blairwood for a year but I was transferred to the Dene last week,' he added, explaining why she hadn't seen him here before.

'Will you stay in the mines when the war's over?' she probed.

He grimaced. 'No! I hate it! Dark, dirty . . . All day bent double in a pool of filthy, stinking water hacking away at a wall of rock nearly half a mile underground, always expecting the whole lot to come down round your head. Och, I don't understand how anyone could want to work in a pit, Evelyn. In winter you never see daylight. I liked the sawmill better. No, as soon as this bloody war's over I'm going to find myself a decent job. I'm going to get out of the pits and I'm never going back. I couldn't

43

stand to spend all my days down there like some of them do.'

There was nothing he could possibly have said which would have impressed Evelyn more. She had been right all those years ago. He was different from the other boys. He had ambition, wasn't content to accept life as it was thrown at him any more than she was. It struck her that of all the boys she knew he was the only one who might offer her a way out, a life away from the mining villages and, above all, away from her mother and Tammy McGurk.

In his pit boots, over-sized, shabby trousers and shapeless jacket he was smaller than she remembered. His sandy hair was shorter than before, making his face seem gaunt but the effect was softened by an expression of permanent good humour which lifted his mouth and warmed his pale eyes. And there was something else different too. Evelyn tried to study him without seeming too obvious. Then she saw what it was. The smooth cheeks of youth had disappeared under a soft haze of sandy stubble. George Innes was, she realised with a sudden bubbling in her stomach, no longer a boy, but a man. And all the more attractive for that.

'What are you doing here at this hour of the day?' he asked.

She smiled up at him, blushing slightly and wishing she had taken more care with her appearance. 'I work up at Cairns Farm. It's an early start.'

'Mind if I keep you company, then?'

'If you like but I only go as far as Lane End. I cut over the fields from there. It's quicker.'

They walked the next half mile in near silence.

'I'll wait for you tomorrow morning if you like,' he offered casually, when their paths divided.

It was her day off but she wasn't going to throw away

44

this chance to get to know George Innes better for something as minor as that. She turned her very best, brightest smile on him. 'Thanks, George. I'd like that.'

He was waiting for her the next morning and for a full week after that, but then he was on a different shift. She missed him.

George Innes had invaded her mind for the second time in four years. She thought about him constantly, glad he was so different from the other boys. Some of her friends rather cruelly said George was 'slow' but, she reasoned, they were only displaying their own ignorance. George was simply quiet and thoughtful, not loud-mouthed and crude like so many of his contemporaries who never thought further than the pit in working hours and the Greyhound in the evenings. No, George was simply biding his time until he could get out of the mines and really make something of himself. On his own admission he had left school at fourteen barely able to read or write, preferring to use his hands rather than his brain. She didn't care about that. Her own formal education had come to an abrupt halt on the day she turned fourteen and she wasn't any the worse for it. Anyway, George had so many good qualities that his lack of schooling was of no real importance. Education wasn't everything and with her at his side to encourage him he was certain to land a clean job with good prospects after the war, maybe in Inverannan or, better still, in Edinburgh or Glasgow. Anywhere so long as it was away from Craigie.

It was a relief to be with a boy who didn't feel the need to brag brazenly about the number of pints he had sunk on a Saturday night, or to try and impress her with the tons of coal he had shifted that week as the other boys invariably did, as if brute strength and drunkenness were qualities which would make them in any way attractive.

Something else she admired in George was his even temper. Nothing ever seemed to upset him. If something went wrong he simply shrugged his shoulders in his boyish way and said, 'There's no point in getting all worked up over something you can't change.' That always made her smile.

But, underneath these mainly happy thoughts, Evelyn felt a small niggle of disappointment. George hadn't said anything about seeing her again. Every morning she rose early and set out for the farm a full hour before she had to in the hope of meeting him and every morning when he wasn't there her heart sank to her stomach, souring the whole day for her. But Evelyn Lennox wasn't that easily defeated. She had set her mind on George Innes and she wasn't going to let him slip away without a fight. If she still hadn't seen him by her next day off she decided that she would simply spend the day hanging around near his house until he appeared. If George wasn't sufficiently interested in her yet to want to intensify their friendship, she would nudge him along until he was.

However, such drastic measures weren't necessary. The next night he was waiting for her when she left the farm. 'I thought you were going to work the night through. I've been waiting here for hours.' His slight, wiry figure detached itself from the shelter of a tree and ambled towards her. 'All right if I walk home with you?'

She was so relieved she could only nod.

It became a regular habit. According to what shift he was on George would either walk her to work or escort her home afterwards but to Evelyn's increasing exasperation he still didn't attempt to kiss her. Nor could she invite him into the cottage as an excuse to keep him with her for a bit longer. She was too ashamed of the place for that and mortified by the prospect of introducing George to her mother and Tammy McGurk and having to explain that relationship. She couldn't bear George to know about that, not yet, never realising that her mother's wanton behaviour had been the talk of the village for two years now. So, she had to be content to allow him to hold her hand chastely while they walked. When they reached her front door he simply squeezed it, said goodnight and continued on his way.

Evelyn couldn't describe the way he made her feel. When he took her hand her skin tingled, when he left her she wanted him to stay, to hold her, to kiss her, so much that she felt a physical ache in her chest. Sometimes, in bed, she cried with the frustration of it all.

In her more rational moments she knew that what she felt for George wasn't love. Desire, yes. The terrible urge of the young and healthy body towards the ultimate, intimate fulfilment, but not love. But, she told herself, love wasn't important and never lasted anyway. What mattered was finding herself a good-natured, reliable man who would take her away from Craigie to something better. Of all the young men she had met in her rather narrow life, George seemed the one most likely to do that. She sighed. At this rate she would still be waiting for him to commit himself this time next year. Evelyn Lennox wasn't prepared to wait that long.

In the end, suspecting that it was nothing more serious than inexperience which was holding George back, she took the initiative into her own capable hands. When he tried to say goodnight that evening she dug sharp nails into the palm of his hand and dragged him into the shelter of the wall.

'It's too early to go in yet,' she whispered, raising her face until her lips were almost touching his, invitation plain in her dark eyes.

In the half-light of the long evening she saw the momentary hesitation before his grey eyes widened in sudden understanding. Then she caught the flash of white teeth as, at last, he bent his head to hers.

The kiss was tentative at first, an uncertain brushing of his mouth over hers, but when he realised she wasn't about to push him away he slipped an arm round her waist and gently parted her lips with his tongue. Her response shocked him but removed any lingering doubts about her from his mind. Coiling an arm down to his firm buttocks she pressed her taut young body into his. Her heart thumped and then missed a beat when she felt the hard proof of his ardour.

'I thought you were never going to kiss me, George,' she teased.

'I wasn't sure you wanted me to,' he admitted, a trifle breathlessly, not adding that he was just a little bit scared of her forthright, confident manner and more than a little puzzled as to why he, of all the young men in Craigie, had been lucky enough to have attracted her.

Having hooked her fish Evelyn gave him no chance to get away. From then on she made sure their walks were punctuated by regular stops to kiss and cuddle, often using the friendly shelter of a tree or hedge and sometimes taking advantage of the privacy on the nearby beach.

Summer merged into a mild autumn. Earlier darkness brought ever greater opportunities for snatched moments of privacy, and steadily increasing temptation. Evelyn longed for release but knew the dangers were too great, knew that no decent girl did what she longed to do before she was safely married and even half-decent girls made sure they had an engagement ring first. And marriage was a word which, to her increasing annoyance, never passed George's lips. For months now she had been absolutely certain that marriage to George Innes was exactly what she wanted, and the quicker the better. It would solve all her problems, get her out of the depressing miners' rows, away from Tammy McGurk and her mother, and give her the independence she craved. With a bit of encouragement from her she really believed that George could earn them a comfortable living, away from the mines, making her the envy of her friends who still scoffed at her ambitions for George. Nothing would give her more pleasure than being able to prove them all wrong. And she would prove them wrong. George was always telling her how much he hated the pits, how he couldn't wait for the war to end so he could find another job and listened seriously when she spoke of her own ambition to move away from Craigie, seeming to agree with her every word. He was no prime minister in the making, she knew that much by now, but he was malleable, good natured and easy-going enough to let her guide him and to give her her own way in most things. Yes, life with George would be an enormous improvement on what she had now. And George Innes, whether he knew it or not, was going to marry her because she had suddenly realised that she had the solution, that she knew the one sure way to trap someone as basically decent as he was.

His hands slipped under her jumper bringing her sharply back to the present. Normally she would have slapped them away but, having made up her mind about what she had to do, she saw no reason to delay. Covering his hands with her own she crushed them to her full breasts, moaning faintly when he teased a bared nipple. When he pushed her softly to the ground she pulled him with her, holding her hips up, rubbing into the heat of his erection and made no protest when his hands edged under the hem of her skirt and on, under the elastic of her knickers. She even moved a little, encouraging him to slide a finger into the moist depths of her. A detached part of her mind knew he was already breathing in rapid pants and wouldn't be able to stop himself from taking what she was about to offer. But, in the end, it was her own ripe body which was tricked by her plan, causing her to forget her determination to stay in control, to be cautious, and drove her desperately onwards. Frantically she fumbled with his buttons until she was holding him, guiding him between her legs, aching for the feel of him inside her, oblivious to everything but her own shattering, burning need. Still not entering her he moved rhythmically, unwittingly bringing her to the point where she could bear it no longer. Aroused past all restraint she guided him hotly to the point of entry, held him there, then thrust up at him. For an instant he froze then, surrendering to his own instincts, pushed against her. Evelyn stifled a gasp at the unexpectedly sharp pain of first penetration then clamped him to her, moving to his rhythm.

In the nick of time he withdrew, shuddering spasmodically with the violent, explosive conclusion to this, his first sexual experience, before collapsing into the fallen leaves at her side.

Evelyn took a surprising number of minutes to regain her composure but when she did feel able to face George again it was with an odd feeling of disappointment, as if he had somehow cheated her. Well, she thought, there was no chance of being pregnant after that fumbling episode. And then she glanced at George's flushed and disturbed face and it occurred to her that, perhaps, it wouldn't be necessary to go that far after all. George was a very old fashioned boy in some respects . . .

'We can't go on like this, George,' she whispered, running a hand over his sweat-dappled chest. 'I'll end up in trouble and then what will everyone say?'

'I'm sorry, Ev,' he mumbled, looking shamefaced. 'I didn't mean . . .'

She took pity on him. 'It was my fault too, George. I wanted this to happen.'

He seemed surprised. 'You did?' According to his father, 'nice' girls certainly didn't want this to happen.

'Of course I did. I love you, George.' She snuggled into his side, ignoring the stone which was grinding into her ribcage. 'But I don't think we should . . . you know . . . do it again. I mean . . . it's far too dangerous. What would we do if I started a baby?'

She waited.

His father would leather him, he was sure of that much. His mother's reaction didn't bear thinking about. 'Maybe we should get married?' he suggested, uncertainly.

It had been even easier than she had expected it to be. 'Married, George?' she asked, injecting astonishment into her voice.

For a moment she glimpsed hurt in his lean face.

'Well,' he stammered. 'There'd be an awful lot of trouble if you did . . . you know . . . I thought . . . now that we've done it . . . it'd be better if . . . You do like me, Ev, don't you? You weren't just saying it?'

'Och, George!' She smiled at him now with genuine affection. 'I told you. I love you. And what would I be doing here with you if I didn't? What sort of girl do you think I am?'

She felt him relax, felt the breath released from his tense body.

'That's all right then,' he said.

'George?'

'Aye?'

'Did you mean it? About us getting married?'

'Aye. If that's what you want.' He had never been good with words and wished he could find something clever to say to her now.

'I do want to, George. But only if you love me, too.'

She paused, wondering if he would be able to say it, knowing it would be alien for him to make an emotional declaration, as it was to all the men in this harsh area. Even her own father had never told her he loved her, though she had always known he did.

'Why would I want to wed you otherwise?' he prevaricated.

'I love you, George Innes,' she whispered into his ear. 'Tell me you love me, too, George.' Suddenly she desperately needed to hear those words.

There was a long, long silence. Then she heard him take a deep breath and felt his mouth brush her ear as he whispered, 'I love you, Ev,' so quickly that the words all rolled into one long, incomprehensible syllable.

She smiled to herself and leant back against his shoulder. It was enough.

He left her at the door of her home an hour later. She burst in, brimming with her news and found the place empty. Only then did she recall that her mother had taken the boys on a rare visit to an elderly aunt. Tammy was likely to stay in the Greyhound until closing time, as usual. Estimating that it would be at least an hour before anyone came in, Evelyn took advantage of the absolute privacy to fill the sink with warm water and wash her hair.

That done she stripped to the skin and lathered herself thoroughly with a tiny piece of sweet-smelling pink toilet soap, jealously guarded since Christmas. Keeping an eye on the clock she towelled herself dry then stood in front of the mirror to brush out her softly shining hair.

Eyes, so alive they were almost feverish, looked back at her, glinting with excitement and satisfaction. She paused, lowered her brush and examined herself more critically. Was she changed in any way now that she had crossed the threshold into true womanhood? Would anyone be able to tell what had happened to her? Stepping back until her top half was visible in the tarnished mirror she cupped her hands under her breasts and swivelled slightly, proud of her feminine outline. Rising on to her toes she pulled her head back, posing theatrically and laughing at her own silliness. Then, still excited by the night's experiences, she slipped a hand between her thighs to where there was still a lingering feeling of tender fullness. Trapped by the unexpected sensations that surged to her touch and still relatively innocent, she slowly rubbed her fingers over the area which now throbbed unbearably while her other hand gently teased a nipple.

·It was a sight which would have broken even the strongest man's resistance. Tammy McGurk, who had glimpsed Evelyn's erotic stance through a gap in the inadequate curtains as he checked to make sure Ina wasn't home yet, found himself wholly unequal to the challenge of restraint. Stealthily he crouched, watching her, his lips moistening with surplus spittle, his hand encouraging the hot urgency of his crotch.

It was in this rather inelegant position, crouching on his knees, one eye peering through the steamed up glass, a hand working furiously on his engorged organ while grunting like a penned pig, that Ina discovered her lover.

Luckily for Tammy the boys were lagging some way behind their mother. By the time they arrived Ina's unexpected and furious appearance had succeeded in deflating the offending member and Tammy was stumbling sheepishly to his feet.

One glance through the gap in the curtains had been enough to tell Ina that Tammy had caught Evelyn in the act of washing while the sudden commotion outside sent Evelyn scrambling into her clothes in record time. Scarlet-faced she unlocked the door, blushing more with embarrassment at what they might have seen had they arrived five minutes earlier than with remembered passion.

'Evelyn! What a time to have a wash,' Ina stormed as she charged through the door.

'I wasn't expecting you back so soon,' her daughter faltered, catching the unmistakably lustful look in Tammy's eyes and understanding that he had seen more than she had first assumed. Ina caught the leering grin too and felt a spurt of jealous anger through her own sagging breasts.

'Have you no sense of decency?' she flared at the girl. 'How do you expect a normal, red-blooded man to react to seeing you like that? You'll get yourself into trouble one of these days if you don't watch out. Not all men are decent, like Tammy here. Are you listening to me?' she screamed, irritated by the look of utter contempt which had settled over her daughter's face.

'Och, I hear you, Mother, and you're a fine one to talk about decent behaviour. But don't you worry your head about me. I'll not be under your feet for much longer. George Innes has asked me to marry him and I've said yes.' She dropped her bombshell with a flourish and turned away, smiling, to brush her disordered hair back into place.

'George . . . ? George Innes?' Now it was Ina's turn to look flabbergasted. 'That glaekit lump?'

FOUR

A̲t last the war was truly over. At Cairns Farm the celebrations were as thorough as only a party of good-natured, thirsty Scots could make them.

'Now,' said George, who had joined Evelyn and her colleagues for the evening. 'We can really make plans.' From his pocket he produced a small box and opened it to proudly display a neat gold band with three modest diamonds set into it.

Evelyn was stunned, caught between delight at this unexpected show of thoughtfulness, not a trait George exhibited very often, and anger at his extravagance. They had already agreed not to buy an engagement ring because they needed to save every single penny towards furniture for their first home.

'Don't worry,' he whispered later, as they said good-night. 'It's not real gold. I bought it at Woolies but nobody will be able to tell the difference. You couldn't could you? And what's the point of wasting hard-earned money on a bit of gold when you can get something as good as this for under a pound?'

With that he sauntered off, leaving his fiancée with tears streaming down her face, not even sure herself if they were of anger or affection.

At least their engagement was official now. As soon as they found somewhere to live they could get married. It was something Evelyn yearned for with even more urgency than usual. Inspired by what he had witnessed on that unfortunate evening, Tammy McGurk's attentions towards her had become a major problem.

Tammy took every small opportunity to be alone with her. Contrary to what she had originally feared, he never tried to touch her now. Instead he attempted to woo her, heaping ridiculous compliments on her and grinning in an appallingly inane way every time he set eyes on her. Evelyn could only pray that her mother never realised what was going on in her uncouth paramour's overheated mind and hope that her own marriage wouldn't be long delayed.

Housing was the big obstacle to their wedding. George was as anxious to escape from his own mother's fussy attentions as Evelyn was to distance herself from Tammy McGurk so, unlike many young couples, they couldn't start their married life with one or other set of parents. What they desperately needed was a home of their own but they could both see that was an impossible dream. But what neither of them immediately realised was that, for the mining villages, the end of the war was to be a turning point.

The mining industry had entered the war in a very weak position. The combination of long hours, low wages and inhuman conditions had driven many men out of the pits and sentenced those who remained to a life of hardship and deprivation. But, as the war progressed it caused a coal shortage which, exacerbated by the lack of manpower, eventually forced the conscription of men into the pits. The government – which had allowed the mine owners to make obscene profits while ignoring the workers' claims for fair treatment – was compelled to admit the economic importance of the miners. For many years the talk in the mining communities had been of nationalisation. The Craigie miners supported the move to take ownership away from unscrupulous private owners who cared nothing for the ideals of safer working conditions, fair pay, reasonable hours and decent housing. Now, at last it seemed that their goal would be realised. A charter setting out the aims of the colliers was presented, demanding that manpower in the mines must be secured by a steady improvement in wages, living standards and working conditions. To the joy of the whole industry the government began to put portions of this charter into effect and a new mood of hope infused the villages.

Craigie was one of the first communities to see positive results. The old rows, originally built by the mine owners, had long been in urgent need of replacement. Because of their deplorable condition, two whole streets of new houses had been built in the village by the county council before the start of the war and more new homes were promised. As a direct result of the miners' strengthened position, by the early autumn of 1945, building work had already started again and long-time residents of the rows looked forward to living in modern houses and flats with running water, electricity and even bathrooms, a luxury beyond their wildest dreams. But George and Evelyn knew they couldn't hope to be housed in the new flats and there was no chance of being offered a place in the old rows. As soon as they emptied they were being flattened. In any case Evelyn had made it plain that she was aiming a lot higher than the rows.

Then, just across the road from the village shop, on what had been an open field, a bulldozer appeared. The villagers watched in amazement as complete houses were erected on to concrete bases, usually within the space of a day. Inside two months a whole estate of tiny, prefabricated bungalows had materialised in the very centre of the rapidly enlarging village. The villagers watched in open curiosity as newcomers moved into these miniature houses; men returning from the war and attracted back to

the mines they thought they had left forever by the promise of improved working conditions; men who had been
factory workers or even fishermen before the war,
tempted by the offer of housing and fair wages. There
was even a scattering of dispossessed Polish mining families who were warmly welcomed into the community.
Everyone was eager to know these strange and somehow
exotic people who were none the less linked by the
brotherhood of the pits. Generous, ill-afforded gifts of
blankets, clothes and even furniture helped these immi-
grant families, most of whom spoke little or no English,
settle into their new life.

Within the space of six months it seemed that Craigie
doubled in size, and went on growing. New houses, a
post office and a row of three new shops, and even a new
church, St Michaels, stretched the village to the point
where an hourly bus service into Inverannan finally gave
them a reliable, affordable link with the wider world.
The original villagers discovered the novelty of regularly
meeting strangers on their streets and suddenly realised
that there were many households whose personal affairs
and family histories were not common knowledge. Even
more fascinating were the several families whose members
had no connection whatever with the pits, and who
brought fresh outlooks and new ideas to the village. But,
while the villages revelled in the new-found, relative pros-
perity which put them on a respectable level with other
working class people, the sense of kinship which had protected the village in the hard years diluted just a little.

'It's wonderful!' Evelyn rushed from room to room in
bubbly excitement.

'It's right wee.' George, whose family were fortunate

58

enough to live in a solid, three-bedroomed council house, was less impressed.

'It's braw,' she insisted. 'At home we have just the two rooms for everything. Here there's two bedrooms, a kitchen, a living room and a bathroom. Indoors!' She clapped her hands in pure glee. It was the inside bathroom which made this place so attractive to her. A toilet, a tiny wash basin and a bath, all in gleaming white. And everything smelt so fresh.

George smiled and put his arm round her. 'If you're sure, Hen.'

'I'm sure, George. When you're settled in a decent job we'll be able to move on but, to start with, this will be just fine.'

She leant against him in perfect contentment. Everything was going to be wonderful. The sooner they were married and she was away from the disgusting Tammy McGurk and her shameless mother, the better. And George really was a decent young man, not at all coarse and rough like so many of the Craigie men. Nor would he be a miner for much longer. He passionately hated the pits and had promised to look for another job just as soon as they were settled. He hadn't actually done anything about it yet, any more than he had made any real effort to find them a house. It was she who went into the council offices in Inverannan almost every week, making sure their name was correctly placed on the housing list and pestering the clerks in the hope that they would find her a house quickly, just to be rid of her. The small, doubting voice in her head which launched the suspicion that George might really be as lazy and unintelligent as her mother insisted he was, was stoutly denied. George Innes, she reminded herself, would take her away from the rows. She could see no further than that.

*

'Do you not feel well enough to go on shift again today, George?' Evelyn asked.

'No, Hen. My head's stuffed up something terrible and my ears ache.'

It was, she knew, nothing more serious than a slight head cold, vastly exaggerated into an excuse to keep him out of the mine for a couple of days.

'But your pay'll not even cover the rent again, George. Could you not make the effort?' she pleaded, `knowing she sounded like an old nag. The trouble with George was that he had no conception of the real value of money. He was perfectly content to hand over whatever was in his pay-packet and leave her to manage the house on it. But he expected miracles. Since their wedding, six months ago, he had had several bouts of sickness and there had been weeks of hungry discomfort because of it.

'I'll go back the morn,' he promised easily, sinking into a chair and closing his eyes.

She sighed. It wouldn't be so bad if she was still working but the farm jobs had been reclaimed by the men returning from the war. In her condition she couldn't work anyway.

She glared impatiently at her husband who, at ten-thirty in the morning and less than an hour out of his bed, was already snoring gently, his mouth hanging open to reveal bare, pink gums. The urge to throw the cup she was holding at his head was only resisted because she knew they couldn't afford to replace it.

It was useless trying to bully George into going to work, or even to look for something which would suit him better. He simply wouldn't rise to it. Sometimes she thought he was too idle even to get angry. Her head throbbed with suppressed temper and she knew she had to get away from George and the claustrophobic little house for an hour or two. Slinging her old coat over her shoulders she slipped quietly through the front door, confident that George wouldn't miss her. Without thinking she allowed her feet to lead her through the growing village and back to the old rows.

It was a different place these days. Most of the families had been rehoused in the new flats and houses which were still being built on the far side of the village. The majority of the old cottages were empty and many of them had fallen into open dereliction with broken doors and shattered windows, the gardens rapidly returning to wilderness. Others had been reduced to piles of rubble which provided an exciting playground for the local children. Only the stink of the privies was the same.

Evelyn's mother's house was one of the few still occupied, the council having baulked at offering one of their new houses to a couple who were living in a state of such overt immorality. Evelyn tapped on the door then shoved it open. Ina glanced up from the table where she was scanning through a cheap magazine, still surrounded by the remains of breakfast and last night's meal.

'Well, well. This is an honour,' she drawled, sarcastically.

'If you're going to be like that I may as well go.' Evelyn turned back to the door.

'Get off your high horse and have a cup of tea with your mother,' Ina rose slowly to her bare feet and filled a cup with greyish, tepid liquid.

Evelyn took the chipped cup and eyed it suspiciously, wondering what on earth had made her come here. She had no real desire to see her mother who never missed an opportunity to have a dig at her about something.

The house was as neglected as ever. Evelyn couldn't help comparing it to her own scrupulously neat house. A pile of dirty dishes littered the table, the boys' mattress was the familiar heap of old coats and stained blankets and the whole place stank. A nauseating combination of stale food, dampness and unwashed humanity, over all of which wafted the ever-present odour of the privies. To think she had actually lived in this hovel! The very thought shamed her.

'How are the boys?' she asked. 'I've not seen them for a day or two.' Her brothers, thirteen, twelve and nine years old now, regularly called at the prefab on the way home to cadge toast and jam.

Ina shrugged carelessly. 'Tammy's told them they're to come straight home for the next week. Little sods that they are.'

Evelyn smiled. She was fond of her brothers who were still a handful despite Tammy's discipline. 'What have they done this time?'

'Chap door run.' Ina allowed herself a thin smile. 'Och, it's harmless enough. All kids do it. But they made the mistake of chapping on your Uncle Harry's door and he came up here raving on about them. Tammy leathered them, and they've to stay in for the rest of the week. Bloody nuisance they are too, hanging round here, bored out of their minds.'

A baby whimpered then broke into a fretful wail. Ina ignored it until the child was bawling. Sighing she eased her swollen body from the chair and lifted him. Evelyn watched her mother fumble with her blouse and swallowed her disgust as the child latched on to a withered, sagging breast. He was a puny, sickly child and she could feel no affection for this unfortunate little half-brother. Nor was she likely to feel any differently about the one her mother was carrying now.

'And how are you then, Mam?' she asked to cover the infant's loud sucking noises.

Ina barely raised her head from the magazine which had reclaimed her attention. 'Tired,' she mumbled. 'The bairn's hard work at my age. Especially with those three still under my feet. I can't say I'm looking forward to having another one.'

'You don't have to have them,' Evelyn retorted, more bitterly than she intended. 'You can use things to stop it happening.' The knowledge that this gaunt, haggard woman, who looked nearer sixty than forty, might be capable of bearing another two or three children disturbed her profoundly. It seemed obscene that Ina and Tammy McGurk did the same things in bed that she and George did, and still without the benefit of a marriage certificate.

'You're a fine one to talk,' scoffed Ina. 'It didn't take you long to let him get you in the family way, did it? And there'll be more. You'll see.'

'I want this baby!'

'I daresay you do. But will you want all the others?' Ina challenged. 'You think you're so clever, coming here and looking down your nose at me. Just you wait! You'll soon have three or four weans trailing at your back. You'll end up just the same as all the rest of us.'

Evelyn swallowed a mouthful of the vile tea and left. She could still hear her mother laughing as she walked away.

Mary Margaret Innes made her damp way into the world two days after her grandmother gave birth to a stillborn son.

She was a demanding, restless baby who cried often and slept little, reducing her mother to bad-tempered exhaustion. Evelyn found herself totally incapable of taking the usual maternal pleasure from simply looking at her baby daughter who resembled nothing more attractive than an ill-natured demon when she was crying. Even when she wasn't, the protruding ears, staring eyes, flattened nose and uncompromisingly bald head gave her a startling like-

63

ness to a baby chimpanzee. She was, Evelyn saw with a sinking heart, very much as George must have looked as an infant.

Evelyn did her very best to love her tiny daughter but failed miserably. It seemed to her that Mary was the unappreciative recipient of never-ending hard work. The washing she generated was, on its own, enough to keep Evelyn fully occupied for the entire week. To her shame the house became cluttered and untidy but dealing with the baby left little time for the finer details of housework.

Most of her contemporaries who found themselves in a similar situation turned to their mothers for support and advice. Evelyn soon saw that there would be nothing other than criticism forthcoming from her own mother who, in any case, was too busy with her own four sons to offer any practical assistance. Ina occasionally called in on her way to or from the shops and, if her son-in-law wasn't at home, would stay long enough to drink a cup of tea and find fault with some aspect of Evelyn's life, usually leaving her daughter discouraged, depressed and angry. If George was at home Evelyn was glad of the excuse not to invite her mother in. Ina Lennox had never bothered to conceal her contempt for him and was the one person the easy-going George Innes ever really detested.

If George had stirred himself to help her, even a little, Evelyn might have felt differently, but he was always too tired and maintained that nursing his baby daughter made his back ache. Evelyn didn't persist. The last thing she wanted to do was hand him the excuse for more time off work. What, she wondered bitterly, had happened to all her fine plans and dreams? How could she have been naive enough to think that she could inspire George to show any interest in clawing his way off of what was very nearly the bottom rung of the social ladder?

In fact, the only time George displayed more than a

passing interest in anything, was in bed. His bad back was no handicap when it came to pursuing his marital rights which he did with an agility which completely belied the condition which kept him away from work when all other excuses failed. She wished he wasn't quite so enthusiastic. Not that she didn't enjoy his demands. It was the results which upset her.

The second result was Linda, born two years after Mary. Catherine was next, less than two years later. Despite the fact that she worked non-stop, the house was untidier than ever, she was permanently drained and George was even less inclined to help.

'No, George. Not tonight. I'm too tired. All I want to do is sleep.'

'Come on, Ev.' His hand was already at the hem of her nightdress.

It was amazing, she thought afterwards, how her body still responded when her mind was close to hating him.

Nine months later, a mere eleven months after Catherine's birth, David was born. And that, Evelyn decided, was more than enough.

'Not tonight, George.'

'Och, aye.'

She slapped his hand away, hard enough to hurt, and turned on her side but still his hand crept to her sore and engorged breasts.

'No, George!' She screamed it at him.

'Why not?' he asked, sounding like a little boy deprived of his lollipop.

'You know fine why not. Unless you use something so I don't get expecting again.'

'Och, Ev, you know I can't get along with those things.' His erection always wilted the minute she even mentioned the subject.

'Well, go without!' Confusingly she felt a stab of annoyance when he simply shrugged, laid on his back and fell asleep within minutes.

It set a pattern. Each time he approached her without protection, she refused. When he did try to use a sheath he invariably failed. After a while he gave up trying. It really didn't bother him one way or the other any more.

Evelyn seethed, cried herself to sleep, then, realising the futility of that, retreated into simmering resentment.

But her days were too full to leave much time for brooding. Weeks passed in the perpetual repetition of the same monotonous tasks. The bloom left her cheeks, the sparkle died in her eyes which drew back into shadowed sockets and her hair hung in limp strands over dry, tired skin. The bounce of confidence was replaced by plodding resignation. She looked precisely what she had vowed she would never be. Just the same as all the other village women, old before her time, bitter and exhausted. She shuddered when she glanced in a mirror and caught unwelcome glimpses of her own defeated reflection.

It seemed the small house was nothing more than a prison, her own family her gaolers. She felt betrayed and cheated, and longed for something else, something more exciting, more rewarding and knew she would never get any of that with George.

The day on which David, her youngest child, started school, was the day which galvanised her into action. He had set out dressed in a worn-out jumper and short, grey trousers, both of which had been bought at a jumble sale. His shirt and shoes had been her little half-brother's. Evelyn hadn't enjoyed being forced to beg Ina for cast-off clothing but there was simply no money for anything better.

Today all she had in her purse was one shilling and a handful of coppers. Every week was the same. Ever since George had managed to wrench his back again they had

66

been subsisting on sickness payments, eeked out by National Assistance. There was no hope of ever having enough money for more than their most basic needs.

She trudged home, trying to forget the shame of knowing that her own son had been the most poorly dressed of the twenty infants who had started school that day. When she pushed the front door open she was greeted by the infuriating sound of George snoring.

'Are you going to stay in your bed all day, George?' she yelled impatiently.

There was a grunt, the sound of a body turning, and more snoring. Furiously she crashed dishes round in the kitchen, making as much noise as possible. The same chipped, cracked dishes. She must have washed them a million times before. Damp washing tangled in her hair as she worked. It smelt stale already, the odours of frying sausages and burnt toast clinging to it as it hung on the high, wooden airer.

She went through her tasks mechanically, tidying the room where all four children slept, jammed together on bunk beds. When she straightened David's blankets she caught a familiar, ammonia-like smell. Stripping the covers back she stared at the damp, dark patch which corresponded with the place his little bottom occupied.

'Not again,' she hissed, tearing away the soiled sheet. Below it the red mattress had a circular maroon patch on it. With great difficulty in the confined space she hauled the mattress off the bed and propped it up in front of the open window to dry off, advertising her son's problem to the whole street in the process. But there was no other way. At least the day was fine and bright, it should dry before evening. She boiled water in the kettle, ready to wash the sheet, then discovered there was no washing soap left.

Not bothering to slip a coat over her wrap-around pinafore or change from her holey, down at heel slippers, she ran across the road to the shop. Two women smiled and nodded as Evelyn went in. Both had taken the trouble to put top coats and outdoor shoes on though neither lived more than a minute from the shop and Evelyn was suddenly aware of how slovenly she must appear.

'Well, Lass. What can I get you?' Mrs McPhee asked.

'Just a bar of laundry soap, Mrs McPhee, please. I'll pay you on Friday,' she added, suddenly remembering that her purse was practically empty. Like most of the village women Evelyn had a small amount of credit at the local shop.

'I'm sorry, Mrs Innes. I can't mark anything more up for you. You already owe five pounds and three shillings. You'll need to clear some of that off first.' Mrs McPhee didn't bother to lower her voice. The conversation between the two women who were still chatting behind them, stopped abruptly. Evelyn flushed red to the roots of her hair.

'I'm sorry. I . . . I didn't realise it was that much,' she stammered, while the shopkeeper pointedly took the soap off the counter. 'I'll call back on Friday.'

It took all her self control not to actually run from the shop, especially when she heard, 'Just like her mother! They're a bad lot, that family,' said just loud enough for her to hear. Never in her life had she been so humiliated. She would be the talk of the village for days to come.

Back home she still had to do something about the soiled sheet and settled for rinsing it through in hot water, releasing some of her temper by pounding it fiercely in the sink.

'What's all the noise about?'

It was nothing more than an idle enquiry. George, sleepy eyed and unshaven, grinned stupidly and scratched his head. She didn't bother to answer him.

'I'm starving. Stick the kettle on will you, Hen, and cut us a slice of bread,' he yawned, opening the back door and settling himself on the top step, his usual morning perch.

Speechless with rage she hacked at the loaf and threw a single mangled slice at him. It bounced off his back and landed on the floor. He retrieved it and picked bits from its surface.

'What did you do that for?' he asked, sounding completely perplexed. 'Give us some jam or something will you?'

'There's none,' she shrieked, dropping the knife into the sink with a clatter.

'Well, give us some money and I'll nip over to the shop for some. I need fags anyway.'

'Money?' she shrilled. 'Money? There's no money, George. No money until Friday. There's never any bloody money and there's no more tick at Mrs McPhee's either. We've a bill of more than five pounds there, George. How am I supposed to pay that?' Hot tears burned behind her eyes.

George levered himself to his feet and emptied his pockets. A grubby handkerchief, a penknife and a single penny. He shrugged. 'Sorry, Hen. I've nothing either. You know you could have it if I had it to give. Never mind.'

He sat down again, looking contentedly out over his small garden. Most of their neighbours cultivated their patches and grew vegetables or at least a square of grass for the children to play on. George was no gardener. Theirs was nothing more than a rambling wilderness of weeds and wild flowers. 'My, it's a braw morning,' he said, as if there wasn't a problem in the world. 'I think I'll take a wee walk along the burn.'

'George.'

'Aye?' He turned weak, greyish eyes on her. Like many of the villagers he had lost his teeth at an early age. He seldom bothered with his false ones. Without them he looked twenty years older. Evelyn stared at him, as if seeing her husband properly for the first time. He grinned back, baring more pink gums, then looked bewildered when she put her hands over her face and sobbed. In ten years of marriage he had never seen her cry before.

He fidgeted in his pockets, shuffling his feet and coughing.

'Just go for your walk, George,' she choked, turning her back on him.

'Aye,' he agreed gratefully. 'I'll be back in time for lunch, Hen,' he called as he escaped.

'What bloody lunch?' she yelled after him. But he didn't hear.

George ambled along the burn enjoying the fresh feel of the autumn air. This narrow stream had once had fish in it. When he was a lad he had caught tiddlers here instead of going to school but, since the new houses had been built, all he could find in the sluggish water was discarded household rubbish. Pausing for a minute to watch some youngsters playing in the slimy mud he then followed the stream through the woods, past the sawmill and on, by the pit railway, until he was a good five miles from the village. Evelyn's strange behaviour had made him slightly uneasy and he wanted to walk the feeling off. By the time he got home she would surely be back to her bright, brisk self. The fact that it had been a very long time since his wife had been bright and brisk eluded him.

George Innes was a contented man. He had a happy family, a comfortable home and lived in a wonderful part of the country. Perhaps he didn't have the small luxuries that some of his friends bragged about but he was a simple man and asked very little from life. His greatest pleasure was this freedom to escape, either into the green country-side or down to the sea-shore, and be totally alone. One shift down the pit was enough to make him yearn for the outdoors and that was the only time he felt true discontent. But, he told himself ruefully, a man had to work, especially when he had four braw bairns and a wife to support. And, thank God, things were easier now than they had been in his father's day. Then he would never have been able to take so much time off on the sick. No work, no pay. That had been the rule then. It certainly made him appreciate how marvellous this new system was. He had his time off, all signed and made official by the doctor and the Ministry gave them enough money to get by on. 'Och, aye,' he sighed to himself as he sat on a rock gazing contentedly into the frothing stream. 'Life's grand, so it is.'

It was well after two before he sauntered back into the village. His stride was long and easy and he whistled cheerfully as he let himself into the prefab and called, 'Put the kettle on, Hen.'

There was no reply. Ev must be at the shop or maybe out back, fetching the washing in. No matter. He could wait for his tea. He slumped into a chair and, within two minutes, was sound asleep.

A loud banging on the front door wakened him two hours later. Stirring gradually, with no sense of urgency, he yelled, 'Ev, get the door, Hen.'

There was no sound from within the house.

'Ev,' he roared. 'The door!'

Still nothing. Slowly, he hauled himself to his feet and shambled into the tiny hall, feeling vaguely irritated. It really was too bad of Evelyn to ignore him like that. She could surely guess how tired he was after his walk.

'Hello, Dad,' his four offspring chanted from the doorstep.

'Oh . . . It's youse,' he grinned. So that was where Evelyn had been, fetching the weans home from the school. 'Where's Mammy, then?'

'She's not here and she promised to come to school and fetch David today because it's his first day but she never came and he had to wait for us for a whole half-hour,' accused Mary in one, long breath.

'Aye, and I waited and waited,' the youngest Innes complained.

'Well, maybe she forgot,' George suggested, puzzled by the first, slow foreboding of trouble.

'Mammy never forgets,' said Catherine, loyally.

'See this, Dad! Och, did you not notice this?' Mary ran back from the kitchen waving a piece of paper jubilantly round her head.

George grabbed it then peered uncomprehendingly at his wife's untidy handwriting. 'Here,' he passed it back to Mary. 'You read it, Lass.'

Mary squinted at the paper. 'Gone to town. Back at tea time. Mind and fetch David from school.'

'Och . . .' George shrugged. 'I went for a wee walk. I never saw that note. Sorry, son. No harm done, eh?'

They forgave him instantly.

'Well, never mind,' he chuckled. 'Come on, we'll play a game. How about that?'

When Evelyn arrived home, half an hour later, she could hear the rumpus issuing from her own house from the other side of the street. The tiny living room was a mass of squirming bodies. She stood silently in the doorway, waiting for them to notice her. It was Mary who looked up first, saw the sour expression on her mother's face and swiftly silenced the others. George emerged from under his children red-faced with exertion and beaming happily.

'Hello, Ev. Did you get your shopping done then?' he asked, innocently.

'Shopping?' She rounded on him, immediately sobering the over-excited children. 'How the hell could I do any shopping? I've no money. I had to borrow from my mother to pay my bus fare.'

'. . . I just thought . . . I mean, why else would you go into town?'

'You lot away and tidy yourselves up. There's bread in the kitchen and tatties ready on the cooker. Mary, you see to it.'

'Aye, Mam.' The ten-year-old girl rounded up her siblings and did as she was asked. They all knew better than to argue with their mother when she was in this kind of mood.

'Put the kettle on, Hen. I'm dying for a cup of tea.'

'I suppose you've had nothing since your breakfast?' Evelyn asked bitterly.

'Well, you weren't in when I got home from my walk,' he admitted. 'But don't worry. I had a wee sleep until the weans came in from the school.'

'You did mind to fetch David home, George?' she asked, suspiciously.

'Eh . . . well, to tell the truth I never saw your note, Ev. But don't go getting yourself all steamed up. There's no harm done. The lassies fetched him home.'

'He was finishing half an hour before them today. It was his first day at school, George! Oh, George,' she sighed but the anger was leaving her now. 'I've got something to tell you.'

'Make us a cup of tea first, Hen. I'm fair dying of thirst.'

73

She surged to her feet in a furious temper again. 'Make it yourself, George Innes! And you had better get used to fending for yourself in future because I won't be here to run round after you.'

'Eh?'

'I've got myself a job, George,' she announced, a satisfied smile playing round her mouth while his fell open.

'A job! What have you got a job for?'

'What do you think I've got a job for? We've no money. We've never got any money because you're too idle to work a full week.'

'You know fine I've got a bad back. And there's enough money. We're not starving. We've got everything we need. A roof over our heads, clothes on our backs and we're right here in the middle of the country, hills to our backs and the sea to the front. What more could you want, Ev? There's not a better place in the world to live than Strathannan.'

'What more could I want?' she screeched, making him wince. 'Everything! Enough money to put decent clothes on the weans' backs; enough to buy good food; enough to buy a bar of soap when one's needed. Enough to get out of this miserable hole!'

She was aware of four pairs of eyes watching them. Never before had she yelled at George in front of the children but even now he wasn't really angry, wasn't making any real effort to argue back. His face merely mirrored confusion and complete incomprehension of her problems.

'What difference does it make if you have to wait an extra day to do your washing? And the bairns are well-enough clothed. They grow too fast to make it worth buying new. I never had new clothes when I was a laddie and it never did me any harm. And we get plenty to eat, too.' He shook his head in wonder at this enraged creature

74

who could get so upset about things which didn't really matter at all.

'Enough to eat, aye. But the bairns aren't getting the right things to eat. They need meat and vegetables and fruit.'

'There's always plenty tatties and carrots and turnips. And home-made soup, like you make, is the best you can get.'

'They need more than that, George. Why do you think they've always got runny noses?' As if to make her point she used an old rag to catch the stream of green slime which habitually ran from David's nostrils.

'All bairns have runny noses. I always had a runny nose. There's no harm in it. He'll grow out of it when he learns to blow it right. Och, Ev, you're making a right fuss about nothing. Maybe you're coming down with a cold. There's no need for you to get a job, Hen. I'll not buy fags this week. That'll help.'

'It's too late, George. I've already accepted it. I start the morn.'

He gaped at her. 'Who'll watch the bairns?'

'You will, George. They're at school all day so it won't strain you too much.' She knew the sarcasm was wasted on him.

'I'll ask your mother . . .'

'You will not! You will look after them, George. You've nothing else to do with your time.'

'What about when I'm working?'

'Mary's old enough to keep an eye on them after school. Between you always being off sick and the shifts you work when you are fit, there won't be many days when they come home to an empty house. And if they do, well, they'll just have to make the best of it. I'm taking that job, George, and that's all there is to it.'

★

75

It was harder than she had imagined it would be. Alessandro's café, just off the High Street in Inverannan, served coffee, tea and snacks all day. The shop was popular because it was inexpensive and cheerful.

Evelyn was on her feet all day, from eight in the morning until six at night, six days a week. The seven mile bus journey added another hour to each working day.

Her feet ached until she thought they couldn't possibly support her for another minute, her head throbbed with fatigue and her throat rasped with calling orders. She loved every second of it. The cheerful banter from the customers – and not a word about shifts, coal or underground conditions – the friendship of the other waitresses, the cheeky repartee from the truanting school children who had made this their favourite haunt and the gentle, teasing flirtation with the charming Mr Alessandro himself, all made the long hours pass with amazing speed.

With her first pay she bought clothes for David. Her second wage was used to make the girls more respectable. Then there was the rent to bring up to date and her bill at Mrs McPhee's to clear. It was three full months before she was able to do anything about her own ailing wardrobe. Even then she had a momentary pang of conscience when she treated herself to two new skirts, a jumper, a blouse and some stylish new shoes, and wondered if the money might not have been better spent to replace the worn sheets on the children's beds. But she often took her breaks at the back of the café with Mr Alessandro himself for company. Without knowing why, she felt it was important to look her best for him.

FIVE

Fifteen-year-old Mary Innes let herself into the prefab, threw her school bag down, put on a large apron and set about clearing away the remains of breakfast. Without pausing she went on to infuse a cup of tea, made a pile of jam sandwiches and called her brother and sisters to come for tea, nagging them to hurry up, to wash their hands, to change out of their school clothes and make their beds while peeling her way through two pounds of potatoes for the evening meal. Then she wiped her reddened hands on her apron and took a cup of tarry tea through to her father who she knew would be asleep in the living room. It was where George spent most of his time since his disabled back and his wife's job had freed him from the burden of working for a living.

'Thanks, Hen,' he mumbled, knuckling sleep from his eyes.

'Just look at the state of this room, Dad! Could you not have tidied it up a bit?' Her heart sank at the prospect of restoring it to some sort of order before her mother saw it.

'You know I can't. Not with my back,' he protested, bending nimbly to retrieve his paper from the floor. 'Anyway, what's wrong with it?' he asked, seeing nothing amiss in the litter of dirty cups, old papers and abandoned shoes.

'Mum'll have a blue fit if she comes home and finds it like this,' Mary chided him, knowing she was wasting her breath. Her father was hopeless, perfectly content to live surrounded by clutter and much too lazy to do anything about it. Mary's exasperation was tinged with affection. Her father was far too good-natured for her to feel any lasting anger towards him.

It was her mother she really resented for leaving her to do nearly everything round the house from making the tea and cleaning to ironing and seeing to the other children. By the time she got her chores done there was very little of the evening left in which to do her homework. Most of that was tackled after she should have been in bed, leaving her tired and edgy in the mornings. It wouldn't be so bad if someone would help her out occasionally, or even if her mother showed some sign of appreciation. But she never did. It really wasn't fair. None of the other girls at school had to do half as much round the house, even though some of their mothers worked too. Because of all the housework she never had time to see her classmates outside school, to go to their houses or invite them back here, like Catherine and Linda often did. That was the main reason why she had no close friends.

Mary would have been surprised to learn that Evelyn was not unaware of her efforts, nor unappreciative, but, she told herself, there was nothing she could do to make her daughter's life any easier. It was simply the lot of the oldest daughter. A small niggle of conscience insisted that she wasn't being fair, that Mary deserved better than this, a lot better. But Evelyn knew that Mary's life was going to get a great deal worse before very much longer.

The children were all surprised when they got up to find their mother in the kitchen making breakfast for them. As a rule she was already on her way to work before they even got out of bed and it was Mary who made their toast and ensured they had everything for school. Even stranger, when they set out that morning, their mother kissed each of them, slipped a whole shilling into each pair of hands and even waved goodbye. Catherine, Linda and David shot across the road to spend their unexpected windfall as soon as they possibly could at Mrs McPhee's sweetie counter while Mary walked to school, so slowly that the others soon overtook her. Her own shilling lay forgotten in her pocket and her mother's puzzling, slightly hurtful words were still ringing in her ears.

'You're a good lass, Mary. Don't think I don't know what you do round the house. Just remember, this is what life is all about once you've gotten yourself saddled with a husband and kids. Work, work and more work. And for what? Think hard, Mary, before you're ever tempted to make my mistake. Don't throw your life away on some idle, good-for-nothing man.

'Aye,' she added, looking critically at her daughter's pasty complexion and the puzzled eyes which seemed to loom out at her from the depths of deeply-shadowed caves. 'But perhaps you'll not get married. You're such a plain wee thing and maybe that's just as well. If you can't get yourself a man then you'll have to learn to fend for yourself . . . to make something of yourself. You'll be happier that way and at least you'll not end up like me.' It was almost as if Evelyn was thinking aloud and she turned away abruptly. 'Away to school with you but be sure and remember what I've said.'

At school Mary made straight for the girls' cloakroom and faced herself squarely in its big mirror. Plain. Her own mother called her plain. And her granny. Even her father never called her his pretty wee thing like he did Catherine and Linda.

The sombre, grey eyes examined every feature and found something lacking in each one. The eyes themselves

– why were they so big and staring, so totally out of proportion to the rest of her face? Like the eyes of a frightened animal. Her nose was tiny and her mouth so small and pale that if she kept it closed it was as if it wasn't there at all. She smiled at herself, a frozen, awkward leer, but at least it showed her tiny, even teeth and made her mouth reappear. And that silly chin! Pointed, like a pixie's. That was what her father called her sometimes. His wee pixie. She knew it was because her ears stuck out, like two ugly toadstools, on either side of her face. They looked even more obvious when her hair was scraped back from her face for school. Scowling she dragged the ribbon out and shook her fine, fair hair down round her face. She would be told off for having it hanging loose but at least it hid those ears. Absorbed in self-loathing she stepped back from the mirror until she could see the rest of her body. Flat. Completely flat. Even when she had no clothes on, her chest was nothing more than a slight unevenness. In school uniform she had nothing, no figure at all. Even Catherine and Linda had more shape. As for her legs they were so thin that her knees were like rheumatic swellings. Above them her thighs actually went in again. Sparrow legs was what the boys called her.

Boys didn't like her. They were always calling her names, especially when she came top in the class tests, which she usually did. Some of her classmates already had steady boyfriends. She didn't. She never seemed to get beyond the first date. Not one single boy had asked her out a second time.

Her mother's words rang in her head. 'You'll have to make something of yourself,' was what she'd said. Well, Mary decided, that was exactly what she would do. She would make something of herself and then no one would notice how ugly she was.

*

When Mary got home from school that afternoon, the house was unnaturally quiet and empty. More astonishingly it was immaculately tidy. A casserole, with huge chunks of steak in it, simmered in the oven and the potatoes were ready peeled in a pot atop the cooker. Puzzled, Mary fed her brother and sisters, put her father's share in the oven to keep warm and settled to her school books.

The evening passed incredibly slowly. By nine o'clock there was still no sign of either parent and the feeling of apprehension which had dogged Mary all day was growing steadily stronger. She chased David off to bed and, with great difficulty, persuaded her sisters to follow an hour later. A little after eleven she gave up waiting and went to bed too. She heard her father stumble in just before midnight. Of her mother there was no sign.

In the morning things were the same as ever. When she got in from school the breakfast dishes were still unwashed and there was nothing in the house for tea. Fighting a rising tide of resentful anger she went to take a ten-shilling note from the housekeeping jar on the mantelpiece so she could buy some sliced white pudding for tea. The shock she got when she looked into the jar, which was more often empty than not, almost caused her to drop it. Instead of the few loose shillings she had hoped to find, it was tightly packed with rolled notes. Hesitantly she took them out and counted them. Forty single pound notes, some silver and, at the very bottom, neatly folded, three five pound notes and a piece of paper. She opened it and recognised her mother's scrawled handwriting immediately.

'This will be enough to see you through for a little while,' Evelyn had written. 'Ask your dad for more before this runs out. Make sure he pays the rent.'

Mary felt her hands start to shake. Slowly she sank into

a chair and stared at the money. It was more than she had ever seen in her whole life but it gave her no pleasure. All she felt was a dread laden hollowing of her stomach.

So little did they normally see of their mother that the others hardly seemed to register her absence. When David asked where his father was, Mary snapped, 'He'll not be in 'till after you're sleeping.'

Her heart racing, her stomach aching with fear, Mary waited alone in the dark until, well after midnight, she heard her father's key fumbling in the lock. As soon as he lurched into the room she knew he was very drunk.

'Are you not in your bed, then?' he slurred, sinking into his chair. 'Make us a cup of tea, there's a good lassie.'

Hoping it would sober him up a bit Mary did as he asked and waited until he had finished drinking it before saying, 'Where's Mammy?'

It was as if he hadn't heard her. He continued to stare morosely in front of him, his shoulders hunched, his face drawn.

'Did you hear me, Daddy? Where's Mammy?'

The expression on his face when he finally looked up at her turned the ache in her stomach to molten lead. 'She's gone, Hen,' he mumbled.

'Gone! Gone where? When is she coming back?' she demanded, frightened to know the answers.

'She's not coming back, Lass.'

'Not coming back?' she repeated, blankly.

Suddenly George made a terrible choking noise and buried his face in his hands. His shoulders heaved, his thin body shook. 'What will I do? What will I do?' he repeated over and over again.

Mary watched in horror, the sight of her father's tears shaking her as much as the knowledge that her mother had abandoned them. Feeling as if there was no strength left in her body she knelt beside him and put a trembling hand on his arm. 'Where's she gone, Dad?'

Still with his face hidden he muttered, 'With that Alessandro. She's run off with that Alessandro, from the café.'

It was as if she had known all along but if that didn't shock her his next words did.

'You'll have to take her place, Hen. Look after the weans. And the house. You're the eldest.' Defeat was plain in every syllable.

Mary let her hand fall from his arm and rocked back on her heels, staring at him aghast, resentment drowning every other emotion.

'That is not fair,' she choked.

'I know, Hen. Life's never fair. But there's nothing I can do about it. I'm not a well man, you know that. You'll just have to make the best of it.'

For the first time, watching her father and seeing no trace of bitterness or anger but only self-pity and selfishness, the unquestioned affection she had always felt for him was tinged with doubt.

'How do you know she's gone off with Mr Alessandro?' she asked.

'She told me yesterday,' he admitted.

'And you let her go?'

'Ah, Lass, what could I do to stop her? He's got money . . . and a big house in Edinburgh . . . Your mother always wanted something better than Craigie.'

'She might have stayed if you'd talked to her, made her feel you really wanted her,' she suggested, naively.

'What was the point? Her mind was made up,' he shrugged, resignation obvious in his watery eyes.

Slowly, Mary pulled herself to her feet and walked out of the room, not trusting herself to do or say anything else. Even the sound of her father's noisy weeping failed to move her. All she could feel for him was contempt.

'Did you know Mammy was leaving us?' Mary, who was truanting from school for the one and only time in her life, faced her grandmother, determined to get an answer.

Ina eyed her wearily. She had been expecting this visit. 'She left me a note, same as you. Shoved it through the letter box. Didn't even have the guts to tell me face to face,' she said bitterly.

'Does she say where she's gone?' Mary pleaded, desperate to find her mother, to beg her to come back.

'See for yourself.'

Ina handed the crumpled sheet of paper across. Evelyn's scrawled message merely said that she was leaving and asked her mother to pass that brief information on to Jackie, Matt, Alec and William.

'Gran, if she writes to you or anything, will you tell me, please?'

'I doubt your mother will write, Lass, and the sooner you accept that the better. She's gone to get away from the lot of you. Gone off with that Mr Alessandro, thinking she'll be happier with him, an Italian, than she is with her own people. She always did want something better than Craigie. Well, now she thinks she's found it. Good riddance to her I say.'

Mary saw there was no comfort to be had from her grandmother who persisted in the bitterness which had driven all but one of her sons to look for work and homes in areas well away from Craigie. Of Evelyn's four brothers and one half-brother, only Jackie remained in the village. Although he and his wife sent Christmas and birthday cards to the Innes children, the families weren't close and Mary knew her mother wouldn't have confided in him.

'But there's so much to do, Gran,' she burst out suddenly, sounding as bitter as her grandmother. 'None of the others help me and I've even got the washing to do now.'

'You are fifteen years old, Mary Innes! Old enough to look after your family without moaning about it,' Ina said curtly. 'And if that was a hint for me to help out, think again. I'm an old woman and I've done my share. Anyway, I don't think that father of yours would be pleased to have me in his house, even for an hour each day.'

That at least was true.

Mary couldn't recall the last time her father had been at home in the evening. Nor could she remember him coming in sober. If she was still bitterly angry with her mother that anger was tempered by an awakening understanding as she saw her father for what he really was. A lazy, pathetic man who would go to any lengths to avoid working and left his young family to fend for themselves while he wallowed contentedly in self-pity.

There were times when she thought she actually hated him, days when, exhausted by the demands of running a home and keeping her brothers and sisters in order, she wanted to shout and scream, to vent her anger and frustration on the nearest living thing. She never did. Responsibility brought self-control. The never-ending battle to keep them all decently clad and fed on a meagre budget made her old before her time. She didn't complain. There was too much pride in her for that and it would have been a waste of time in any case.

'Can you spare a bit for a pint, Lass?' It was a whining request her father made at this time every week.

'There's nothing left,' she snapped, reminding him of Evelyn.

'Just two bob?' he begged.

'Not even two pennies. And all you're getting for tea the night is stovies.'

'Nothing wrong with stovies,' he laughed. 'Still, there'll be more money to spare once you're out to work.'

'What?' she gasped, hoping she had misheard him.

'Well, you've already turned fifteen. What's the point of wasting more time at school when you could be out earning good money?'

She rounded on him, an angry flush staining her cheeks. 'I am not leaving school. I'm staying on for my exams.'

'What for?' He was genuinely amazed. 'The lassie Meachin's got a braw job, sewing skirts and things at that clothing factory near the bus stance, in the town. She didn't need exams for that and they pay a fair wage. Her father was telling me last night.'

'I am not going to work in any factory. I am going to college to train to be a cook.'

'You can already cook! You make braw meals.'

'I want to be a proper cook.' The idea had been simmering in the back of her mind for a long time. She loved cooking and properly qualified she could get a job which would be more interesting and with better prospects than any factory could offer. When she had time to daydream she saw herself living in a smart house, somewhere miles away from Craigie, perhaps in one of those pretty coastal villages – like the one her mother's Aunt Maureen and Uncle Maurice lived in – and running her own successful restaurant. Her father's bland assumption that she would leave school at the first opportunity and take whatever job happened to be available suddenly solidified her ambition.

Keenly aware of the fact that she was unattractive she knew that, unlike the majority of girls who only took a job to mark time until they caught themselves a husband, she would need to choose a career which would support her throughout her life. As a professional cook she would have wonderful opportunities and, from what her domestic science teacher had told her, some catering jobs were residential, making them all the more attractive.

George Innes always knew when he was beaten. 'Och, well, I suppose we could manage for a wee while longer, if that's what you want, though I don't see the point in it myself.'

Dismissing his daughter from his thoughts he settled into his old armchair and waited for his tea to be brought to him. As for his drinking money, well, Bob Mathie at the Greyhound would put a couple of pints on the slate, just as he always did.

SIX

Mary ignored the feeling of guilt which persistently niggled away at her and got on with writing the letter accepting her very first job. As an assistant cook at St Elphin's college, in St Andrews, she would have a small but regular salary, a secure job and her own room. It was what had kept her plodding stolidly through her school certificates and three years at college while most of her classmates left school to work in local factories. Most of them seemed to find husbands and get married within a year or so.

Her father, though never understanding her desire to make something of herself, offered no serious opposition. Neither did he display the slightest interest in her course. But, when she finally brought her diploma home to show him, he was roused to emotional praise. No one he knew had ever gained any sort of paper qualification and he boasted about his 'clever lassie' to all his cronies at the Greyhound.

He was just as pleased when she told him she had a job. Admitting she was leaving home was another matter.

'What do you want to do that for?' he complained, looking almost crestfallen.

'I want a decent job, Dad. I told you that, years ago. What was the point of all that training if I don't intend to use it?' she said in her quietly lilting voice. She had worked hard at taking the rougher edges off of her Craigie accent, knowing a better speaking voice would give her more chance of success at interviews. The result had been the label 'snob' from people who had known her all her life. People she had been at school with mocked her for her ambition and hardly bothered to say hello when they met on the street.

'There are cafés in Inverannan. What about that place your mother used to work in?'

'Dad!' It amazed her that he could even bring himself to talk about Alessandro's let alone suggest she go to work there.

'But they would be glad to have you with they qualifications. And all the factories have canteens. Or even at the pit. They're always looking for women to help out in the kitchens.'

'I am going to be a cook, Dad, not a waitress or a potato peeler.' Though she suspected that that was exactly what she would be, at least to start with.

He shook his head, not understanding her at all. 'I don't get it,' he admitted. 'Why go all the way to St Andrews when you could stay here in your own home? What will you do with yourself up at that fancy university place? They'll all be stuck up, cleverer than you. Your fancy way of talking won't make you one of them. You should stay with your own kind.'

How could she ever make him understand her burning desire to get away from her own kind, to escape the sort of life that had driven her mother away? The kind of life that would trap her, too, if she stayed. And who in their right mind would prefer Craigie to St Andrews?

'Aye,' Linda, who had been working in a factory since her fifteenth birthday, chimed in. 'Are we not good enough for you now?' But there was no real malice in her teasing tone.

'Well, I think you're right stupid,' Catherine said later, when George had gone on his nightly pilgrimage to the

Greyhound. 'And what about us? Stuck here with all the housework?'

'It'll do you good,' Mary retorted. 'It's about time you started to pull your weight. I've been doing the lot since I was old enough to get my arms in the sink. Now it's your turn. Anyway,' she added. 'You're the stupid one. Imagine getting yourself engaged at your age. You're hardly old enough to leave school. Before you know it you'll be running round after a man and half a dozen snotty-nosed kids. And you haven't been anywhere or done anything yet!'

'You are just like your mother,' Ina Lennox sneered when Mary finally plucked up the courage to go and see her grandmother who stubbornly refused to enter her son-in-law's house on the grounds that she had never been welcome when her daughter was there. It was a flimsy excuse made so she would not be trapped into taking on some share of the household chores and Mary knew it. In truth, the children weren't fond of their grandmother whose acid tongue so obviously delighted in finding fault and George was frankly terrified of her. They were all relieved to limit contact with her to a once weekly 'duty' visit. 'She ran away from her responsibilities and all. Thought she was too good for Craigie and look how she ended up! Running off with a Tally and him a Catholic! As if him having money made it all right,' she went on.

But at least Evelyn's Tally had had the decency to make things legal and respectable which was more than she had been able to persuade Tammy McGurk to do. Despite her constant nagging Tammy had never been able to bring himself to marry her and she had only returned to some semblance of respectability after he died, late the year before, leaving her nothing more than his clothes. Ina's eyes glittered briefly with the fury, tinged with envy, she still felt every time she thought about the happiness and

90

wealth her daughter had found with her new husband. Happiness which was obvious in the letters Evelyn wrote to her mother at odd intervals begging for news of the children she had abandoned and giving snippets of information about herself and her new life. Ina had made a single trip to the prefab to show George one of his wife's letters but, more deeply wounded by Evelyn's treachery than his children would ever know, he had refused to read it, preferring to sever all painful links and genuinely, if mistakenly, believing it would be better for his son and daughters to forget their mother. So, it was left to Ina's bitter and barely literate hand to keep her daughter up to date with the progress of her family.

'I am not running away,' Mary pointed out as reasonably as she could.

'You're leaving your father and the weans to cope on their own. That's running away.'

'They're not weans! Even David is old enough to look after himself now. It'll do them good.'

'You are the eldest. It's your place to look after the family. That soft-headed father of yours will never manage on his own.'

'He's not going to be on his own.' Mary wanted to scream her frustration. Her face coloured hotly and she clenched her fists into tight little balls in an effort to control her rapidly rising temper. 'Linda and Catherine are quite capable of taking care of the house. I was doing it long before I was their age.'

'They'll be married before you can sneeze. You've not got a man of your own yet so it's only right that you should be the one to look after your father.'

'That's not fair,' spluttered Mary. 'Father is quite capable of fending for himself. He's not crippled. Why shouldn't he be the one to run the house? He's got nothing better to do with his time. Anyway, if you're so worried, you go and look after him. But no one is going to tell me what to do with my life, Gran. I am not going to end up like all the others, married to some ignorant miner who spends half his life underground and half his pay on booze. I am going to have a decent career, a home of my own somewhere nice and, one day, my own business. Just you wait and see. St Andrews is just the start.'

'I've heard it all before,' Ina snapped. 'Almost word for word. Like mother, like daughter and I'll tell you what I told your mother all those years ago. You've ideas above yourself, my girl, and you'll soon see you're no better than all the rest of us.' She broke off, a slow smile spreading across her wrinkled face. 'Mind you, perhaps you're right about being able to support yourself. I can't see any man wanting to take you on.' Her granddaughter was far too outspoken, too stubborn and independently-minded to ever make a good, submissive wife. Ina turned away so that Mary couldn't see the openly twisted smile of victory which bared her gums.

'That is not why I'm doing it,' Mary said coldly. 'Why won't any of you understand?'

She turned away. Her head throbbed, her eyelids burned with the effort of restraining the tears which threatened to trickle down her face. But she wouldn't give the old woman the satisfaction of seeing how much that last comment, which she wrongly assumed had referred to her looks, had hurt. Had she understood her grandmother's true meaning she might even have been pleased.

The bustling university town of St Andrews was a full two hours away from Craigie by bus. Mary made the journey in a state bordering on euphoria. Even the overcast sky and drizzling rain could do nothing to dampen her enthusiasm.

By the time she had dragged her single, heavy bag from the bus stance to the college she was bedraggled and very conscious of the fact that she looked far from her best and hardly likely to make a favourable impression on her new employer. St Elphin's college loomed on a street corner, greyer and more forbidding than it had seemed when she had attended her interview on a mellow, sunny, late summer day, a month ago now. Its double doors swallowed Mary and disgorged her with a clang into a dingy, green corridor. A peeling arrow indicated the direction of the domestic bursar's office. Mary hesitated, her confidence melting in the overpowering gloom, and attempted to ignore the combined smells of dust, age and Jeyes fluid which were making her eyes itch. Behind her the doors crashed open again. A student, her arms full of books, hurried through looking businesslike and purposeful. Mary pretended to be absorbed in an untidy notice-board until a corner hid the girl from view.

Well, she told herself, no one is going to come and lead you by the hand. You're independent now and responsible for yourself. Buoyed up by the thought she marched down the corridor, a slight but determined figure, dragging her one suitcase behind her.

Twenty minutes later, still clutching her bag and trying desperately to hide her apprehension, Mary followed a junoesque woman along another, narrower passageway and into a lift which clanked and groaned alarmingly as it took them to the very top of the old building. The corridor which awaited them there was even more depressing. Doors, in a uniform, sludgy brown, lurked like cavern entrances in walls of unrelieved, sickly green.

'This is your room, Miss Innes.' The bursar, a severe woman with flint-like, very direct, grey eyes, pressed a heavy, metal object into Mary's hand. 'Here is your key and a list of rules. Be in the kitchen at six sharp in the morning. You'll meet cook then. Remember the kitchen and the dining room are in the basement. The lift takes you right down. The other floors are off limits.' With those encouraging words of welcome she was off.

Mary grappled with the stiff lock, stepped into her room and shut the door quickly, hiding the dreadful corridor from view. She expected her room to be little better but, as she gazed cautiously round, her mouth gradually lifted into the hint of a smile.

It was big, almost as big as all the rooms of the prefab combined. Along one wall was a single bed, its cheerful coverlet dotted with bright cushions. Another wall was dominated by a set of shelves, already partially filled with books and small ornaments. The third wall housed two deep, casement windows which were allowing the newly-emerged, early afternoon sun to flood in. In the centre of the room three easy chairs were grouped round a low table and, on that table sat a television set, a luxury they had never been able to afford at home. In the corner, at right angles to the windows, was a door. Timidly she opened it, not sure if it might lead to another employee's private room, and discovered her own, personal, bathroom. It was all, she decided, perfect.

In a sudden burst of energy she flung open her case and started to pack away her few things in the huge wardrobe which completed the furnishings. Already hanging inside was a creamy white overall and, on a shelf above it, a puffy, white hat. Pinned to the pocket of the overall was a green badge with white printing on it. Miss M. Innes. Assistant Cook. Miss M. Innes, Assistant Cook, laughed aloud.

Alone in a room at night for the very first time in her life, Mary simply couldn't relax enough to get to sleep. Disembodied voices, distant laughter, quick footsteps and the restless, creaking, shifting of the old building kept her tossing and wakeful in her new bed. From across the quadrangle the college clock struck the hour and it was only after she had counted four that she finally drifted into sleep. Her alarm woke her at five-thirty but, exhausted by her restless night, she allowed herself to drift back into a light doze. It was a quarter to six before she opened her eyes again. With only fifteen minutes to go before she was due to report for her first day at work, she jumped out of bed with a start. Panicking she washed, dressed, tidied her hair and ran from the room with three minutes to spare.

It was after two that afternoon before she found her way back upstairs. Her new duties promised to be exhausting but at least she had managed to get through the day without making any ghastly mistakes. Breakfast had been easy, few students seemed to bother with more than toast and cereal, but lunch-time had been a different matter. The spacious dining hall had been crammed with students, all eager to have a cheap, filling meal as quickly as possible. By the time the last dinner had been served, Mary barely had enough energy to eat her own lunch but the rest of the day was hers. Tea and the evening meal were seen to by other staff and she was already looking forward to getting her turn at that, too.

Excited by all that had happened to her and eager to share it with her family she sat down as soon as she got back to her own room and wrote a long, descriptive letter to her father, keen to make everyone at home understand that she had made the right decision, that despite all that had been said to her she was going to be happy and successful in St Andrews.

Mary's natural warmth and the friendliness of her new colleagues made settling in easier than she had expected. Professionally it didn't take her long to establish herself as an efficient and original cook who accepted responsibility eagerly, never flapped in a crisis and had a remedy for every disaster. When she was left in charge of the kitchen, which happened frequently, she managed the other staff, all older than her, with an easy, firm authority which completely belied her slight build and youthful appearance.

As the weeks passed she began to recognise many of the students and staff of the college. Most of them had a friendly word for her and some of the boys even flirted a little. She knew better than to take them seriously, she knew how unattractive she was – she had been told so often enough. Even so, it was a new experience for her and she enjoyed it openly, responding to them all with a cheerful smile and unflagging good humour. And she made a friend.

Janette King was one of the two other assistant cooks and had the room next to Mary's. She was about two years older than Mary, dark haired, plump, sociable and outspoken. In fact Janette was the precise opposite of her new friend but the two young women took to one another on sight and quickly fell into the habit of spending much of their free time together.

'Why don't we go to a pub on Friday night, just for a change? Or there's a dance at the community hall. That'd make a nice change,' Janette suggested, about a month after Mary's arrival in St Andrew's. The two young women were sharing a cup of coffee in Mary's room, directly after finishing work for the day.

Mary laughed tolerantly. Janette was extroverted and lively, and was forever telling her she needed to get out more. 'I'm not going to any dance.' The idea frightened her, giving visions of her being the only one to have to sit out, too ugly for anyone to want to dance with, while everyone else had a wonderful time.

'But you never do anything more exciting than going

to the pictures, Mary. How on earth do you expect to meet people that way?'

'I meet plenty of people here, in college,' Mary retorted.

Janette sighed. 'I mean boyfriends . . . you do like boys, don't you?'

'Yeees . . .' Mary coloured uncomfortably.

'Well then! A dance is a great place to meet boys. You'll enjoy yourself once you get there.'

'No I won't,' Mary snapped.

Janette bit off the sharp reply that sprang to her own lips and looked at her friend thoughtfully. 'Have you ever been to a dance before, Mary?' she asked.

Mary shrugged. 'I don't remember,' she lied, colouring hotly. Then looking up and catching her friend's raised eyebrow and disbelieving expression. 'OK. OK. No. I've never been to a dance.'

'Not even at school? Surely there was a leaving dance, or one at Christmas?'

'There was one when we left but . . .' She dropped it, hoping she wouldn't need to go into detailed explanations.

'But?' Janette insisted.

'No one asked me to be their partner . . . I couldn't go on my own . . . without a date . . .' It was a dreadfully painful admission, one she could have made to no one else. 'I couldn't have gone anyway. We didn't have a lot of money. I wouldn't have been able to buy a decent dress to wear.'

'So, you've never been out with a boy!' Janette exclaimed.

'I didn't say that!' Mary protested.

'All right. I apologise,' Janette laughed now.

'That's all right. I know it seems unbelievable but I have had a couple of dates.'

'Why should it be unbelievable?' Janette asked, shocked by the obvious vulnerability she saw in her friend's face.

Mary directed a look of such pure scorn at Janette that, under different circumstances, the older girl would have been hurt. As it was she sensed the pain her friend was valiantly trying to hide. 'You know why,' Mary muttered.

'No I don't! Oh,' she sighed in exasperation. 'What's this all about, Mary? Why should the thought of you having a date be so unbelievable?'

'Don't try to be so nice all the time, Janette. We're friends. You don't have to pretend with me. You can't hurt me with the truth. I know I'm ugly. Even my parents told me how plain I was. And it's not as if I can't see it for myself every time I look in the mirror. There's no point in trying to meet boys, they just make fun of me.'

'Your own parents told you you were plain?' Janette was appalled.

Mary nodded. 'You should see the photographs of me when I was a baby! Horrific!' she laughed, weakly.

'Most babies are and there's nothing wrong with you now!' Janette asserted strongly.

'You're only saying that because you're my friend.'

'No I'm not! You're not perfect, any more than I am, but, if you want to know the truth, I think you're quite pretty. And you've got a marvellous figure. I'd kill to be as slim as you.'

Mary surged to her feet, marched to the wardrobe and threw it open. Standing stiffly she stared at her own reflection in the long mirror on the inside of the door. It was truly awful. 'How can you say that? Look at me,' she wailed in despair.

She was still in her uniform. The long, off-white coat did absolutely nothing for her, hanging like a flour sack and hiding what little shape she did have. Nor did her practical, black shoes help, making her legs seem even more spindly than they really were. But that was nothing compared to the effect of the white hat which covered her hair. The thick band, pulled low on to her forehead, drew attention to her eyes, making them even larger and darker, while the netted crown gave her head a peculiar, flattened shape. It was a shape that perfectly emphasised her ears which stuck out flagrantly, determined to be noticed. How she hated them! They were ridiculous. Her whole appearance was laughable.

Furiously she tore the hat from her head and turned to face her friend.

'How on earth could you expect any normal boy to fancy someone who looks like this?' she demanded.

Janette chuckled, forcing Mary to a wry smile. 'Good God, Mary, surely you wouldn't go dancing dressed in that?'

'Don't be daft.'

'That uniform would make anyone look ridiculous,' Janette assured her. 'I can't bear to look at myself when I'm wearing mine.'

'I can't bear to look at myself even when I'm not wearing it,' Mary confessed.

Janette's heart went out to her friend. 'But that's stupid. What on earth's given you the idea that you're so hideous?'

'I told you. Everyone says I'm plain. They always have.'

Janette looked at her closely. 'Well, you're certainly not plain now. Perhaps you were when you were a kid, but people change as they get older.'

'Not that much.'

Janette snorted her impatience. 'For goodness sake, stop feeling so sorry for yourself and look into that mirror again but this time look properly.' Mary turned reluctantly and stared at her own unhappy reflection. 'Right,' Janette said. 'Tell me what's wrong with you.'

Mary shrugged, suddenly self-conscious.

'Come on,' Janette insisted. 'Let's get to the root of it.'

'Everything!' Mary shouted. 'My mouth's too small,

mean looking. My nose is ridiculous. My eyes are too deep in my head and look at my ears!'

She dragged her hair out of the loosened pony tail she had worn all day and scraped it back off her face so that her ears stuck out in the most ludicrous way.

Janette studied her friend's features. 'You're right about the ears,' she admitted eventually. 'They do stick out. But you could hide them.'

'See, I told you so,' Mary said, sounding childishly peevish.

'But the rest of you is perfectly OK,' Janette went on, ignoring the outburst. 'Your eyes are wonderful. Huge, a lovely colour and such long eyelashes. Your mouth is fine, especially when you smile because your teeth are nice and even. And your nose is beautifully neat. As if that's not enough you've got all this wonderful, blonde hair. Women pay a fortune in hairdressing bills for hair like this,' she laughed, lifting a silky strand and running it through her fingers. 'I'll admit you're thin but that's fashionable. You'll look great in tight skirts and trousers.'

Mary was staring at herself as if she found her friend's words impossible to believe. 'I don't see the person you've just described,' she smiled at Janette in the mirror, still convinced she was simply being kind.

'Well, it's you all right. The trouble is, you don't make the best of yourself. You could try a bit of make-up, like the rest of us do. And I'll bet you've worn your hair like that since the day you started school. Your ears are your one bad point. Instead of disguising them, like anyone sensible would do, you've chosen the style which will make them look even worse.'

'What else can I do with it? I have to get it out of the way for work. I suppose I could have it cut . . .'

'No! It's beautiful. For goodness sake, don't do that,' Janette pleaded, sending them both into fits of laughter.

'Look, I'll just nip to my room and fetch my make-up. I'm dark and you're fair so the colours won't be quite right for you, but it'll give you the general idea. I'll bring some clips and things for your hair too if you like, and we could try out some different styles.'

'OK,' Mary agreed, her eyes sparkling in anticipation.

For the next hour they experimented with make-up and hair-styles as they struggled to find some way to hide those dreadful ears. Mary's long, shining tresses were coiled and twisted, brushed and pinned into a variety of styles until at last they thought they might have found the solution. Now her hair was gathered at the nape of her neck in a loose knot but, rather than pulling it back behind the ears, Janette had drawn it over them, so that nothing more than the small, pink lobes were visible.

'I'll take you to have your ears pierced tomorrow,' Janette promised. 'You'll suit ear-rings.'

Conditioned from childhood to believe she was hopelessly plain, Mary stared at her reflection critically and saw nothing of the soft beauty which was only just emerging from the pinched, urchin-like features of childhood. But she had to admit that the face that looked back so gravely was much improved over the one which had so depressed her an hour ago. The new hair-style softened the effect of her huge, grey eyes, allowing the honey blonde of her hair to complement the delicate tone of her skin, rather than draining it. Yes, she thought, that was better, more mature, almost sophisticated.

'My family won't recognise me when I go home this weekend,' she laughed at Janette.

The Mary Innes who went self-consciously into the kitchen to work the next afternoon attracted compliments from her workmates and even a wolf-whistle from one admiring student. Caught back in its new style her hair framed her face in shining gold, neat gold studs twinkled in her pinkened ear lobes, a faint dusting of newly-purchased rouge gave unexpected shape to her delicate cheekbones and her pale lips were lent definition by the merest hint of lipstick. She looked bright, attractive and confident. And that was exactly how she felt.

SEVEN

Mary's new-found but fragile confidence in her appearance was further boosted when one of the professors who regularly used the dining room appeared to be taking more than just a passing interest in her. Mary had often noticed Professor Paul Kinsail. Not because he was particularly good-looking. In fact he was just the opposite. His face was pale, his brows heavy and his nose too large but the overall effect was of unusually fascinating and attractive ugliness. But it was his manner rather than his looks which had first claimed Mary's attention. Compared to other members of staff he was aloof and cold. Despite the fact that he was one of the youngest professors and less than ten years older than most of his students they treated him with unnatural and wary formality, often getting nothing more than an arrogant, disinterested stare in response to a perfectly polite greeting. It was obvious that he was extremely unpopular. Nor did he appear to have any friends among his colleagues who left him to dine alone, usually immersed in papers.

But, to Mary, he was charming, his manner towards her impeccable. When she was on duty he always had time for a polite word, asking if she was settling in, whether she was making friends in the town and how she liked her job, then listening attentively while she answered. Of course, in so doing, he conveyed the unlikely impression that he was genuinely interested in her.

Vastly flattered to find herself singled out by such an

eminent person, Mary still couldn't let herself believe that there was anything more to it than pure good manners on his part. But she couldn't stop herself from hoping. Lacking the experience which might have equipped her to deal with him, it was natural for her to want to discuss Paul Kinsail with Janette, from whom she had few secrets. But, to Mary's dismay, Janette gave the distinct impression that she was anything but pleased for her friend. Sounding almost angry she told Mary she was being a fool to even contemplate a relationship with a member of staff, something which was strictly forbidden in the long list of college rules, and added, with some acerbity, that he was far too old for her before deliberately changing the subject. Mary was careful never to mention his name in front of Janette again.

Mary was browsing through the magazines in a town centre newsagents when she became uncomfortably aware that someone was staring at her. Pinkening slightly, she glanced up, frowning her annoyance, and found herself looking into Paul Kinsail's pale brown eyes. He was watching her from the opposite side of the rack.

'It is Miss Innes, isn't it? I wasn't sure at first. I've never seen you with that wonderful hair loose before. It suits you like that. You really are a very beautiful young woman.'

Despite her better instincts she couldn't help smiling at the unaccustomed compliment. 'Or without that awful white hat,' she laughed, marvelling at how attractive she suddenly felt, simply because someone had told her she was beautiful.

'Are you in a hurry? If not, I was just going to have a coffee. Would you like to join me?' he asked, following her to the till.

Mary wondered if she was being picked up and half-hoped she was. 'I have to be at work for two,' she answered, doubtfully.

'There's plenty of time then,' he decided, taking her arm in a solid grip and leading her to a nearby café.

She sat down nervously, wondering what on earth she could find to say to this charismatic professor, frightened that he would think her dull or uneducated, dreading that half-surprised, half-contemptuous look of haughty disdain she had seen him levelling at more than one unfortunate student.

She need not have worried. Outside the confines of the college it was as if he were a different person, an impression heightened by his care to exercise his well-practised charm on her. Not at all aloof he chatted comfortably, entertaining her with wicked anecdotes about various faculty members. Relaxed and laughing she forgot to fret about the impression she was making on him, allowing the natural warmth of her personality to shine through, making her eyes sparkle and bringing fresh colour to her cheeks. Paul Kinsail noted, with some satisfaction, that other customers were looking at her with open admiration and at him with envy.

It seemed they had only been there for a few minutes when he looked at his watch and exclaimed, 'It's a quarter to two! You had better hurry if you don't want to be late.'

She gasped. 'I didn't realise that was the time!' Frantically she gathered her shopping and dashed for the door. 'Thanks for the coffee,' she called back as she ran towards St Elphin's.

Kinsail followed, more slowly, then stood on the pavement and watched as she dodged nimbly through the traffic, her hair rippling round her shoulders as she ran. There was a thin, self-satisfied smile curling his lips when he made his own leisurely way back to college.

★

Because it was cook's day off, Mary was in charge. As always she took her responsibility seriously, determined that she would give no cause for criticism. When the last student had finished his supper she checked that everything was in order in the kitchen then went to make sure the dining room was tidy, clean and ready for breakfast. To her surprise there was still one figure at a table, his back to her, apparently unaware that the room had emptied around him.

'Professor Kinsail,' she laughed, feeling her pulse quicken. 'I'm sorry but the dining room is closing now.'

He flapped his book shut and smiled up at her. 'So, you're evicting me?'

''Fraid so.'

'Actually,' he confided, 'I was waiting for you.'

Her heart leapt painfully. 'For me?'

'You left your magazine in the café yesterday.' He held the offending book out to her.

Mary was mortified to know he had been looking through her book of hair and beauty tips. 'Thank you,' she muttered, snatching it from him as a blush crept relentlessly over her face. For one crazy moment she had thought he was here for a much more personal reason. She fussed with the chairs, trying to hide her disappointment, and her reddened face, from him. As she did so a strand of hair escaped the knot at the nape of her neck and flopped forward. Now she felt untidy as well as gauche.

'So, what about tomorrow?' he was asking, in a slightly raised voice.

She stared at him blankly.

'If you would stop fiddling with those perfectly tidy chairs you might hear what I am trying to say.' He raised a quizzical eyebrow and waited.

She thought he sounded like an impatient schoolteacher. Well, it served her right for behaving like a schoolgirl.

For a moment her father's warning came back to her. Maybe he was right. Perhaps she wouldn't fit in here with all these clever, sophisticated people. She dismissed the idea before it had time to settle. She was as good as any of them, she told herself. She was intelligent, well-educated and if she wasn't particularly articulate that was only because she was innately shy. It was Janette who was right. All she lacked was experience, she needed to get out, to mix more.

'I'm sorry,' she offered in her best accent. 'Please, go on.'

'I said, would you have dinner with me tomorrow night?'

'I . . . I don't know,' she lied, not wanting to appear too keen.

'You're not working, are you?'

'No . . .'

'Well then, that's settled. I'll pick you up at eight-thirty. Outside.'

He was gone before she could answer.

Mary was ready a full hour before she needed to be and then had to stand and wait, frightened to sit down in case her only decent dress creased.

He was ten minutes late. She fretted, fumed and paced the pavement, trying not to believe that he might have changed his mind. She was on the point of giving up when a very smart, red car screeched to a halt, fifteen yards in front of her. The horn blared once and he gestured impatiently for her to get in. So relieved was she that she overlooked the fact that he didn't bother to apologise for his lateness.

Mary's experience of cars was strictly limited but she knew, at once, that this one was very expensive. Knew too that he was driving it much too fast. They flew into a blind corner with a screech of tyres which made her gasp and grip the side of her seat in blind terror. Paul Kinsail glanced at her, chuckled quietly to himself and took the next bend even faster.

Ten minutes later, some miracle having saved them from a horrific accident, he was steering her into the restaurant he had selected. It was Chinese, the food a completely new experience for her. So, too, was the wine which he ordered and encouraged her to drink. 'To the most lovely woman I know,' he toasted her, bringing a blush of pleasure to her face. She recognised flattery when she heard it but how wonderful it was to be able to dare to think she was at least averagely attractive. Just being here with Paul increased her growing confidence, for there was no doubt that he was not the sort of man who would be seen with a plain girl on his arm.

'I've never had wine before,' she admitted naively after the first glass, privately thinking she hadn't missed much.

'And you have never eaten Chinese food either.' He smiled tolerantly as he said it but it still made her feel uncomfortable.

'I didn't realise it was so obvious,' she retorted.

He smiled again, patronisingly, she thought. 'Relax. I was teasing. Have some more wine. It won't do you any harm.' He refilled her glass and watched her closely for a minute or two before announcing, 'You really are most refreshingly innocent.'

Instantly she was back on the defensive. This evening was not turning out to be at all what she had hoped for. Her reaction to Paul was veering erratically between dislike and adoration, always tempered by a strange excitement. 'And what, exactly, do you mean by that?'

He frowned, surprised by her spirit. 'I'm sorry. That wasn't very tactful, was it? I guess I'm a little out of practice. My career doesn't leave me much time for this sort of thing. All I meant was that you are wonderfully young and natural. It was supposed to be a compliment.' He looked so contrite that she forgave him instantly.

'I was hoping it didn't show too much,' she admitted, draining her glass and allowing him to refill it. By now her head felt distinctly odd.

'Don't ever try to be something you're not,' he told her with smooth hypocrisy. 'You are absolutely perfect the way you are.' He took her hand over the table and kissed it lightly. She prayed he hadn't noticed how her hand trembled.

Seeking refuge in her meal she attacked it with assumed gusto, barely tasting what she was eating, aware that he was still watching her, unaware that his expression was now speculative. Perhaps, he thought, that innocence was genuine after all. If so, what a catch she would be. From the way she sparkled in the dining room he had assumed that it was all an act, that she was nothing more than an accomplished little flirt. It seemed he might have been wrong.

It was almost midnight before they got back to his car. Paul settled into his seat and fired the engine at once. He had to exercise a great deal of self-control to resist the temptation to take advantage of the dark and begin the serious campaign for her body. She would, he decided, be well worth a little patience.

To her astonishment he drew up on the main road, a good walk from the college. 'I think I would be wise to drop you here. I wouldn't want any of the students to see us together. They would tease you mercilessly if they thought you had been out with me. And the bursar would definitely disapprove. You could even lose your job.'

It sounded plausible enough. Plausible but, she wondered as she walked hurriedly towards the college, was it her reputation or his own that he was really concerned about? What a confusing night it had been. He hadn't even tried to kiss her. But maybe that was the difference between a mature man and the few boys she had gone out with in the past. They had wanted nothing more than a quick fumble under her blouse in return for the price of the cinema tickets. No, she decided, Paul was too well-bred to play silly games like that.

As she slipped into sleep that night Mary was smiling, still amazed that someone as distinguished as Paul Kinsail could possibly want to get involved with anyone as plain and unattractive as she was. But perhaps Janette was right and she was pretty after all, maybe she was growing to be more attractive as she matured. Paul had told her she was wonderful, said she was lovely, that she was perfect. She giggled sleepily to herself. Wasn't it marvellous what a new hair-style and some make-up could do?

Paul planned his campaign of attack and pursued it meticulously, wooing Mary with intimate dinners, small, inexpensive gifts and repeated assurances of his deepening affections. It was a terrible nuisance that this little affair had to be played out well away from the intimate confines of the historic university burgh but there was no point in taking unnecessary risks. He was very well-known locally and word of this latest dalliance could too easily get back to his wife. The last thing he wanted to do was put his marriage at risk when all he really needed was a little light relief until after the birth of their fourth child. And Mary Innes was just the person to provide it.

As the relationship ripened, Mary felt herself being drawn irresistibly under the spell of Paul's strong personality. It was not a comfortable sensation. It was as if all her confidence, all her determination and even some of her self-respect melted away when she was with him. The only thing that mattered then was pleasing him, keeping him.

She spent her entire life waiting to be with him again and was constantly disappointed that they could only meet once a week when she yearned to spend every free minute in his company. But, as he explained, he had a very demanding job which required him to work most evenings.

Paul was adamant that their affair remain a secret. He had explained, very early on in their relationship that he and his wife were separated, awaiting a divorce because of his wife's infidelity. Naturally, under the circumstances, he was resisting her outrageous maintenance claims but it was, he stressed, almost every time they met, crucial for him to protect his own innocent reputation, at least until after the divorce hearing. Too many of his colleagues had wives who were still friendly with his wife and he couldn't take a chance on one of them telling her that he was seeing another woman. In any case, it was against college rules for staff to become involved with students or other employees.

Mary understood the reasons for Paul's caution but was sometimes hurt by the cool, almost contemptuous manner he was capable of showing towards her if he thought she had been too familiar with him when they met on college premises. It got to the stage where she hardly dared to look at him when he came into the dining room. It disturbed her, too, that Paul tried to dominate her, ordering her food – expecting her to like what he liked – and even telling her what to wear. Over their shared meals he frequently asked what she thought about some item of topical interest then patiently corrected her if her, usually well-considered, views differed from his. There were times when she felt she was sitting some sort of exam. Desperate to convince him she really was worthy of his affection she took to reading two, politically opposed, papers each day, trying to anticipate what he would choose to talk about. Deep down she despised herself but took some consolation from the knowledge that she was at least becoming better informed because of him. In any case, as soon as they were alone together he was so wonderful, so able to stir her physically, that it was impossible for her to feel resentment for very long.

It was hurtful that although her campaign of self-improvement was working and she felt increasingly confident of her ability to offer informed opinions in a well-spoken, lucid manner, her family could only mutter about her, 'acting better than she was' and 'putting on airs'. Her grandmother was particularly scathing and even her father laughed and said she sounded like she had a mouth full of marbles. Fed up with their taunts she cut her visits home from one a week to just once every month. But it was all worthwhile if it helped her relationship with Paul.

The usual end to Paul and Mary's evenings together was in some secluded spot where he could park the car and indulge in an hour of intimacy. Their favourite place was in the depths of the Coutsmuir forest, just outside the town. But lately the time they spent there had been turning into something of a battle. For weeks she had held him at bay, even when he hinted, unsubtly, that he wasn't prepared to wait much longer. She knew she must give in to him soon or lose him. That wasn't a risk she was prepared to take. And perhaps he was right. Perhaps it really was up to her to prove her feelings for him. From the chatter in the kitchens she knew that most girls with steady boyfriends slept with them. After all, it was 1967 and not 1867 as Paul was so fond of pointing out. But still she hesitated, something stopping her from making the final commitment before she was absolutely ready.

'Come on. Let's get out of the car. It's a lovely, warm night,' Paul insisted one evening about two months into their relationship. He sensed she was near surrender and he had no intention of taking her messily on the back seat of the family car.

'All right,' she agreed readily enough, as eager as he to avoid another undignified scramble.

Behind the forest lay a stretch of unspoiled and relatively unknown beach. Paul led the way until he found a suitably sheltered hollow and spread a blanket on the sand.

He had her in his arms almost before she could sit on it. His mouth was punishingly hard and demanding, his hands impatient at her breasts. Gasping, dizzy with the enormous amount of wine he had plied her with, she was less inhibited than usual and made no attempt to stop him when his mouth found her nipples.

Paul had been very careful to control his impatience, taking Mary just a little bit closer to the inevitable each time but overriding his urge to ignore her protests with greater and greater difficulty. Tonight he had waited long enough. As he slipped a hand under her skirt and between her legs his breathing was unusually fast and ragged. The dampness there convinced him she was ready so he pressed on, moving his fingers to her most private area. In his mouth her tongue stopped moving.

'It's all right,' he mumbled hotly into her ear, forcing his way further on. Her thighs closed painfully on his wrist.

'No, Paul.' But she was as hot as he was and breathing even faster.

'Yes,' he insisted, stroking her until she was writhing underneath him. 'You want this as much as I do, Mary. Show me you really love me.'

Suddenly resistance seemed pointless. She did love him. She did want him. The full effect of the potent wine he had so carefully fed her and the disturbing urgency of his fingers finally overcame the last shreds of her reluctance. He felt it the instant she capitulated. It was her mouth which came back to his, her arms which pulled him closer.

She tensed when he entered her and he heard the small whisper of pain as he broke her body's natural barrier. It only increased his desire, driving him to ram himself into her, not caring that he might be hurting her, intent only on his own gratification.

After that first, searing pain she moved with him, giving him everything, her body, like her heart, open and generous. The sensations she felt were too new to be disappointing but afterwards, when she desperately wanted him to hold her, to be tender with her, to reassure her of his love, he was in a sudden, frantic hurry to get dressed, to shake every last grain of sand from his clothes and from the blanket, and hurry back to his car, leaving her to readjust her clothing and trail back after him. As well as the dull ache between her legs her head was throbbing and starting to spin as the heady effects of the wine wore off into something far less pleasant. In the end she was simply relieved to get back to her own, quiet room.

Mary had given Paul everything, never doubting that their relationship was special, dreaming of the future they must surely build together when his divorce came through and picturing her pride when she introduced him to her family. Even her grandmother wouldn't be able to sneer at a university professor. Each time they made love his hold over her strengthened. Even when, now that he had achieved his goal, Paul drove straight to the beach, no longer bothering with the expense of wining and dining her, she saw it as evidence of his desire for her and loved him all the more for it.

*

As winter drew in the evenings became steadily colder until even the friendly trees couldn't protect them from the wind lashing in from the North Sea. Mary didn't care, she never noticed the cold when she was with him, but Paul, rapidly tiring both of her and of the need to painstakingly remove all traces of sand from his clothing before his wife could become even more suspicious, finally baulked.

'It's too cold tonight,' he decided.

'Why can't we go back to your flat?' she suggested after an uncomfortable coupling on his back seat which had left her disgruntled by the reluctant, almost resigned, performance of her lover. The fact that he had been less than fully aroused, even when she had done her very best to excite him, had been impossible to ignore.

Still recovering from the sheer physical exertion her young body demanded of him, he was off guard. 'I said no,' he snapped.

'Why not, Paul?'

By now he had had time to think. 'I've told you before, Mary. It's too risky.' He had told her he shared a flat with colleagues.

'You can't think your own flatmates would go running to your wife and tell her about me? We've been together for six months now, Paul. They'll have to know sometime.' How she wanted to be seen with him, to let people know that this wonderful man was hers. To show him off to her sisters.

'No, Mary.'

She should have had more sense than to argue with him when he used that tone of voice but, foolishly, she persisted. 'We can't hide forever, Paul. Let's tell our close friends at least. No one will think any the less of us when they see we're serious about one another.'

He wouldn't argue but fired the engine with a tense,

jabbing motion. The anger emanating from him was palpable, like a red, shimmering mist between them and finally reduced her to wounded silence.

It was, he thought, as he harried the car dangerously along the dark, wooded track, more than time to put an end to this. Mary Innes had been an amusing diversion, a necessary relief. Nothing more. The naivety he had once found so appealing was simply irritating now and she had become so clinging, so demanding, starting to act as if she had some sort of right to his company.

Mary watched the taut, angry line of his jaw and the undisguised hostility on his face. Even the way he was handling the car was a reflection of his mood, crashing the gears and stamping on the brakes as if he could take his anger out on the machinery. Too late, much too late, she began to doubt him.

'Will I see you tomorrow?' she asked when he dropped her off, even further away from the college than usual.

'I'm going to be busy,' he muttered, revving the engine.

'When then?'

'I don't know! I'll let you know. Just get out of the bloody way will you.'

It was so virulent that she stepped back, visibly shaken. Kinsail pulled away in a violent blast of exhaust smoke, leaving her to stare after him with the bottom dropping out of her world.

A week passed. Paul avoided the dining room and made no attempt to contact Mary.

Two weeks, then three weeks and still nothing. She could hardly eat, barely slept and never smiled. Wrapped in misery she went about her duties with one eye always on the diners, hoping for a glimpse of him. She snapped at her colleagues and escaped after work to brood alone in her room.

Finally, in what she knew to be pathetic and demeaning

desperation, she took to hanging round in the foyer, hoping to catch him as he arrived for work. It was a full week before that strategy succeeded.

Paul Kinsail saw Mary the second he stepped through the doors. The temptation to turn round and hurry away was overwhelming but a body of students crushing in behind him made escape impossible. Trapped, he acknowledged her with a long, cold stare then walked stiffly to his office, knowing she was unlikely to follow him there.

What little colour she had drained from her face. Paul's expression had told her everything he had been too cowardly to put into words. Irritation, anger and even contempt had all been there, quite nakedly. A month ago he had still been telling her he loved her. Today she had seen that he didn't even care that he was hurting her.

When she went on duty later that day her hair was scraped back behind her ears, she wore no make-up and her eyes were puffy and swollen.

'Are you sure you don't want me to ask one of the others to work your shift for you?' Janette, who had a shrewd idea of what was going on, offered.

'No,' Mary snapped ungratefully and turned her back.

Mary was already preparing for bed and the oblivion of sleep at eight-thirty the following evening when there was a light tap on her door.

'It's Janette. Let me in, Mary.'

Listlessly Mary threw open the door.

'Want to talk?' Janette offered, settling on the bed.

'Not really. I'm tired. I'm going to have an early night.' Mary locked herself in the bathroom, hoping Janette would take the hint. But, when she emerged, dressed in her pyjamas, a full ten minutes later, her friend was still there, propped up against her pillows, smoking and tapping ash into a pot plant.

'Use an ash tray if you must smoke in here.' Mary tossed her an old saucer which she kept specifically for her friend's visits.

'That's better. If you can still nag at me about smoking there's some hope for you.'

Mary had the grace to smile wryly. 'Sorry, Janette. I didn't mean to snap your head off.' She was guiltily aware that she had been a very poor friend to Janette lately and regretted letting Paul come between them. Janette's friendship was much too valuable to be taken so lightly.

'Don't worry about it. I can see you're upset,' Janette smiled, easily. 'It might help to talk and you know I'm not a gossip.'

'I know you're not but there's nothing to talk about really.' She attempted a ghastly smile which certainly didn't deceive Janette but this was too humiliating to share, even with her best friend.

'OK. If you're going to be stubborn, I'll tell you what happened,' Janette went on ruthlessly. 'Professor Wonderful has dumped you. And it hurts like hell.'

Had their affair been that obvious? Mary felt the bed lurch, saw the ceiling spin. 'NO! . . . Yes . . . Och, I don't know what happened. He's not speaking to me. I saw him today and he looked right through me, as if I didn't exist. No, worse than that. He looked at me as if he loathed the sight of me.' She swallowed hard, fighting to keep the tears at bay.

'I'm really sorry, Mary. I know how you feel but it had to happen sometime. He's married.'

'I know he's married!'

'But you still went out with him?' Janette asked, sounding shocked.

'Of course I did. It's not as if they're living together or anything.'

'What do you mean?' Janette asked, warily.

'They've split up. He's getting a divorce,' Mary said, defensively.

'So that's what he told you . . . ?'

'What do you mean by that?' Mary demanded.

'He told you he and his wife are getting a divorce?'

'That's what I just said,' Mary retorted, ignoring the sinking sensation in her stomach.

'So, where is he living?' Janette was relentless.

'In a flat. With colleagues.'

'Have you ever been there?'

'NO! What are you trying to say, Janette?'

'You've never been to his flat because it doesn't exist. Paul Kinsail isn't divorcing his wife. They live in one of those big, old houses, near the castle.'

'Yes he is. I haven't been to the flat because he doesn't want people to know about us. If his wife finds out before the divorce is heard she could claim huge maintenance payments from him. It would ruin him.'

'And I bet he never takes you anywhere in St Andrews where you might be seen together.'

'For the same reason! He only left his wife a few months ago, Janette. I don't suppose it's common knowledge yet.'

'No, Mary! He keeps you hidden away so that he can have his little bit of fun while his wife is pregnant.' Janette knew it was cruel but it had to be said.

'His wife is pregnant?' Mary whispered it, her face dropping in horror.

'With their fourth child. I'm sorry, Mary, but it's true.'

'They've got children?' Why hadn't he ever mentioned them? How could he pretend his own children didn't exist? In her heart she knew it was over but still she fought. 'All right, how do you know all this?' Mary rounded on

Janette, angrily. 'And if you knew why didn't you tell me before? You're supposed to be my friend.'

'I am your friend,' Janette assured her, taking Mary's cold hand in her own warm ones.

'I know,' Mary smiled briefly. 'But you're wrong. It's simply not true. He's waiting for a divorce. He's annoyed with me about something that's all. It's probably because he's seen me joking about with the students. He's very jealous you know. He'll call in a day or two and everything'll be OK.'

'For goodness sake! Listen to me will you!' Janette resisted the urge to shake her young friend. 'I know how much you're hurting, Mary, honestly I do. And I did try to warn you, but you wouldn't listen. Remember?'

Mary knew her friend was speaking the truth, pride stopped her from admitting it aloud. 'I don't want to hear any more about this, Janette. I really would like to go to bed now.'

'No! You are going to hear me out. Don't you realise that everyone knows about you two? You're the talk of the college.'

'We can't be. We've been so careful.'

'Careful?' Janette laughed. 'You made it so obvious. You never took your eyes off him and he actually smiled at you when he snarls and looks down that big nose of his at everyone else. Then, all of a sudden, he stops coming to the dining room and you're as miserable as sin . . .'

'Oh no . . . he said I was to make sure no one found out. That must be why he's so angry.'

'Will you wake up! You know that's just rubbish. It's over, Mary. They say his wife is very attractive. Got money too, so I hear. He wouldn't leave her, he's got too much to lose.'

'No . . . How could he do this to me?' All hope evaporated leaving Mary cold and shivering. Janette hugged her tightly, trying to offer some sort of comfort.

'The best thing to do is pretend you don't care. Even if you're dying inside, don't let him see it. And don't go crawling to him, hoping he'll take you back.'

'But I love him,' Mary whispered, pathetically.

'Not any more you don't,' was her friend's brutal response. 'Look at the way he's treated you, Mary. Think of all the lies he must have told you. And now you've given him what he wanted he's tossed you aside like a dirty hanky. And don't think you're the first. There were rumours about a girl in the Dean's office. He even tried it on with me, but I've met his kind before.'

'Janette . . .'

'Have some pride, Mary. You may not think so at the moment but you will get over him. You don't need the likes of Paul Kinsail. Forget him.'

Mary tried to speak but her throat was too tight, closed with emotion. Instead she hugged her friend tightly.

'He's a bastard. Put it down to experience and don't waste any more energy on him. Now, slip into bed and try to get some sleep. There's a whole generation of young men out there and on Friday night we are going out on the town. I am going to make sure you have a good time, without Paul Kinsail.'

Janette pulled the covers down and Mary crawled into bed, feeling totally drained.

'Thanks, Janette,' she whispered. 'I'm sorry I've been such a pain.'

'You've not been a pain. And anyway, what's a best friend for?' Janette planted a soft kiss on Mary's brow and crept out of the room.

In the lonely darkness Mary buried her head in her pillow and cried until she could cry no more.

*

Mary felt dreadful. Her night out with Janette had been a miserable failure. Work sickened her. The students with their inane chatter only heightened her depression. No matter how often she told herself that she had to forget Paul she just couldn't put him out of her mind.

Lethargy dragged at her. Her head ached incessantly and her stomach was a cauldron of acid. It had always been the same whenever she was upset. It reminded her of the way she had felt when her mother walked out.

Seven weeks after she had last been with Paul she hauled herself out of bed, aware again of the nausea gripping her stomach. In the kitchen the sight and smell of food made her feel even worse. Her head swam, her face beaded with cold sweat. One look into the pan she was stirring, at the revolting, creamy mess of porridge, was enough to warn her that she had to get away. She made a desperate lunge for the door but collapsed untidily on to the floor before she could reach it.

'And you've been feeling sick every morning?' Matron, brisk and efficient, was perched on the edge of her bed. Mary had no recollection of being brought here.

'Yes,' she nodded miserably, feeling wretched.

'And have you any idea what might be causing this, Lass?' The middle-aged woman watched Mary closely, allowing no expression to cross her calm face. She had seen it all before.

'No . . .'

'Are you certain?'

Mary knew Sister McNulty wouldn't be satisfied with a plain denial. 'I had a shock . . . it's personal . . . I've been a bit upset . . . off my food, that's all.' She attempted a wan smile. Damn Paul for doing this to me, she thought. And what a fool she was, letting herself get into such a state. As soon as she was over this sickness she really was going to get on with her life as if Paul Kinsail had never existed.

'Something to do with a boyfriend?' Sister suggested casually.

'Yes,' Mary admitted reluctantly.

'Well, Lass, the best thing to do now is sleep. I've asked Doctor Cathcart to look in later, just to be sure there's nothing seriously amiss.'

Mary nodded and slipped down into bed, closing her eyes gratefully.

Doctor Cathcart washed his hands in Mary's bathroom and re-emerged, his face professionally unreadable. Sister McNulty caught his faint nod and folded her arms over her ample bosom. Stupid young girl, she thought disdainfully, looking at Mary's bleached face.

Mary sat trembling on the edge of the bed. The questions the doctor had asked had shocked her profoundly, the physical examination had nauseated her but by then she already knew why she was being sick each morning. The normal irregularity of her cycle and the overwhelming absorption in her misery had blinded her to the obvious, until the doctor had so coldly pointed it out to her. Innocent she had been, stupid she was not. She should have realised this for herself long ago. Shame and fear were her overriding emotions now.

'Don't forget, Miss Innes. The bursar's office. Two o'clock tomorrow,' was Sister McNulty's final instruction as she and the doctor left.

Mary sat rigidly tense, her heart pounding wildly. Never had she felt so afraid. Nor so angry. Abruptly she leapt to her feet and went to the mirror to face herself. If anything she was thinner than ever, her face was ashen and her hair a tangled disgrace. With painfully hard strokes she brushed it, dragging at the snarls until tears blinded her. When it was smooth again she rearranged it into the neat little knot at the nape of her neck which always seemed to make her feel smarter and more confident. Make-up disguised the worst of the shadows under her eyes and rouge lent her a misleadingly healthy colour. Finally, dressed in a plain but smart skirt and blouse, she let herself out of the room.

'Mary!' Just finished work for the day, Janette shouted from the other end of the corridor. 'Are you OK?' she asked as soon as she got close, looking at her friend critically, her mind on the rumours which had been flying round the kitchen all day.

Mary took a deep breath. 'I'm pregnant,' she said. 'But I suppose you all know that. I can't believe I was stupid enough not to realise what was wrong with me.'

'Oh God! Oh, Mary, I'm so sorry. And you're right, most people have guessed. But only after that little drama you put on for us this morning,' she admitted in her usual, frank style. 'But I didn't suspect a thing. I should have done really, shouldn't I?'

'If I was too stupid to see it why should you?' Mary tried to laugh but there were tears in her eyes.

'What will you do? Will you be able to stay on here for a while?' Janette asked, fighting tears of her own.

'I've to see the domestic bursar tomorrow . . . but I doubt if they'll want me to stay. In the meantime I'm going to see Paul Kinsail. This is as much his responsibility as mine.' Now the tears were gone and there was a hard glint in her eye that Janette had never seen before.

'Good for you! Do you want me to come with you. Give you a bit of moral support?' she offered.

Mary considered it for a minute. 'No, I don't think so,

thanks all the same. This is something I have really got to do for myself.'

'OK. Good luck.'

Mary had never before ventured into the college proper and soon became lost. Not to be deterred she asked a student for directions which took her to a corridor on the first floor. On each door there was a brass nameplate so she simply walked on until she found the one with his name on it. She didn't hesitate before knocking sharply. If he wasn't there she would simply wait. He was bound to return to his office at some point during the day. But his voice rumbled a deep 'Enter.'

Head high, back rigidly straight, she walked in. Paul was engrossed in paperwork and didn't even look up. 'I'll be with you in a minute,' he said.

'No, Paul. Now,' she answered, her voice deceptively sweet.

His head jerked up and she had the satisfaction of seeing a rush of horror cross his face. And, disconcertingly, she felt a flicker of the old attraction. Maybe . . . maybe, when he knew the truth . . .

'What the hell are you doing here?' he hissed, his face contorting with fury and destroying her fragile illusion.

'I need to talk to you.'

'We have nothing to talk about. Now, I suggest you leave, before I call the porter and have you thrown out. You know as well as I do that domestic staff are not permitted in this part of the college.' He stalked round the desk and threw the door wide open. She saw sweat globules on his upper lip.

'This will only take a little of your precious time,' she insisted, wondering how she could sound so calm when her insides were about to erupt.

'I would have thought I had made my position perfectly

clear by now. There is nothing I wish to discuss with you.'

'Please, Paul,' she pleaded.

'Out! It's over. Finished. There is nothing to say. How dare you come here. Did anyone see you? My God, the whole college will be talking about us if you go on like this.' Still the door yawned open.

'I'm pregnant. And the whole college knows about us anyway.'

He span round, gaped at her then, very slowly, closed the door. 'What did you say?'

'You heard.'

'My God.'

'Please, Paul, help me. I don't know what to do.' She put a hand out and touched his arm. He flinched away as if she had bitten him.

'What the hell do you expect me to do about it?' he snarled. 'If you were careless, that's your fault. Not mine.'

'Careless?' she screamed.

'Keep your voice down,' he hissed.

'You have got to help me, Paul.'

'You aren't serious?' He was sneering at her now.

'I don't know what to do,' she repeated. 'You must help me, Paul. This is your child I'm carrying.'

'Is it?' he asked, with devastating cruelty. 'You can't prove that.' He moved closer to her, so close she could feel his breath on her cheek. 'You listen to me. I want nothing to do with you, or your little bastard.'

'But it is your – '

'SHUT UP!'

She backed away, terrified of the anger which poured from him.

'Get out of this office and don't ever come back. If you try and involve me I shall simply deny it and destroy you in the process.'

'You can't,' she whispered.

'Can't I? It is not unknown for young women to have crushes on older men, especially in places like this. It has happened with the students here before now. I will deny there was anything more to it than that. Who do you think will be believed? A distinguished member of the faculty or you, an ignorant little kitchen hand from some dirty mining village? Who on earth would believe that someone like me could ever get involved with the likes of you?'

He opened the door and waited, his face a mask of victory.

Beaten, she fled.

Less than twenty-four hours later Mary was in the domestic bursar's office, flanked by Sister McNulty.

'I am deeply shocked,' the stern-faced bursar was saying. 'This sort of immoral behaviour cannot be tolerated in a college of this reputation. You will, of course, have to leave.' She glanced up, expecting Mary to make some sort of defence for herself. 'Have you nothing to say?' There was no hint of understanding in those flinty eyes.

'No.' Mary's attitude was defiant.

The bursar shook her outraged head and stared at Mary with something akin to hatred on her face. 'I need to know if a student is responsible. If so he will be disciplined.'

'It was not a student.'

The bursar sighed her relief. 'That's something to be grateful for.'

'Grateful?' Well, she would give them something to think about. 'It was Professor Kinsail.'

The woman's head snapped up, the expression on her face like a beached fish. 'What are you saying?' she rasped.

'The baby is Professor Kinsail's.'

'Now look here! You are in quite enough trouble without making serious accusations, unfounded allegations . . . Professor Kinsail is a married man. A respected – '

'Professor Kinsail is a first-class bastard,' Mary said, quietly but quite distinctly.

The bursar lumbered to her feet as fast as her bulk would allow. 'You will leave this college at once. Think yourself lucky that I will allow you one month's salary in lieu of notice. Vacate your room before tonight. Is that clear?'

'Perfectly.'

Lingering only to write an emotional note to Janette, Mary was packed and on her way back to Craigie before Paul Kinsail answered the Dean's summons. He arrived at the wood-panelled office only two minutes after a grim-faced Janette had left it. The interview was not a pleasant one. Of course, he hotly denied that there had been any involvement; was even confident enough to admit he had known the girl in question had a crush on him. But that, he assured the Dean, was as far as it had gone.

The Dean was far from convinced. An apparently retiring man who, none-the-less, missed very little of what happened in his college, he, too, had heard the rumours. Added to that, he had just spent a very informative fifteen minutes with a young woman who had been courageously outspoken on behalf of her unfortunate friend. In any case, this was a scene which had been played out before. Last time the young woman had been a valued clerk in his own office. Paul Kinsail's name had also been mentioned in connection with a brilliant young history undergraduate who had left hurriedly two years ago. Coldly he reminded the unpleasant and abrasive professor of these two previous cases.

Kinsail responded with the precise amounts of anger and outrage the Dean had anticipated and ended by threatening to resign if the Dean did not retract his words, confident that he had called the senior man's bluff. To his horror the Dean declined and accepted Kinsail's resignation with a surge of glee which he couldn't quite conceal.

Paul Kinsail emerged from that interview a shaken and dangerously angry man with much explaining to do to his already suspicious wife.

Mary Innes was a girl he would have cause to remember for a very long time.

EIGHT

Mary endured the bus ride through Strathannan in a state of numbed shock. Everything had happened so quickly. She hadn't even had time to consider what she would do next. Not that there was any real alternative to returning to Craigie. There was nowhere else to run to. But, at that moment, her overwhelming emotion was anger. All those extra years of school and college so she could better herself and get away from Craigie. All for nothing and there was no one but herself to blame.

The bus ground into the stance at Inverannan. Mary waited until everyone else was off before dragging her case on to the pavement. As she stepped down the Craigie bus started to pull out of the neighbouring bay. She let it go. It would be an hour before the next one. Time to think about what she was going to tell her father, her brother, her sisters. Her grandmother. Huddling miserably in the corner of the filthy shelter she shivered in the biting wind.

'Give us a wee smile then, Mary.' The familiar, laughing voice made her look up. A flash of violent red hair caught her eye and she found herself face to face with Archie Cree.

Archie was a Craigie boy, a couple of years older than her and badly crippled by a twisted spine and club foot which had made him the butt of much cruelty when they were children. In spite of that he was invariably cheerful and, with his bright red hair, freckled face and bright, blue eyes, quite good-looking in a boyish sort of way.

Mary had always liked him, had in fact been quite friendly with him until she realised that he wanted much more than simple friendship. It hadn't been his disability which had made her turn him down but her own burning ambition to get away from the village.

'Hello, Archie,' she responded, dully.

'You've just missed the bus,' he volunteered needlessly. 'It's a while before the next one.'

'I know.'

'Come on, then. There's time for a fish supper.' Before she could stop him he had her case in a strong grip and was limping across the road with it.

'I'm not really hungry, Archie,' she panted, running after him. 'I'd rather just wait here.'

'Don't be daft! It's freezing out here,' he called back over his shoulder.

She had no choice but to follow him into the busy café where he managed to find a table at the back. The familiar, mouthwatering smell of frying chips, fresh fish and vinegar filled the room making her realise that she was, in fact, ravenous. She allowed Archie to buy her a fish supper without arguing about it.

'Thanks, Archie. I was hungry after all,' she smiled at him at last.

He grinned back. 'How long are you home for? Just a holiday is it?'

'No, I'm home for good.' She hoped he hadn't heard the catch in her voice.

'Oh? To hear your father bragging about your wonderful job I thought you were all set to stay up there. Did you not like St Andrews then?'

'I liked it well enough.' She gulped at her coffee, trying to avoid his clear, blue eyes. 'The bus'll be in soon.'

'Aye, so it will,' he agreed cheerfully, picking up her case.

She deliberately chose to sit on the upper deck, hoping he would find the stairs too difficult with his lame leg but, to her consternation, he followed her. 'This leg of mine doesn't hinder me much though some folk seem to think it addles my brain and all,' he chuckled, settling beside her.

Instantly she was ashamed. 'Sorry, Archie . . . I know people are cruel sometimes. I didn't mean to hurt you. It's just . . . I really need to be on my own right now.'

'Well, sorry, Hen, but I'm stuck here now,' he chortled.

When the bus pulled away they were still alone on the upper deck. Mary stared morosely out of the window. This was it. She was going home in disgrace. How could she face everyone? All too soon they would be able to see for themselves exactly why she had come running home and she could imagine what life would be like for her then. Tears rolled unheeded down her face. A grubby handkerchief materialised under her nose.

'Here, use this. It's not that bad. I've not blown my nose on it or anything.'

Keeping her head averted she mopped her face miserably.

'Well, I can see you're not in the mood for cheering me up,' said Archie. 'So why don't you tell me what's got you feeling so sorry for yourself?'

She shook her head.

'It helps to talk about things, Mary.'

'Talking won't help me, Archie.'

'But maybe I can?'

'No one can.'

He was silent for a few minutes, waiting for her to stop crying. 'Better now?'

'Yes, thanks.' But her face was still etched with anguish.

'Come on, Mary. This is stupid old Archie. We've known each other since we were bairns in nappies. You can tell me anything. And I hate seeing you so miserable.'

She sighed, feeling a need to talk this through with someone.

'I've been sacked. I don't know what I'm going to tell my dad.'

'Your father isn't the sort to go off his head about a thing like that.'

'He will this time.'

'Why? What did you get the sack for?' He was amazingly persistent. 'You know, if you need help you've only got to ask for it. I'll do what I can.'

The unexpected kindness was too much. Fresh tears flooded her eyes. The handkerchief reappeared. 'Thanks,' she sniffed.

'Well, are you going to tell me?'

Mary sighed. 'Why not? Everyone will know before long anyway. It's not the sort of thing you can keep hidden. But you won't think much of me when I've told you.'

'Don't talk such rubbish! You know fine I've always liked you. You can't have changed that much. Tell me what happened and we'll see what we can do about it. And remember, I'm used to dealing with problems. My life is one big problem.'

'I'm pregnant.' There was a long pause. 'There, I told you you wouldn't think much of me.' It was almost triumphant the way she said it.

'I guessed as much and aye, that's a problem right enough.' He ignored the glare she levelled at him. 'Your father doesn't know?'

'I only found out about it myself yesterday.'

'What about the bloke, the one who did it to you?'

'He's married. Oh, I didn't know it at the time. Not

133

that it would have made any difference. He dumped me anyway.'

The rest of the journey passed in silence. When they arrived in Craigie, Archie took her case and hobbled off towards the village centre. 'What are you going to do?' he asked at last.

'I don't know. I haven't had time to think about it.'

'Well, I've just one suggestion for now. Say nothing at all yet. Make some excuse, homesickness or something. It'll give us time to work something out.'

'Like what?'

'Just say nothing while you're still so upset. Best leave it a day or two at least.'

'I'll see. It might be better to get it over with.' They were already outside the prefab with its broken gate and untidy garden. The air was heavy with smoke and lingering dampness. A bitter, ugly contrast to the sharp, clean air of St Andrews.

Archie broke into her unhappy thoughts. 'I'll call for you tonight. We'll go for a drink and talk it through.'

She smiled softly. 'Thanks, Archie, you've already made me feel easier. You must be shocked.'

'No . . . surprised maybe. I would have thought you were too smart, too ambitious to be caught like this. I'll call for you at eight. We'll talk about it then. OK?'

'I don't feel much like going out, Archie, and I certainly don't want to go anywhere where people will start asking questions.'

'Then we'll go out of the village. Come on, Mary. I've carried your case all this way. The least you can do is have a drink with me,' he teased. But then his tone changed and she thought she detected a bitter edge to his voice. 'You know, no other lassie would be seen dead with me, what with the back and the foot and all. I never thought it bothered you though.'

The last thing she wanted was to make him think she didn't want to be seen with him. 'It doesn't bother me, Archie Cree and well you know it!'

'Good. Eight o'clock then.'

'OK,' she laughed now. 'You win.'

It was as if she had never been away. The girls were both at work and David was at school. Their father was in exactly the same place as he always was, sound asleep in the living room, snoring gently, his mouth hanging open to show pink gums.

'Hello, Dad,' she whispered, half-hoping he wouldn't wake up.

He stirred, opened sluggish eyes then peered at her as if he couldn't believe what he was seeing. 'Well, if it's not our Mary!' he said at last. 'What are you doing home?'

'I've left my job, Dad. You were right. I didn't fit in up there.'

'Och well, never mind. Stick the kettle on, there's a good lassie.'

Archie stood whistling on the pavement outside the prefab where he had stood every night for the past fortnight, waiting for Mary. The difference was that tonight he had his best jacket and trousers on, his unruly hair was combed into partial submission and he had a wad of pound notes in his back pocket.

'We'll take a taxi home,' he promised as they boarded the Inverannan bus.

She laughed. Archie had been wonderful. Each day was endurable only because she knew he would be there in the evening with his cheerful, undemanding company. He was the one person she didn't have to pretend to. 'A bus is quite good enough for me, Archie Cree.'

He took her to a Chinese restaurant. 'I bet you've never eaten Chinky before,' he said smugly.

'No, never,' she assured him, her face perfectly straight.

As they followed the waiter to their table she was aware, not for the first time, of the open stares, or worse, the embarrassed avoidance which greeted Archie. His lurching, tilting waddle made him an object of fun or pity wherever he went. When they sat down a man at an adjoining table stared so openly that Mary flushed with anger.

'It bothers you then?' Archie asked, watching her.

'What?' She pretended she didn't understand.

'When people stare at me like that, it bothers you?'

'No,' she shot back, then, 'Yes,' she admitted, raising her face to look directly into his keen, blue eyes. 'But only because it makes me so angry that anyone should dare to look at you that way.'

'You're not ashamed to be seen with me then?' He asked her this nearly every night.

'Don't be ridiculous. How many times do you want me to tell you the same thing? To be honest I only notice your limp when other people draw attention to it. I guess it's because I've known you for so long. It's just you, isn't it?'

'Aye, and that's the way it'll stay. Cripple Cree.'

'Archie! Don't! That's awful.'

'That's what they used to call me at school. You know. You were there too.'

'They were just children. They didn't know any better. We're adults now.'

'Aye, but they still think of me in the same way.'

'I'm sorry, Archie. I don't know how you stay so cheerful.'

'Don't waste your sympathy on me, Hen. I don't need it. I just wanted to be sure of how you feel about being seen with me.'

'I wouldn't be here with you now if I felt embarrassed,' she retorted hotly.

'Good. That's what I thought. But, enough of me. We're here to talk about you.'

'Must we? I don't want to spoil my meal. I have all day long to think about me and it doesn't help, believe me.'

'Have you decided what to do about the bairn?' he asked, leafing through the menu.

'No. I'll have to tell Dad soon though. He's bound to wonder why I'm not looking for another job. And my grandmother will have to know.' That was the encounter which was scaring her the most. Ina's tongue was acid at the best of times.

'What about an abortion? Have you thought about that?' he asked, watching her reaction closely.

'Of course I've thought about it. I've thought about throwing myself off the Forth bridge too!' she retorted angrily but then relented. 'Sorry, I don't mean to get angry with you . . . I have thought about an abortion but I can't do that, Archie. I'd never be able to live with myself afterwards. Anyway, I wouldn't even begin to know how to get one.'

'I've been making a few enquiries . . . carefully mind, and I think I've got the name of someone . . . Expensive, but she's meant to be good. If money's the problem I could help you out a bit . . .'

'No! No . . . thanks for trying to help, Archie, but I couldn't . . .'

'OK . . . Don't get upset. I just wanted to make sure you'd thought about it. Now, I've a wee suggestion. I think I've found the solution.'

'What?' she stared at him. 'Tell me, Archie. What solution?'

'After we've eaten,' he said infuriatingly. The waiter chose that point to come for their order. Archie grinned at her. 'Since you've never eaten Chinky before I'll order for you. OK?'

She nodded and kept silent while he selected all her least favourite dishes. Although Mary pleaded with him to tell her more, Archie stubbornly refused and attacked his meal with exaggerated concentration. Watching him she knew he was relishing her mounting suspense.

'Now will you tell me?' she demanded as soon as the table was cleared of everything but their coffee cups.

'Och, you're an awful impatient woman, Mary,' he chuckled.

'You've got a kind-hearted aunty who lives on a remote island and specialises in taking in fallen women?' she suggested but there was little humour in her face. Any mention of her problem brought a return of the depression which was souring every waking moment.

'Better than that. Och, much better than that.'

'Archie! Will you please just get on with it,' she begged.

Suddenly he was deadly serious. 'Right. But you'll hear me out. I'm not much good at this sort of thing so don't interrupt.'

'OK.' She would have agreed to standing on her head in the corner by now.

'Well, you're not embarrassed by me, are you?' She shook her head. 'And you do like me a wee bit?'

'You know I do.'

'Then marry me, Mary.'

'What?' she gaped, her coffee cup poised midway between saucer and mouth. Then she had the terrible urge to giggle and knew that would be unforgivable. Whatever

138

else she did she must not laugh at him. 'Archie! That's not fair.'

'I'm serious. Do you think I would try to make a jest out of something as important as this?' He sounded very angry and now that she looked at him more closely she saw the intensity in his eyes, the hard line to his mouth and the sweat beading his forehead.

'But I'm pregnant,' she whispered.

'You surely think I haven't considered that? Maybe you being pregnant is my good fortune. I know fine you wouldn't look at me twice otherwise.' It was said with bitterness but he went on before she could protest. 'I know I'm no great catch, what with the leg and all, but I'm game if you are.'

'I don't know what to say . . .'

'So, you don't like me after all? What you said wasn't true.'

'That's not it, Archie. You've taken me by surprise, that's all.'

'Are you sure that's all it is? You don't look like a lassie who's just been proposed to,' he challenged her acidly.

'Archie, how many times do you need me to tell you I like you? Your leg and back make no more difference to me than your red hair does. You have to believe that. But I'm hardly the catch of the month, am I? And the last thing I expected tonight was this. You have rather sprung it on me.'

'Just listen then. I'll tell you the truth, though I can't promise you'll like what you hear. With my disability no lassie will even pass the time of day with me, let alone think about getting married. And I want to be married, Mary, just like any normal bloke. I'm the same as all the rest . . . I mean . . . I can be a proper husband . . . in bed.' He flushed to the roots of his carroty hair. 'You know what I mean. And I can afford to keep you and the bairn.'

'But there's more to marriage than sex and money, Archie. I always thought I would fall in love first. I do like you, honestly I do, but I won't pretend to love you.' She tried to soften the harsh words by letting her fingers link with his across the table. 'I might make you very unhappy. I wouldn't want that.'

'You won't. And who said anything about love? I'm not stupid enough to expect that. Not yet. But maybe it would come, in time.'

'I don't know . . .' she shook her head. 'I don't deserve this.'

'Why don't you try thinking of it like I do? As a business proposal?'

'A business proposal?'

'Aye.' He laughed at her now. 'It's as good a way to start a marriage as any other. I've my own wee business, as you know. A mobile butchery. I'm needing help if I'm to expand the way I plan to. Aye, Mary, I've got big plans. My own shop. A whole string of shops. But I can't do it on my own. With a wife to help me, well, that would be different. It won't be easy mind, but it'll be our own future we're working for. With a bit of hard work we could really make something of ourselves.'

'I'll have a baby to look after.'

'You'll manage. You're a cook. I've got it all worked out. You can stay at home at first, make the pies and bridies for me. Good quality pies and bridies mind. None of that muck some butchers think they can get away with selling. Ours will be the best. So good everyone will want to buy them. They'll come to the van for their pies and bridies and while they're there they'll buy a bit of sausage for the tea, or some mince, maybe a chicken once in a while. They'll soon see that Archie Cree doesn't cheat on them. They'll come back time and time again . . . And you can help with the books too. My mother's been helping out a bit but she's got a heavy hand with pastry and the books are in a worse state now than they were before she started.'

'But I'm having a baby,' she repeated, helplessly. 'Another man's child.'

'I'll treat it as my own,' he promised quickly. 'And when we get a proper shop you can help me serve.' His eyes lost their focus as he pictured himself as the proud owner of a string of shops, his attractive wife at his side. Then no one would have cause to jeer at him.

'No, Archie. I can't. It wouldn't be fair.'

'What's not fair about it? We both know what we're getting into. Doing one another a favour if you like. Don't say no too quickly, Mary. You're not likely to get a better offer in your condition and things'll not be easy for you in Craigie with a bairn to raise up and no man to support you. I think we could make a go of it between us. And,' he added almost as an afterthought, 'don't think I'm only doing this for the business. You know I've always fancied you.'

'The baby will be born too early. Everyone will talk.'

'Let them. So long as they think it's me you've jumped the gun with.'

She sank back in her chair, her brain reeling. 'It still feels wrong somehow. As if I'm using you.'

'It doesn't feel wrong to me.' He finished his coffee in a series of long gulps. 'Let's go home. Think about it, Mary, but don't take too long. That bairn's not going to wait and I'm not wanting you the size of a battleship when we get wed, that'll really start the tongues wagging. If we do it we'll need to be as quick as we can.'

Beyond sensible comment she followed him from the restaurant in silence. 'I'll leave you to think about it for a

141

couple of days,' he said when he left her outside the prefab. 'I'll be back for my answer on Tuesday night.'

'Janette!' Mary welcomed her friend with a suffocating hug. 'Oh God. I'm so pleased to see you,' she said, her eyes filling with tears.

'Me too.' Janette was too choked with emotion to say much more.

Mary's family had heard so much in praise of her friend that Janette was given a very warm welcome and they all chatted together for most of that first day. It was evening before the girls each left for dates, David went off to see a pal and George, as usual, took himself down to the Greyhound, leaving the two friends alone at last. But just seeing Janette again had made Mary feel more optimistic.

'I warned you this place was tiny,' Mary laughed, as her friend finally managed to stretch her legs out in the cramped little living room.

'Where will we all sleep? I never realised how difficult it would be for you when I said I'd stay the night.'

'Don't worry! Amazing though it may seem there is a bed for each of us. David always sleeps in here now. The settee makes into a bed. When we were kids all four of us slept in two sets of bunks in the bedroom. They're still there so we're perfectly all right for tonight. But it's a good job we all get on well, isn't it?' Mary laughed, something she had done very little of recently.

'That's nothing,' Janette insisted. 'When I was a kid my sister and I had to share a single bed, right up until she got married. Me at one end, her at the other. She snored, farted and to top it all had smelly feet.'

They both dissolved into gales of laughter.

'Come on then,' Janette said, wiping tears of mirth from her eyes. 'Now that we have the place to ourselves, tell me how you are. Have you decided what to do yet? What about your folks? Haven't you told them yet? You should do you know . . .'

That was typical of Janette, Mary thought fondly. 'I think I might be getting married,' she said softly.

'What?' Janette stared at her, mouth agape.

'So, what do you think?' Mary asked when she had told her friend the details.

'I don't know, Mary. This Archie, he sounds as if he might have a bit of a chip on his shoulder. And are you sure he's not the kind who will spend the rest of his life reminding you of how grateful you should be to him?' Janette was her usual, frank self.

'I don't think so. The way he put it I was doing him at least as big a favour.'

'A business arrangement?'

'That's what he called it.'

'Some arranged marriages are very successful,' Janette said.

'But?' Mary prompted, hearing the doubt in her friend's voice.

'But, are you sure you wouldn't be better just to admit you're pregnant, have the baby and bring it up yourself? Leave any decisions about marriage until later. Your dad seems a smashing sort of a bloke, I'm sure he'd get used to the idea and your sisters are lovely too. They'd help.'

'Yes. Yes, I know they would but can't you see how unfair that would be? For a start there's nowhere to put a baby in this place. And this is just a village, Janette, things are twenty years behind the times here. Unmarried mothers are still looked down on. Some of that would rub off on Catherine and Linda . . . people would say they were like me . . . You know the sort of thing.'

'To start with, maybe, but not for long. They'll soon forget.'

'No they won't! There was a girl who was at school with me who had a baby, about eighteen months ago. You should hear what they call her. Instead of just seeing her as some poor kid whose boyfriend let her down, most people round here won't even talk to her, won't let their kids speak to her. They call her little lad a little bastard and that's how they'll always think of him, until he grows up and moves away. But they'll always think of that girl as immoral, even when she's sixty.'

'Sounds like you've already made up your mind,' Janette said softly.

'If I had some money so I could move away, go somewhere I wasn't known, even have a place of my own, it might be different but . . .'

'There's social security. The State won't let you starve.'

'Don't talk to me about social security! I'm an expert. I was brought up on it. Never quite enough to eat; never enough money to warm the house properly; haunting jumble sales for second-hand clothes; never taking a bus when you could walk! No, Janette. I will not go back to that. Never. I want something better for this baby. And for me.'

'Och, Mary. It sounds like you're marrying this Archie just because of what people will say. Think about it, please.'

She had. Quite apart from her father and sisters there was Uncle Jackie and his wife, Uncle Harry and Aunt Hettie, and all her mother's other brothers and their families who would all be outraged by the shame of illegitimacy. And then there was her grandmother. Mary shivered.

'Archie will make a good husband,' she insisted, quietly, knowing the decision had been made.

'You could always come and live with me,' Janette offered suddenly.

'In college!' Mary exclaimed.

'Surely we could find a cheap flat to share in St Andrews.'

Mary took her friend's hands and squeezed them affectionately. 'Janette, I couldn't pay my fair share. And even if I could, what about you and Jamie? I thought things were getting serious between you two.'

'It's early days yet.' But Janette blushed slightly and smiled just to think of her boyfriend.

'And you wouldn't want me and a screaming baby getting in your way. It might even cause trouble between you and Jamie, especially if you were subsidising me.'

Janette sighed. 'So you are going to become Mrs Cree?'

'I think so.'

'Just remember that I'm still your friend, Mary. If you need me, I'll come and the offer of finding a flat together is still there if you change your mind.' Tears fogged her eyes and thickened her words.

'I know. I know . . .'

Talking to Janette had cleared her mind. The more Mary thought about it the more attractive Archie's proposal seemed. And he was right about one thing. She wasn't going to get a better offer. No man in his right mind would want her when she had an illegitimate child. It wasn't as if she didn't like Archie and admire the way he coped with his disability. But, at night, her sleep was disturbed by visions of Archie, serving raw meat from his van and her there, serving with him. Was that what her life was going to be after all her grand plans? No, she told herself, it would not be like that because Archie, like herself, had ambition. Perhaps he was right and they really could make a success of marriage together by treating it like a business contract.

Archie accepted her decision without surprise, giving her the impression that he had never seriously doubted the outcome. They posted the bans and set a date a bare three weeks away.

Now she had to tell the family, including her grandmother. Archie had already broken the news to his own parents and reported a surprised reaction.

'Mother thought I would never manage to get a woman of my own,' he laughed, judging it wisest to keep most of what his mother had had to say on the subject to himself.

In fact Mrs Cree had been appalled. A strong-willed, overbearing, self-righteous and narrow-minded woman, she was the self-appointed matriarch of Craigie. The only person who had ever been brave enough to stand up to her was the equally sharp-tongued Ina Lennox. Mrs Cree's soft-voiced opinion of Ina's immoral co-habitation with Tammy McGurk had resulted in loud, public battles between the two protagonists. When Ina's daughter, Evelyn, then walked out on her own family, running off with another man, Mrs Cree had circulated the gossip, suitably embroidered, with high glee, attracting Ina's renewed wrath. So, to have her favourite son announce his intention to marry into the most notorious family in the village was the most humiliating moment of Mrs Cree's life. She cajoled, threatened and stormed, using language more generally confined to the pit bottoms, all to no avail. Archie remained stubbornly determined. But so was she. Nothing would ever make her utter even a single good word about Mary Innes and only a holy commandment, written in stone from the Almighty Himself would get Mrs Cree to the wedding.

'That wee cripple?' was Ina's astounded reaction. 'What the hell do you see in that wee freak?'

'He is not a wee freak,' Mary screamed back. 'He's good and kind and generous.'

'Oh aye . . . ?' Ina laughed, looking hard at her grand-daughter. Mary had the horrible feeling that Ina saw right through her to the child in her womb. 'He's no good, Lass, you mark my words. And do you really want Mrs Cree as your mother-in-law? She'll make your life hell . . .'

'I'm not going to change my mind just because you and Mrs Cree can't get on!' Mary retorted.

'Aye, well, you know best. As usual! But don't say you weren't warned.'

Ina also found that pride prevented her attending the wedding of her eldest granddaughter to the son of her oldest enemy and the potential for social disaster was averted.

George's reaction was predictable. 'If that's what you want, Hen, though I can't see what you see in him.'

'He used to fancy you at school, though I never knew you liked him back,' was Linda's puzzled response.

'You're mad,' snorted Catherine, comparing the crippled Archie to the strong collier she was engaged to.

David wasn't really interested one way or the other.

Mary and Archie were married in Inverannan registry office.

Cost being a limiting factor the guests were few. Archie's two brothers, Arthur and Samuel, with their wives and children, were his only supporters.

Mary's side was represented by her sisters and their boyfriends, and her Uncle Jackie and his silent wife. Janette, naturally, was Mary's best maid and James who had also been invited took photographs and showered everyone in confetti. George was so nervous that he had to be fortified with two whiskies before he felt equal to giving his daughter away, a duty he eventually performed faultlessly.

After the ceremony there was a celebratory meal in the local co-operative hall.

Mary flicked a crumb of steak pie from the skirt of her suit and felt tears smarting behind her eyes. Since childhood she had harboured every girl's dream of a white wedding, the church full of flowers, a smart reception, and a handsome groom. She sneaked a sideways glance at Archie, who was three quarters drunk and swopping lewd jokes with his unappealing brothers, and sudden panic enveloped her. Anything, she would give anything, just to put the clock back by two hours. Her clothes felt too tight, as if they were choking her, sweat dampened her hands, her head span. Desperately she looked round, searching for some way out. Janette, watching and understanding some of her friend's feelings, was on her feet in a second, giving Mary a glass of cold water and squeezing her shoulder. When Mary raised bright, tear-glazed eyes to her, she deliberately misread their message, knowing it was too late for sympathy now.

'Something went down the wrong way,' Janette explained to Archie who was scowling at her. 'OK?' she asked the bride when he had turned away again.

'Yes . . . Thanks.' Mary smiled wryly, feeling in control again and released her friend to go back to her own seat before they attracted too much attention. To her dismay Archie and Janette, who had met only yesterday, had taken an instant dislike to one another and the frosty atmosphere between them was obvious. Janette was much too loyal to voice her own opinion about Archie but he had no compunction about labelling Janette as bossy, stuck up and – ludicrously – jealous, making it perfectly plain that he did not approve of his wife's friendship. Mary wondered if this wedding had already claimed its first sacrifice then vowed that nothing would ever be allowed to spoil things between her and Janette.

As soon as the meal was over Archie made it plain that it was time to go to the ground-floor council flat which was to be their home, and take up her duties as Mrs Archie Cree. A noise to her left distracted her as she rose to collect her coat and she looked round in time to see her father's head hit the table in a drunken stupor, spilling a tumbler as it went.

Her abiding memory of that day was of Catherine and Linda's boyfriends hoisting the insensible George upright and dragging him outside into the fresh air.

NINE

When Archie said hard work would make a success of the business, hard work was what he meant. Mary spent all day and much of the evening making pies, bridies and sausage rolls for him to sell from his van the following day. The flat stank of meat. Archie stank of meat. She was sure the baby, when it came, would stink of meat too. At night she collapsed exhausted into bed, yearning for rest.

Archie had been a surprise in that area. Far better than she had expected him to be. Gentler than Paul, more demanding too, complaining if she missed an opportunity to take the initiative, sulking if she was less passionate in her response than he thought she should be and, occasionally, angry when she failed to reach a convincing climax. It wasn't all acting on her part. He consistently stirred her to a far more satisfying reaction than Paul had ever done. But she did wish he was a little less determined to make love to her every single night. She felt there was something unhealthily desperate about it, as if he was trying to prove something.

And she missed Janette. The two young women had only managed to meet twice. The first time, about six weeks after the wedding, Janette had visited Mary and Archie's council flat where she had had no option but to sit in the kitchen all day while her friend worked to keep up her normal quota while chattering non-stop. Even so she had fallen behind, attracting acid criticism from Archie which Janette had been quite unable to stop herself answering, just as sharply. In the end Janette had also rolled up her sleeves and set to with a will and the friends had worked together to make up for lost time but Mary felt angry and resentful that she wasn't able to treat her best friend to anything better.

A little over a month later Mary travelled to St Andrews to spend a Saturday with Janette in the little house she and Jamie had bought in preparation for their wedding. She had been looking forward to this for ages. The weather was beautiful and the scenic bus ride should have contributed to her enjoyment. As it was, the whole day was marred by the row she and Archie had before she left. Saturday was the only logical day for her visit because – there being no round on a Sunday – it was the one day of the week which wasn't fully occupied with cooking Archie's supplies for the following day. For him Saturday was his busiest day. When he finished, sometime after five o'clock, he came home briefly to wash and change before going off to the Greyhound for a couple of hours. As a rule he came back for his evening meal soon after eight o'clock. Today Mary intended to be home in time to have dinner ready for him as usual, so, in fact, he would hardly be aware of her absence. Archie had known about the planned visit for more than a week but left it until she was on the point of leaving for her bus before raising objections. He started by sulking and pretending she hadn't told him of her plans. When that failed he told her angrily that her place was with him, accused Janette of being a bad influence and finally ordered her to stay at home. Mary suspected that Archie was actually jealous of her relationship with Janette and resisted the temptation to argue back, guessing correctly that he was more than likely to be apologetic by the time she got home. Nevertheless, the incident upset her.

Not that she had very much to complain about. On the

whole, their unlikely marriage was proving to be much more successful than either of them had dared to hope.

And then it all began to go wrong. The day started out much like any other. Archie left their cheerless council flat in Craigie just before six in the morning to bone and roll his meat in a room he rented at the back of the old church hall. By eight he was back with the lamb offcuts she needed for her shell pies, steak for the bridies and oddments for the meat and potato pies she made so well. By this time Mary had been hard at work for well over an hour and had already made her pastry. While he was out on his rounds she would cook the meat and vegetables then fill the pies, ready for baking that evening.

When he brought the meat in, Archie called to Mary to take the pies she had made yesterday out to the van. Stacking the trays until she could barely see over the top of them she staggered towards the front door. She was proud of the fact that since she had taken over, his sales of cooked pies, bridies and sausage rolls had increased dramatically and he had even managed to get contracts to supply both the local shop, and the Greyhound, on a daily basis. The amount of work was steadily increasing and already occupied her from morning to night so that her back ached and her feet swelled but it was worth it just to see the money they were making. Another two or three years and the shop would be more than just a dream.

The front door of their flat was at the top of eight concrete steps. Mary hurried through it knowing Archie would be impatient to be off on his round. But somehow she missed her footing and felt herself starting to fall. Hampered by the swell of her eighth month of pregnancy she struggled, determined not to lose her grip on the trays. The weight of them pitched her forward towards the flagged path where she landed heavily on her right hip.

'Are you all right?' Archie was at her side, hauling her painfully to her feet.

Mary brushed herself down and winced slightly. 'Yes,' she snapped, angry with herself. 'Oh, just look at the mess!' A good proportion of yesterday's work was strewn over their little front garden. An opportunistic dog slunk through the gate, grabbed a best steak bridie and scuttled off with it hanging from his slobbering jaws.

Archie assessed the damage rapidly. Only about a dozen and a half items were actually on the ground. The rest were safely, if untidily protected in the trays. 'Not to worry. I'll soon have this tidied up.' Hurriedly he rearranged the trays. 'There, nothing more than a flake of pastry missing here and there. It's the Greyhound's delivery that's spilt. I should get them to him for lunch-time. Tell you what, I'll call in about half eleven. That should give you time to make some more.'

'I've got tomorrow's orders to see to,' she protested, rubbing her back, already feeling exhausted.

'I know that fine! But these are ordered for today. If I'm to make a go of this I can't go letting folk down, Mary. It'll not take you long and it was your fault.' With that he hobbled to the van and drove off, leaving her to clear up the mess.

Resignedly she swept the broken remains on to the patchy grass and watched angrily as birds and dogs swooped on their unexpected feast. Archie was right, she thought as her temper cooled, they couldn't afford to let his hard-won customers down. But she had the unpalatable feeling that he had been more worried about them than about her.

All morning she worked like a demon and just managed to have a fresh batch ready when Archie called to collect them, which he did without a single word of appreciation. And she still had most of tomorrow's order to deal with.

She mixed and rolled more pastry furiously, gritting her teeth against the ache in her lower back which was growing steadily worse.

By tea-time the pain was so bad that she was frightened and starting to wonder if she had done more than just bruise herself.

The pies were neatly lined up, ready for the oven and there was just one batch of bridies to be made when the pain changed abruptly, running viciously through her back and into her abdomen. She gasped, clutched at her swollen belly and ran to the toilet. The smear of crimson blood on her panties told her her worst fears had been realised.

Abandoning the kitchen she crept to bed. Archie would be home soon and could call the doctor for her.

While she waited she thought about the baby fighting for its life inside her. At first it had meant little to her, worse than that, it had been a cruel reminder of Paul Kinsail, living, permanent proof of her own stupidity and of the hurt which still stabbed at her in unguarded moments. But gradually she had come to see the child as an independent, blameless human being, something deserving love and care. Now she was frightened more for it than for herself and lay rigidly, scared to move and perhaps make things worse.

Archie found her, white-faced and weeping, an hour and a half later.

'It's the baby, Archie. That fall . . . I think I'm losing it,' she stammered through stabs of ferocious pain. 'Please, call the doctor.'

He seemed flustered. 'Aye . . . right . . .' She heard the kitchen door open and a few seconds later he was back in the bedroom. 'You've not finished the order for the morn! There's a dozen bridies short.' It was an accusation.

She could hardly believe her ears. 'Archie! To hell with your bridies! I'm bleeding. Just get the doctor. Quickly.'

Without another word he stomped from the house, leaving her in tears. But now they were tears of anger.

By midnight it was all over. The child, a boy, was born dead. Weakened by loss of blood and desperately sad, Mary lay silently in her hospital bed, waiting for her husband to visit her, to comfort her.

Early the following morning her family arrived, subdued and awkward, none of them knowing what to say to make her feel better. In the early afternoon a nurse brought a message from Janette, who had been contacted by a thoughtful Catherine but it was evening before Archie finally turned up.

'I thought you would have come before this,' she accused as soon as he appeared in her doorway.

'I had to see to the round. My customers were expecting me.'

'You could have called in for a minute or two.'

'And then I would have been late,' he retorted angrily. 'Folk won't wait, Mary. If I don't turn up when they're expecting me to, they go off to the local butcher's shop. Anyway, I knew you were all right. I phoned last night and they told me it was all over. I didn't go to bed until I knew you were OK.' He shuffled his feet uncomfortably. 'I'm right sorry about the bairn,' he offered at last.

'So am I,' she whispered.

'Still, not to worry, eh? Maybe it's for the best after all,' he said, oblivious to the tormented expression on her face.

'The best?'

'Aye. You know what I mean . . . It wasn't mine was it?'

'It was a human being and you promised to treat it as your own,' she reminded him, coldly.

'Aye. And I would have done. But it's better this way. A bairn would have been in the way, wouldn't it?' He

155

hurried on before she could argue with him. 'I need you to make the pies for me, Mary. You couldn't have made so many with a bairn to look after.'

Mary dissolved into strangled sobs and eased her sore body on to its side, away from him.

Archie stared at her thoughtfully. 'Don't be upset, Hen,' he muttered at last. 'I was only trying to make you feel better. Maybe it was the wrong thing to say but I was trying to be practical. Come on now, stop that crying. I wasn't trying to be cruel.' Still her shoulders shook. 'When can you come home?' he asked, searching for a safer subject. 'I do miss you, you know.'

Mollified slightly she choked back her tears and tried to sound more cheerful. Archie did have the unfortunate knack of saying the wrong thing. She should know that much by now. 'Friday. The doctor says I should be able to go home on Friday.'

'Friday?' He was horrified. 'But that's three days away! You're all right aren't you?'

'Yes,' she assured him, touched by his concern. 'Sore, and I lost a lot of blood but I'll be all right.'

'Friday,' he repeated, half to himself. 'What am I supposed to do about the pies and things? I'll lose half my business.'

'Damn your bloody pies, Archie Cree,' she yelled, shoving him away from her. 'Just go away. Get out of my sight.'

'Aye. Maybe I'd better,' he agreed, backing away from the wildcat on the bed. 'I'll ring in tomorrow, see how you are.'

He fetched her home on Friday night, after the day's business. All through Saturday she rested, still feeling totally drained. When Archie came home he was wonderfully kind and considerate. Obviously, she thought, trying to make amends for his earlier thoughtlessness. But, on Sunday morning he roused her at eight o'clock.

'Come on, Mary. The meat's all ready for you, in the kitchen. You'll have to make a start if you're to have the orders ready for tomorrow.'

'Not already, Archie. I'm not fit yet. Can't you let me have another couple of days?'

'Another couple of days?' he roared. 'In another couple of days you'll not need to bother. My customers'll be buying from someone else. I'll give you a wee hand with the vegetables and I've fetched a high stool from the storeroom so's you can sit down while you work and not tire yourself too much.'

'No, Archie. I can't. Not today.'

He moved a step closer to the bed, looming over her threateningly. 'Get out of that bed. Now,' he ordered in a furious temper.

'No.'

He slammed his hands down on the dressing table, causing it to rock dangerously, then turned to face his wife again, his fists clenched at his sides as he struggled to control his surging temper. For the first time she was frightened of him, sensing his previously hidden capacity for violence.

'If you don't get out of that bed, I'll drag you from it by your hair,' he threatened. 'You had better remember, we made a bargain, Mary Cree. I married you on the understanding that you would help me to make this business a success. So far all you've done is damn near ruin me. We'll never get anywhere if you take to your bed at the slightest little excuse.' Now he grabbed her arm, tight enough to leave a bruise, and dragged her to the edge of the mattress. 'My mother had three weans and she never had more than a day in bed in her whole life.'

'If your mother's so wonderful why don't you ask her

157

to help?' Mrs Cree senior was constantly being held up to her as an example of perfection. Mary heartily disliked the older woman who was over-critical, sour-tempered and did nothing to hide her disapproval of her son's choice of wife.

'Get your clothes on and get to work, and leave my mother out of this,' he growled.

Realising he fully intended to haul her on to the floor she struggled into a sitting position and started to pull her nightdress over her head.

'That's more like it.' He stepped back at last then sighed heavily. 'I didn't mean to be rough with you, Mary. But it's for your own good. I'm really sorry about the bairn, Hen, but I know you'll feel better with something to take your mind off it. It's no good lying there all miserable.'

'Go to hell, Archie Cree!' she spat at him, limping her way to the bathroom and slamming the door behind her.

Somehow she struggled through the day. Archie helped where he could but, tiring of her continued bad temper, took himself off to complain to his delighted mother who, aided by the contents of a whisky bottle, encouraged him to believe that all his complaints were justified. His unhappy wife, who might have responded to a comforting arm and a shoulder to cry on, fell into bed long before he came home again and another opportunity was lost.

A week after the miscarriage an invitation to Janette and Jamie's wedding arrived. A beautiful, silver-edged card invited her and Archie to attend the ceremony and reception in Janette's home town of Carnoustie, just to the east of Dundee. From the long letters she and Janette exchanged every week, Mary knew this wedding was to be the sort of fairytale occasion every girl dreams of and longed to be with her friend on this very special day. If it hadn't been for the fact that the wedding date was within a fortnight of the day on which Mary's baby would have been born, she would have been her friend's matron of honour. Both girls had laughingly agreed that a hugely pregnant woman, decked out in pink satin and organza, was not likely to be the most attractive of prospects and Mary had limited herself to promising to be there if humanly possible, vowing that only the onset of labour would keep her away. But she had failed to predict Archie's reaction.

'It's on a Saturday!' he protested when she showed him the invitation.

'Most weddings are,' she laughed, never imagining he would raise serious objections.

'Saturday's my busiest day.'

'I know that, Archie, but this is a very special occasion. Couldn't you take a day off for once?'

'And what about my customers?' he demanded.

'Warn them in advance. So long as they know you'll not be round on the Saturday, they can stock up the day before. All you'll have to do is carry some extra stock.'

'They're used to me coming every Saturday. Anyway, I do a different round on Friday and Saturdays. Monday, Wednesday and Friday in Craigie and the other mining villages. Tuesday, Thursday and Saturday in Inverannan. So I can't just sell extra the day before. If I take Saturday off I'll lose a whole day's takings. Half my customers will buy their stuff from someone else and I'll never get them back.'

'Of course you will.' She ridiculed his assertion. 'You know your prices are cheaper than the shops and if your stuff's as good as you say it is, your customers will be only too keen to come back to you.'

'Even so,' he insisted doggedly, 'I can't afford to lose a day's takings.'

'Are you saying you are never going to take any time off?' she exclaimed, disbelievingly.

'Not for the first couple of years.' Why wouldn't she understand how precarious a mobile round was, how fickle housewives were, how easy it was to lose everything you'd worked for years to build up? 'I'm not trying to be difficult, Hen. And it won't be forever. When we're a bit more secure we could pay someone to fill in for me for a week or so and take a proper holiday.'

'What about Catherine's wedding? It's in less than two months! Are you saying you won't take time off for that either?'

'That's different. Catherine and Bobby are getting wed at four o'clock. I'll make sure I'm finished by then. All I have to do is warn everyone I'll be round a wee bitty earlier than normal. I don't have to take the whole day off for that. It'll be the same when your Linda weds her Mick, next year. But Janette's wedding's in Carnoustie, at eleven in the morning . . .'

'Archie! Please. Janette is my best friend. She'll be hurt if I don't go to her wedding.'

'No . . . she'll understand. You've got a good excuse. Tell her you're still not strong enough after losing the wean,' he suggested with unwitting callousness.

'No! I want to go to her wedding, Archie.'

'It'll cost a fortune.' Thoroughly aggravated now by what he saw as pure selfishness he found another excuse. 'You'll be wanting a new rigout, there's a present to buy and that hotel where the reception's being held sounds right posh. Drinks'll be over dear. No point in going if you can't afford to have a good drink.'

'I can wear the suit I got married in, and you can wear yours, too, so we don't have to buy any new clothes. And I'm going to buy them a wedding present whether we go or not, so you can't save any money there. As for drinking. Well, we're not so poor that we can't afford a night out once in a while, are we? Anyway, I don't think it's a particularly posh hotel. Janette's family are just ordinary folk. And surely you don't have to get rolling drunk just to have a good time?'

His arguments demolished, Archie resorted to stubborn refusal. 'I don't care what you say, Mary. We're not going and that's that . . .'

'This is all because you don't like Janette. It's nothing to do with the money, or the lost trade,' she accused him, truculently.

'You're right! I don't like her,' he admitted. 'She's stuck up and smart mouthed and, and . . .'

'And she's my best friend! You can't ask me not to go to her wedding.'

'If you go, you'll go on your own,' he decided, triumphantly.

'Fine! I'll enjoy myself better without you to spoil the day,' she retorted instantly.

Between then and the wedding they barely exchanged a word that wasn't absolutely necessary.

Mary went to Janette's wedding and cried her tears of happiness and sadness alone. Apart from the bride and groom she knew no one else there so, as soon as Janette and Jamie had been decently sent off on their honeymoon, she started on her way home. The journey gave her plenty of opportunity to review the state of her own marriage. Janette and Jamie's touching exchange of vows had reminded her sharply of the pledge she and Archie had made to one another so short a time ago and by the time she stepped off the bus in Craigie she was in a more positive frame of mind, willing to make excuses for her husband who was, after all, a man and naturally not as sensitive as she was. Perhaps all they needed was more time to adjust to one another.

TEN

Despite all that Archie had said about a baby being in the way while they were trying to build up the business, he was as excited as a small boy when she announced she was pregnant again, almost exactly a year after their wedding.

'We'll celebrate,' he told her, grandly. 'I'll take you out and you can buy yourself a new dress.'

'Do you like it?' she asked, as she slipped the shimmering, blue creation over her head. It was the most elegant thing she had ever owned. And the most expensive. Archie had actually blanched when she had confessed exactly how much it had cost. But it suited her colouring. Her blonde hair, waved and brushed softly on to her shoulders, shimmered as much as the satiny material. Her figure, not yet showing her twelve-week pregnancy, was nevertheless slightly fuller and more shapely now, and was displayed to perfection by the low-cut, but not immodest, bodice, fitted waist and tight skirt. 'Do you like it, Archie?' she repeated, pirouetting in front of him.

'I suppose the colour's OK,' he grunted but his expression was anything but appreciative. 'But it's too tight. You'll have every man in the place ogling you in that thing.'

The sparkle died in her eyes, leaving them grey and lifeless. 'I bought it to please you, Archie.' But he was almost impossible to please these days.

'Considering what you paid for it, it makes you look

cheap. You'll not see any of the other women dressed like that.'

'Just where are you taking me, Archie?' She had assumed it would be somewhere special, an intimate dinner for two, which was why she had chosen this particular dress.

'The Miners' Welfare. They have a dance every Saturday night.'

'The Miners' Welfare!' She was staggered, horrified. It was the roughest place for miles around. A place even her easygoing father had forbidden his daughters to go to. 'We won't get in. We're not members.'

'My father is. He and mother go every week. There's a wee bit of a dance and they say it's a good night. They're going with us. And my brothers, too.'

She groaned. 'But it's so rough, Archie.'

'Not good enough for you, eh?' he taunted. It often seemed to him that on the strength of her college diploma, Mary thought she was too good for Craigie, and, by implication, for him. 'Anyway, you're wrong. It's not that bad. I go there a couple of times a week.'

'So that's where you get so drunk?'

'Don't start! I'm entitled to a drink, just like any other man. I earn the money and I can spend it any way I damn well please.' It was an argument they had all too often these days.

'So you keep telling me. But I work too, don't forget, so don't complain when I buy myself a dress, especially when it's the only thing I've bought myself since we got married. I wore the suit I got married in to both my sisters' weddings and to Janette and Jamie's.' Catherine and Linda had both married local men within the last months and were now settled in homes of their own in the village with their first babies on the way.

163

'It's not the price I'm complaining about. If you want the truth you look like a whore.'

Mary looked at her reflection. It wasn't true. For the first time in her life she thought she looked truly attractive. It was a sophisticated, glamorous dress, the first of many if their business prospered. But it was entirely unsuitable for a night at Craigie Miners' Welfare Club.

The night was ruined before it had even begun. When she insisted on wearing the dress, not because she was being stubborn but simply because she had nothing else to wear, Archie sulked. As soon as they got to the club he surrounded himself with his father and brother and dedicated himself to downing as much whisky as he could before the bar closed. Despite the band playing and the other couples who were dancing on the cramped floor, he ignored Mary who was forced to make stilted conversation with his censorious mother.

Mrs Cree had disliked Mary from the moment they met and nothing would induce her to be even mildly pleasant to her newest daughter-in-law. She was a formidable adversary. Built like a bus and with considerably less charm, she presided over her family like a malevolent Buddha. Her husband and grown sons were in awe of her and no woman could ever hope to be an acceptable wife for her offspring. Like her two unfortunate sisters-in-law, Mary avoided her whenever possible.

Tonight Mary was forced to endure her unpleasant company for over an hour. When her own sister, Catherine, and her new husband came into the crowded hall she gladly muttered an excuse into Mrs Cree's unattractive ear and joined them.

It wasn't long before Bobbie, Catherine's strapping husband, took Mary up to dance. After that Matt Donnelly and Ian Mathie, both of whom she had known at school, also danced with her. Suddenly the evening was turning out to be enjoyable. Perhaps, she thought as she and Ian executed an inexpert waltz, this was the best place to have come to after all. It was a long time since she had had the chance to gossip with old friends like this. Archie was far too possessive to let her have friends of her own and, in any case, she was always much too busy. As if to endorse her thoughts Archie glared at her in undisguised fury as they shuffled past. Well, she thought, smiling sweetly at him, this was supposed to be her celebration too and she was as entitled to enjoy herself as he was.

All the time they danced, Archie stared balefully at her, his face getting redder and redder, sweat pouring from his face and soaking his shirt. When she saw him taking a fresh drink to his mother she went over to talk to him.

'Come on, Archie. Dance with me. This is supposed to be our celebration.'

'You know fine I can't dance. I'm a cripple,' he spat at her while his mother tut-tutted her disapproval.

'Of course you can dance,' she retorted, meaning it. In truth she was so used to Archie's limp that she rarely thought about it. 'Come on. Let's try. We've never danced together.' She took his damp hand and attempted to pull him on to the dance floor.

He shook her off violently. 'You just want to make a fool of me so all your fancy friends can take the piss out of me,' he roared, drunkenly.

'You know that's not true,' she shot back. 'And as for fancy friends, they are people we were both at school with, people who could be friendly with you, too, if you'd just give them the chance.'

Ignoring her he picked up his empty glass and staggered back to the bar for another drink.

'Don't think I don't know what your game is,' Archie's mother scowled at her. 'I warned him you couldn't want him for himself. How could you, him being like he is?

All you're interested in is a share of the takings to throw away on fancy clothes.' She fingered the blue satin of Mary's dress contemptuously and scattered ash all over the skirt.

Mary had had enough. 'You evil old woman,' she hissed. 'You've done nothing but cause trouble between us – ' She would have gone on to say a lot more if Ian hadn't reappeared at that precise moment.

'Come on, Hen. One more dance.'

Willingly she allowed him to lead her back into the throng. Like nearly all the men there, Ian was following the hallowed Saturday night custom of sinking as much drink as he possibly could in the space of three hours. It was this custom which accounted for the extraordinarily subdued air of the village on Sunday mornings. With two solid hours of drinking behind him, Ian was far from steady on his feet. He draped himself heavily over her shoulder and his left hand strayed to her right buttock and clamped itself firmly there.

'Shift your hand, Ian.' Mary suddenly realised she had made a mistake in agreeing to dance with him again. He merely grinned stupidly and tightened his grip. Sighing she let him lean on her as they lurched round the hall. When they reached her table she would say she was too hot and escape.

But, before they had the opportunity to get there, Ian seemed to rise into the air, propelled aloft by Archie's two brawny brothers and helped on his unexpected way across the room by a hefty punch to his jaw. He landed in a confused heap but scrambled quickly to his feet, yelling obscenities and lunging for the Cree brothers. The dance floor erupted into an arena with every available man and not a few of the women attaching themselves to one faction or the other.

Mary watched in dazed abhorrence as Archie, no less

166

drunk than the others, waded into the fray, not at all hampered by his leg and landed several heavy blows on the unfortunate Ian's face. 'Keep your filthy, fucking hands off my wife,' he snarled and spat full in the other man's face. Mary gagged. Samuel and Arthur, Archie's brothers, dragged him off before he could inflict serious damage and Mary found herself being hauled outside by her mother-in-law.

'Now see what you've done,' she accused, hustling the younger woman on to the street just as the police car roared up. It was a rare Saturday night when they weren't called here.

Samuel, Arthur and Archie arrived, breathless and dishevelled, and harried the women along the road, eager to avoid trouble. Moving with remarkable speed considering his handicap, Archie had Mary's arm in a grip like an animal trap.

'You're hurting me,' she protested.

'You'll be hurting even more when I've finished with you,' he promised, shoving her through the gate.

Too late Mary realised that the rest of the family had melted away. Even her mother-in-law's poisonous company would have been welcome at that moment.

They were hardly through the front door when he landed his first blow, an open handed slap which sent her crumbling back against the lobby wall, her head spinning.

'That's for making a fool of me,' he screamed, sounding completely deranged. 'Do you not think I get enough stick the way I am without my own wife carrying on with other men, as if I'm not enough for you?'

Archie was so drunk, so angry that he was unable to control the small, twitching movements his head made, spittle dribbled from his mouth and his whole body shook with paroxysms of fury. Terrified she shielded her face behind her hands as he closed on her, raining furious, uncontrolled blows all over her body. Groaning she slid to the floor and curled into a foetal ball, whimpering with pain and shock. Then, abruptly, the attack stopped. Cautiously she opened her eyes and saw Archie, his red hair standing on end, an expression of drunken confusion distorting his slack face, swaying over her. Expecting him to hit her again she cowered but he stumbled away. Seconds later she heard him retching in the bathroom. As soon as she was sure he was safely in the bedroom she picked herself off the floor and laid her aching body on the settee in the living room.

In the middle of the night she woke with terrible cramping pains in her abdomen. There was no need to look for bloodstains to know she was losing her second child.

So early in the pregnancy it was physically less traumatic this time. One night in hospital was all it took before she was allowed home. She escaped in shame. The bruises covering her body had been all too obvious and the doctor attending her had left her in no doubt that he understood precisely what had happened to her. At one stage he even asked if she wanted to talk to the police, or a social worker.

Archie was a chastened, sober and frightened man when he took her home. 'I'm sorry, Hen. Oh, God, I'm sorry, Mary,' he repeated time and time again, tears filling his tired eyes. 'I don't know what got into me. I've never hit a woman before . . . It was the drink talking, that's all. I saw you with all those men, looking at you – my wife – I didn't know what I was doing . . . I thought you were taking the piss out of me, trying to make me dance . . . Oh God! I'll stay off the booze. Honest I will. I'm sorry, Hen. I'll do anything to make it right between us,' he pleaded.

'You killed your own child,' she retorted, hating him more than she had believed it possible to hate another human being and wanting to make him suffer too. 'Your own flesh and blood, Archie Cree. But perhaps it was for the best. After all, a baby would have been in the way, wouldn't it?' She threw his own words back at him and exulted when she saw the look of raw pain on his face.

'Bitch,' he choked.

'I don't care what you think of me, Archie, or what names you call me. You can't possibly hurt me more than you have already done. But if you ever hit me again, I'll leave you,' she threatened. And before that if she could get enough money together somehow.

A wave of terror burned through his body. What would he be without her? How could he admit he hadn't been able to keep his wife? Everyone would mock him, just as they had done in the past . . . The pain and confusion, the shame at what he had done emerged as an angry shout. 'No! You can't leave me, Mary.'

Misunderstanding she stepped back, feeling threatened but refusing to back down. 'No? Well, we'll see about that if you so much as lift one finger against me ever again,' she promised him defiantly, refusing to be cowed this time.

She half-expected him to lash out at her again. Half of her wanted him to, to force her into action, the other half of her knew she had nowhere to go. Pride would prevent her from running home to her father and advertising her plight to the whole village. And this was something she could not even bring herself to tell Janette about.

'Don't leave me, Mary,' he pleaded. 'I know I was wrong. But I need you. You're my wife. I'll not do it again, I promise, only please, don't ever leave me, Hen.'

She looked at him coldly, totally sickened by this pitiful display. 'I hate you,' she said, turning her back on him.

ELEVEN

Nothing was ever the same again. There was nothing they wanted to say to one another, no thoughts or experiences they wanted to share. Hating the tense, resentful silence which marked their few shared evenings, Archie spent his days in the van, his evenings in the Greyhound. He knew that despite all his attempts to make her understand how much he regretted what had happened, no matter how sincere he was in trying to make her see how jealous he had been, how inadequate she made him feel, that all the feelings he had kept bottled up had simply exploded that night, Mary would never forgive him. He responded by drinking even more. At least that way his problems didn't seem so enormous.

For her, every time he came home drunk it was a terrifying reminder of that dreadful evening when whisky had inflamed him to the beating which had resulted in her second miscarriage. It was impossible for her to even look at him then without starting to shake with remembered terror and she couldn't bear him to touch her. She took to going to bed early to avoid him.

Mary had watched Archie trying to make amends for what had happened to her but her heart had remained hardened and untouched. She knew that it was her unforgiving attitude which had driven him back to hide in drink but there was nothing she could do about it. His violence had destroyed everything, including her hope for the future, and had taught her to hate with a bitterness which scared her, made her incapable of seeing any shade of good in him. Every time he was drunk, each time he sounded even slightly irritable, she felt threatened. It was as if the menace of violence, once unleashed, could never be restrained even though he had hardly even raised his voice to her since then. She had seen the way he stopped himself, holding his temper in check with a physical effort that was visible and frightening in its fragility. One day she knew the slender threads of self-control would break again. Before that happened she promised herself, she really would leave Archie.

All this had a disastrous effect on his business. In the mornings Archie was often so hungover that he didn't get out on his round until lunch-time. His regular orders were cancelled because he could no longer be relied on to make his deliveries on time. Takings fell dramatically. Some days he didn't even make enough to cover the cost of the petrol he used, though he never admitted as much to Mary.

Day to day existence became a struggle. Bitterly, Mary thought that this was just the way it had been when she was a child. Her purse was always empty and she was forced to plead with Archie to give her money for every little thing she bought while he still spent every last penny in the pub, buying pints for his pals, desperate to make them all see what a fine lad he was; that cheerful Archie Cree, despite his disability, had a happy home, an understanding wife and a thriving business; that Archie Cree was as good a man as any of them, a success. Mary watched him hobbling along the street, calling out to his friends, even to his in-laws, as if he hadn't a care in the world and wept to think that she was the only person who ever saw the other, darker side to Archie's character, the side that seemed to emerge as soon as he stepped through the front door.

Then, just as she thought things couldn't get any worse, she got a long letter from Janette with the shattering news that she and Jamie were going to emigrate to Canada. Jamie, she wrote, had relatives in British Columbia who had offered them a temporary home. A joiner by trade, Jamie had the written promise of a job and arrangements had already been made for him to start work in slightly less than six weeks' time. Reading through her friend's letter Mary realised Janette and Jamie must have been making their plans for a very long time and felt a spurt of resentment that her best friend had excluded her from her confidence.

Janette drove to Craigie to make her farewells a couple of days before she was due to leave Scotland.

'We've known we'd be emigrating since before we married,' Janette admitted through streams of tears. 'Jamie has always been determined to go over there. If I hadn't agreed to go too, he would have gone without me. I love him, Mary. What could I do?'

'But why didn't you tell me before?' her distraught friend demanded.

'The worst thing about going to Canada is leaving everyone I love. Especially you, Mary. And you've been so unhappy recently. I didn't want to make it any worse for you.'

'Oh God, Janette. I'm going to miss you so much!' Mary sobbed.

'Don't,' Janette pleaded. 'I can't bear to think that I might never see you again.'

'No! Don't say that! I'm going to save every spare penny so I can come and visit you. And you are sure to come home again. You've got to see your parents . . .'

'I'll write, send postcards, photos . . . and you've got to promise to do the same for me.'

'I will. I will . . .'

Mary watched her friend drive out of her life with unashamed tears streaming down her face. Despite all their fine words both women knew it was unlikely that they'd ever meet again. Mary knew she had lost something utterly priceless.

Not content to sit at home and watch her husband drink their future away, Mary decided it was time to get herself a job but Archie wouldn't even consider it. He would give no one reason to think he couldn't support his own wife, and, more to the point, he wanted her at home, where he knew where she was and what she was doing. Who knew, he reasoned, what an attractive woman like Mary might be tempted to do away from her husband's watchful eye? Especially when that husband was as horribly crippled as he was.

So, she was confined to Craigie. Business was so bad that there was no longer any point in making pies and bridies so there was very little to occupy her time. Her sisters were busy with their own jobs while her father had his contented routine of idleness which he saw no reason to disturb – even when Mrs Morrison, a wholesome but desperately lonely widow, tried to train him up to be her new husband, a hopeless task which resulted in her own rapid defeat. Even Mary's neighbours had friends of their own and no real desire to pass the time with someone who had been too busy to notice them in the past. Her days stretched before her like long, grey tunnels of boredom. Her life had no purpose, no point to it. No point in doing her hair, to putting on make-up or dressing in anything smart. Who was there to dress up for? She certainly didn't want to make herself attractive for Archie.

There was absolutely no resemblance in this tired, dowdy woman to the cheerful, neat and attractive girl who had first caught Paul Kinsail's eye. Mary's hair straggled mousily over a too-thin face. Her complexion was blotchy, the underlying skin greyish, her eyes huge and dull, her mouth unsmiling. If she caught a glimpse of herself in the mirror she looked away quickly, despising the poor, hopeless creature she saw there.

She was trapped, tied to a man she loathed, to a life she detested. How, she wondered, could her life have turned out so badly? So much for her mother's advice. If only she had been wise enough to heed it and stay away from men, but, if anything, she had ended up worse off than her mother who had been brave enough to take her future into her own hands and at least her father had never been a violent man.

She found herself wondering what her mother was doing now, where she was, whether her life was a happy one, if, perhaps, there might be room in it for her daughter. On a day of abject depression she even considered trying to trace her. Surely she, of all people, would understand, would help. But no one even knew where she was. Mary was certain her father had had no contact with his ex-wife since the divorce and when she probed her grandmother for information, Ina denied knowing anything more than George did. Mary was glad to escape from her grandmother that day and knew she had made a grave error in going there. Such sudden interest in her mother's whereabouts had instantly alerted Ina's unsympathetic suspicions about the state of her marriage and nothing could persuade Mary to confide in her grandmother who had always predicted that her marriage to Archie would end in disaster.

With Janette, her only possible ally, gone, there was no one she could turn to. The only way she was going to get out of this marriage and away from Archie was by falling back on her own depleted resources of strength, confidence and self-reliance. Qualities she had once had in abundance but which had faded along with her hopes for the future. But one day, when the slowly increasing store of pound notes which she had started to hoard was big enough to take her well away from Craigie, she would make her bid for freedom. One day . . .

Late in the afternoon of a long, dismal day, her unhappy musings were disturbed by an insistent rapping on the front door. Two strange men, grim-faced but smartly dressed, stood on her shabby doorstep.

'Mrs Cree?' the younger of the two asked.

'Yes.'

'We are from Strathannan council. Rent arrears department.' They watched her closely, obviously expecting some sort of reaction. She noticed that one man had his foot wedged in the door so she couldn't close it.

'Yes?' she asked, her heart starting to hammer with apprehension.

'May we come in? This might be better said in private.'

Mary realised that her nearest neighbour was blatantly eavesdropping from her doorstep. 'I suppose so.' She stepped back and ushered them inside, aware as she always was when anyone came into the house, of the poor furnishings and decoration.

'We have written to you several times, Mrs Cree, but the outstanding rent is increasing every fortnight. You must realise that we cannot allow this to continue,' the older man said as soon as they were in the living room.

Mary felt as though someone had delivered a chopping blow to the back of her knees. 'What?' she gasped.

'The rent arrears are considerable, Mrs Cree. Nothing has been paid for the last nine fortnights. Now, if your husband is unemployed, there are agencies which might be able to help. You might even be entitled to a rebate.' His voice was firm and not at all sympathetic.

She shook her head. 'My husband works. He has his own business.'

Then, her strong practical streak overcoming her initial shock, she sat up straight and faced the officials with a determined look on her face.

'Please,' she said, mustering all the dignity she was capable of. 'Tell me again.'

'You, or rather your husband, as the tenancy is in his name, is seriously behind with the rent on this flat. Nothing has been paid since last April.'

'My God!' It completely stunned her. 'I'm sure there must be some mistake. Archie . . . my husband, he pays the rent every other Monday morning.'

'Where does he pay it, Mrs Cree?'

'At the rent office. In Inverannan. Every other Monday morning.'

'Not for the past four months, Mrs Cree. And we have written to you about it several times.'

'Archie hasn't said anything about any letters.' On his insistence she left all the mail for him to open.

'Perhaps you could let us see the rent book?'

'Yes!' She sprang to her feet. 'Of course! Archie keeps it with all his other papers. In the bedroom. I'll not be a minute.'

But it wasn't in the old biscuit tin with all their other documents. Desperately she shuffled through everything then started to turn out the drawer where it was kept. At the very back, buried under the lining paper, she discovered a large paper bag, stuffed with papers. With shaking hands she emptied a heap of crumpled letters and torn envelopes on to the bed. The blue-backed rent book was easy to spot. She opened it nervously, already knowing what she would find. The officials were right. The rent hadn't been paid for months. Furiously she sorted through the creased letters and found three from the council, each one more threatening than the last. The most recent of them was dated almost two weeks ago. Also lurking in the pile of unpaid bills was an electricity demand, more than three weeks old, and a letter from the meat wholesalers demanding immediate payment of their overdue account. The amount made her mouth dry up. Trembling she sat on the bed, the papers dangling loosely from her hands.

'Mrs Cree,' one of the men called. 'Have you found it?'

'I'm coming,' she yelled back. Taking another minute to try and regain some composure she went to face them. 'It's here.' She held the worn book out to them. 'You're right. Nothing's been paid. I found some letters too.'

'I take it that you were unaware of the situation, Mrs Cree?' the younger man asked.

She shook her head. 'He never said anything to me. The business . . . it's not doing very well, but I didn't understand it was this bad.'

'I am sorry, I know this must have been a shock for you, but the fact is that something must be done to clear these arrears.'

'Yes. I do understand that but it's such a lot of money. We haven't got that much.' Not even with her secret bundle of pound notes and there was no way she was going to use them. That much was clear in her mind already.

'It may be possible to come to some arrangement.'

'Yes. Anything. What do you want me to do?' Her initial shock was forgotten. In its place was explosive resentment against Archie and, almost as strong, deep, stomach-curdling humiliation. To know that these men saw her as a debtor, to see herself reduced to the same level as some of her idle, shiftless neighbours when she had had such grand plans, rankled more than anything else.

The young man was still talking. 'As the rent agreement is in your husband's name I am afraid it is up to him. Ask him to call at our office within the next forty-eight hours.'

'I'll do that,' she agreed readily, anxious only to get them out of her home.

At the front door the older man turned to her again. 'I have to warn you, Mrs Cree, that unless your husband can make a considerable payment within the next few days, we will serve him with an eviction order.' That said they hurried to their car.

'Behind with the rent are you, Hen?' Mary's neighbour called from across the low front fence, her face avid. Mary knew it would be all round the village by nightfall.

She dived back inside her poorly furnished home and slammed the door.

She let Archie eat his tea, waiting for her moment with barely concealed fury. He seemed so unconcerned. How could he be acting so normally with such terrible debts hanging over him? She shivered and eyed the drab kitchen morosely. Everything they earned had gone into the business, leaving nothing to spare for furniture or decoration, or so Archie claimed. As a result, this flat was even worse than her father's prefab, shaming her so much that she no longer invited anyone here, not even her sisters. They would be shocked if they knew how far she had fallen.

'I'm fed up with egg and chips,' Archie complained, shoving his empty plate away from him. 'Can you not even be bothered to cook for me now? Am I not worth feeding any more?'

Ignoring the barb, so common these days, she took the envelope from the shelf where she had hidden it and calmly emptied the contents over the table in front of him. She was gratified to see him pale visibly.

'What's this?' he asked, sweat breaking out on his upper lip.

'A pile of unpaid bills. You had them so well hidden that I would never have found them if the men from the council hadn't come about the rent arrears. That's when I had to go and look for the rent book. Stupid of me but you see, Archie, I was so certain you'd paid the rent.'

'I have paid it, Hen, honest,' he lied monstrously.

'Don't waste your time lying to me, Archie Cree. You've not paid the rent since April. There's an unpaid electricity bill and threatening letters from the meat suppliers. Oh . . . and they're coming to take the telly back tomorrow. What are you doing with all the money, Archie?' she demanded, losing control at last and screaming at him.

'All of what money?' he countered sullenly. 'I don't even take enough to cover the expenses on the van.'

'Then find another job.'

'Who would employ a cripple like me?' He tried for sympathy and found none.

'Don't give me that. You use that back of yours as an excuse for anything that doesn't suit you. I used to admire you, Archie, for the way you coped but now . . . now you're just pathetic.'

'You cow,' he bellowed, hauling himself to his feet.

She backed towards the door, seeing all too clearly where this was leading but unable to curb her tongue. 'If you didn't drink so much you'd be able to get yourself out of bed in the mornings and do a decent day's work like any self-respecting man. When was the last time you came home sober? When was the last time you got into that van before midday?' He closed on her, full of menace but still she taunted him. 'What happened to all our fine

dreams, Archie? What about all those big plans now? I'll
tell you shall I? You drank them all!' Still yelling at him
she backed against the wall while he prowled round her
like a predator closing for the kill.

'It was you,' he accused. 'You . . . thinking you're too
good for me, eyeing up other men . . .'

'That is not true!'

'How do you expect a man to feel when his own wife
can't stand him to touch her? I've seen the way you look
at me, Mary. I'm not made of stone,' he was almost
weeping now, it hurt so badly, the rejection, the humiliation. 'If I drink it's because you've driven me to it . . .'

She couldn't keep the curl of contempt from her lips.
'That's right. Blame someone else for your own failure,'
she taunted.

'Bitch!' He spat it at her.

'I'm leaving you, Archie,' she said. 'I've had enough.'

'You're going nowhere! You are my wife,' he snarled.
'We made a deal and I won't let you walk out on that.'

'Bastard,' she sobbed, expecting him to hit her. But the
blow never fell. Instead Archie stared at her with hatred
burning in his own eyes then took a deep, ragged breath
before deliberately picking up his cup of tea and hobbling
out of the kitchen. Seconds later she heard the television
being switched on and the squeak of the chair springs as
he settled down to watch the news, as if nothing at all out
of the ordinary had happened.

A tide of anger first immobilised her then built inside
of her until she was almost screaming with frustration.
The belief that any such outburst would bring Archie
storming back ensured her silence.

Shaking still she tiptoed to the bathroom and swallowed
two aspirins for the pounding headache which was making
coherent thought almost impossible. Why had she let him
get her into this state, she asked herself? Why should she

live her life in terror of him? Anyone with any guts would have walked out on him long ago. But today's discovery had been the final straw, the final incentive.

Quickly she sluiced her face in cold water, patted it dry then opened the door quietly to make sure that Archie was still in front of the TV. Pausing only to grab the bottle of aspirins from the window sill she slipped out of the bathroom and into bed, huddling under the covers and shivering convulsively.

Ten minutes later she heard the living-room door open followed by Archie's uneven footsteps along the corridor which ran the full length of the flat. The bedroom door opened quietly and he stuck his head round to check on her. Mary was curled up in bed, apparently fast asleep. Closing the door again he shrugged himself into his jacket and let himself out of the flat.

As soon as she heard the front door snap shut, Mary was out of bed and hauling her daytime clothes back on. Archie had probably gone to the Greyhound as usual so there was plenty of time, but even so she ran to the cupboard by the front door and rummaged frantically until she found their only suitcase, a battered hand-me-down from her father. Back in the bedroom she stuffed clothes carelessly into it, threw in a few personal items, a photo album, some old jewellery and her diploma and closed the lid. Then she scrambled under the mattress until she found her secret hoard of pound notes. It wasn't much, but enough to tide her over for the first couple of days. She stuffed two into her purse but the rest she hid behind some of the photos in the album.

The case was overfull and she simply couldn't shut it. Impatiently she dragged it onto the floor and knelt on it, eventually managing to close first one side and then the other.

Ignoring her painful face and throbbing head she tore

along the corridor, grabbed her coat then manhandled the
case to just behind the front door, meaning to make sure
there was no one about when she left. Tonight she would
stay with her father and by this time tomorrow she would
be miles away from Craigie and Archie Cree.

Her hand was actually resting on the latch when the
door was shoved open and Archie burst in.

'I knew you were up to something,' he snarled.

'Archie!' Her heart was hammering against her ribs so
hard that it actually hurt.

'Where the fuck do you think you're going?' he
demanded, shoving her hard against the wall.

There was nothing she could say to defend herself, the
evidence against her was all too apparent in the bulging
suitcase. She shook her head and stayed silent.

'Where?' he demanded. 'Where were you going? Tell
me, Mary, or I'll beat it out of you,' he threatened, his
face flushing an ugly, deep red, his veins bulging with
temper.

'To my father's,' she said.

'Your father's? You were leaving me to run back to
your stupid father?' It was as if he couldn't believe she
would really go. 'You were walking out on me? You
bitch.' He hung on to his self-control with a huge effort.

'NO!' She denied it in a feeble attempt to calm him
down. 'I just thought it would be better . . . just for a
couple of days . . . until we could sort something out.'

'There is nothing to sort out,' he bellowed, sending
flecks of spittle into her face, clenching his fists at his sides.
'I'm warning you, Mary. You walk out on me and I'll
come after you and drag you back. I'll make your life as
miserable as you've made mine. Look what you've done
to me! After all I did for you, you've ruined me.'

'NO!'

'You've done your best to make me the laughing stock

of the village. What about the way you behaved that night at the Miners' institute? Ogling all the men. You still do it. I've seen you, eyeing up every man who passes within a hundred yards of you.' Something snapped inside his head.

'That's not true!' Mention of that night had started her shaking.

'Liar!' He raised his hand.

'No, Archie. Not again,' she pleaded, recognising the incipient violence in the tension of his body, knowing it would explode at any second. 'Please, Archie. Not again!'

She didn't even feel his fist in her face.

TWELVE

The next thing Mary was aware of was a heavy, throbbing pain in her forehead. When she cautiously raised her cramped body it sharpened, stabbing viciously into her brain, making her feel sick and giddy. Very carefully she lowered herself and waited for the spinning in her head to subside before opening her eyes again. When she did, the darkness was so absolute, so impenetrable, that for ten terrifying minutes she thought she had gone blind.

By now she knew she was lying on a floor, the cold, unyielding concrete told her that much. Every bone and muscle in her body was stiff and aching. Warily she moved her legs and winced when they started to tingle with renewed circulation. The pain gradually subsided allowing other, equally unpleasant, sensations to invade her battered system. She was cold, chilled to the point of numbness in her fingers and toes, and nauseated by her spinning head. Then memory returned.

Reeling with dizziness she forced herself to struggle to her feet, groaning at the excruciating pain thundering in her head, the knives behind her eyes. Now she could just make out a faint lightening of the darkness. Blindly she staggered towards it but crashed heavily into something and lurched to the floor. Groping in front of her she grasped the wooden leg of an upturned chair. More carefully now she picked herself up again and gingerly felt her way round a huge table and another chair. The lighter patch was, she realised when she felt cold glass, a window, but shuttered from the outside and letting very little light through. Slowly she turned and peered into the unrelieved gloom but still she could discern nothing.

Panicking she called out, 'Archie! Archie! Are you there?' But there was nothing, just complete and total silence. The silence of night. But there was something she recognised. Gently she sniffed through her damaged nose, causing a sharp pain where his blow had caught her. The smell was unmistakable, making her retch. Raw meat. Now she knew where she was! It was the room at the back of the disused church hall where Archie boned and rolled his meat.

Her heart sank. The church hall was isolated and never used. About a quarter of a mile from the church it had once served it was derelict and hidden in an overgrown clearing, not far from the old sawmill. Mary knew it would be a waste of time and energy to scream for help. There was no one within half a mile who could possibly hear her.

Keeping one hand on the wall as a guide she worked her way round the room until she came to the two deep, stone sinks which stood against one wall. Creeping on she found the door and, next to it, the light switch. With a sigh of relief she flicked it down. Nothing happened. Suddenly dizzy again she slipped down on to the floor, her back against the door, her aching head cradled in her hands.

When her reeling head had steadied she hauled herself back on to her feet and rattled furiously at the door. It was locked from the other side, as she had known it would be. Angry and frightened she kicked out at it then hammered on the unyielding wood with her bare fists. Still there was nothing. No light. No sound. Nothing.

Defeated and exhausted she crumpled on to the floor,

hugging her arms round her chilled body in an effort to get warm.

When she next opened her eyes light was filtering through the cracks round the edges of the shutters. Grey shadows loomed at her but, as her eyes adjusted to the dim light, they solidified into the recognisable forms of the table and chair she had felt before.

Her head was still throbbing, her entire body ached after the hours she had spent on the cold, hard floor and she felt nauseous. Holding on to the table for support she pulled herself to her feet and groped her way to the sinks. The water was icy cold but she let it run up her arms then splashed it over her damaged face until the pain was numbed. Her mouth was sore and dry. When she took a drink, the water made the cuts on her gums sting but cleared her mind.

How, she wondered, had Archie managed to get her all the way down here? All she could recall was the anger in his face and the awful fear she had felt when he had come through the front door and caught her with her case. After that her mind was a complete, merciful, blank, though her bruised and swollen face told its own story of what had happened. Logic suggested that Archie must have brought her here in his van, probably late at night when no one was likely to see him. Then he had callously dumped her in this cold, dark and foul-smelling room, locked the door and left her there. For all he knew she could be dead. Anger overwhelmed the pain and made the blood pound unbearably in her aching head.

From outside she could hear the muted twittering of birds and, once or twice, the distant sound of a car engine on the back road to the Dene colliery.

Time dragged, it seemed hours later before she caught the unhealthy chug and rattle of the approaching butchery van. Her heart started to thud behind her ribs and her hands dampened with sweat in an agonising alloy of anger, fear and relief.

The van's sliding door scraped open, followed by the boom of the church hall's outer doors crashing back. Archie's limping footsteps echoed harshly on the bare floorboards of the hall itself. And then there was total silence. Mary sensed that her husband was on the other side of the locked door, listening, trying to tell whether she was conscious. Perhaps he was even wondering if she was still alive.

Frozen in horror she hunched against the far wall, desperate to be released but dreading seeing him again, petrified by what he might do to her this time. The sound of his key in the lock was deafening after the protracted silence. Mary watched the handle in awful fascination and held her breath when the door inched open.

'You bastard!' she screamed, her anger igniting as soon as she saw his face. 'I could have died.'

The initial relief he had felt on seeing her conscious and on her feet disappeared instantly. He glared back at her from a face suffused with hatred, giving her no hint of the horror her unconscious body had raised in him or the panic which had driven him to bring her here, frightened that she really might die. 'You'll wish you had,' he promised, 'if you don't start behaving like a decent, loving wife.'

The sheer force of venom in his voice warned her to stay silent. For a long moment he stared at her. She met his eyes, refusing to look away then, mustering all the courage she possessed, pushed past him and ran for the door. But she was weak and still in pain. Despite his handicap he got there before her and slammed it shut.

'Where do you think you're going?'

'Away from you, Archie Cree.'

'Oh no you're not.' He spat it at her, his face flushing

an ugly puce, then grabbed her arm. 'I warned you. My wife does not walk out on me. Until you accept that you are going nowhere.'

'Let go of me,' she screamed.

'Shut up,' he snarled, hitting her across the face with the back of his hand, splitting her lip and drawing fresh blood.

'You can't make me stay here,' she challenged, unwisely.

'Why not?' he sneered. 'No one's going to miss you. I've already told your father you've got a bad dose of 'flu. Even if you yell yourself hoarse no one will hear you down here.' He dropped her arm and laughed.

Mary backed away, truly terrified now. 'You're mad,' she whispered. 'No sane person would do this.'

He surged after her, grabbed her by the throat and forced her head back against the wall. Panting, he shoved his face into hers. Mary's stomach heaved at the smell of his fetid breath.

'I'm your husband. I can do what the hell I like to you. I can keep you here for the rest of your miserable life if I want to.' He jerked on her neck, sending pain through her shoulders and into her arms. 'You are going to stay here until I am sure you've learnt your lesson. Until you understand that I will never, ever let you go. We made a bargain and you are going to stick by it. You'll stay here until you realise how well off you are.'

'Well off!' she choked. 'How could I be well off? I'm married to you and you are a bastard, Archie Cree. You killed my babies and damn near killed me too. Now you've lost your business and in another week we won't even have a home. Bastard! Bastard! Bastard!' she shrieked.

He silenced her with a powerful slap to her face. She tasted blood.

'Shut up! Shut up and listen to me,' he rasped, his voice hoarse with barely controlled anger. 'I worked hard for you, Mary. I stuck to our bargain. I gave you everything . . .'

'You gave me nothing!' she cried. 'You destroyed everything.'

'It was you . . . you ruined it all . . . I know what you did when I wasn't there . . . all those other men . . . I know . . . I know.' He was driving himself into a frenzy of jealousy, feeding the disappointment, resentment, and frustration caused by her rejection, her selfishness, her coldness. Keeping a tight grip round her throat he jerked her around and shook her until she thought her head would burst then threw her down on to the table causing her injured head to thump against the wood. For a moment everything dissolved into swirling redness. Fighting for consciousness she rolled limply then slid heavily to the floor. He was on her before she stopped moving, hauling her to her feet and slamming her back on to the table, leaning over her, pinning her there. Her reeling senses cleared sufficiently to recoil in sickened horror when she understood exactly what he intended to do.

Panting, drooling slightly, enraged and excited beyond all control, Archie was wrenching at his trousers. In nauseated disgust she felt him hot on her thigh.

'NO!' she screamed frantically, rolling from side to side. He held her with difficulty then silenced her again with another hard blow, stunning her and making her choke on the blood from her nose which poured down her throat. Then her reeling brain registered that the violence was adding to his lust. In an instant she froze, refusing to move, keeping even her facial muscles completely immobile, betraying neither fear nor the agony she felt. She blinked, took a sharp breath and refused to let him see any other emotion.

'Bitch,' he spat, tearing at her clothes, slapping at her wildly another three or four times, trying to wrench a reaction from her. Mary laid as if dead, her eyes closed, making no attempt to protect herself from him, allowing him to open her legs and finger her intimate area without a flicker of expression on her face. All the time she was telling herself that he had taken her hundreds of times before, that this wasn't worth fighting for, that she would deny him the satisfaction of the forcible rape he so obviously wanted. He thrust at her brutally but failed to penetrate. Mary could feel him softening, knew she had beaten him, but hardly dared to breathe.

Shouting the most foul words at her he moved away. 'Bitch. Bitch. Bitch,' he repeated time and time again.

When she risked squinting up at him there were tears streaming down his face.

Exhausted he turned away and stumbled from the room, locking the door after him and leaving her still lying on the foul-smelling table.

Later, much later, she got to her feet and washed her face. Under the sink she found a bundle of old newspapers which she spread out over the floor under the table. Then she crawled into her nest and curled up like a foetus.

She was aware of nothing until the following morning when the door opened quietly and a paper bag containing some sandwiches was placed beside her.

'Mary . . . Mary . . . ' he whispered.

She lay silently, refusing even to look at him and after a minute or so he crept away again.

Her pain-filled face, her swollen tongue, her bruised throat and screaming head rendered all logical thought impossible. The only time she forced herself to move was to creep to the sink for a drink or to crouch over the bucket she found in a corner.

Sometime later in the day she woke to find herself

covered by two old tartan blankets and some dry biscuits at her side. At last her mind was clear and though her head still ached the sharp edge of pain had gone. She shuddered when she recalled what had happened and knew Archie would never forgive her for that final humiliation.

Forcing back nausea she made herself sit on one of the two, hard chairs and nibble at a biscuit. She had no idea how long she had been there. The light filtering round the shutters told her it was daytime, other than that she knew nothing. After a couple of hours she felt steady enough to walk across the room. Her head was spinning but there was no unbearable pain, just the constant ache of the bruises which covered her face.

Carefully she examined the window, seeking some way of escape, but it was screwed into immobility. The external shutters would be impassable even if she broke the glass. The door was equally daunting, solid wood with double locks and she was sure she had heard the sound of a bolt that morning. It was hopeless. The only way she would get out of here was by persuading Archie to release her.

Dusk fell, throwing the room into ever-deepening greyness until night finally brought utter blackness. She dozed a little then fell into a deep, natural sleep until dawn. She judged it to be around midday when she heard the instantly recognisable grind of Archie's van.

This time she was in control of herself and prepared for him. With relief she saw his mood was calm and normal, almost normal.

'I'm sorry, Archie,' she greeted him, as soon as he was in the room, willing to say almost anything to get out of here.

He looked at her suspiciously. 'Had enough, have you? Ready to see sense now, are you?'

'Yes.' She hung her head. 'Please, Archie, can I go home now?' she begged.

'Do you think you've learnt your lesson?' he asked, watching her closely.

'I have, Archie. Honestly I have,' she pleaded, convincing tears in her eyes. Promise him anything she told herself. As soon as she was out of here she would find a way to get away from him, forever.

'I don't know . . . ' He sounded doubtful.

'Please, Archie, don't make me stay here for another night. Please.' Ignoring the feeling of revulsion in her stomach she reached out and touched his arm lightly. 'Take me home, Archie. Please. I'm really sorry for what I said.' How she wished she had the courage to tell him the truth, that she hated him, that the very sight of him made her stomach heave. But she wasn't that brave.

'All right,' he agreed at last. 'But cross me once more, Mary and next time I'll beat the fucking life out of you.'

She believed him.

Mary was surprised that Archie had allowed himself to be so easily persuaded but had no way of knowing that Archie's mother had become suspicious about her daughter-in-law's sudden disappearance. Sensing something very wrong in Archie's evasiveness and noting too that he was abnormally restless, it hadn't taken her long to draw the truth from her unbalanced son. Horrified, she quickly persuaded him to bring Mary back from her prison before he was tempted to do something which might incite the interest of the police. The old woman acted from purely selfish motives, tempered by not a single shred of sympathy for Mary who, to her mind, had broken her son and deserved everything she got. All that mattered to Mrs Cree was the necessity to guard her family from a possible scandal and protect the son she doted on.

Archie hustled Mary into his van and locked her in

before hobbling to his own side. 'Keep your face down,' he ordered, knowing that the mass of disfiguring bruises would cause comment, even in this village where it was far from unusual to see a woman with facial injuries.

Too ashamed to risk anyone seeing her Mary complied willingly enough and so didn't realise where they were going until he pulled up outside his parents' home.

'Oh no,' she breathed but didn't dare challenge him openly.

'Thank God it's raining. Here, use this umbrella to shield your face. We don't want any of the neighbours seeing you like that. You're a right mess!' He said it as if it was her fault.

She took it and hurried up the short path to her in-laws' unwelcoming house.

He halted her just inside the door. 'If my dad asks about your face you're to tell him you fell out the back of the van. And don't think you can sneak off to your father's when I'm out. My mother's going to keep an eye on you. We're living here now. I've already shifted all your stuff up to my old room. You go on up and don't come down until I tell you you can.'

'All right, Archie,' she answered tonelessly, still anxious to convince him she was the obedient little wife he wanted.

Upstairs, the case she had packed for herself was on the bed. Eagerly she ran to it and rummaged around until she found the photograph album. Tucked behind the pictures, exactly where she had hidden them, were her pound notes. They were enough to bring a faint smile of hope to her mouth.

Mary knew she must wait before attempting to run away again. The hideous bruises and scabs which disfigured her face had to be given time to heal and she was weak, still inclined to dizziness if she moved too quickly. But, by the start of the second week she was much stronger and itching to get away from Archie and his awful mother. The problem was she was as closely confined here as she had been in the old church hall.

At night Archie shared her room, though mercifully he made no attempt to share her bed, and slept on a truckle bed across the door. During the day when he was out, trying to rebuild his ruined business, Mrs Cree found innumerable chores for Mary and never let her out of her sight. If the old woman had to answer the call of nature she first locked her daughter-in-law into the bedroom and never left the house without taking the same precaution. Nor could Mary bang on the walls and shout to attract the attention of the neighbours. The bedroom was on an outside wall and anyway, it was doubtful if her incredible story would be believed. Craigie people preferred to stay well away from one another's marital problems, each man believing in the others' right to deal with misbehaving wives in whatever way seemed appropriate. In any case, drawing attention to herself was no way to slip away unnoticed which was crucial if Archie was to be unable to trace her. She was frightened enough of her husband to believe him when he said he would come after her if she ever left him and knew, when she went, she had to go as quietly as possible and give herself time to be well clear of Craigie before he discovered she was missing.

She was constantly searching for opportunities, especially early in the day when her chances of success were at their highest but it was as if Mrs Cree could read her mind. Wherever Mary went the old woman was there with her disparaging remarks and withering looks. The outside doors were all locked, the windows nailed up and she spent hours locked in her room.

'When are you going to let me live like a human being again, Archie?' she asked, angrily, when he came to bed one night.

He laughed, an unpleasant, sneering sound. 'When I know I can trust you,' he said, locking the door and shoving the key into his pyjama pocket.

One of Mary's first tasks every morning was to fetch up the coal for the two fires. The houses were built on a steep hill, the back gardens sloping away towards the burn. A flight of twenty steps led down from the back door to the garden. In the space created by the fall of the land was a large coal cellar which ran the full width of the back of the house. The coal itself was delivered through a hatch in the back garden which opened high on the cellar wall but there was also a narrow stairway into the cellar from the kitchen. It was this dark staircase that Mary had to use.

On this particular day Mrs Cree sent Mary down with two buckets to fill. Mary had almost finished shovelling coal into them when the dim bulb which illuminated the cellar popped and died. Knowing her mother-in-law was in the kitchen, waiting for her, Mary simply shouted, 'The light's gone out.' Within a second or two she saw Mrs Cree's massive form silhouetted at the top of the stairs.

'Stay there,' the old woman ordered. 'I'll fetch a new bulb down.' She then shut the door, leaving Mary in total darkness. Less than a minute later she opened it again and struggled down the steps carrying a kitchen chair and the new bulb.

'Here,' she handed the bulb to Mary who jumped on to the chair and reached for the light. Even when she stood on tiptoes it was an inch or two beyond her.

'For goodness sake get down from there and let me do it,' her mother-in-law snapped impatiently.

Mary watched as the old woman hauled herself on to the chair which wobbled dangerously under her weight.

'Careful,' she warned, steadying it while Mrs Cree stretched for the light. Mary felt the chair tip and instinctively tightened her grip on its back. Then, appalled by the idea, but unable to resist, she let go and stood back. The chair lurched, throwing the massively built woman off balance. The lightest touch from Mary would have sent it over but, eager though she was to escape, she couldn't bring herself to deliberately injure another human being, even one as obnoxious as Mrs Cree senior.

Above her the old woman felt the chair tilt again and struggled for balance, throwing her weight against the back of it. It was too much. The chair steadied for an instant then seemed to pirouette on one leg before falling backwards, launching Mrs Cree into the air. With the full force of her sixteen stones behind her the landing was both painful and undignified.

In the gloom, Mary caught a glimpse of voluminous, pale underwear and an unsavoury, musty smell which suggested it was less than clean. In the same instant she saw that the leg which protruded from the sloppy elastic was resting at a very unnatural angle. Nor was the old woman moving. She moaned softly but didn't wake up when Mary removed the large bunch of keys from the pocket of her pinafore.

In less than ten minutes Mary had rushed upstairs, washed the coal from her hands, repacked her case, shoved her coat on and was at the front door, ready to flee, knowing she was unlikely to get a better chance.

Conscience took her back to the cellar to check on the old woman who still hadn't regained consciousness but was moaning softly to herself. Mary made her as comfortable as she could then hurried back up the stairs and propped open the cellar door with a chair so Archie would immediately know where to find his mother. Finally she picked up her case and let herself out of the house, taking care to leave the door open behind her.

Twenty pounds, ten shillings and a broken nose. That was the sum total of her miserable marriage. And she wasn't even sure that she was entitled to the money. Even the scruffy suitcase really belonged to her father. Only the equally worn clothing and few personal bits and pieces inside it were undeniably hers. But she was forgetting about Aunt Minnie's tarnished and old-fashioned brooch with matching necklace and ear-rings. They had been the best her elderly aunt had been able to give as a wedding present. They were far too ugly to be worn. Sentimental value, nothing more. Not even that really. She had barely known her father's older sister who had lived in the west. The only reason she had brought the jewellery with her now was the faint hope that she might be able to sell it. She had the feeling that she might be very grateful for the five pounds it might bring.

Mary allowed a mocking smile to widen her mouth which still bore scars to remind her of Archie's violence. That awful jewellery! It was like an encapsulation of her life so far. Too ugly to be displayed and worth very little. But from this moment on things would be different. Never again would she abase herself for a man or place her reliance on another human being. Nor would she repeat the mistake of allowing her emotions to rule her mind. It had been a punishingly hard lesson. Between them Paul Kinsail and Archie Cree had almost destroyed her but they had been excellent teachers and she had learnt it perfectly. She didn't let herself brood on the past. The future was what mattered now. One step at a time, she told herself. And the first step was to get herself as far away from Craigie as she could before Archie came home and discovered she was gone.

Resolutely she gripped her case and walked away from the drab, forbidding house, tossing the keys defiantly into one of the front garden's mildewed rose bushes as she went. After a second's thought she tore her wedding ring from her finger and ran back to place it on the doorstep, where Archie could not fail to see it.

With the ring she jettisoned the past. And poor, pathetic Mary Cree who was nothing more than a victim. From this second on she would be Maxine. Maxine Lennox. She liked the sound of it and Lennox had been her mother's maiden name so it wasn't entirely alien.

Maxine Lennox, twenty-three years old, strong, self-reliant, dependent on no one and with a whole, exciting life still in front of you, she told herself.

Without a backward glance she hurried to the bus stop.

THIRTEEN

Maxine's only thought was
to get away from Archie. She ached for peace, for a safe
retreat where she could nurse her wounds and find some
purpose to her ruined life, a place where he would never
find her. Somewhere well away from Craigie and, she
realised with a pang of sadness, from her family.

Not that there would have been any comfort from her
father. He would have sheltered her willingly enough but
would have expected her to fall back into the old pattern,
to look after him as thoroughly as if he was a child.
Maxine's desperate need for solace and reassurance would
find no responsive ear there, only the burden of more
domestic responsibility.

Her sisters were both adjusting to their own relatively
new roles as wives and mothers. An embittered woman
with nothing but regrets for her own marriage would be
an unfair burden in either of their households. Nor could
she face her grandmother who would resort to the 'I told
you so' attitude which had been lurking, ready to surface
at the first sign of marital disharmony. Maxine was too
proud to bear that.

When the bus pulled into the stance in Inverannan,
Maxine still hadn't decided where she would go. In fact
she had spent most of the twenty-minute journey agonising over the fate of Mrs Cree, worried that the old
woman might even die of her injuries. If that happened
she would be a fugitive from the law as well as from
her husband. Her original intention had been to call an

ambulance from the phone box by the bus stop in Craigie, but it had been vandalised, the glass smashed, the door broken off and the receiver ripped away from the coin box. So, as soon as she got off the bus, Maxine hurried to the nearest call box and dialled 999. It eased her conscience and, satisfied that there was nothing else she could do for her mother-in-law, she turned her mind back to her own escape.

Lugging her suitcase she resorted to wandering past the various bus stops and reading the destination boards on the parked vehicles.

Edinburgh was the most obvious place and the hourly bus was ready to leave. It would be the most obvious place to Archie too but, in a city as large as the Scottish capital, surely he wouldn't be able to find her. She started towards the bus then changed her mind and stopped abruptly causing a woman, following close behind her, to stumble into her. Maxine apologised quickly and stepped out of the way but the woman muttered angrily and carried her complaint on to the bus causing several passengers to stare curiously at the unhappy-looking girl who still hesitated by the bus stop. Maxine, still wondering whether she should go to Edinburgh, was unaware of their interest. She hated big, noisy places. On the few occasions she had visited the Scottish capital she had always been relieved to come home again, even to a place as grim as Craigie. Edinburgh was too busy, too impersonal, intimidating. How could she ever hope to be happy in such a hostile place? What she was looking for was her new home and it was vitally important to make the right decision, to find a place where she could settle, somewhere she could belong to and never have to move away from.

'You getting on, Hen?' the conductor called from the steps.

She shook her head. 'No.'

He shrugged and the bus moved off in a cloud of choking exhaust.

Beyond it was the blue Stirling bus. Perhaps that would be a safer choice. Stirling was a smaller town, not much bigger than Inverannan, but still, it was not a place she liked. It seemed grey and uncharitable, cold and oppressive, the whole place dominated by the blackened castle which loomed over the town as if to remind everyone who lived there of past horrors.

Beyond that, the bus just drawing in was bound for St Andrews. It was a beautiful little place and one where she would have been happy to settle if it hadn't been for the memories it held for her.

Still she lingered, oblivious to the people hurrying round her, knowing she had to make some decision soon. As she waited the driver wound on the destination board, displaying all the places the bus would pass through on its way to St Andrews. Cairney, Sauchar, Kilweem, Anstruther. Most of them were pretty coastal villages and she had always harboured a seemingly impossible dream of living in one of them. A dream inspired by happy childhood memories of a time before her mother had left, when the whole family had sometimes clambered on to a bus for a day at Kilweem to visit relatives of her mother's. It had been an infrequent treat and all the more memorable for that. Maxine, indeed all the Innes children, had good reason to recall their Aunt Maureen and Uncle Maurice, who were clearly fond of children, with affection. The aging couple were her grandmother's unmarried sister and brother and ran the Kilweem village bakery between them. Tea-time, in their old-fashioned, upstairs flat into which filtered the aromatic, mouthwatering smells of the downstairs bakery, was a delectable feast of fresh bread, fruit tarts and iced cakes. The children were always sent home with paper bags full of crisp biscuits and fancy cakes and the whole family dined on Uncle Maurice's sausage rolls and bridies for days afterwards.

Maxine smiled at the memory, regretting that her family had lost touch with the kind-hearted couple several years ago. The details had rarely been discussed but she knew Uncle Maurice and Aunt Maureen had taken over the family business from their father, her own great-grand-father. Their younger sister, Ina, had been alienated from her family after leaving the village in shame to marry her handsome collier, only three months before the birth of their oldest child, Maxine's Uncle Jackie. After the death of their parents Maurice and Maureen had been keen to mend the rift with their only remaining relatives. Ina's stiff pride had prevented her own return to Kilweem but she had been unable to stop her daughter, Evelyn, from responding to the couple's invitations to visit with her own family. But, after Evelyn's defection, George had made no effort to keep the friendship alive and they had all simply lost touch.

But perhaps, Maxine thought excitedly, it was not too late to contact them again. And surely it would be more sensible to go to a place where she knew someone, had some sort of contact, however fragile. Aunt Maureen and Uncle Maurice were family. Surely, when she explained her circumstances, they would let her stay with them, just for a day or two. And, she realised with a sudden lifting of her heart, these quaint villages which were the pride of Strathannan, were becoming increasingly popular with the tourists. There were sure to be rooms to let and even jobs in the cafés and boarding houses which were springing up, so it wouldn't be a case of simply dumping herself on her great aunt and uncle. She should quickly be able to support herself and find somewhere of her own to live.

The small seed of doubt which insisted that she would be too close to Archie for real security, withered and died under the reasoning that he would assume she had fled to one of the large cities like Edinburgh, Glasgow or Dundee. He knew nothing about Uncle Maurice and Aunt Maureen so had no reason to look for her so close to home. The chances of him discovering her whereabouts accidentally were almost non-existent. Archie disliked the sea and his twisted mind could find no beauty in the charming fishing villages so he was hardly likely to visit them. Decisively she hoisted her bag on to the bus, stowed it on the luggage rack and found herself a window seat.

It was an extremely pretty ride through ever-changing countryside, unmarred by the pit bings which corrupted the area round Craigie. On the flat bed of the Strath, around the river which gave the area its name, prosperous, arable farms and thriving villages were connected by a good network of roads giving easy access to the towns. But further out, hillsides heavy with heather, gorse and peaty grassland were cropped by hardy, thickly fleeced sheep and dotted with remote stone farmsteads, a reminder that these hillfoots were the precursor of the highlands. As the bus made its circuitous way towards the sea the sheep gave way once more to an undulating patchwork of fertile fields and dairy farms. The coast road itself was sheer delight meandering round inviting niches in the coast which invariably revealed one of the picturesque fishing villages which characterised the Strathannan coastline.

The skies were blue, the day fairly warm and Maxine felt her spirits soar as the narrow streets and trim houses of the villages ambled by. Kilweem, bathed in sunlight, was especially lovely. The bus rounded a bend in the road and there, sheltered by a kink in the coast, was the old harbour with its fishing boats bobbing peacefully on azure-blue water. It was so beautiful it made her gasp, but the breathtaking view was quickly lost as the bus clattered on along the setted streets of the tiny village centre and eventually came to a halt at the Tollbooth. Maxine retrieved her case and stepped out on to the cobbled road. She sucked in a lungful of sea air, revelling in the sharpness of it then looked round hopefully. Although she recalled the Tollbooth itself, simply because that was where the bus had always dropped and collected passengers, the rest of the village seemed totally unfamiliar. Certainly she could see no sign of any bakery. In her mind she carried a clear enough picture of its interior but the outer façade and location were lost to her. Still, she told herself, the village was small so finding her great aunt and uncle's establishment couldn't be an impossible task. Picking up her case purposefully she walked to the other side of the Tollbooth, which was set, like an island in the middle of Marketgate, and there, immediately opposite, on the seaward side of the road, was the little bakery. Relieved, Maxine started briskly towards it. But then she slowed, hesitated and made her way slowly back to the Tollbooth where she sat herself down on one of the two benches there. What on earth was she going to say to her great aunt and uncle? How could she just walk in and introduce herself and expect them to offer her shelter when she hadn't seen them for almost ten years? She sat, lost in thought, for ten minutes or so and only moved on when she was joined by two local women who eyed her with ill-concealed interest. Hoisting her case again she lugged it across the wide street, her heart hammering with nervousness. What would this couple, who must be quite elderly by now, think of her uninvited arrival? Surely they would help her, just for a day or two until she could find a job and a place to stay. Outside the bakery she paused for one last second, pulled herself up straight, fixed a determined smile on her face and shoved the door. Nothing happened. She tried again, pushing harder this time, then when it still wouldn't budge, stood back and

204

looked into the small shop. It was deserted, the counter bare, even the window display limited to empty baskets and plastic flowers. Maxine's heart sank. Perhaps the shop was closed. Her great aunt and uncle must be getting on in years so it was perfectly possible that they had retired. Only then did she see the handwritten sign in the window announcing the fact that the shop was closed for a three-week holiday.

Three weeks! What on earth was she going to do now? She had only come here because she had hoped they would give her a bed for a night or two. Well, she decided, refusing to be discouraged by this first failure in her plan, Kilweem was a beautiful place and she was determined to stay here so she would just have to find somewhere else to live. Maxine's initial disappointment rapidly gave way to a mood of buoyant optimism. Much better to introduce herself to her aunt and uncle after she was settled with a job and a place to live. That way she wouldn't be asking them for anything other than their friendship. It would have been humiliating to simply arrive and throw herself on their mercy as she had intended to do. Perhaps things would be marginally harder for her this way but at least she could retain a thread of self-respect. Maxine picked up her case again and started to walk through the village.

The most pressing thing now was to find somewhere to stay. She had expected there to be some signs of the tourist trade in the form of boarding houses or holiday flats but a quick walk round the village centre revealed absolutely nothing. In the end she waylaid a housewife who directed her to the far side of Kilweem. There, at the very edge of the growing village, parallel to the beach, Maxine saw a wide strip of common grassland. A small travelling fair was clustered at the far end where the low dunes would protect it from sea breezes. On the other side of the road, facing the grass and looking out to sea, was a short terrace of post-war, stone-built houses, the very last houses in the village. To her relief several of them displayed signs advertising bed and breakfast. She chose the one at the village end of the row and knocked firmly on the door, full of newly-emerging confidence.

It was opened by a thin, harassed-looking woman. 'Yes?' she snapped.

'I was wondering if you had any vacancies?' Maxine asked, smiling brightly and completely forgetting the yellowing remains of the bruises and the two red scars, one by her eye, the other just above her mouth, which disfigured her face.

'Are you on holiday?' the woman asked, suspiciously.

'No . . .'

'I only let to families on holiday,' the woman muttered, slamming the door in Maxine's face.

The new confidence blew away like sand in the breeze, leaving her crestfallen and despondent on the gleaming doorstep. Slowly she retrieved her case and moved on along the road. 'Don't be stupid,' she told herself, aloud for extra effect, 'that was only the first house. There are plenty of others.'

At the next one she was determined to make a better impression. 'Good morning,' she beamed as soon as the door opened. 'I need to find somewhere to stay in Kilweem. Do you have any rooms available?'

'Where are you working?' this woman asked. She was older than the first one and less miserable looking.

'Nowhere yet. I need somewhere to stay first,' Maxine explained reasonably, the sun catching the fading bruises perfectly.

'Sorry.' Again the door was slammed in her face.

Enquiries at the two remaining houses elicited the same response. The last one, where she thought she might, at last, be lucky, demanded an outrageous deposit. Without the means to pay it, Maxine was forced to leave.

Disappointed she crossed the road, walked over the strip of grassland and emerged, through a gap in the low dunes, on to the beach.

It was the most beautiful beach she had ever seen. More wonderful than even her nostalgic childhood memories had suggested. Pale, clean sand stretched for more than five miles from the rocky point which sheltered Kilweem's tiny harbour to the next headland. In the distance children played in the sand and someone splashed at the water's edge, but too far away to be heard. Maxine sat on the sand with her back against a dune and felt the tension drain from her. It was a full half-hour before she made her way back to the village itself and by that time she was feeling positive that somewhere in this beautiful village she would find a place to stay.

After walking fruitlessly through the village again she resorted to knocking on doors and simply asking if anyone knew of a room to rent, anxious to find anywhere, no matter how shabby, at least for tonight. Although the villagers were unfailingly courteous, no one was able to suggest anywhere other than the houses she had already tried.

It was after four o'clock and Maxine was certain she had knocked on every likely-looking door in Kilweem. Now her stomach was growling with hunger and her feet were sore and swollen. As evening approached the morning's light breeze had an increasingly chill edge to it. Disconsolately she wandered back to the main street, looking for a shop where she might buy something to eat. Apart from the bakery with its tiny tea-room attached, there was a general store, a butcher's and a newsagent's-cum-post office. To her dismay, every one of the small shops was closed. Wednesday, she realised, early closing.

The first real gnawings of trepidation stirred in her stomach, combining with the hunger to make her feel slightly sick. It had all seemed so easy this morning, so straightforward. It had never occurred to her that anyone might distrust her, that a poorly-dressed and bruised young woman with one battered suitcase, no job and very little money might be regarded with suspicion. Now she was stranded in a strange place with nothing to eat and nowhere to sleep.

Her unguided steps took her back to the harbour. On an evening like this it was wonderfully peaceful. Proud, old boats bobbed on the gentle waters, the quayside houses were nearly all neat and trim, advertising the pride their owners took in them, and two or three fishermen sat smoking pipes and chatting while they mended nets. Maxine saw nothing of it. She wandered blindly along the narrow, setted streets until she found herself outside a small public house. The rusting sign above her head proclaimed it to be the Lobster.

Hesitating for a second, never having gone into such a place on her own before, she finally opened the creaking door and walked into the public bar. Fortunately it was still early and there were few customers. Those men who were there paused in their drinking and stared at her as she crossed to the bar. An unaccompanied female was unheard of in here and they considered her entry an intrusion into exclusively male territory. Aware of their hostile scrutiny Maxine's cheeks glowed crimson as she waited for the barman to come to her.

He took his time then said, 'Yes?' gruffly.

'I was wondering if you had a room to let?' she asked, boldly.

'Rooms to let?' he scoffed. 'No, Lass. This is a pub, not a hotel. Best try the boarding houses on the far side of the village.'

'I have.'

He shrugged and turned away.

'Is there anywhere else I might try?' she persisted.

'Not that I know of,' he muttered. He had seen the yellowing bruises, obvious even under artificial light, and wondered, fleetingly, what had happened to her. But it was none of his business and he certainly didn't want an unattached female hanging round his bar and giving his customers the wrong idea. 'If you want a drink you'd better get yourself round to the lounge bar, otherwise you'll have to leave. I don't want any trouble.'

'Trouble?' She glared at him, then, holding her head high, hauled her bag to the door.

An unshaven, thickset and thoroughly disgusting-looking man scraped his chair back and rose ponderously from a nearby table then held the door open for her. Surprised, she was about to thank him when she realised he was blocking her way with his filthy, booted foot.

'If it's a bed you're looking for, Hen, I'm sure I'm more than willing to share mine,' he offered loudly, grinning through fat, wet lips. 'And I won't charge if you don't.'

Behind him, his companions dissolved into guffaws of ribald laughter. Maxine knew she would lose any verbal battle so contented herself with stamping heavily on his foot before barging her way back on to the street.

The sun was sinking now and although it wasn't truly cold she knew the temperature would fall sharply during the night. And still she had nowhere to sleep. It was too late now to even return to Craigie but she would rather sleep on the beach for the rest of her life than face Archie Cree again. Her heart plunged towards her bowels when she realised that sleeping on the beach might be her only option, at least for tonight. Tired and hungry she decided she might as well head there now. At least the sand would be soft and she could rest her aching feet.

Earlier that morning she had noticed the small, travelling fair on the stretch of grassland between the dunes and the road. Now the showground was brightly lit and loud with distorted music. But what Maxine noticed most were the mouthwatering smells drifting towards her. Candyfloss and toffee apples, sticky sweets and, best of all, an unmistakable aroma, issuing from a trailer parked near the back. Hot chips! She chuckled to herself. Of course! Why hadn't she thought of this before?

They were the best she had ever tasted. Wiping greasy fingers on her clean handkerchief, she leaned against the side of the trailer, trying to make herself inconspicuous. The food revived her flagging spirits a little. She bought a second cup of tea and warmed her hands on it while she watched the revellers with a smile on her lips. Excited youngsters, squealing with delight one minute then dissolving into tired tears the next; exuberant teenagers, the boys showing off to the girls by winning cheap prizes of tacky toffee apples and tatty teddy bears; weary adults, worn out by the demands of their children. Above it all came the thick drift of diesel fumes and the thumping cacophony of competing pop music as each ride tried to drown out all the others. Well-muscled young men in checked shirts and oily jeans flirted with girls in the crowd, trying to entice them to spend their money while the show women called out to passing youths, seeming to guarantee a lucky win with wide smiles and outrageously flirtatious looks. Nearby a circular stall attracted a good sized crowd to play bingo, encouraged by a dark-skinned man who laughed and teased his, mainly middle-aged, female customers to stay for just one more game with a never-ending stream of bawdy patter. The atmosphere was earthy, loud and crude and in impossibly sharp contrast to the sleepy little harbour of Kilweem which sheltered behind a rocky headland, less than a quarter of a mile away.

It reminded Maxine poignantly of her childhood when her father had always, miraculously, managed to produce enough pennies to take his family to the shows when they came to Inverannan, once a year. His enjoyment had always been at least as great as theirs, marking a high spot in an otherwise dreary existence.

Still Maxine lingered, reluctant to leave the tenuous security of these garish lights and smelly rides and make her way on to the beach to find a sheltered spot for the night. Once more she wandered round the booths, never having a go on anything, her small store of money was too precious to be wasted on such frivolity.

By ten-thirty the crowd had thinned. The younger children had been taken home to bed long ago and only the adolescents were left. Some of the stalls were already closing, drawing wooden shutters over floating ducks and shooting ranges. The music stilled and the lights faded and as they did the atmosphere changed. The shadowed stalls seemed vaguely menacing, the painted clowns which decorated the rides were suddenly grotesque and the few people still around emphasised her aloneness, her isolation from them all. And behind it all the blackness of the dunes was inpenetrable. Cold now and thoroughly apprehensive of what lay ahead of her that night, Maxine returned one last time to the trailer on which had been roughly painted, 'The Tea Wagon'.

'Back again?' The fat, garishly made-up woman behind the counter frowned, causing her pencilled eyebrows to disappear under a row of tight, black curls. 'That's the pot drained, Hen. It's not fresh so there's no charge.' She handed Maxine a chipped cup and went back to the business of clearing up. Maxine sipped slowly, making the cup of already tepid tea last for more than fifteen minutes, determined not to leave the shelter of the fairground until she absolutely had to.

'Finished?' the woman asked, leaning over the counter so that her ample breasts bulged alarmingly.

'Yes. Thanks.' Maxine handed the cup back reluctantly.

'You supposed to be meeting someone here? Stood you up has he?' The old woman was eyeing Maxine closely.

'No . . . I just came for a look at the shows,' Maxine mumbled.

'Well, Lass, I'm finishing now. Best make your way home. We don't like people hanging round after we've closed up.'

'I was just going anyway. Thanks again for the tea.' Maxine picked up her case hoping she looked as if she had a home to go to then started to walk off in the direction of the beach.

'Just a wee minute, Lass.' The woman had spotted the suitcase, as well as the strange direction the girl was taking. Considering her vast bulk she was out of the trailer and facing Maxine with amazing speed. 'The village is that way,' she said, pointing in the opposite direction. Then, 'Are you in some sort of trouble, Lass?'

'NO!' Maxine knew she had answered too sharply. 'I've done nothing wrong, if that's what you mean,' she added.

'Nae, Lass. I didn't think you had but there's more than one kind of trouble. I'm not blind, nor stupid either. To my mind a girl with a suitcase and a face full of bruises, hanging round a place like this on her own, is in trouble of some sort.'

Maxine's fingers flew to her face. Until now she hadn't given those lingering marks a thought. 'It's nothing.'

The old woman's sharp eyes noted the waist on Maxine's finger where the wedding ring had rested until so recently. 'If you want an old woman's advice, Lass, you'll go back to your man. He'll likely be ready to say he's sorry by now.'

'No . . . I can't . . . ' Maxine stammered, caught off

guard by what this old woman had been able to work out about her. 'Anyway, there's no bus at this time of night.'

'You're not a Kilweem lassie then?'

'No.'

'Ah . . . ' The old woman nodded her strangely curled head knowingly. 'And where are you spending the night?'

'I don't know. I'll find somewhere,' Maxine said, refusing to meet the old woman's keen eyes.

'At this time of night! What in the Lord's name are you thinking of?' the old woman exclaimed. 'You'll end up wandering the streets all night.'

'It's not what you think! I came to stay with my aunt and uncle for a few days, but they've gone on their holidays. But I'll be all right. I can look after myself. I'll sleep on the beach if I have to,' Maxine shot back defiantly, feeling foolish and exposed under those shrewd old eyes.

'The beach!'

'There's nowhere else,' Maxine shrugged, pretending indifference.

'Have you tried over the road there, at the boarding houses?'

Maxine nodded. 'This morning.'

'And in the village itself?'

'Yes. I've even been to the pub. There's nothing available,' she admitted.

'Then I suppose you'd better come with me.'

Maxine gaped at her. 'I can't . . . '

The woman rounded on her, plump cheeks shining with indignation. 'And why not? Are show folk not good enough for you? Is that it?' she demanded.

'I didn't mean that,' Maxine retorted hotly. 'It's just that . . .'

'Yes . . . ?'

'I don't want to be a nuisance,' she ended lamely, though the truth was the old woman scared her.

The rigid curls shook again. 'What you mean is you're too proud to accept an honest offer of help from an old woman who lives in a caravan.' Her chins wobbled in outrage. 'Well, it's up to you. I'll not beg you. If you think the beach is better than a good, clean bed, then go rot on it. There's a dry, warm place in my van – the offer's still there – but make your mind up fast. I'm not hanging around here all night.'

Maxine still hesitated, not knowing what to make of this startling old woman who was now walking away, her rolls of fat bouncing dangerously with each step. She looked frantically towards the dark gap in the dunes which led to the beach, felt a stab of cold from the lively breeze and a spear of pure fear in her stomach.

'Wait!'

'Changed your mind, have you?' the woman chuckled, glancing back. 'Well, follow me, Lass.'

Less than a dozen caravans circled the showground. All were brightly lit, the chrome on the bodywork glinting, even in the artificial light. The old woman stopped by one of the smaller vans and squeezed herself through its narrow door. Maxine tried to follow her but found her way barred.

'If you're to be my guest I should know your name.'

'Maxine . . . Maxine Lennox.' The new name sounded strange, even to her own ears.

'Maxine? Well, Maxine, they call me Rosie. Come on in, Lass, and welcome.'

'Thank you.' With great difficulty Maxine squashed past the old woman's soft body.

'There's just the one bedroom,' Rosie was saying. 'My son, Douglas, used to sleep out here but he's got a van of his own now so you can have his bed. It's quite comfortable.'

Maxine peered into the semi-darkness and just made out

the shape of a couch built against one side of what was probably the living area. 'Thank you, Rosie,' she said. 'I can't say I was looking forward to spending the night outside.'

'Aye, well, no decent woman would leave a young lassie to sleep rough. The beach isn't safe, even in a braw place like Kilweem. Now, put your bag down and I'll brew us a decent cup of tea.'

Maxine laughed for the first time that evening. 'I don't think I could drink another cup,' she admitted.

There was a series of little splutters as Rosie moved round the room, lighting the gas lamps which dotted the walls. They hissed into bright life one by one and Maxine gasped audibly. She had been expecting something fairly primitive but this was neater, smarter and much more luxurious than any house she had been in. Although the caravan looked small from the outside it was, in fact, deceptively roomy. The furnishings were plush, a range of colourful ornaments decorated the shelves, red velvet cushions softened the brightly upholstered seats and a richly patterned carpet warmed the floor. It was gaudy but fresh smelling and scrupulously clean, and nothing at all like her idea of a caravan.

'This is beautiful,' she murmured.

Rosie looked at her sharply. 'And what did you expect?' she challenged. 'A blanket on the floor and candles to see by? You folk are all the same,' she ended, disgustedly.

'I didn't know what to expect,' Maxine admitted frankly, confused by the old woman's mercurial temper. 'I just didn't think a caravan, any caravan, could be so homely.'

'No one of your kind ever does,' was the hostile response.

'My kind? What's that supposed to mean?' Maxine was

starting to wonder if she would end up on the beach after all.

'Town folk. You and your smart houses. You always think you're so much better than us.'

'Rosie, my father lives in a prefab, not much bigger than this van and a lot more untidy! When I was a kid there were six of us living in it. If we were all in the living room at the same time there wasn't enough room to stretch your legs out without kicking someone else and two of us had to sit on the floor.'

At last Rosie laughed. 'I've never lived in a house, Lass. Spent all my days in a van. Wouldn't want it any other way. It's a grand life when you're young. Never in one place long enough to get sick of it. It's folk like you who spoil it for us with your stupid laws and rules, your prejudices! You think, just because we're show folk, we're ignorant, live like animals and steal anything that's not nailed down. But you're wrong, all of you. Too close-minded to see the truth. My, you should see some of the vans. Proper palaces they are. This is tiny compared to most. There's not one that's dirty or uncared for. The kids are all loved and well fed and the menfolk take good care of their families.' Fierce pride rang in every word.

'I never thought like that, Rosie. How could I? I've never met anyone like you before. But I do know that in Craigie, where I come from, no one would take a stranger from the street and offer them a bed for the night.'

'Craigie, eh? Well, I can believe that of Craigie.' Rosie brought a pretty cup and saucer and settled her bulk beside Maxine, wheezing slightly with the effort. 'Don't let me upset you, Hen. I was raised to say what I think. Then we all know where we stand.' She patted Maxine's hand. 'But I was speaking the truth. It's the same wherever we go. Even here and we've been coming to Kilweem since the war. These little villages are the worst. Village folk

216

are always full of suspicion. Anything happens while we're here and this is the first place the police come to. It makes you bitter in the end, knowing none of them are any better than you.'

Maxine was aware of a growing liking for this outspoken woman. 'You should see the houses in Craigie,' she confided. 'Some of them are a total disgrace. But,' she added in defence of her own people, 'miners don't have much money. And those villages are ugly places, not like this. Everything in Craigie is so dark and depressing. It's hard for some of them.'

'Life's hard for everyone, Hen. You have to make the best you can of it. I've no patience with them who sit back and moan because they're too idle to help themselves.'

A picture of her father, splayed out in his chair and fast asleep at eleven o'clock in the morning sprang into Maxine's mind. 'I guess you're right.'

'Maybe. And maybe I'm just a bitter old woman who's letting her tongue run away with her.'

They sat in companionable silence while Rosie finished her tea. Maxine stifled a yawn then jumped when Rosie took her hand and drew it into her ample lap, palm up.

'I expect this is exactly what you think all us show women do,' she chuckled. 'And this time you'd be right. My mother was the greatest reader there ever was. Truly gifted she was. Made her living at it. But it drained her. I've never wanted to be like her. It's too much of a responsibility, something as strong as that. Not everything you see is good and I've never wanted to tell folk bad news. But it can be useful, helps you to see what to do next . . . understand?'

Maxine nodded doubtfully.

'Shall I have a look, then?'

'If you like.' But she was anything but sure about this. Rosie chuckled and bent her head over Maxine's palm.

217

When she looked up again her face was grave. 'You're a young lassie to have known so much unhappiness,' she said, slowly.

'The state of my face is enough to tell anyone that I'm not exactly on top of the world,' Maxine smiled grimly, unimpressed.

'It's not your face that tells me about miscarriages and men who use you for their own purposes,' Rosie insisted.

Maxine felt a shiver spread through her body and tried to draw her hand away. To her consternation she couldn't. Rosie had it clasped firmly between her own hands but, rather than examining the palm, she raised her head and stared ahead, concentrating intensely. Very gradually Maxine became aware of a sensation of deep warmth, spreading slowly from her hands and through her entire body.

'Relax, Lass. I'll not harm you,' Rosie said suddenly. 'My mother could see a person's whole life like that. I can't, thank God, but I can pick up bits and pieces sometimes. Nothing more than glimpses of things. Do you want to know what I saw?' she challenged, dropping Maxine's hand rather abruptly.

'I'm not sure.' Maxine didn't know whether to giggle or be angry.

'I'll tell you then. Maybe it'll help you, maybe it won't.'

'Is there anything awful? I really don't want to know if there is.' She desperately needed to hold on to the conviction that she was going to transform her life into a sparkling success.

'No one's life is full of happiness. We've all got our bad times to get through.'

'All right. What can you tell me?' Despite herself she was interested.

'I know you've had a lot of pain. Some of it was your own fault, but you already know that much. You think you've got away from him but he's not finished with you yet. Not for years. He's not right.' Rosie took Maxine's hands again but this time held them as if to offer comfort. 'Does that make sense to you, Lass?'

'Archie . . . my husband . . . he's got a bad back,' Maxine said. 'His spine's deformed and he's got a club foot, too.'

'No, Lass. It's his mind I'm talking about. Twisted. Rotten. And he'll not let you go without a terrible struggle.'

'I know that,' Maxine admitted. 'He always said he'd come after me if I tried to leave him.'

'And he will.'

'Oh God. I don't want to hear this,' Maxine groaned, fear making her heart beat faster.

'Not listening to me won't stop it happening. At least this way you'll be on your guard. And you will be all right. In the end. But . . .' The old woman seemed about to add more and then thought better of it.

'And? You've got this far. You might as well tell me the rest of it,' Maxine prompted.

'I couldn't see very much,' Rosie muttered, then, looking at Maxine's worried face added, 'Och, Lass, in the end it'll work out fine. When things are hard all you have to do is remember that. There will be times when you think life's not worth living, but you'll be wrong. Happiness is waiting for you, Mary, even if it's a long way off yet.'

'What did you call me?' Maxine asked, the colour draining from her face.

'Mary. It is your name, isn't it?'

'Yes. Mary Cree. Lennox was my mother's name and Maxine is just something I read somewhere . . . I wanted a new start, Rosie. I wanted to put it all behind me, everything, even my name . . . But how did you know?'

'Goodness knows, Lass. Goodness knows. I can't

explain it. Perhaps that will make you pay heed to what I told you?'

Mary smiled wryly. 'Perhaps . . . Rosie?'

'Yes, Lass.'

'You will keep what I've said to yourself, won't you? I don't want Archie to find me. I shouldn't really have said anything . . .' She was starting to regret the confidences this old woman had managed to ease from her.

'The others,' Rosie nodded towards the neighbouring vans, 'are bound to wonder about you, Lass. But, since you've asked, I'll not betray a trust.'

'Thanks, Rosie.'

'Aren't there people who will be worried about you, Lass? Didn't you say your father lived in Craigie? He'll likely be worried sick. Can't you phone him, tell him you're safe?'

Maxine sighed sadly. 'He's not got a phone. Neither have my sisters. But I don't think they'll know I'm gone yet.'

'You don't think your father will be the first person your husband goes to?'

'Oh no . . . I hadn't thought of that,' she admitted.

'Here, Lass.' Rosie opened a cupboard and produced paper, envelopes and a stamp. 'Just write your father a line or two. It's only fair.'

Maxine nodded. 'You're right. I'll do it now and post it first thing.'

'Good. Well, I think it's about time I got off to my bed. You too, Lass, when you've written that letter. It's been a long day and tomorrow won't be any easier.'

Before slipping into bed Maxine wrote a short note to her father, telling him only that she was safe and well, and would stay in touch. She ended by sending him her love and promising to let him have an address later. If she posted it tomorrow he would get it the day after. Later,

220

when she was settled she would write again and that would be the time to write to Janette too.

Tired though she was, Maxine found sleep impossible. Still she fretted over the fate of Mrs Cree. And, by leaving her like that, she had given Archie even greater reason to want to find her. Rosie's strange warning only heightened her unease and as the night deepened she tossed restlessly, pondering her own uncertain future.

FOURTEEN

George ambled happily through the coal-coloured village, stopping from time to time to exchange a few words with people he had known all his days. In the distance an ambulance siren wailed. He paused to listen. Some poor soul in trouble, he thought sympathetically.

It was barely eleven o'clock and his belly was already growling with hunger but he decided to hang on for an hour or two yet. The chippy didn't close until two. If he went in a couple of minutes before then, Dougie Willis would likely give him extra chips, rather than waste them. He'd been lucky that way before and eating a big meal at that time of the day meant he could get by with a piece of bread and jam in the evening. To take his mind off his stomach he'd have a wee walk down to the beach, see what the tide had brought in.

An hour and a half later he strolled back, following the burn which ran through the steep-sided park, dividing the village into two halves. He stood idly on the wooden bridge looking down into the dirty stream for a moment. It must be thirty years since any fish was brave enough to make its way up here. In those days this had been a bonny wee glen with a sparkling burn running through it. Many's the time he'd had a drink from it. You couldn't do that now though. The burn was filthy, full of old prams, garden rubbish and broken bottles, and worse. Everything in the village had changed and not much of it for the better. When he was a young man Craigie had been nothing more than the miners' rows and one street of two-storey houses. Everyone knew everyone else and you were all the same with no need for toffee noses. But just look at the village now! Houses on both sides of the burn and out along the road as far as Tower Hill where the stuck-up folk who had bought the new houses there thought they were better than folk like him who had lived in the village all their lives. Folk who had never even lit a fire made with coal never mind been down in the bowels of the earth to dig it out.

George sighed with nostalgia and wondered what to do with the next hour or so. He thought about calling in at the bookies but then remembered that he had only just enough for a fish supper and nothing to spare for a wee bet until he drew his money from the Post Office, tomorrow.

Looking up, he realised that he was gazing into the back of the Crees' house. Well, Mary was living there now and he hadn't seen her since she and Archie moved out of the flat. She'd had a right dose of the 'flu, according to Archie who had warned him that it was highly contagious. But she should be well on the way to recovery by now so she'd likely be pleased enough to see her old dad and give him a cup of tea.

Whistling softly he climbed the steep path out of the park then stopped on the edge of the footpath to light another cigarette and smoke it before he knocked on the Crees' door.

Disappointingly there was no one in. Mary must be out with the old woman, probably fetching in the messages, more than likely from the local shops, so he might bump into her anyway on his way down to the chippy. Pity, he thought, as he sauntered off up the road, he could have just done with a nice cup of tea before his chips but at least it meant she was feeling better.

By three o'clock, exhausted by his walk and the effort

of digesting a huge fish supper, George had made himself a pot of tea and settled into his comfortable chair, fully intending to sleep away the rest of the afternoon. His siesta was rudely interrupted by someone who was apparently trying to demolish his front door.

'Can you not wait?' he roared irritably, hauling himself out of his chair and shambling sleepily to see what all the fuss was about. 'Och, it's you is it?' he said, eyeing his son-in-law uncertainly. Archie was clearly in a towering rage.

'Is she here?' Archie demanded, shoving roughly past his father-in-law and marching into the living room.

'Is who here?' George's brain was still befuddled with sleep.

'Mary! Where is she?'

'What would she be here for, Lad?' George scratched his thinning hair in puzzlement and watched while Archie searched every small room of the cramped house.

Finally, looking bewildered and no longer so angry, Archie limped back into the small living room and dropped on to the settee. He shook his head slowly and muttered, 'I thought she'd be here.'

'No, Lad. If Mary calls here it's always in the mornings, on her way to the shops. She never comes at this time of day.'

'Have you not seen her at all today?' Archie said, sounding angry again. Surely she'd tell her own father where she was going.

George finally understood that this was more than a simple case of Archie getting home to find his wife gone out shopping and no meal ready.

'No, I've not seen her since she had the 'flu. You told me to stay away in case I got it, so it's been a couple of weeks . . . Mind you,' he added, 'I did call at your

mother's house this morning . . . on the off chance . . .
but there was no one in.'

'What time?' Archie demanded quickly.

'Och, I don't recall exactly . . . Twelve . . . No, about
one o'clock it'll have been.'

Archie grunted. 'She was already away by then.'

'Away where? Would you tell me what the hell's going
on here?' George said, roused to irritation at last.

Archie eyed his father-in-law balefully, but he quite
liked George who was an easy-going sort of bloke and
had never, ever made any sort of derogatory comment
about his disability, seeming to accept him into the family
as easily as if he had been whole and able-bodied. In any
case it wouldn't help to get on the wrong side of Mary's
father who might be able to find out where she was. 'She's
left me, George.'

'Left you! What do you mean, left you? Where's she
gone?'

'I don't know where she's gone! I hoped you'd know.'

'No. Don't you?'

Realising the conversation was starting to go round in
circles Archie tried another approach, aiming to get
George firmly on his side. 'We had a terrible row last
night, George.'

'Is that all? Well, our Mary always comes right out and
says what she thinks. Give her time to calm down and
she'll be back. She's likely gone to one of her sisters.'

Archie already knew that wasn't the case. 'No. I've
already checked. She's not there. To tell you the truth I'm
right worried about her, George. She's been that depressed
lately, what with us moving into my mother's place and
all. They don't hit it off at all and it's been getting Mary
down. And she's been proper poorly with this 'flu . . .'

'Aye. I can see she'd be upset, losing the house like that.
Eviction's a terrible thing.'

'It is that, George. And I tried my best. But you know I relied on Mary to make the pies and things for my round, to do the books and ordering for me. But after she lost the bairn, well, she didn't seem interested any more. We lost the orders, some of the bills weren't paid . . .' In his mind he had already convinced himself that the failure of his business was all Mary's fault.

'Pity you never said anything at the time. Maybe I could have had a wee word with her. She's a hard worker, my Mary, and if things were getting on top of her she must have been feeling pretty bad. You should have got the doctor to see her. And you could have asked someone to help her out after she lost the wean. Our Cath or Linda would have been glad to help . . .'

Archie realised he had nearly overplayed his hand. 'Don't misunderstand, George. I'm not blaming Mary for what happened to the business. I know I was expecting too much of her. I blame myself. But, George, how's a man supposed to understand how a woman feels at a time like that . . . ?'

'Aye . . . I suppose you've a point there. Women are strange creatures right enough.'

'Look, George. I love Mary and I want her back. It's just a stupid misunderstanding that's behind this. If she gets in contact, let me know, will you? Please. Tell her I'm sorry. Ask her to come home and I'll find us somewhere else to live. We were all right when we had our own place but you know what my mother's like, she's not an easy person to live with . . .'

George considered it, trying to imagine where Mary could have gone but failing. But he liked Archie well enough, he was a good fellow, one of the lads, and always stood his round at the Greyhound. Very likely this was just a row that had got out of hand, probably because Mary was depressed after the 'flu. And what Archie said about his mother was true enough. Living with Mrs Cree would be enough to drive most people to distraction. 'All right, Lad. I'll let you know if I hear anything,' he agreed.

'Thanks, George. I'll appreciate that . . . Look, I'll not be at the Greyhound tonight, just in case Mary comes home, and anyway, my mother's not too good . . . Just keep this to yourself will you? I wouldn't like it to get out in the village, start people talking. That'll not help Mary when she comes home.' He couldn't stand to have everyone gossiping about him, crowing over him because his wife had walked out. It was hard enough deflecting the talk that moving back with his mother had caused. Rumours were already circulating about the eviction and yesterday Jock Moran had asked him outright whether the business had gone bust. If he didn't get his wife back he would never be able to hold his head high again.

'I knew there was something amiss with that pair. That lassie hasn't looked right since she lost her first bairn,' Ina said the next morning.

'She looked right enough to me,' George said, irritated as always by her manner. Only a sense of duty had brought him here. He had to tell the old woman about Mary before the village gossips did it for him.

'Och.' Ina grunted her contempt. 'You never see past your television and the bar at the Greyhound, George Innes! When did you last look at her properly?' She stretched her gaze to include Mary's sisters who had come to offer their father moral support. 'Youse are all too wrapped up in your own business to even see what's happening right under your noses. In my day folks cared about one another . . .'

Catherine, the younger of the sisters, was very like her father in that she liked to see everyone round her living

227

in perfect harmony and could find nothing unpleasant to say about anyone, with the occasional exception of her own grandmother. She shuffled uncomfortably but Linda was less reticent.

'So why did you not say anything when you realised there was something wrong, Gran?' she demanded, the cold tone of her voice making her anger plain.

Ina didn't even blink. 'It's not my place to run telling tales. Mary wouldn't have thanked me for interfering. Proud! That's her trouble. Just like your mother. Well, I hope she thinks she can sort her problems out by running away from them,' she snorted derisively.

'Maybe she can!' Linda defended her sister stoutly. 'I think she just needs some time on her own, to sort things out. She's had a horrible time, what with losing the babies and everything . . . and then she was right upset when Janette went off to Canada. And Archie can be very moody sometimes . . .'

'She knew that when she married him. Still, that's what you get for jumping the gun . . .' Ina preached, forgetting that jumping the gun was exactly what had condemned her to live out her life in this depressing little village.

'Well,' George had had enough. 'We'd best be on our way, Ina. I just thought I'd see if you knew where she might have gone. Archie's right worried about her. Still, I daresay it was just a tiff. They'll be back together again in a week or so.'

'Aye. Maybe,' Ina sounded doubtful. 'You've heard about Mrs Cree, then?'

'Heard what?' Linda asked quickly.

'Broke her leg,' Ina cackled, wickedly. 'Yesterday. They say she fell off a chair in the coal cellar – changing a light bulb she was – laid among the lumps of coal for so long she'd peed her breeks when they finally got to her. Aye, serves her right and all. Evil old woman that she is. She gave our Mary a real hard time of it. Wouldn't surprise me if the lassie didn't shove her off the chair herself before running off.'

Still chuckling she settled back in her chair and left them to see themselves out.

The chink of cups woke Maxine. Stirring blearily she was unable to get her bearings at first.

'Did you manage to get some sleep last night?' Rosie's slightly wheezy voice brought it all back to her. 'I wondered if I said too much. I didn't mean to upset you.'

In the friendly light of morning Maxine was more inclined to view Rosie's reading with scepticism. 'I slept fine thanks,' she lied, rather than upset the old woman, then scrambled into her clothes before turning to face her hostess. The shock forced her to sit back on the bed.

Gone were the stiffly disciplined curls of the previous night. Gone, too, was the heavy make-up and glittering jewellery. Most alarming of all was the disappearance of the perfectly aligned, white teeth. Rosie's bottom jaw now met her top one half an inch under her nose. Her hair, which was plastered to her scalp, was thin and completely white.

The old woman threw back her head and cackled wickedly at Maxine's obvious discomfiture. 'Don't fret, Hen. It's still old Rosie.' Not in the least embarrassed she lumbered back to her bedroom and re-emerged bearing the discarded wig. 'I've got three of them,' she chuckled. 'One for my head, one at the hairdresser's and one spare. Even an old woman has to keep up appearances.'

'I could do with one of those myself,' Maxine laughed, patting her own dishevelled hair.

Breakfast, in the form of toast and sausages, was cooked and eaten in an atmosphere of relaxed friendship.

'Thanks, Rosie. I don't know what I would have done last night if you hadn't taken pity on me. I'm sorry if I sounded ungrateful.'

'It was nothing, Hen, and you were right to be wary of strangers. But . . . much as I've taken to you, to tell the truth the others here don't like outsiders and I like my privacy so I won't offer to let you stay.'

'I understand. I never expected to be here for more than the one night.'

'So, what will you do tonight?'

'I don't know. I tried everywhere in Kilweem yesterday. I suppose I'll have to move on to Anstruther.'

'Did you try Mrs Dalgleish?'

'Mrs Dalgleish? I don't think so.'

'Big, fancy house . . .'

Maxine laughed. 'I didn't try anywhere like that. I thought people who could afford big houses wouldn't need lodgers.'

'Then you were trying the wrong places. And to be honest, Lass, with those bruises, you're not making the right impression. I daresay that's why none of the villagers sent you to see Mrs Dalgleish. And those holiday land-ladies, they aren't interested in a permanent let. All they want is a bit of extra money in the season. Most of them aren't even locals. They've moved in from Dundee or Edinburgh to cash in on the holiday-makers. A bit like us show folk!' she laughed. 'I'll give you Mrs Dalgleish's address. It's in the village centre. She lets out furnished flats and rooms, not in her own house but in an old place she has, near the Tollbooth. They're decent enough. Nothing fancy mind but about in your price range I should think. Old Ruthie Muir – she used to help me on the Tea Wagon whenever we came to Kilweem – she had the attic. But poor old Ruthie passed on a month since, while we were still in Kirkcaldy. Such a shame, she was a kind-hearted soul . . . Still I don't think her rooms have been re-let yet.'

Maxine gathered her things together, anxious not to overstay her welcome. 'Right, I'll go and see this Mrs Dalgleish then. What do I owe you for last night, Rosie?'

'Owe me?' Rosie seemed on the point of losing her uncertain temper but then just shook her head and laughed. 'If I had wanted to charge you for the use of my couch and a couple of old sausages I would have made that plain from the start. Now,' she went on over Maxine's stammered apologies. 'Let's get you sorted out. Mrs Dalgleish is a stern, church-going sort of woman and she'll not be letting you have one of her rooms if you go there looking like that. At least let me try to hide those bruises. They're starting to fade so it shouldn't be too difficult.'

Maxine found herself shoved back into a chair while Rosie dabbed thick make-up over the offending areas.

'There!' she exclaimed after ten minutes of concentrated effort. 'That's much better!' She handed Maxine a mirror.

'That's marvellous! You can't see the marks at all.'

'I've had lots of practice,' the old woman admitted wryly. 'Right.' She was all bustle again. 'Off you go. If Mrs Dalgleish offers you a room she'll want twenty pounds in advance. Have you got that much?'

'Yes . . .'

'But?'

'It's all I have got,' Maxine admitted. 'I can't afford to use all my money, especially when I've no job.'

'But you have got a job,' Rosie chuckled gleefully. 'Get yourself back to the Tea Wagon for five o'clock. You can help out there.'

'Doesn't your son do that?'

'Douglas? He'd eat the profits. No, Lass, he works the dodgems and to be truthful I could really use another pair of hands. Old Ruthie always helped out while we were in Kilweem before, but now she's gone . . .'

'I don't know what to say,' Maxine stammered.

'Don't say anything. Just be there at five o'clock.'

The address Rosie had given Maxine turned out to be a large, detached house of grey, weathered stone, just off Marketgate. It sat in its own spacious grounds and was screened from the road by a dense hedge.

The door was opened by a tall, hawk-nosed woman, leaning heavily on a walking stick. She merely stared at Maxine.

'I've come to see Mrs Dalgleish,' Maxine said, ignoring the woman's bad manners.

'I am Mrs Dalgleish. What do you want?'

'My name is Maxine Lennox. I've just arrived in Kilweem and I was told you might have a room to rent.'

'I see . . . Do you have a job?'

'Yes I do,' Maxine answered confidently.

'Where?' persisted the old woman.

'I'm helping Rosie in the Tea Wagon for now but I . . .'

'I never rent to show people!' The door was already closing.

'NO! I'm not from the shows. I came here to look for a proper job, in catering, that's what I'm trained in. This is just temporary until I can find something better.'

The door opened again. The woman frowned then subjected her to a humiliatingly long inspection. Despite Rosie's skills with make-up, Maxine was sure her bruises wouldn't go unnoticed. But, if Mrs Dalgleish did see anything unusual she made no comment. 'I'll need a deposit,' she said eventually.

'I can manage ten pounds,' Maxine offered hopefully.

'Fifteen. Refundable when you leave. Minus any damage and breakages, naturally.'

Thoroughly rattled by now, Maxine retorted, 'I must see the room first, Mrs Dalgleish. I have to be sure it's clean and dry.'

For a moment she thought she had gone too far. The door closed and all she could see was the woman's retreating back through the frosted glass. Then, just as she was about to ring the bell again she heard uneven footsteps returning along the hallway.

Mrs Dalgleish emerged, dressed now in a heavy astrakhan coat which gave off the distinct smell of camphor. A large bunch of keys dangled from one hand and she held her walking stick in the other. 'Follow me, Miss Lennox,' she ordered.

They crossed Marketgate and walked slowly towards the other end of the village. Not far from the Tollbooth they came to a tall, granite, tenement-style building, tucked into a corner. A heavy front door led into a shadowy, varnished passageway. Maxine followed Mrs Dalgleish along it, then up several flights of stairs to where three doors formed three sides of a perfectly square landing, illuminated by a skylight. Panting for breath Mrs Dalgleish unlocked the right-hand door and threw it open. Then she stood back and allowed Maxine to precede her into the room.

It was dark so, at first, she could see very little. However, when her prospective landlady dragged back the heavy curtains, the sun streamed in, illuminating spirals of disturbed dust. Through the grimy window Maxine caught the sparkle of the sea and knew, if she opened it, she would be able to smell it too.

'Well?' Mrs Dalgleish settled herself on an upright chair and banged her stick impatiently on the floor.

'Can you give me a minute or two to have a proper

look please, Mrs Dalgleish?' Maxine asked, remembering her new resolutions and asserting herself as she intended to do from now on.

It was a large, adequately furnished room with a single bed, a wardrobe at one end and two battered armchairs and a huge, comfortable-looking but old-fashioned sofa at the other. Under the window was a small table and two upright chairs. An electric fire clung to a patch of wall at the bedroom end but, in the living area, there was an open grate. The floorboards were partially covered with bright rugs and the walls were painted a dull cream colour.

'Five pounds a week. Electricity by your own meter, in that cupboard,' Mrs Dalgleish used her stick to point to cupboards which flanked the fireplace. 'Bathroom and kitchen are behind the other doors on the landing. No noise, no men, no animals and no mess. Any complaints and you're out. Understand?'

'I'd like to see the bathroom and kitchen, please,' Maxine insisted, though secretly she was delighted with the flat which she knew was far cheaper than anything similar would be in a town.

Mrs Dalgleish smiled grimly then stood up stiffly and limped on to the landing where she unlocked the other two doors. The bathroom, behind the middle door, was cramped and basic, but clean while the kitchen was old-fashioned but fairly well equipped and spacious with a wonderful view of the sea between roofs and chimneys.

'When could I move in?' Maxine asked.

'As soon as you pay me.'

'Today?'

'As soon as you pay me,' Mrs Dalgleish repeated flatly.

Maxine took fifteen pounds from her purse and offered it to her new landlady.

'Twenty pounds, Miss Lennox. Fifteen pounds deposit and five pounds advance rent.'

Reluctantly Maxine handed over her last five pounds, leaving nothing more than a handful of silver and some coppers.

'Good. The rent is due every Friday. Someone will collect it. If you miss him call at my house on Saturday morning, before eleven. And I will not tolerate arrears.'

With that she handed the keys to Maxine and limped away.

Maxine spent the rest of the day cleaning the flat. All the rooms were stuffy and slightly musty smelling, probably because they been closed up for too long. Every floor was swept, each surface dusted and buffed using rags, brushes and polish from a cupboard in the kitchen. With a huge effort she managed to wrestle the windows open allowing the clean, sharp tang of the sea to surge into the room.

Much to her relief she soon saw that everything was clean and well cared for. Only dust, disuse and dirty windows had made the rooms feel dull and stale. And this, she told herself, surveying her handiwork with real satisfaction, is home. Home where she didn't have to worry about unpaid bills and a brutal husband. Home, a place to live and save and make plans for the future. Already she felt some of the old strength and determination flowing back.

FIFTEEN

It was a tired but much happier Maxine who presented herself back at the Tea Wagon a little before five o'clock that night.

'Everything all right?' Rosie asked, handing Maxine an apron.

'Fine thanks, Rosie. The rooms are quite big, the furniture's old-fashioned but – '

'Right then, there's a lot to be done so let's get to work. Put those pies in the oven and make sure they don't burn. Then these tatties need peeling and chipping.' With that, Rosie busied herself setting out vinegar, salt and sauce, plastic spoons and clean cups, displaying no further curiosity about Maxine's new home. Maxine took the hint, rolled up her sleeves and got to work.

'You'll have to learn to do all this by yourself,' Rosie said after the first rush of customers had been dealt with. 'I like to have at least one day off in the week and you'll have to cope when I'm not here. You'll even have to come in in the morning and cook up the pies.'

Maxine chuckled. 'I could do it now, Rosie. I'm a proper cook. I used to make pies and bridies for my husband's mobile butchery round. Some said they were the best in town,' she added, with a rare touch of pride.

'Did they now?' Rosie eyed her new employee speculatively. 'I think you and I will get along very nicely, Lass. Very nicely.'

Douglas, Rosie's son, turned up to introduce himself half-way through the evening. Like his mother he was grossly overweight. His belly hung obscenely over the top of his greasy jeans and a multitude of chins obscured a thick, bull-like neck. Long, lank hair was dragged back into a limp pony tail and his ragged fingernails were rimmed with oil. His manners were crude and his conversation was coarse, but, aware of how much she owed his mother, Maxine did her best to be friendly.

The fair was the only one to visit this part of Strathannan and drew visitors from all the surrounding area. Maxine loved to watch, catching some of the crowd's excitement. The atmosphere was always lively, exciting and somehow mysterious. The long evenings seemed darker here where the bright, fairground lights plunged the surrounding area into comparative blackness. The pungent smells of diesel, chips and candyfloss mingled and settled over the grass, lingering until early dawn when the sea breeze blew across the dunes, clearing the air for another day.

It was like another world, something strange and foreign sent to transform the sleepy fishing village for six hours every night. But, when morning came it was a ghostly scene, deserted and silent, discarded papers blowing in the fitful wind, the generators still, the rides shrouded in flapping canvas.

During the course of the evening, Rosie allowed Maxine one fifteen-minute break. Glad to escape the close confines of the hot, greasy van, Maxine usually strolled round the booths and rides, always hoping for a friendly response from the show folk. Always she was disappointed. The men simply ignored her while the women glared at her with dark, arrogant eyes, leaving her in no doubt that they resented her presence among them. It hurt and then angered her that they all seemed to have made up their minds to dislike her without making the faintest effort to get to know her. And it was a dislike which, despite all her determined efforts to be pleasant, was increasing with every passing day. The young women pointedly turned their backs when they saw her coming. Older women stared at her with hatred in their dark eyes and sometimes even hissed as she walked by. As a result her steps invariably led to the dodgems where at least Douglas could be relied upon for a few minutes of friendly, meaningless chat.

'You don't want to be seen talking to Douglas so much,' Rosie warned her after a week of this.

'Why not?' Maxine demanded. 'At least Douglas *will* talk to me which is more than the rest of them do.'

'Showfolk keep to themselves and you'd be well advised to do the same,' was Rosie's sharp advice.

Irritated by the older woman's manner Maxine turned away and busied herself serving the small queue which had built up. Rosie was something of an enigma, often pleasant, frequently hostile for no obvious reason. Maxine was already tiring of the unpredictability of Rosie's wildly swinging moods and had been looking for more conventional work, fearing her aunt and uncle, when they returned, would be shocked to know she was working on the showground.

'Och, Lass, try to understand,' Rosie said later, as they closed up for the night. 'We showfolk, we have to keep ourselves to ourselves. No outsider can ever hope to be accepted. We're too close. We've been together for too long . . . not like some of the showfolk these days. Two hundred years our families have been together, that we can prove, it's likely even longer than that. Aye, I suppose it must seem strange to you though,' she added wistfully. 'And this happens time and time again. Even old Ruthie wasn't liked, poor soul.' She smiled grimly at Maxine. 'We have to stick by each other here, Lass. We get enough bad words from outsiders without all falling out among ourselves. I'll always take the side of my own people. I have to live with them for the rest of my days. If I broke faith again, they'd never forgive me. I'm an old woman, Hen. The day's not far off when I'll need them. Even I can't go on working forever.'

'Again . . . ? You said if you, "broke faith again," ' Maxine prompted gently, sensing something deeper in Rosie's rambling speech.

Rosie stared at her for a moment then sighed. 'I suppose there's no harm in telling you . . . My Peter, Douglas's father, he wasn't one of us . . . Oh, I loved him all right. More than anything in the world, I loved him.' She laughed harshly. 'I bet you can't imagine old Rosie in love, can you? But I was. I'd have died for him. But it was no good. I always knew it was hopeless. They stopped me seeing him . . . my father, my uncles, everyone. Even when they knew I was pregnant . . . I don't think Peter even knew about the baby . . . They warned him off. I don't know what happened to him. My people, they stood by me, supported me and Douglas, but they've never really forgiven me, or let me forget. Why do you think they let me work the Tea Wagon on my own? None of the women will help. They say I betrayed them. It was twenty-five years ago but they still talk about it as if it was yesterday.'

Maxine was appalled. How could Rosie have let them treat her so badly?

'That's terrible, Rosie.'

'It's our way. The right way,' the old woman said with absolute conviction.

'I think it's cruel to treat anyone so harshly,' Maxine insisted, wondering if they could ever understand one another.

*

Tired out by each evening's work, Maxine slept late, seldom rising before ten o'clock, enjoying the freedom of her new home, a place to call her very own. It was wonderful to be able to do exactly as she pleased. Often she collected her paper from downstairs and spent a luxurious hour reading it before attending to the little bit of housework which was all that was needed to keep the place tidy. And, during that first week, she sat at her table in the window and wrote to her father, enclosing loving notes to both her sisters, assuring them all that she was perfectly safe and happy and had no intention of coming back to Craigie. After much thought she also penned a letter to David, now based in the south of England with the navy, telling him the bare details and giving him her new address. But it was to Janette that she poured her heart out, filling page after page, keeping back nothing and admitting for the first time to the violence and fear which had doomed her marriage. It was cathartic. When it was finished she felt cleansed, ready to put it all behind her and start again.

One of the advantages of working in the evenings was that the best of the day was hers, giving her plenty of opportunity to explore the small village.

Despite the line of new houses which had sprouted up along the coastal road and the ever-increasing number of tourists, the heart of Kilweem, round the quayside and Tollbooth, was unchanged. Behind the wonderful old harbour setted wynds clambered up a steep brae to the main streets of Marketgate and Kirkgate. Many of the buildings retained their original character and most were still inhabited by families such as the McArdles, McLeans, Moys and Camerons who, because their families had lived in the village for generations, regarded it as their own kingdom and viewed all newcomers with suspicious hostility.

The harbour itself still sheltered some elderly fishing boats, though many fewer than before the war which had claimed so many vessels. One of Maxine's favourite pastimes was to stand on the broad quayside and watch the boats negotiating their way through the narrow harbour entrance, followed by flocks of gulls looking for an easy meal. The business of selling the catch by auctioning the boxes of gutted fish fascinated her, as did the way the men conscientiously tended their nets, checking for tears which were patiently repaired before the nets were finally stowed away, ready for the next trip. Occasionally she persuaded one of the gruff fishermen to sell her a freshly netted fish and went home triumphantly with a glistening haddock, loosely wrapped in a piece of old newspaper.

Round the coast from the rocky point which shielded the harbour lay the wide, sandy beach. At weekends it was dotted with holiday-makers and day trippers but, during the week, the farther reaches were a haven of peace.

Maxine had always loved the sea. As a child she had often walked with her father along the small beach at Craigie. It was rocky and gravelly, strewn with lumps of sea coal which they collected gratefully, and backed by scrubby, reluctant, hillocks of sand and patches of coarse grass. Like Craigie itself the beach was bleak and stark. Even the sea was uninviting, edged with yellow scum where it lapped lethargically at the rocks.

Kilweem was a bare fifteen miles along the coast from Craigie but here the beach was soft, golden and clean, a wide swathe of rippling sand which filled the shallow bay for almost five miles to the next headland. The dunes were wide and inviting, filled with grassy hollows which offered privacy and protection from the wind.

Maxine revelled in the wildness of it, the isolation, the

beauty and in the calming tranquillity she found there. The contrast between Kilweem and the harsh, impoverished ugliness of Craigie could not have been greater. In those first weeks she spent many hours walking on the beach, simply enjoying the sights and sounds of the ocean, feeling that the fresh, tangy air and the regular rhythm of the waves were healing her. Already she was so much more relaxed and confident. More the girl she used to be. Before she married Archie Cree.

When Linda turned up unexpectedly, anxious to see for herself that her oldest sister really was as well as her letters said she was, it was to the beach that Maxine led her. There, protected from the breeze by the dunes, Maxine described her marriage to her shocked sister but then pledged her to silence.

'I don't want everyone to know about this, Linda. It's enough just to say Archie and I don't get on. OK?'

'There's nothing to be ashamed of. He's the one in the wrong. Not you. You shouldn't have to hide away like this. Come home, Mary. You don't have to go back to Archie. You are welcome to live with us, or with Cath, or Dad. Even Gran would be pleased to have you.'

'You've got your own lives to live. And I've got mine. I can't come back, Linda. Every time I walked down the street and bumped into him, or that mother of his, it would just bring back too many rotten memories.' Maxine had been relieved to learn that Mrs Cree was recovering well. 'This is a fresh start for me. I'm going to stay here.'

'Yes.' Linda kissed her sister's cheek. 'I understand. I'd probably feel the same.' She shivered briefly and looked out to sea. 'But why here, Mary? It's so lonely. So . . . wild,' she said, sounding thoroughly perplexed.

'I know,' laughed her sister. 'It's perfect.'

*

'You mean she's left you?' Mrs Cree roared incredulously at Archie.

Behind them her husband slipped unobtrusively out of the room. When she was in this kind of mood he didn't want to be within a mile of his wife.

'Yes,' Archie admitted, sounding sulky. Pointless to insist that Mary's escape had been his mother's fault because the old woman remembered nothing later than breakfast that day.

'And you didn't have the bloody guts to tell me before now,' she sneered at her unfortunate son who was still out of breath from the effort of wheeling his mother's wheelchair into the house from the taxi which had delivered her home from hospital.

'You weren't well . . .'

'You stupid, bloody fool, Archie Cree! Can't you see what she could do to you? Is your brain damaged as well as your back?'

'No!' Even his own mother had to torment him about his deformity.

'Well think! Think what you did to her. My God, if she ever told anyone, you could end up in jail.'

'I'm her husband . . .'

'What sort of husband beats his wife's face half to pulp then knocks her out and leaves her in a deserted church hall, eh? She could have bloody well died!' she screamed.

'But she didn't.'

She ignored him. 'You get that little bitch back here, where we can keep an eye on her, before she opens her mouth and lets us all in for it.'

'Nobody knows where she is.'

'Of course they do! She wouldn't walk away from her family and not tell them where she was. If she had really disappeared the whole bloody lot of them would be beyond themselves with worry. Old Ina would have been up here murdering you with her bare hands. She might do that yet if she ever suspects what you did to Mary.' She spluttered with rage, heaving herself about so wildly that the wheelchair creaked and her injured leg, projecting stiffly in front of her, slipped from its support. She swore obscenely, then groaned in pain while Archie struggled to lift it back.

'I've tried to find out where she is,' Archie said in the ensuing silence while his mother re-mustered her strength. 'But she could be any-bloody-where.'

'Then bleeding well find her! The Innes's know where she is. I'd put money on it.'

'I'll ask George again.'

'You do that. And make sure you get an answer this time. And if he tells you he doesn't know anything don't believe him. Just think about what would happen if she decides she wants a divorce. The whole bloody thing would come out in court. You could go to jail and take me with you, you stupid little sod. Assault. Kidnapping. Imprisonment . . . you've done it all, Archie Cree. That girl is Ina Lennox's granddaughter. She'll want to make you pay . . .'

'I'll talk to George again,' Archie promised. 'Tonight. At the Greyhound.'

His mother had ignited his innate fear of the law and Archie would indeed do his very best to trace his missing wife. But, terrified of the police though he was, Archie's biggest motivation was still the knowledge that people were starting to talk, to speculate on the condition of his marriage. More than anything else he wanted no one to know of his failure.

But Mrs Cree was too impatient to wait for Archie. While he made his way to the Greyhound she nagged her unwilling husband into pushing and shoving the heavy wheelchair right through the village to Ina's home. It was a two-bedroomed house and little better kept than the one she had occupied in the old rows, long since demolished.

'Ring the bell,' she ordered her exhausted, panting spouse.

After a few seconds the hall light went on and Ina herself opened the door. 'Well.' She looked down on her immobilised foe with a satisfied smile on her thin lips. 'Had an accident have we?' she chortled, patting the plastered limb enthusiastically.

Mrs Cree kept a determined smile on her bulldoggish face. 'I've not come here to discuss my health, Ina Lennox.'

'Well, what the hell are you dirtying my doorstep for?' Ina demanded.

Thin as a stick with long fingers and feet and a sharply pointed nose, Ina was the physical antithesis of her arch rival.

'I think we should have a wee talk, you and me, Ina.' Mrs Cree's neck was aching from having to constantly look up at Ina but the stiff smile stayed firmly in place.

'I can't think of a single thing I could ever want to discuss with you, Mrs Cree.' Ina started to close the door. Both women knew the plastered foot was in the way and Mrs Cree clenched her hands round the arms of her chair, expecting an onslaught of pain. But Ina stopped just in time.

'Move your foot,' she ordered.

'I am here to talk to you about your granddaughter. My daughter-in-law,' Mrs Cree roared. Already, several windows had interested faces at them and across the street two women listened in with no shame at all.

'What are you looking at!' Ina bawled at them. 'All right, in you come,' she agreed at last.

'Come here, Sid! Come here!' Mrs Cree bellowed at her

husband who had moved out of range and was smoking a cigarette on the street corner.

Hearing her at last he dropped the butt into the gutter and galloped to his wife's aid. Much to the hilarity of the spectators he tripped on Ina's uneven path and cannoned into Mrs Cree's chair.

'You stupid bastard,' she snarled. 'Get me in there. Hurry up.'

'Are you coming in or not?' Ina got a measure of pleasure from adding to their confusion. But at last Mrs Cree was ensconced in her untidy living room, Mr Cree had been dismissed to the back garden and the two women were facing each other.

'About your Mary,' Mrs Cree started, when it was obvious that Ina had no intention of breaking the silence.

'What about her?' Ina knew the answer very well but wasn't going to make this any easier than she had to.

'She's gone off. Left my Archie. Run out on him . . .'

'Clever girl,' Ina said approvingly.

'Just like her bloody mother!' Mrs Cree exploded, goaded beyond endurance. 'It runs in your family, Ina Lennox . . . You're a right bloody bad lot! You're all the effing same . . .'

'Language, please, Mrs Cree!' Ina tutted, delightedly. 'This is a decent house.'

'Decent!'

'If you want to know anything about our Mary you'd best watch what you say to me.'

'Where is she?' Mrs Cree spluttered.

Ina laughed. 'If you think I'd tell you, even if I knew, you're even dafter than you look.'

Mrs Cree bit her tongue. 'You don't understand . . .' she floundered. 'Archie . . . he really loves the lass. It's nothing more than a wee misunderstanding. If he could just have a wee talk with her they'd sort it out.'

246

'. . . Archie really loves the lass,' Ina mimicked. 'Aye, Mrs Cree, that much is obvious.'

'You have got her address?' Mrs Cree persisted.

'Now look here you, I wouldn't tell you where the lassie was even if you were going to pay her a million pounds to talk to that twisted little demon you call a son. I don't know what went on with those two but I do know it was nothing good. Our Mary's well out of it. You'll get no help from me, or anyone else in this family, so go and boil your head in a bucket of shit.'

While the hapless Mrs Cree still gaped at her Ina grabbed the handles of the wheelchair and whipped the other woman round as if she weighed nothing more than a child. Before she knew it Mrs Cree found herself ignominiously marooned in the middle of Ina Lennox's front path. Crimson with fury she screeched for her husband who was still round the back.

'Sid! Sidney! Sidney Cree! Will you come here when I call you.'

Encouraged by the cheers of Ina's neighbours Sid scurried round the side of the house, grabbed his apoplectic wife's chair and almost gave himself a hernia, straining to push her home.

Meanwhile Archie was having another go at George.

'No, Lad,' George lied. 'Apart from that first note, I've not heard a thing from her. Still, at least we know she's all right.'

'You would tell me, wouldn't you, George, if you heard from her again? If she gave you an address?' Archie asked, watching George closely and noting how uncomfortable the older man seemed.

'Aye! Of course I would, Archie.' George was never at ease with untruths but in each of the two letters she had sent him, Mary had begged him never to give Archie her address. Privately he had been tempted. He didn't like to think of her all alone like that, not that she didn't sound happy enough. But she hadn't given poor old Archie a chance to put things right between them and the lad surely deserved that much. He remembered how hurt he'd felt when Evelyn walked out on him. But George was stopped from saying anything by the knowledge that he would have to answer not only to Catherine and Linda – who were formidable enough – but to Ina too. All three women were, for once, unanimous in agreeing that Mary should be allowed to keep her whereabouts secret.

'Come on, George. No hard feelings, eh? I'll buy you a pint.'

'No hard feelings, Archie. You're still family, Son. Still family.'

Archie quickly put a frothing beer in front of his father-in-law. When that was finished he replaced it with another. And then another and another, with a whisky thrown in for good measure. By nine o'clock George was at the happy, expansive stage Archie had been aiming for. He watched his father-in-law polishing off his fifth pint with as much relish as the first but didn't offer to buy him another one. After all, the man would be no good to him semi-conscious.

'Och, George,' he said, slipping into the neighbouring seat and slinging his arm companionably round the older man's neck. 'You know something?' he slurred, sounding as drunk as George though, in fact, he was utterly sober.

'What, Lad?' George asked.

'I miss her, George. Oh God, I miss Mary.' The emotional catch he inserted into his voice was so good he almost convinced himself. 'I love her. I'd do anything, George. Anything, just to be able to have a few wee words with her. Just to tell her I'm trying to find us a house of our own. And I'm out every day on the van, George. The business is making money again.'

'Good for you, Son!' George said happily.

'But, George, there's no point. Not without Mary . . .'

'No . . .'

'George, let me tell you something?' Archie put his face closer. 'It's the bloody women. Och, they all think they know best. They're all the same.'

'Aye. You're right enough there,' George agreed.

'What right have they got to come between Mary and me? They know where she is. YOU know where she is, George! But the bloody women have told you not to tell me.'

'I . . .'

'It's all right, George. I understand. My own mother's the worst of the lot! There's no going against her, George. Her and Ina, well they're two of a kind . . . old cows.'

'Cowwshh,' George giggled.

'We've got to stop them, George. We can't let the old cows get the better of us.'

'NNNNever.' George hiccoughed his agreement.

'They're stopping me and Mary getting back together. They're stopping Mary from coming home, George.'

'Old cowwsshh.'

'What's her address, George? Tell me Mary's address then I can bring her home and we can tell the old cows to go fuck themselves.'

'Fuckkk,' George repeated.

'What's Mary's address, George?'

'Address . . . in my jacket . . . inside pocket,' George mumbled.

Archie had his hand inside the jacket before George had finished slurring the sentence. He found the letter easily, scribbled the address on the back of a cigarette packet and replaced the letter. That done he went to the bar and ordered a double whisky and a pint of heavy which he took to his father-in-law. 'Drink up, George. I've got to go now but you drink up and enjoy yourself.' With any luck the silly old fool wouldn't remember a thing tomorrow.

He was right. Come morning George's aching head was completely fuddled. But, with a feeling of vague unease he did recall talking to Archie.

On the Friday of Maxine's third week in the village the weather suddenly changed. A keen wind, bringing the warning of rain, drove her home from the beach much earlier than usual. The evening was cold and a slight mist crept in off the sea, shrouding the dunes in a shifting, grey haze.

Inside the Tea Wagon it was warm and greasy. Outside customers shrugged themselves deeper into summer jackets and shivered. Trade boomed as people sought warming drinks and filling snacks. Maxine and Rosie were so busy that they hardly had time to glance at each customer as they took the orders. Beaten by the unexpected chill the crowd thinned earlier than normal and by nine-thirty the last customers were buying a final drink before making for the warmth of their beds.

'See to these last two while. I pull the shutters half down,' Rosie instructed. 'Looks like we'll be having an early night.'

Maxine handed her customer his change and turned to serve the remaining man. 'Yes?' she asked brightly, wiping the counter with a cloth and picking up the teapot as she went, ready to pour.

'First I'll take a cup of tea. Then I'll take you home with me,' he growled.

Maxine felt the blood drain from her face and forgot that her hand was clamped to the burning pot. 'Archie!'

she gasped, letting go of it and sending it crashing to the floor.

'Get yourself out here,' Archie ordered, anger glittering dangerously behind bloodshot eyes.

'No!' Maxine shrank back against the far wall of the Tea Wagon. 'Go away, Archie. Go away and leave me in peace.'

'Get off with you.' Rosie summed up the situation in two seconds and imposed her solid form between the ugly little man and her terrified assistant. Archie actually spat at her and hobbled swiftly to the door of the van. Before either woman could do anything he was inside and wrestling with his wife.

'You are coming home with me, Mary,' he grunted, grabbing Maxine's wrists.

'I am not!' She screamed her defiance, struggling to break free, smelling the drink on his breath and knowing what that would mean if he managed to get her on her own.

His face flushed, clashing with his carroty hair. 'You are my wife,' he hissed. 'And no one walks out on me, especially you, after all I've done for you.'

'I am never coming back, Archie.' Her voice trembled but she faced him bravely.

'The lassie doesn't want to go with you. Now why don't you just go home and sober up,' Rosie suggested, making things worse.

'Out of my way, you old cow!' Archie shoved the elderly woman with unnecessary force, sending her backwards to stumble heavily against the counter. 'If you don't come with me, Mary, I'll smash this place to matchwood,' he snarled, sweeping a tray of clean cups on to the floor where most of them smashed.

'Douglas!' Rosie screamed. 'Douglas!'

'Shut your face,' Archie growled, rounding on her and

shoving her down on to a stool, then running a hand along the counter and sending everything from it on to the dirty, churned ground below.

'I am not coming back to Craigie, Archie.' Anger gave Maxine strength. She held her back straight and spoke defiantly.

Archie grinned horribly and kicked at the low cupboards with his good foot, splintering the plywood.

Rosie screamed again. 'He'll ruin me,' she blubbered, as Archie sent his foot into the splintering wood again and again. 'Stop him.' Then she was on her swollen feet, facing Maxine. Behind them Maxine saw several of the showmen running towards the wagon. 'This is your problem, Maxine. Get it out of my van or it'll be the worse for you. If my folk have to sort it out for me they'll make you wish you had never set foot in the showground.'

As she finished speaking the whole van shuddered as Douglas leapt into it. Archie span round, a broken cup in his hand, ready to fight, but seemed to shrink back against the counter when he saw the size of man who was challenging him.

'This is my mother's van,' Douglas growled, menacingly.

'I've come for my wife!' Archie yelled, desperately. 'I've come to take her home. Is a man not allowed to claim what's rightfully his? I'll not harm the old woman and Mary'll pay for any damage. Let us through so's I can talk some sense into her,' he babbled, then grabbed Maxine's arm, and tried to haul her towards the doorway.

Douglas simply brought the edge of his hand down on Archie's bicep. Before Archie's yelp of pain had died away Douglas had him by the collar and was manhandling him out of the van. The crowd of showfolk parted then closed again, forming a ring round the two men.

Maxine ran from the van, pushed her way into the crowd. 'What are you doing?' she screamed at Douglas.

'What does it look like?' he asked, rolling up his sleeves. The crowd guffawed at her.

'He's my husband!' she yelled, hating Archie but not wishing to witness anything as vile as this.

Douglas dragged the terrified Archie across to where Maxine was standing. 'This little runt wrecked my mother's van! He needs a good lesson teaching him,' he snarled at her before hauling Archie away again.

She turned and tried to beat a way out of the crowd but strong arms caught her and turned her back. Appalled she closed her eyes, refusing to watch.

Gradually she realised that she could no longer hear the thuds and grunts which had marked Douglas's progress. Very slowly she opened her eyes. Archie lay curled into a ball at Douglas's feet, crying and whimpering softly.

Douglas hawked and spat on him then grinned at the appreciative crowd. Maxine gagged.

'I don't think he'll be bothering you again, Hen,' Douglas laughed into her face while behind him Archie struggled into a crawling position. 'Don't worry, I've not killed him. He's not worth the trouble,' he laughed horribly, displaying decayed teeth. 'I've just made him understand that he can't mess with showfolk. He'll not come back, you can be sure of that.'

Maxine stayed silent while Douglas dragged Archie to the edge of the grass. With one shove of his massive hand he tossed the crippled man on to his hands and knees then watched while Archie dragged himself up. Beaten, bleeding and totally humiliated he hobbled slowly away to the jeers of the show people.

Too shocked for speech Maxine returned to the Tea Wagon to collect her coat.

'See what that man of yours did!' Rosie screamed at her as soon as she opened the door.

Maxine stared at the shattered cupboards, the broken cups. 'I'm really sorry, Rosie. I didn't think he'd find me here.'

'I warned you, that first night, I told you he'd find you. It's a good thing my Douglas was around,' the old woman added with a touch of pride. 'Or you'd have got more than a black eye this time.'

'I got more than a black eye last time,' Maxine retorted. 'Oh, I am grateful to Douglas, Rosie. I just wish he hadn't been so . . .'

'So what?' the older woman rounded on her furiously.

'So violent. I thought he was going to kill Archie.'

The old woman guffawed hideously. 'You've got a lot to learn if that's what you thought. Douglas wouldn't risk trouble with the law for the likes of you. And he didn't do it for you! He did it for me, his old mother, because that man of yours was breaking this place up. If he helped you out at the same time, all the better. Aye, he taught that man of yours a lesson he won't forget in a hurry. That's our way. Take no nonsense. Let everyone know where you stand. It's the best way. In this life you have to fight for things to make other people respect you.'

'By half-killing them?' Maxine was seeing Rosie in a new light, one she didn't admire.

'It's the only way with some folk.'

'You're wrong,' Maxine insisted angrily.

'Am I? Not so wrong just now though. You were glad enough to see my Douglas then. If it wasn't for him you'd be on your way to the hospital now, or worse. And I'm warning you, Mary, or Maxine, or whatever you call yourself, I'll not have this sort of carry on here! I'm a decent, clean-living woman. I don't hold with a woman walking out on her man. In my book marriage is for life.

254

And if you got a beating you probably deserved it. But I suppose that's your business.'

'Too damn right it is!' Maxine exploded. She grabbed her coat from behind the door and shrugged herself into it. 'You can send any wages on to me. You know my address,' she called back as she walked away.

Tomorrow, she promised herself, she would find a proper job, something to secure her future and allow her to build a respectable life for herself in this beautiful village. She had been searching for work ever since arriving here, to no avail and now her need was urgent again, not least because her great aunt and uncle must be returning within the next couple of days if they were to re-open their bakery on Monday as their notice promised.

She threaded her way quickly through the showground driven on by her anger, anxious to get away from the place and these strange, hostile people. A sound from behind made her falter. She turned sharply but saw no one so carried on, quickening her step slightly. When Douglas stepped out from behind the shelter of a generator lorry she jumped and only just managed to stifle a scream.

'No need to take fright, Hen, it's only me,' he grinned, his huge belly rippling with mirth.

'I'm just on my way home, Douglas,' she said coldly, totally unamused by him.

'What's the big hurry?' He barred her way solidly and caught at her arm. 'Why don't you and me go for a wee walk along the beach?'

She could think of nothing she would rather do less. 'I'm tired.'

'I'll walk you home then,' he persisted, still grinning broadly.

'No,' she yelled, starting to feel pressured now and in no mood to put up with it.

'Why not? It's what you want isn't it? You've been

hanging round after me ever since you arrived. And you do owe me a favour, after tonight.'

She laughed, struck by the sheer, awful absurdity of the situation. 'Don't be ridiculous, Douglas. And let go of my arm!' But his grip tightened and he pushed her back against the side of the lorry.

'You're a braw wee thing, Maxine,' he drooled, ignoring the look of utter abhorrence which crossed her face as he brought his damp lips close to hers. All she could see was the yellow slime which coated his teeth. Her stomach heaved and she jerked her head aside.

'Stop it!' she shrieked, squirming to get away from him. His fat body pressed into her, jamming her where she stood. Horrified she felt one of his hands sliding over her breasts while the other grappled with the hem of her skirt.

'This is what you want, isn't it, Maxine? I'll show you what a real man is like,' he panted into her ear.

Now she could feel him, stiff and warm against her skin, and smell him too. 'NO!' she shouted, revulsion churning her stomach.

'Yes,' he grunted, forcing himself against her, hampered by his own huge belly.

She resisted with all her strength, dug her nails deeply into his puffy flesh, kicked and wriggled, all to no avail. Then, just as she thought he really was going to rape her, Douglas pulled away abruptly, his head twisted awkwardly to one side.

'You cheating bastard,' an angry, female voice hissed. 'Get away from her.' She tugged hard on his pony tail and her voice rose to a shrill screech, accompanied by thuds and thumps as her flailing fists attacked his gross frame.

Covering his head with his hands, Douglas scurried away in the direction of the caravans, unmindful of his exposed manhood which, wilted in defeat, flapped before him as he ran.

Maxine stepped away from the lorry and found herself facing a pair of dark, blazing eyes. A young woman, one who worked one of the rides and who had never done more than glower at her, challenged her, hands on hips, her long, dark hair tumbling in wild curls to a tightly clinched waist. Her feet were planted squarely apart in the most aggressive stance Maxine had ever encountered in a woman. Before she had time to register more than the most obvious details a slim hand, tipped with ferociously long, red nails, shot out and slapped her resoundingly across the cheek. Maxine gasped, astounded by this unexpected attack from someone she had thought was rescuing her.

'Stay away from him, you cheap little tart,' the girl spat, fire snapping from her eyes. 'We've watched you. Everyone knows what you've been up to. But Douglas McGuinness is mine and don't you forget it. One more look in his direction and I'll give you a face no man will ever want to look at. Starting with those pretty little teeth. Understand?'

Turning her back the girl, dressed in indecently tight, lurex trousers and ludicrously high heels, strutted after her lover.

The anger pounding through Maxine's veins made her head feel as if it was about to explode. She stood in the shelter of the lorry and waited until she calmed down a little before finally turning and walking out of the showground forever.

Archie summoned enough strength from somewhere to drag himself away from the fairground with the jeers and catcalls of the show people still ringing in his ears. His old van was parked down at the harbour, and every step he took over the cobbled wynd which led down to it sent spears of pain through his body, every breath he took seared through his cracked ribs.

The effort of unlocking the high door and pulling himself up into the van almost made him faint. The drive back to Craigie was more than he could face tonight. Wishing he had never come to Kilweem, Archie eased his aching body along the bench seat at the front of the van and closed his eyes.

He woke when the morning sun sent shafts of light into the cab and on to his face. For a moment he was totally confused, unable to place where he was, but when he tried to move, a fierce, stabbing pain in his ribs brought it all back. And then a feeling of complete, bitter humiliation drowned even the pain.

Eventually he eased himself into a sitting position and, when the expected agony failed to materialise, he opened the door of the van and slid out. Apart from a few hopeful gulls the quayside was still deserted. Archie shielded his eyes against the light which was reviving his headache. He had stiffened up overnight and felt bruised all over. His face, particularly his nose, was throbbing with dull pain. A cautious examination of his body revealed no serious damage apart from a cracked rib or two which promised to make the drive back to Craigie a painful one. But when he peered at his reflection in the van's wing mirrors he groaned at what he saw. The pulpy, swollen face that looked back from the puffy slits of eyes, made his stomach heave and reminded him uncomfortably of the way his wife's face had looked after his last attack. The memory made him even more bad-tempered than he already was. One look at his face and everyone would be talking, speculating. He'd never be able to hold his head up in Craigie again. He aimed a kick at a discarded lobster crate, sending it rasping over the cobbles but also sending spears of pain through his body. Cursing he walked to the harbour's edge and relieved himself into the peaceful waters before finally inserting himself gingerly behind the wheel of his old van and driving off.

'Morning, Archie. It's a braw morning.' Ina was on her routine trip to the shops and just happened to be in the vicinity when Archie's van drew up. She got herself across the road to stand outside his home with amazing speed for a woman of her advancing years. 'Ochhhh . . . that's a right mess you've got yourself into there, Son. What happened? Did your mammy give you a good licking?' she taunted, cackling horribly and bringing the bat-eared Mrs Cree to stare out of her window. Seconds later the front door clanged open and Archie's mother, her leg still firmly encased in plaster from hip to toe, hopped out, teetering wildly on her crutches.

'What the hell do you want, Ina Lennox,' she snarled, 'and what in the name of God happened to you?' she demanded of her battered son, barring his escape by planting herself in the gateway.

'Oh, so it wasn't you did this to him then?' Ina commented innocently.

'Mind your own bloody business, Ina Lennox,' Mrs Cree hissed, almost losing her balance.

Ina chortled. 'What a sorry pair you are,' she laughed.

Archie, whose pride was fragile at the best of times, abandoned all pretence and roared at her. 'Your bloody granddaughter did this to me . . .'

Ina's smile stiffened a little. 'Well, Archie, I always said you were a poor specimen but to let a wee lassie like our Mary do this . . .'

'Eff off,' he snarled, shoving past her.

'Where is she then? Haven't you brought her home?' Mrs Cree demanded, still blocking his path. A dreadful thought occurred to her. 'You didn't . . .' The words were too terrible to say easily. '. . . I mean she is . . . You didn't *do* anything to her, did you, Archie?' More than anyone she understood how dangerous Archie could be when his temper snapped.

'Where is she? Is that all you can ask? What about me?'

'Is she all right?' his mother asked again, her voice rising to a demented squawk.

'Of course she's all bloody right. And no, I've not brought her home. I wouldn't have her back if she came gift wrapped in eighteen carat gold. She's brought me nothing but bloody trouble . . .' He clutched his broken ribs in agony.

'Well, seems to me you got a taste of your own medicine, Archie Cree,' Ina said quietly. 'And not before time. If I was a younger woman I'd have given you a hiding myself for what you did to our Mary. George may be daft enough to believe all your tales of little misunderstandings and sudden attacks of the 'flu but you and I know better than that, don't we, Mrs Cree? Och, aye,' she nodded, 'I may be getting on in years but the brain's still working. You're lucky I don't get the law to you. If I'd known what was going on . . .' She left the rest to Archie's imagination.

Archie growled and faced his mother again. 'Will you get inside the bloody house before the whole street comes to see what's going on.' He couldn't face any more humiliation.

'That's right, Archie Cree, run away indoors where your mammy can look after you,' Ina taunted. Then, 'How did you know where to find her?' she yelled after him.

Archie was going to ignore her but suddenly saw a way

to make trouble for the Innes's. 'George let me see a letter from her,' he yelled back before disappearing into the welcome darkness of his parents' home to lick his wounds.

Ina watched him with a grim smile on her thin lips. Settling her old shabby coat more firmly round her shoulders she redirected her steps to the prefab. George Innes would feel as sorry for himself as Archie did by the time she'd finished with him.

SIXTEEN

Maxine spent the next two days trudging round the boarding houses and cafés in the thriving coastal villages, desperately seeking work. Without success. It was the worst possible time to be job hunting. The season was drawing to a close so the landladies were gradually shutting up their rooms and winding down for the approaching winter. So, too, were the few cafés. Even without the disadvantage of the season she knew that as soon as she admitted to working with the show people many prospective employers lost interest.

Back in her rooms she counted the very few pounds she had managed to save and faced the fact that she could soon be destitute. Much as she loved Kilweem she knew there was no chance of her remaining there throughout the winter unless she could find a job locally, and that possibility was becoming more and more remote with each passing day. Reluctantly she faced the awful prospect of moving on, to a larger town, possibly Dundee or even Edinburgh. The idea appalled her but she knew there was no logical alternative.

Oh God! she thought. Why did she have to make such a hash of everything? Why did everything in her life turn sour? First her mother walking out and destroying what should have been a carefree childhood; then Paul Kinsail and, she admitted, her own stupidity, putting an end to any chance she might have had of a successful career; she then compounded all the mistakes she had made there by marrying Archie Cree and turning her life into a hellish, living nightmare. And now her frantic bid for freedom in ruins, simply because she couldn't find a decent job.

Well, she wouldn't let it happen. 'I don't want to leave Kilweem.' she told herself, looking fondly round the room that was hers to do what she liked in, relishing the total independence she had found here. 'I won't leave Kilweem.' Even if she had to scrub floors she was staying right here. Yes, she decided, this was where she wanted to live and this was where she would stay. To give in now and move on would be to become a victim of circumstance, again. For the sake of her pride she couldn't let that happen. This was her life and she was in control. She was happy in her little flat, loved the village and respected the proud reservation of the villagers, even if that trait did mean she had not made any friends yet.

Although there were six other flats in the building, two on each of the floors below her attic rooms, Maxine had been disappointed in her fellow tenants. Not that they were unpleasant, far from it. Most were friendly and would nod and pass the time of day for a minute or two, but there was no one with whom she was likely to strike up a real friendship, no one who would share some of her lonely hours. An elderly couple had one of the ground-floor flats and the other was occupied by a couple with two young children. The young woman, a girl not far from Maxine's age, looked permanently harassed and could be heard shouting at her children, even in the attic. Above them were two old ladies, sisters, Maxine guessed, who entertained other elderly ladies to bridge afternoons, and an elderly gentleman who was very rarely seen. On the floor below Maxine was what she had assumed was an empty flat but turned out to be inhabited by a merchant seaman who had appeared during the last week. He was a middle-aged widower, jolly and talkative, but was home for less than two months in every year. The remaining flat was occupied by the spinster headmistress of the local primary school. In an effort to be friendly Maxine had smiled and offered her the same cheerful greeting she gave to her other neighbours, only to be ignored. She persevered for a couple of weeks before finally accepting that the woman simply refused to acknowledge her. Maxine suspected her connection with the showfolk was to blame. Still, she consoled herself, her great aunt and uncle would be returning home any day now, and surely they would offer some sort of friendship.

But she had more pressing problems than her lack of companionship. If she wanted to stay in Kilweem she had to earn the money to pay her rent. Perhaps Mrs Dalgleish could help . . . she might be able to use some help round the house . . . anything would do. Or maybe she could work as a barmaid. Or even, when she had explained her situation to her Uncle Maurice . . . but no, pride wouldn't let her ask him for a job.

A loud knock at her door startled her, breaking her line of thought just when she felt she might come up with some inspired idea. Feeling rather irritable she opened the door a crack and peered round the edge. 'Yes?' she asked the rather solemn young man she found on her threshold.

'Ah . . . Miss Lennox?'

'Yes.'

'I am Callum Mackie,' he introduced himself. 'The Curate of St Peters, the Episcopal church . . . on Fishergate?' She nodded. 'Your landlady, Mrs Dalgleish, is one of our parishioners. She happened to mention that you have just moved to the village. The Rector or I try to get round to seeing everyone who comes into the area, in case there's anything we can do to help. And, of course, to say that you are very welcome at St Peters.' He offered it all as a well-rehearsed speech and without the trace of a smile.

'I don't go to church,' she said flatly. 'And if I did it

wouldn't be to St Peters. I'm Church of Scotland.' She was certainly much too preoccupied with the problem of finding a job to care if that sounded terse and ungrateful. In any case, this young man was rather too sincere.

'That's what they all say,' he agreed, sadly. Mrs Dalgleish had hinted that the girl might be finding it hard to make friends in the village. And no wonder if she was as rude as this to everyone. Still, it was his Christian duty to do what he could for her. 'Do you think I might come in for a minute?' he asked, half-hoping she might say no. 'I can give you the times of the services and there are a fairly good range of other activities too. Women's group, young wives, open discussions, that sort of thing.'

There was no way she could refuse without being downright rude. 'I suppose so.' She stood back and ushered him inside, wishing he would just go away and leave her to think through all possible ways of finding a job to see her through the winter in Kilweem.

'Well, Maxine . . . it is Maxine, isn't it?'

She nodded, thinking him unbearably pompous for such a young person.

'How are you settling into Kilweem?' Forced cheerfulness disguised the fact that he was very well aware of what she thought of him, masking too his uneasiness when meeting people for the first time. This particular aspect of his job made him feel more like a door-to-door salesman than an ordained clergyman.

'OK,' she replied, non-committally. 'Would you like a cup of tea or something?' He looked so cold that she felt duty-bound to offer something.

'Please.' He smiled at last, giving her a brief glimpse of the real Callum Mackie. Not realising how difficult he found it to maintain the rather dour façade which the older ladies, who made up the bulk of his congregation, seemed to expect of him, she was astonished by the change that grin wrought on his features, making him look much more approachable.

'Give me a couple of minutes.'

She escaped to the kitchen and returned, five minutes later, with a tray bearing tea things. Always careful of his manners, Reverend Mackie jumped to help her. As she moved his coat flapped open revealing his clerical collar. It suited him, she thought, giving him a rather distinguished air which was emphasised by the surprisingly stylish cut of his plain, grey suit.

They applied themselves to their tea, making the insubstantial small-talk which was the backbone of his professional visits, and took the opportunity to assess one another more closely.

Callum Mackie was, she guessed, in his late twenties and of average height and build but his broad shoulders hinted at an athletic physique which wasn't immediately obvious as he sat muffled in top coat and suit. He had thick, dark blond hair which had a tendency to wave at the ends and watchful, rather intense, blue eyes. They were set in a square-jawed, determined-looking face. It was the sort of face, she thought, that invited you to rely on its owner. His voice was deep but softly pitched and tightly controlled, giving Maxine the impression that he thought deeply before committing anything to speech. In fact he was altogether too serious. He should smile more often and get rid of that slightly worried expression. Actually, she realised with surprise, he was quite good-looking when he smiled. It was rather a waste, she thought irreverently, for a clergyman to be so handsome.

'Do you visit everyone who comes to Kilweem?' she asked, aware that a pause in the lurching conversation had become uncomfortably long.

'Either myself or the Rector. Though to be honest we don't recruit many new parishioners that way. But I do enjoy getting to know everyone, whatever their beliefs. Ours is the only Episcopal church in this part of Strathannan and the parish includes most of the fishing villages. I'm sure it's one of the most beautiful parishes in the whole country.'

'Really?'

'I hear you're working with Rosie at the shows,' he said when it was obvious she wasn't in the least bit interested in his scattered parish.

'I was. You seem to know a lot about me,' she challenged, more sharply than she had meant to.

'It's the nature of the job. People tell you things.' Now he was uncomfortable. 'I'm sorry if you think I'm prying. You don't have to tell me anything. That's not why I'm here.'

'Why are you here?'

'As I said, Mrs Dalgleish happened to mention you. She's a very well-meaning woman really. I know she can appear to be a bit stern and abrupt but that's because she's in constant pain from her arthritis. Most people would have given in and taken to a wheelchair by now, but she refuses to give up her independence. She's a very strong-minded woman. She seems to be a fair landlady too, really cares about her tenants. When old Ruthie was ill, Mrs Dalgleish spent hours up here, looking after her, doing things more suited to a nurse. Far more than the old woman's family ever did for her . . . I expect you've heard about old Ruthie? This was her room.'

Maxine was seeing her landlady in a rather different light. 'Mrs Muir? Yes, Rosie told me about her.'

'Well, you see, I happened to ask Mrs Dalgleish if the room had been re-let and she told me about you. She's worried in case you were feeling a bit lonely on your own. So I thought I'd call in.'

'To cheer me up?' she teased him now.

He reddened slightly. 'I know how difficult it can be, settling into a new place. Especially a village like this. People tend to stick with the folk they've known all their lives and regard anyone else as an interloper.' He was smiling at her now, a smile of genuine friendliness which softened his blue eyes and banished the perpetually worried expression which marred his face.

'I know what you mean,' she agreed. 'The villagers seem to keep pretty much to themselves but at least they aren't openly hostile, like some of the showfolk were.'

'Yes. The locals aren't that bad, thank goodness,' he sighed. 'I have tried to get to know the show people, after all they are here for two months every year, but they simply walk away or else say something they know I'll find offensive. They're a completely closed community. With no time for the likes of me. They're due to move on soon, will you go with them?'

'No . . .' She shrugged and met his eyes directly for the first time. 'Like you say, they don't accept outsiders easily. As a matter of fact I'm not working there any more.'

'So, what will you do? Have you found another job?'

'No. Not yet.' She wished he wouldn't keep asking questions.

'What about the boarding houses, would they have something?'

'Not at this time of the year.'

'Ah . . . And the other villages? Anstruther's a fair size, you might have a better chance there.'

'I've already tried.' She saw he'd finished his tea but didn't offer to replenish his cup. The sooner he left her in peace the better.

'What sort of work are you after? Waitressing? Cooking? What about shop work?'

She sighed, loud enough to be sure he heard her. 'Anything really, though I'm a trained cook so I'd prefer to get something where I can put my diploma and three years at college to good use.' She put that in on purpose, eager to make him understand that she wasn't just some shiftless, casual worker. 'The trouble is, this is the wrong time of year to be looking for anything like that in this area.'

'But you will stay here?' he watched her carefully.

'Oh yes, I'll find a job of some sort,' she said with impressive conviction. 'I love Kilweem. It's such a beautiful village. So peaceful. I really do want to stay.'

'It is lovely, isn't it?' he agreed enthusiastically. 'I was absolutely delighted to be sent here. I fully expected to be packed off to Glasgow or somewhere. I don't think I would take to city life very easily, though, of course, it's my duty to go wherever the Church needs me.'

'You've not been here long, then?' she asked, feeling obliged to make an effort.

'Six months in Kilweem but I do come from Strathannan. My parents live in Coustrie. Your accent sounds pretty local, too.'

'I'm from Craigie. It's a mining village on the other side of Inverannan. That's why I love it here so much. I remember it from day trips when I was a kid, to visit my mother's aunt and uncle.' She deliberately avoided enlarging on that, feeling he knew far too much about her already. 'It seemed such a magical place then and so different from the mining villages. No bings, no ugly pits, no one coughing themselves to death and the air's so clean here. You would never think it's only fifteen miles from somewhere as awful as Craigie.'

'Yes,' he said, thoughtfully. 'Those villages can seem pretty dreadful, but, even so, they've got tremendous character of their own. But perhaps it's hard to see if you've lived there all your life. Some of the locals here seem to take Kilweem so much for granted, don't see anything at all special about the place.'

269

He was obviously the sort who looked for good in everything, she thought disgustedly.

'You'd be hard put to find anything attractive about Craigie,' she insisted, a hint of bitterness in her voice which he didn't miss. 'It spoils Strathannan. The river, the hills, the pretty little towns and this marvellous coast and then, just when you're least expecting it, there they are, Craigie, Blairwood, Oakdene and Valleydrum, like four warts, spoiling the countryside for miles around . . . Oh, I would hate to go back.'

'You're not thinking of doing that, are you?' he asked, the worried frown marring his face again.

'No,' she said with absolute certainty. 'I am going to get a job, somehow, and stay here. I don't suppose you need any help at St Whatsits, do you?'

He chuckled with delight. This girl really was different. 'St Peters. No, we're quite well served thanks. Unless you fancy your chances with the Brownies – voluntary work, naturally.'

'Eh . . . no, maybe not. I was thinking more along the lines of earning some money to pay the rent.' She was beaming back at him now.

Abruptly he sprang to his feet, checking his watch. 'I didn't realise the time! I'd better go. I've a whole list of people to see. Some of them rely on me turning up at precisely the same time every fortnight. Thanks for the tea, Maxine. And good luck with the job hunting.' He was half-way through the door before she could answer. Then he turned back suddenly, almost bumping into her. 'Maxine, please remember that I am always available if you need anyone to talk to, or if there's anything I can help you with.'

She smiled, embarrassed now. 'Thanks, I'll remember.'

'And it really doesn't matter, you know,' he shouted back from half-way down the stairs.

'What doesn't?' she called, leaning over the banister to catch a glimpse of his rapidly disappearing form.

'That you're not an Episcopalian,' he called back. 'It makes no difference to me and I suspect God doesn't mind either. You are very welcome at St Peters, whatever your denomination.'

She laughed aloud, waved then went back into her room, still smiling. Initially Callum Mackie had been humourless, intense, slightly smug and altogether irritating but, amazingly, in the end, she had enjoyed his visit.

When she sat down to answer Janette's latest letter she included a whole paragraph describing him.

Ina hated using the telephone. Especially when the conversation was as difficult as this one was likely to be. She had been trying this number without success for a week before she finally thought of calling the local post office. If Craigie was anything to go by the post master would know almost everything there was to know about the Kilweemers. She had been right. Mrs and Miss Archibold were on holiday and weren't due back for another week yet.

That week had given Ina plenty of time to consider whether this course of action was wise. After all, she had refused any contact with her family since she was a mere nineteen years old, pregnant and disowned by them.

She had met Joe Lennox when he and some friends had come to Kilweem, full of laughter and confidence, and had fallen instantly in love with her broad-shouldered miner. The lads had been brash and loud, attracting the attention of the whole sleepy village which had looked at these rough miners with silent disapproval. Ina's family had been very quickly alerted to the fact that she had been seen hanging on the arm of some dirty collier by the entire village. Furiously they had banned her from ever seeing him again, turning the unhappy Joe away from their door each time he came calling. But it had already been too late.

In the end, when her ballooning abdomen could no longer be decently contained by any of her clothes, they had been forced to confront the truth. Ina was called a number of names which she simply could not forget and then cast into solitary confinement, for all the world as if she carried some contamination. Joe Lennox found himself face to face with Mr Archibold and his oldest son, Maurice who punched him squarely on the jaw, breaking several teeth before demanding that he do the decent thing. A month later nineteen-year-old Ina, cast off without so much as a farthing by her moderately prosperous family, found herself in the meanest village in Strathannan, married to the man she loved but living in squalor in a cottage so base and filthy that she hadn't thought such places existed, a place no self-respecting Kilweem fisherman would dare to call a house. There was no furniture, no running water, no warm bread, fresh from her family's oven and no hope of them relenting and responding to her appeals for help.

Her son, Jackie, was born on the floor without even the aid of a midwife. From that day to this Ina had refused all contact with her family, even when her brother together with her older sister, had formally taken over the bakery on their father's death, and invited her to visit them, even offering her a home. Nothing could persuade her to go creeping back there, taking what would be their charity. The fact that Evelyn had felt sorry for her aunt and uncle, now alone in the world, had been a source of bitter disagreement between them. But now the time had come to swallow her pride and ask for their help. But only Mary, her favourite grandchild, though she would never admit to liking any of them much, could ever have brought her to this situation. Damn the stupid girl for acting so foolishly, when she herself had warned her where her ill-advised marriage would lead.

Ina walked quickly through the dark village and slipped into the phone box. By some miracle, although the box itself was daubed with obscenities and the glass was lying inches deep on the concrete floor, the actual telephone was in working order. She coughed, fiddled with her change then dialled ponderously. Maurice and Maureen should be home by now.

Callum saw the light was on in the Archibolds' flat as he hurried from his visit to his newest parishioner. On impulse he made his way round to the back of the bakery to their entrance. One ring on the bell was enough to bring Maureen to the door.

'Reverend Mackie!' she exclaimed, her pleasure unfeigned.

'Good evening, Miss Archibold,' he greeted her, cheerfully. 'I saw your light on so I thought I'd just say hello. When did you get back?'

'Half an hour ago,' she laughed, looking up at him. Maureen resembled nothing more than a busy little bird when placed up against the solid figure of the curate. Even while she spoke to him she was unable to be still, her hands, her feet and her face, all in constant motion.

'Oh . . . I didn't realise it was so recent . . . I won't disturb you now, you must be tired after your journey. I'll catch you during the week, unless I see you at church before then.' He turned to go.

'Och, come away in, will you. You know we're always pleased to see you and Maurice will be glad of some male company after having to listen to me wittering on for the past three weeks.' She was off up the stairs before he could object. 'Maurice is in the sitting room. Just go on through. I'll be with you in a wee minute,' she added when he caught up with her on the upper landing.

'Well, Reverend Mackie, it's good to see you. Good to be back in my own home, too,' Maurice rumbled, rising with difficulty to shake the younger man's hand then towering over him, his bulk seeming to fill the room. 'You'll take a wee dram with me, I hope?'

A tumbler of neat whisky found its way into Callum's hand and he raised it to Maurice. 'Thanks. To your good health, Maurice.'

'And yours.' Maurice tipped the amber liquid into his mouth and rolled it round his tongue appreciatively. 'Well, Reverend. It's not the warmest of nights to be out and about but this'll warm you more than any thick coat or woollen long johns would do.' He regarded the younger man good-humouredly from under rather wild, white eyebrows.

'That it will. I've been visiting a new parishioner and saw your light on when I drove past. I really only called in to see if you'd enjoyed your holiday.'

'You're welcome at any time, and you know it, I hope, by now,' Maureen said, bustling into the room with a plate of freshly-made drop scones.

'Maureen! I hope you haven't made these for me,' Callum said.

'Indeed I have! Two minutes' work. See you've not even managed to drink your whisky in the time it took me to make these. Now, eat them while they're hot. Here's the butter.'

'Thanks.' Callum tucked into the fresh pancakes with obvious enjoyment. 'So,' he asked, licking butter from his fingers. 'How was your holiday?'

'I can't imagine why Maureen thought we should travel more than two hundred miles just to see mountains that are not a patch on what we've got in the Highlands,' Maurice grunted. 'And what's more it rained most of the bloody time!'

'Maurice!' Maureen wailed.

Callum laughed. 'I take it the Lake District wasn't to your taste then?'

'Well, it might have been if a man had been allowed just to sit and enjoy himself but I was obliged to visit every square inch of the place, wasn't I? Coach tours round miles of soggy hills, boat trips down windswept lakes, in and out of gift shops and tripping over Americans in every village.'

'Maurice's idea of enjoying himself was visiting every bakery he could find then criticising everything it produced in front of other customers. It was very embarrassing,' Maureen chuckled, thoroughly enjoying the sparring match with her brother. 'Actually we both enjoyed it. It made a change and it is the first holiday we've had in years.'

'And what about your arthritis, Maurice?' Callum asked, knowing full well that it was ill health which had forced the elderly man to embark on his first real holiday in years. 'I thought you looked a little less stiff when I came in.'

'Aye. It's no worse anyway.' Maurice levered his huge frame out of the chair and tried to pour another generous shot into Callum's glass. The curate hastily covered it with his hand.

'I've another two visits to make. I can't be turning up on people's doorsteps reeking of whisky! I'll have to chew on some mints as it is.'

Everyone laughed and Maureen asked, 'Didn't you say

you were visiting a new parishioner before you came here? Is it someone new to the village then?'

'Yes. She's a very young woman, in her twenties I should think. Small, blonde, very attractive. I'm sure you'll see her about the place. She's one of Mrs Dalgleish's tenants. That's why I went to see her. Mrs Dalgleish asked me to look in on her.'

'She's a good-hearted old soul, Mrs Dalgleish,' Maurice commented.

'And are we likely to see this young woman at church?' Maureen, who liked to keep abreast of what went on in the village, asked.

'I doubt it . . .' Callum admitted. 'But you might have her calling on you to ask for a job. She's looking for work in the village . . . Good Lord, look at the time! I really must get on now. I was late even before I stopped in here. Thanks for the dram, and the scones. I'll see you both at church.' The impatient ringing of the phone cut their farewells short.

'Well!' Maurice set the phone back in its cradle and eased his aching limbs into his high-backed chair. 'Well, well, well.'

'Are you going to let me in on the secret?' Maureen demanded impatiently, returning from the kitchen, where she had been washing up, eager to know who had been calling at this hour.

'That was our sister . . .' Maurice said.

'Ina!' Maureen gasped.

'Unless you know of another sister no one's told me about.'

'Good God! After all this time. What did she want, Maurice? Oh Lord, it's not bad news is it?' Something traumatic must have happened for Ina to get in touch after all this time.

'No, no, nothing like that . . .' Maurice mused, still

startled by his sister's request. 'Just listen for a minute or
two and I'll tell you what she said.'

Maxine saw the light over the bakery and knew her great
aunt and uncle were home. Half of her longed to see them.
The other half, the proud half, was reluctant to introduce
herself and have to admit that she was unemployed, almost
destitute, that a whole series of failures had driven her
here. Maxine decided to have one more day hunting for
employment before calling on her elderly relatives. It
would be so much better if she could visit them as a self-
sufficient, independent young woman.

When she left her flat to catch the bus down to Sauchar,
hoping there might be work for her there, she saw at once
that the bakery was open for business again. Unable to
resist the temptation she ambled across the road and risked
a quick look inside, wondering if she would even recognise
her aunt and uncle after all this time. But the tall, generously proportioned woman who was serving behind the
counter was definitely not Aunt Maureen who was,
Maxine recalled, tiny. She peered into the back of the
shop, then moved to the adjacent window and peeped into
the café, but it was deserted. Then, just as she was about
to move off, her eye was caught by a postcard in the
window which hadn't been there yesterday.

WANTED.
BAKERY ASSISTANT
MUST BE QUALIFIED AND EXPERIENCED
AND WILLING TO SERVE BEHIND COUNTER
apply within

Maurice and Maureen had discussed their great niece's
plight long and hard before finally deciding on this plan.

If the girl needed a job then she would certainly see this notice and, if she was interested, apply. That way she wouldn't think the post had been manufactured specially for her. Indeed, they did desperately need some help in the bakery.

For the past twenty years, the brother and sister had run the bakery together, taking pride in producing items of exceptionally fine quality. Other than employing local women as part-time counter assistants in the shop and café, until now they had refused to consider hiring professional help in the bakery, loath to risk losing the personal touch on which their reputation was built. But, as Maurice's condition steadily worsened and every task took longer, there were more and more days when he knew he had failed to meet his own exacting standards. Maureen found too much of the workload falling on to her own shoulders.

Their problems had been compounded over the past five years as the village expanded, bringing new customers who rapidly grew to appreciate the bakery's products while the influx of tourists during the summer months injected new life into the quiet little café. During the most recent summer season it had become clear that the brother and sister could no longer manage without expert help. To find that their niece, a qualified cook, had come to the village and was apparently looking for work, seemed like a minor miracle.

Unable to believe what she was reading, Maxine hesitated for a full minute before finally walking into the shop and explaining to the surprised assistant that she had come about the job, advertised in the window.

'Job . . . Well, Hen, the best thing to do is take a wee seat in the café and I'll tell Miss Archibold you're here.'

Maxine waited, getting more and more nervous as the minutes ticked away.

Meanwhile, Maurice was busy cleaning flour from his hands while Maureen waited for him impatiently.

'Remember,' she hissed at him as they made their way to the still-deserted café. 'She mustn't know Ina called us about her. We did promise.'

Maxine leapt to her feet when the door behind the counter of the café swung open. There was absolutely no mistaking Uncle Maurice. He seemed to reduce the café to toy town proportions. Beside him Great Aunt Maureen was equally recognisable, as restless and lively as she had always been. 'Good morning, Lass,' Maurice greeted her affably, as he would any other applicant. 'You've come about the job, then?'

'Yes.' Maxine nodded then gave her new name, relieved that they hadn't recognised her. It would be better, she thought, to apply for this job and be judged purely on her merits. That way she wouldn't feel unduly indebted, if she was successful, and the elderly couple wouldn't feel obliged to employ her simply because she was their niece.

'Well, you've not had a lot of experience,' Maurice said after a tour of the bakery and a lengthy interview. Maxine's heart fell into her stomach. She had been so sure she would be successful. 'But,' he added, looking back at his notes, 'your qualifications are first class. I don't see why we shouldn't suit one another, provided you are prepared to work as hard as you say you are. What do you say, Maureen?'

'Do you still want to work with us here?' his sister asked.

'Oh yes. Very much,' Maxine confirmed, eagerness shining from her eyes.

'Then when can you start?' Maureen smiled.

'As soon as you like. Today . . .'

'Och, I think tomorrow would be just fine, Lass,' Maurice said, exchanging a look with his sister that was

279

part satisfaction, part puzzlement. Would this young girl admit who she really was? He hoped so. She had struck him as an honest young woman, giving candid reasons for her presence in the village without going into unnecessary detail and he would be disappointed in her if she felt unable to reveal her true identity now that she had the job. It could make things very awkward for them all if she didn't.

Maxine thanked them, feeling jubilant but then knew she had to do the decent thing. The ageing couple listened in silence while she explained her situation in more detail.

'Please don't think I was trying to deceive you,' their great niece pleaded when they had expressed their surprise. 'I thought if I told you who I was first, you might feel you had to give me the job . . .'

'Och, Lass.' Maureen, feeling hugely emotional took Maxine's hand over the table. 'I'm just sorry we weren't here when you arrived . . . As for the job, it's yours, fair and square.'

'Aye,' Maurice chuckled. 'You'll be treated just like anyone else. Hard work for fair pay. But we're glad to have you, Lass. Very glad to have you.' Even Maurice's eyes seemed more rheumy than normal.

'Right then.' Businesslike again, Maureen looked at the wall clock. 'Eight-thirty tomorrow morning. We'll see you then, Lass, but now we have to get back to work.'

Anxious to be in good time for her first day at Kilweem's village bakery, Maxine was up and dressed before eight o'clock. She walked briskly up Marketgate, hunching against the stiff breeze which gave the first hint of approaching winter, thinking wryly about the change in her life. What big plans and ambitions she had had when she left college, even when she and Archie got married. What wonderful opportunities wasted. Not that she could ever regret leaving such a bitter and violent man, but now she was nothing more than a bakery assistant. No better than those girls she had so pitied who had left school at the first opportunity to work in factories and shops. But not for long, she promised herself. A working bakery with a small café attached would offer her plenty of chance to broaden her experience. It was up to her to make sure she benefited from it and learned everything she possibly could about running a business, ready for the day when she would buy a small restaurant of her very own. But, as she walked into the small bakery on that first day, those ambitions seemed impossibly far-fetched. The wages she would be paid here would never allow her to save the sort of money needed to set up in business on her own.

Maxine arrived at the bakery with ten minutes to spare but it was obvious that her great aunt and uncle had been watching out for her. They greeted her warmly, introduced her to the other staff then sat her down with a cup of coffee while they outlined her responsibilities. They were warm and friendly and already Maxine knew she was going to like them and felt she would be at home in the small but busy bakery and tea shop.

Her childhood memories of her aunt and uncle had been little more than a vague recollection of a huge, kind man and a tiny, talkative woman. But, during her interview, Maurice and Maureen Archibold had both made very strong and individual impressions on her. Filling in some gaps in her knowledge of the family history, Maurice had told her he had trained at his father's side in this very bakery, more than fifty years ago. It was obvious that he prided himself on his skill as a baker and confectioner. A huge mountain of a man he delighted in producing delicately iced, feathery-light cakes which were a miracle of dexterity from someone with hands as big as his were. But now, in his early seventies, he was suffering from arthritis. Moving around was increasingly painful and the joints of his hands were stiff and inflamed making his work at the craft he loved more and more arduous. He warned Maxine that he could be bad-tempered at times.

His sister, Maureen, was only two years his junior. A natural organiser, her responsibilities included the running of the shop and small café attached to it, and all the associated paperwork. As tiny as her brother was large she was quite unable to sit still for more than two minutes at a time. Despite the forty years which separated them Maureen could easily match Maxine in terms of sheer energy. Her mind, like her body, was brisk, neat and precise.

Maxine soon saw that Maurice and Maureen were strict and exacting, allowing no compromises in the quality of their products. However, they also controlled their small empire with fairness and discipline, commanding respect and affection quite effortlessly from everyone on their small staff. Maxine was no exception. In her element in the scrupulously clean and efficient bakery and café, she sparkled with life and boundless vitality, and felt an instant rapport with her elderly employers.

As he had warned, Maurice could be tetchy at times, apt to become frustrated by the limitations imposed by his disability and inclined to be sharp with anyone who tried to help him with something he had determined to do for himself. Sympathising deeply and knowing he was an otherwise fair and cheerful man Maxine took it all in good heart and soon learned when to help and when to step back. She felt deep admiration for his refusal to give in and treated him with precisely the right combination of respect and affection which the normally reserved Maurice found himself returning wholeheartedly.

Maxine's warm personality, her obvious talent for cooking and baking, along with her keen approach to her job, won all-round approval. It was easy to do well in such a happy environment.

The only place in Kilweem which served any kind of hot food, the café attached to the bakery was incredibly busy during the holiday season. But, as summer cooled into a damp and dismal autumn followed by wintery storms and freezing mists which finally chased even the hardiest visitors away, the café reverted to being a warm refuge for local women on their daily round of shopping. Women who wanted nothing more than a cozy chat, a good, plain scone and a piping cup of strong tea. When she was working in the café, Maxine gradually found she was greeted cheerfully by the majority of regular customers, young and old. None of them offered close friendship and by now she had come to understand that the real villagers, although they were invariably polite and offered a brief greeting if they passed her in the street, would never see her as truly belonging to their tight knit community.

However, she wasn't entirely alone. Eileen Crombie, who worked at the post office, next door to the bakery, and whose widowed mother ran one of the guest houses on the far side of the village, was inclined to be friendly and often chatted to Maxine for a few minutes over lunch. Before long the two young women found they were sharing the occasional shopping trip or a visit to the pictures.

Even more than her new friendship with Eileen, Maxine valued the warm relationship she was building with her aunt. Despite the vast difference in their ages the two women were delighted when an instant liking for one another had developed into an unlikely but close friendship. Maureen became Maxine's trusted confidante, the willing keeper of her hopes and dreams, and encouraged Maxine to believe that, one day, those dreams would become reality. Maxine shared Maureen's concern for

283

Maurice's health and caught some of the older woman's irrepressible zest for life. They enjoyed shopping trips, companionable evenings over a bottle of wine and moments of wonderful humour.

But, glad as she was of Eileen's rather light-hearted company and much as she valued her friendship with Maureen, there could never be anything like the unselfish, caring intimacy she had shared with Janette.

As was her habit Maxine wrote to Janette, telling her every detail of her life. The equally long and descriptive letters she got back from her friend were treasured monthly highlights. It made her achingly sad to know that Janette and Jamie were not as idyllically happy as everyone had supposed they would be. From Janette's letters Maxine knew that their dream of a wonderful future in Canada had disintegrated leaving them disillusioned and homesick. Things had started to go wrong from the day of their arrival when the job which had been promised to Jamie had turned out to be nothing better than poorly-paid day labouring. Then they had discovered that Jamie's uncle, who had promised there was plenty of room for them to live in his house until they were established, could offer them only a bed settee in the living room for which he expected to be paid a sum amounting to the whole of Jamie's wages. His wife obviously looked on Janette as a personal maid and unpaid nanny to her four children. After two weeks the young couple moved into an apartment of their own which Janette described as miserable, depressing and outrageously expensive. Their misfortunes were crowned by an accident at work which left Jamie with a broken ankle and swallowed every penny of their savings in medical bills. Despite her qualifications and experience, which were similar to Maxine's, Janette found herself working shifts in a hospital canteen as nothing more than a lowly kitchen hand. Desperate to find a well-paid job

Jamie had left Janette in their flat in Victoria and gone into the mountains to work in the mines there. From her latest letter Maxine knew her friend was lonely and depressed, that her relationship with Jamie was in danger of breaking down under the enforced separation. Janette longed to come home, even for a visit, but knew it was impossible. Maxine wrote back quickly, trying her best to sound positive and encouraging and regretting that she could do nothing more practical to help.

SEVENTEEN

'Maureen, can I ask you something?' Maxine said one night, as the two women shared a cup of coffee after the shop and café were closed.

'Sure. Fire away,' the older woman said, watching her niece closely.

'Well . . . what happened, Maureen? Between you and Uncle Maurice and my family. We used to come here as kids but that was years ago . . . I had almost forgotten you lived here.'

Maureen sighed. 'Those were great times, weren't they, when you all used to trail up here for the day . . . ? It was lovely for Maurice and me . . . To have all you children rushing round the place, waking us up . . . making us realise what we'd missed, not having families of our own. I'm surprised you remember much about it, Lass. You were just a bairn then.'

Maxine laughed. 'It was coming here, to see you, that made me love these villages. I used to think they were in a different country, they're so different to Craigie. Have you ever been there, Maureen?'

'Yes. Just a couple of times, though. I called to see your father, after your mother went . . . And I went there to see Ina . . .'

'I don't remember.'

'No . . . you were too young and the day I called to see George, after your mother left you all,' Maxine heard the disapproval in her great aunt's voice, 'you were all at school.'

'And was that the last time you saw my father?'

'Yes. Och, Maurice and me, we went there to see if there was anything we could do . . . stupid really. Insensitive. It was too soon after your mother walked out. Your father, he was shattered by the whole thing you know. I see that now but at the time he just made me mad.'

'What happened?' Maxine was intrigued.

'Well, we walked in . . . the place was a complete mess . . .'

'It always was,' Maxine laughed, loyalty to her father preventing her from adding that it still was.

'Aye. But with four youngsters and no wife . . . and those places are so small, even a teaspoon left lying looks untidy. But you see, I've never had children. I didn't understand what it must be like for him . . . anyway I started to clear up, you know me. I can't be still. If something's needing to be done then I simply have to do it. Your father didn't take it very kindly.'

'No . . . I suppose he wouldn't,' Maxine agreed.

'But to make matters worse it wasn't even lunch-time and your father had been in the pub when we arrived. The woman next door told us where he was and Maurice went to fetch him home. Well, he was hardly able to walk! I was shocked I can tell you. Out of his mind before midday and with four weans to look after. Maurice gave him a piece of his mind and they ended up roaring at each other. In the end George told us to get out and not bother coming back.'

'And that's what you did?' Maxine asked, incredulously.

'Aye, Lass. Real stupidity, eh? You see, your father was drunk right enough but it was less than a week after your mother left him. He was still in shock, but we made no allowances, none at all. The sad thing is we'd come to see what we could do to help. Maybe take you children for a holiday in the summer, maybe even have one of you to live. We wondered about David coming to stay with us, learning the trade . . . or you. Any one of the four of you would have been welcome . . . And look what happened. We ended up not speaking. Haven't spoken to this day to your father . . .'

'You sent me a wedding present,' Maxine reminded her.

'Aye. We'd a line from your Uncle Jackie about that. He always keeps in touch. Christmas cards and the like, though we never see him, either.' Her voice was laced with regret. 'So you see, Lass, when you turned up in Kilweem, it was the best thing that could have happened to us. We've no one else but our Ina's family.'

'Why did you and Uncle Maurice never marry?' Maxine asked, determined to find out as much about her family as she could.

'Maurice never had time to find himself a wife. He was married to the business,' Maureen said with deceptive lightness.

'What about you, Maureen? Why didn't you get married?' Curiosity was getting the better of good manners.

But Maureen was not offended. 'I was never asked,' she answered, simply.

Maxine gaped. Her aunt, though aged, still bore signs of the woman she must once have been. Her face was small, heart-shaped with high cheekbones and a skin which, even now, was smooth and healthy looking. Her eyes were bright and lively, frequently sparkling with laughter – Maureen had a well-developed sense of the ridiculous. Surely she must have been a very attractive young woman. 'Why not?' she asked without thinking.

'I never had the chance,' her aunt admitted, wistfully. 'When my mother died someone had to look after Father. Maurice was busy with the shop, Ina, your grandmother, had already gone to live in Craigie . . . but you already know all about that. I was the only one who could do it. Then, when Father died, Maurice couldn't manage the bakery on his own, so I stayed . . . and I'm still here now.' She smiled again and looked up at her sad-faced niece. 'Don't you go feeling sorry for me, Lass. From what I see of marriage in this family it's just as well I stayed single. And I've been happy enough.'

'I'd say you did the right thing,' said Maxine, with some feeling.

'Och, Lass, don't let this Archie make you bitter,' Maureen warned. 'There's other men, decent men, in the world. And I don't see you as a single woman somehow.'

'Well I do! I can make my own way without some bloke in tow. I'm going to have my own business one day, Maureen and I don't need a man to help me do that.'

'I know how ambitious you are but making money isn't what life's all about.'

'It's not the money! It's independence. Not having to rely on someone else. Proving to myself that I can make a success of something. God knows I've managed to make a mess of everything else so far.'

Maureen sighed, frightened that her niece was going to let bitterness and guilt mould the rest of her life. 'You have got to learn to put your marriage behind you, Maxine. Forget about it, about him and don't let it sour the rest of your life.'

Maxine smiled at her aunt fondly. 'Let's not talk about me any more. We always seem to get round to me and what I want. Tell me more about you.'

'Like what? I've had a very dull life. There's nothing left to tell.'

'Then tell me about my gran. Why do you and Uncle Maurice not speak to her? I know about the baby and everything, but surely that was between her and your parents?'

Maureen looked momentarily disconcerted. 'Ah . . . That's difficult. Let's just say we've all been too stubborn and proud.'

Maxine sighed. 'That sounds like our family doesn't it?'

Maureen smiled wryly. 'Aye. Pride has been the cause of most of our troubles and your grandmother has her fair share of it, that's for sure.'

'Do you and Maurice really want to get back together with the family again after all that's happened?'

'Och, you'll never know how much we've wanted that. More so as we've got older. And wiser,' she added ruefully. 'There's nothing like knowing you're running out of time for making you regret how much of it you've wasted in the past. But it's too late.'

'Maybe not . . .' Maxine murmured to herself. 'Maybe not.'

Maurice, with the aid of a driving school, had been teaching Maxine to drive. It was a traumatic experience for both of them. Terrified by what he considered to be her unbridled confidence and her insistence on driving on the speed limit rather than the full ten miles an hour below it which he felt to be sensible with all the mad drivers on the roads these days, Maurice invariably ended up yelling at her. Aware that Maurice's habit of driving along the main road at twenty miles an hour was a major source of dangerous frustration for those unlucky enough to be caught behind him, she ignored his bad temper and used their outings as a time to practise what she had learned in her latest session with the Strathannan School of Motoring. When she passed her test at the first attempt she was delighted. Maurice was amazed but magnanimous.

'You can use the car any time you want. Think of it as yours,' he told her generously, pressing the keys of his

Morris into her hand. 'You know it's hard for me to drive now but I still like to get out now and then and I know Maureen's been missing her Sunday outings. You can give us a wee trip out from time to time and we'll call it quits. How's that suit you?'

In answer she stood on the tips of her toes and managed to plant a kiss on his chin. 'Thanks, Uncle Maurice,' she said. 'And our first trip out will be on Saturday afternoon. We close at twelve-thirty so we've loads of time. I've got it all planned already.'

'Maurice, the girl is a perfectly fine driver and she's passed her test now so you do not have to tell her what to do every time we get to a corner or meet another car.' Maureen poked her brother in the shoulders from behind and winked wickedly at her niece whose eye she caught in the rear-view mirror.

Maxine chortled. 'It's OK. I'm used to it,' she assured her aunt, grinning at Maurice who had been on the point of sulking.

'OK. OK. Forgive me for wanting to live through this experience,' he laughed.

'Concentrate on the scenery, Maurice. It's a glorious day and the trees all look marvellous at this time of year. All those reds and yellows. We should make the most of this weather. The winter will be on us soon enough.'

Maxine had driven them practically all round Strathannan, taking care to stick to back country roads which she was hoping they wouldn't recognise. But Maureen wasn't so easily duped.

'I'm sure we crossed the river Annan just now so that must be Inverannan down there,' she pointed through a gap in the hills. 'Look, you can see the Forth from up here, see Maurice, on the left. So we're still heading east. That right, Maxine?'

Damn, thought Maxine, but only admitted to a non-committal, 'Probably.'

She circled round the village, going almost to the coast then coming back to it from the west, hoping to delay the moment of recognition until the last minute. But the time came when it was all too obvious where they were.

Fortunately the day was one of the best, warm and mellow, and, Maxine thought, even Craigie seemed softer, more welcoming. No one had a fire lit in this weather so the smoky fug which seemed to hang permanently about the place had lifted, taking most of the more unpleasant smells with it. Even the kids, still filthy, but bare-legged and naked-bellied in the sun, looked healthier, the winter greyness replaced by rosy cheeks and freckles. Their mothers, lounging splay-legged on their front steps, rousing themselves to blast some offending child with a stream of invective before settling back in the sun, were a timely reminder that underneath the sunshine, Craigie was just the same. The broken windows, vandalised telephone boxes and graffiti-scrawled walls and even her father's prefab, lost in a veritable field of grass, were all depressingly familiar. So why did she feel this sudden emotional fondness for the place?

As she pulled into the kerb the NCB bus drew in opposite and twenty or so miners got off. They all looked exhausted she thought, staring after them. Old trousers, worn out jackets, heavy boots and a canvas bag for their piece boxes. It was like a uniform. She watched after the bus pulled away again, empty now, while the miners plodded up the road, shoulders bent, some of them coughing, but still laughing and calling to one another as they reached their separate homes. Once, her father had been one of them, and her grandfather and Uncle Jackie, and

Uncle Harry. How could she ever feel ashamed of coming from a village like this where people had to work so hard, in such awful conditions underground and yet emerged each day uncowed?

'Maxine?'

Just for a moment Maxine had forgotten why she was here. She turned and found Maureen looking at her with something close to anger in her face.

'It's time I was making a visit home,' she offered nervously. 'I thought you'd like to come too.'

By now Maurice had scrambled out of the car. 'I think you should have told us what you were planning,' was his comment. 'We're old, Maxine, but we're not children. You should have consulted us before bringing us here.'

Maxine saw all her grand plans collapsing. 'I'm sorry,' she started. 'But, now you're here, couldn't you – '

'Aunty Maureen! Uncle Maurice! Gosh, I would have recognised you both anywhere.' Warned in advance by Maxine, Linda had been watching from inside her father's house and now rushed out to greet her aunt and uncle, her delight unfeigned.

'Come on in. Father will be so pleased to see you. I've got a lovely tea ready for us . . . It's a bit of a squash . . .'

The elderly brother and sister found themselves propelled into George's tiny living room which seemed to be bursting with people. George, who had wondered why both his daughters and their husbands, each with a baby in tow, should choose to visit on this hot afternoon when all he really wanted to do was doze, stared at Maurice and Maureen as if he couldn't believe his eyes.

'Good God! Am I seeing things or what?' was his ingenuous reaction.

Maurice was the first of his unexpected guests to recover. Realising this reception committee was friendly he immediately stepped forward and offered his hand.

Delighted, now that he was recovering from his initial surprise, George clasped it and pumped it up and down heartily before turning to Maureen. For a moment neither quite knew what to do but then she laughed and opened her arms to him. George hugged her then gave her a peck on the cheek.

'Well,' commented Catherine, *sotto voce*. 'I've never seen Dad do that before.'

Maxine laughed then took control again by introducing her sisters, their husbands and their unimpressed babies, one girl, one boy, to Maureen and Maurice. Suddenly everyone was laughing and talking at once and one child, startled out of a post-feed slumber, started to howl its displeasure. In an instant Maureen was delving into the carry-cot. She emerged with a rather surprised infant who was, however, prepared to smile for this gentle-handed stranger.

Maxine heaved a huge sigh of relief and took herself off to the kitchen, followed by her sisters. Their husbands, having done their duty, sloped off to share a packet of cigarettes in the overgrown back garden. After the young women had hugged and exchanged news they settled down to preparing tea, leaving the older generation to make their peace in privacy.

By the time they took the loaded trays into the living room everyone was perfectly relaxed and smiling. As Maxine gave Maureen her cup of tea the older woman grasped her wrist. 'You little wretch,' she laughed.

'Well you can't blame me for taking things into my own hands, Maureen. I've been hinting for long enough. But you two can be so stubborn . . .' She shook her head, grinning widely.

'Aye, well, it must run in the family,' Maureen retorted.

Maxine presided over tea, helped by Catherine who also

had the job of changing nappies. No one seemed to realise that Linda had vanished.

'And tell me about David,' Maureen asked, looking at the photograph George kept on the television. 'I must say he looks smart.'

'He's in the navy. His ship's stationed at Devonport but he's at sea now and won't be home for eighteen months.' Catherine supplied the answer. 'I think Dad misses him more than he says.'

'He must do,' Maureen agreed, looking at George who was in animated conversation with Maurice. 'Still, your father's a lucky man to have you two girls, and your families, living so close. I suppose you see quite a bit of each other.'

'Not as much as you'd think, Aunty Maureen. Dad's got his life organised to suit himself. He's got so many friends. Most of them are retired now so he's never on his own. He goes bowling nearly every afternoon in summer, curling in winter and he walks for miles and miles. Linda and I take it in turns to do his washing and cook Sunday dinner but, apart from that, he likes to be left to get on with it himself.'

'Good for him,' applauded Maureen.

Behind them the door opened again. Maurice was the one who looked up first. His face froze.

'I've brought someone else to see you, Aunty Maureen, Uncle Maurice,' Linda said, standing aside to allow one more person into the crowded room.

'If I'd known . . . What the hell do you think you're playing at, Linda?' a furious voice yelled. 'What sort of trick is this?' Ina stood rooted in the doorway, her face a mask of anger. 'If I had wanted a bloody reunion I'd have sorted one out for myself. Without you lot as witnesses.'

'Gran – ' Maxine began her plea for common sense.

Ina rounded on her furiously. 'Oh, so you're here are you? I might have known you'd be at the back of it.'

'Bloody hell,' muttered George. 'That's a perfectly good afternoon in ruins.'

'You might as well come on in and have a cup of tea with us, Ina, now you're here,' Maureen coaxed her younger sister.

'I've tea of my own at home,' Ina yelled.

Grunting with the pain of movement Maurice levered himself to his feet. Seeing the agony flitting across his face, Ina was silent, for just long enough to let him speak.

'Will you shut your bloody face, woman, and sit on your backside,' he roared, making Maxine gasp in astonishment. 'Since your granddaughters have gone to so much trouble on our behalf the least you can do is try to keep a civil tongue in your head for the time it takes you to drink your tea. If you really can't stand the sight of your only brother and sister, after so many years, then we won't force you to stay longer than that.'

Grunting he sat down. The silence was so intense you could hear the babies breathing.

'All right,' Ina said, ungraciously. 'Give us a cup of tea then.'

Maxine jumped up from her seat on the settee next to Maureen, forcing Ina to sit by her sister, then cursed as her grandmother stared straight in front of her, her face as stiff as Maurice's collar.

'By God, you're a stubborn woman, Ina Lennox,' George exploded suddenly. 'And I've never seen anything as sour-looking as you. It's like you've a stick of rhubarb up your arse.'

Maureen spluttered then lost control altogether and howled with laughter until tears streamed down her face. Behind her the three sisters clung to each other as they choked on their laughter. Maurice's face turned red and

296

his shoulders shook with mirth while George and Ina stared acidly at each other. But the laughter all around them was infectious. George succumbed first, his mouth trembling, his nose twitching, his cheeks ballooning until he could contain himself no longer. And at last Ina, too, gave in.

When they had all regained control, more or less, Maurice wiped his eyes and regarded his youngest sister sternly. 'Well, Ina. Now we're all together there's one or two things that need to be given an airing. We've spent the best part of our lives at loggerheads and I see no reason for it to continue. What say we ask the young 'uns to give us an hour or so on our own?'

'Aye, Maurice. I see you've still got to be giving out the orders,' was the nearest she would come to agreeing.

'Nae, Lass,' he rumbled. 'I passed that hat on to Maureen, years ago.'

Three hours later Maxine parked Maurice's car outside the bakery and turned to say goodnight to her great aunt and uncle. The journey home from Craigie had been made in silence, each having a great deal to think about.

'I'll see you on Monday,' she said, as she locked the car.

'Aye. Monday . . .' agreed Maureen, smiling at her through misted eyes. 'Och, Maxine . . . the day you decided to come to Kilweem, well that was the best thing in the world for Maurice and me. Thanks for today, Lass. Thank you so much . . .' Tears made the words almost inaudible and Maureen clasped Maxine in an emotional hug before hurrying upstairs.

'Aye, Lass. I wasn't too pleased when I understood what you were doing but you were right. We're just three stubborn old duffers who needed someone like you to put us right. I'll always be grateful to you for that.' Maurice,

EIGHTEEN

Torrential rain had kept most sensible people indoors one Friday when a familiar figure settled in a seat in the temporarily deserted café.

'What can I get you, Sir?' Maxine asked, wondering if he would remember her.

He did. 'Ah, Miss Lennox. I'm frozen,' Callum Mackie complained, rubbing his hands together and blowing on them noisily. 'Hot, sweet tea and something hot to eat too, please Maxine.'

'How about a bacon roll? The rolls are fresh from the oven and the bacon's Ayrshire.'

'Perfect,' he nodded, gravely. 'I'm on my way to the harbour master's office. It's been a bad night for the boats to be out. I don't think anyone expected it to get as rough as this.'

'They're all safely in,' Maxine told him. 'The *Isobel* was last, half an hour ago.' In bad weather the welfare of the few remaining fishing boats was the over-riding concern of the villagers. Word of their safe arrival was passed from neighbour to neighbour on the street and in the shops with eager relief.

'Thank the Lord.' Callum closed his eyes. Maxine wondered if he was praying and felt oddly uncomfortable for a second or two. But that was quickly followed by a surge of admiration for this young man whose beliefs were so much stronger than her own, who so obviously cared about his fellow human beings and who had chosen to devote his life to such a demanding career.

Later, when she had taken him his order, she watched him covertly as he devoured his food with a healthy and unclergymanlike enjoyment then went eagerly to see if there was anything else he wanted.

'No thanks. I'd best be getting on my way or the Rector will want to know what I've been doing with my time.' He smiled at her now and she blushed slightly as she realised, again, just how attractive he really was. 'I had hoped to see you in church,' he ventured quietly. 'Not that I want you to feel obligated, no, that would be quite wrong, but it can be a very good place to get to know people.' He reached out and touched her arm lightly, an unconscious gesture of friendship and sincerity.

Behind them the door opened and Eileen Crombie, from the post office, ran in, laughing and shaking rain from her hair. She greeted Maxine warmly, smiled at Callum and sat behind them, clearly waiting for Maxine and inadvertently destroying the warmth which had been growing between her friend and the young curate.

Callum nodded politely at her then turned back to Maxine, drawing her towards the door with him, away from Eileen's finely-tuned ears. 'I can see you've made friends of your own without the intervention of the church. I should have known you would,' he smiled, wryly.

'Yes,' she said, desperate to keep the conversation alive. 'But I have to admit I was pretty lonely at first. Still, that was a year ago now.'

'That long?' He looked at her in astonishment. 'It doesn't seem more than a couple of months. I did call back at your flat once or twice but you must have been out. I wanted to see how you were getting on. Then, of course, I realised you were working here, with your aunt and uncle.' He stopped, seeming embarrassed.

'That was a nice thought,' she smiled. 'Thanks. I'm

sorry I missed you. But I've settled in very well now. Mind you,' she added, 'I can't imagine that anyone could not like living in a place as beautiful as this.' She glanced outside at the teeming rain and laughed. 'As beautiful as this place usually is,' she corrected herself.

'Good,' he murmured, raising his rather serious face to look at her again. 'As I said before, if you ever need anyone to talk to, Maxine, I'm always available.'

'I don't think . . .' she stammered. The idea of him getting to know her better, of confessing anything of her past to this disturbingly attractive clergyman was horrific. What could he possibly make of her background, her disastrous marriage and the terrible, shameful reason for it? What would he think of her if he ever found out she had allowed an elderly woman to fall and injure herself and had then left her to suffer agony? How could anyone like him ever hope to understand what she had been through? She doubted if he had ever known deprivation, desperation or even unhappiness and he had certainly never experienced physical abuse and degradation in the way she had. Everything about him, his cultured manner, his refined accent and even his stylish dress spoke of someone from a very comfortable background.

Callum watched the emotions chasing across her lovely, open face and knew he was in danger of alienating her, something it was suddenly very important not to do. This mysteriously self-contained girl had hidden depths which were intriguing him. 'I'll probably see you next week. I have visits to make in Kilweem most Fridays and if the weather stays cold I'll be looking for something warm to keep me going.' With a deliberately casual smile he was back on the wet street.

Maxine turned to her friend who had been watching with undisguised interest but, when Eileen launched into a detailed description of her latest disagreement with her fiancé, Maxine found she was only half-listening.

Fridays were transformed into the high spot of the week. Maxine made special efforts with her appearance, washing her hair each Thursday night and arranging it with extra care on Friday mornings. Sometimes she even added a dusting of powder to her cheeks in an effort to disguise the pink blush the heat of the bakery brought to her face.

Maureen Archibold, who missed very little, smiled to herself. In the year Maxine had worked for them she and Maurice had grown extraordinarily close to her. Not simply because she was their niece, not even because she had managed to effect the reunion they had thought impossible, but also because she was an excellent worker who had rapidly risen to be their deputy, solely on her ability, without upsetting the half dozen other women who worked in the bakery. She was also honest, kind-hearted and genuinely fond of her elderly aunt and uncle. In all the time Maxine had been with them she had never tried to take advantage of the fact that she was their great niece. If anything the opposite was true. Maureen knew that the girl frequently did more than her fair share of the work in an effort to spare Maurice, whose condition had worsened during the bitterly cold winter. For weeks now it had been Maxine who had cheerfully started work in the bakery in the wee, small hours of the morning, knowing that Maurice's health wouldn't allow him to leave his bed in the middle of the freezing nights. When they tried to thank her, knowing that without her their business would certainly have collapsed, she simply shrugged and said she was glad of the chance to get the experience she would need if she was to open her own café or restaurant one day. She repeated it as she sat with Maureen, absorbing the intricacies of book-keeping and ordering. Maxine's dream was growing stronger every day but they all knew that on her modest salary, her chances of ever going into business on her own were remote. Which was why Maureen was so delighted to see the spark between Callum and Maxine. Even if the girl never realised her commercial ambitions perhaps she would find happiness in another way, though Maureen realised with a sudden sharp pang, losing Maxine would be like losing a daughter.

Maxine knew things were coming to a head with Callum. For more than a month he had been making a point of coming into the café almost every day, and had hinted, more than once, that he would like to take her out.

Maxine's feelings for Callum were ambiguous which was why she seemed deaf to his suggestions. Much as she enjoyed talking to him, her previous experiences with men had been bitter ones and she wasn't at all sure that she was ready to become emotionally involved with anyone, especially Callum. His obvious devotion to his religion scared her. The thought of the explanations she would have to make about her complicated and shameful past, and the reaction that he, as a minister of the church, was bound to have, was more than enough to ensure that she maintained a certain distance between herself and the young curate.

But Callum Mackie was a very determined young man. Good looks and impeccable manners had brought him his share of girlfriends. His calling had not prevented him from enjoying those relationships, but his moral principles had made certain that he had done nothing of which he was ashamed, unlike most of his peers. His training and his work in the parish had matured him but also isolated him from people of his own age who, because of the strength of his beliefs, tended to regard him as something of an oddity. As a result he was increasingly aware of a lack of female companionship, of a very real void in his life. In short, at twenty-six, Callum Mackie was level-headed, sensitive, unashamedly devout and ready to settle down. And the person he thought he wanted to settle down with was Maxine Lennox, though he was having incredible difficulty even persuading her to have dinner with him.

In the end, sheer persistence on his part paid its dividends and Maxine found her resistance weakening.

'I don't know, Callum.' Men had brought her nothing but misery in the past and, more importantly, she was still married, something Callum was unaware of. Perhaps she should tell him before she even agreed to go out with him, but the right words were so difficult to find and hardly the sort of thing you blurted out in the middle of a busy coffee shop. 'You don't know anything about me,' she stammered out at last.

'I have been trying to remedy that for several weeks now,' he countered with perfect solemnity, belied only by the twinkle of merriment in his disconcertingly direct eyes. 'Have dinner with me tomorrow night?'

'All right,' she laughed. 'You win.'

'I'll book a table at *L'Escargot* for nine. OK?'

'That'll be fine.'

'I'll call for you at eight.'

'No!' She preferred to meet him on neutral ground. 'Pick me up at the Tollbooth. It'll save you parking your car.'

He looked at her quizzically then smiled, revealing even, white teeth. 'If that's what you want. Eight o'clock. Yes?'

'I'll be there,' she called back, walking away to serve another customer.

He watched her with a slightly perplexed look on his face. He was as sure as he could be that she liked him but as soon as he suggested getting to know one another better he sensed her withdrawal. It was almost as if she was afraid of a closer relationship. Maybe it was his calling which intimidated her. Many people seemed incapable of normal behaviour in the presence of a clergyman, but surely Maxine was too intelligent to fall into that category. She was also unpredictable, exciting, and there was something else too, something sad and unreachable in her. And that made her all the more attractive.

It was a mistake. She should never have agreed to meet him. And certainly not here, on the windiest corner in Strathannan. The last thing she needed right now was another man to complicate her life, especially not a clergyman who would expect her to be something she was not, had never been and never could be. The truth was, she told herself, she simply didn't have time for romantic entanglements. Maurice and Maureen needed her and a man would only get in the way of her ambition to have a restaurant of her own one day. Any involvement could only spell more unhappiness, for Callum, too, and he was too nice, too thoroughly good, to be hurt. Her whole being shrank from telling him about her past but she knew the only acceptable course was for her to be totally honest with him as soon as possible. The first thing she had to tell him was that she was still, technically, a married woman. There had been no sign of Archie since the fairground incident but unable to face the exposure of her personal life in court, she had taken no steps to obtain a divorce. In fact she had heeded Maureen's advice and done her best to file Archie Cree away in the furthest reaches of her mind and leave him there, as if he had never existed. But exist he did and she had to tell Callum about him tonight, give him the chance to back out before it was too late. She caught a glimpse of her windswept appearance in a window. There would be no need, she thought glumly. Callum would take one look at her bedraggled hair and flee.

It had taken her a full hour to get ready but the wind had tangled her long hair as soon as she stepped outside. By now the tip of her nose was probably glowing red and those dratted ears would be quite horribly obvious with the wind whipping her hair back like this.

The Tollbooth clock struck the hour, making her jump. That's it, she thought. He's not coming. She settled her bag over her shoulder and prepared to walk home.

'You must be frozen.' His voice, from behind, startled her. He chuckled, a deep, comfortable laugh. 'The car's over there. Let's get in and warm up.'

They accomplished the short drive to Sauchar in companionable silence. Maxine allowed herself to be led into the restaurant feeling slightly out of place. She had never been anywhere quite like this before. How wonderful it would be to be the owner of a restaurant as impressive as this one. An impossible dream.

The *maître d'* hurried towards them with a deferential smile and a small bow. 'Your table is ready, Sir.'

Maxine slipped out of her only coat, glad she had worn her smartest dress and smiled to see that Callum had left his clerical collar off for the evening. He had opted, instead, for a white shirt and dark tie but somehow it didn't look right and she noticed him fiddling with it, as if he was uncomfortable.

He caught her looking at his neckline and grinned, something he found himself doing a lot in her company. 'Off duty, but I have to admit it feels odd, as if I'm not properly dressed.'

'Would you care to see the wine list, Sir?' A waiter

interrupted before she could tell him that she actually preferred the crisp, white dog collar.

'Wine, Maxine?'

'No thanks. Just fruit juice. Orange, with ice.'

'For me, too, and may we see the menu?'

'Certainly, Sir.'

'I hate wine,' he confided, leaning towards her. 'Tastes like drain cleaner, makes me talk far too much and leaves me with a thumping head.'

For Maxine wine evoked painful, shameful memories of those nights when Paul had plied her with the stuff, for reasons which had become all too apparent. 'Me too,' she said and lapsed into tense silence.

Callum also seemed to have been deserted by his usual reliable line of small talk. After three or four awkward minutes he groaned and asked, 'What's happened to us? We don't normally run out of things to say. And there's so much I want to ask you, Maxine.'

Her heart sank. 'Like what?' she asked, panicking. She wasn't ready for her dreadful confession yet.

'Everything . . . Let's start from the beginning,' he laughed, extending a well-manicured but uncompromisingly male hand across the table. 'Callum Anthony Mackie. Curate to the parish of St Peters in Kilweem. Only son of Mrs Agnes Mackie and Mr James Drummond Mackie, solicitor. Father always hoped I would follow him into the family firm so I'm afraid I'm something of a disappointment to him. Still, he's taken it rather well on the whole.'

She allowed her own carefully lotioned hand to rest in his for one delicious moment and answered. 'Maxine Lennox. Once an assistant in a seedy tea wagon, now deputy manageress in the village bakery. Aspiring to my own business and fortune. But, my real n – '

'So that explains it!' He interrupted her just as she had found the courage to tell him something of her past.

'Explains what?'

'Why you work so hard. What sort of business are you after?'

'I work hard because Maurice really isn't fit any more. There are days when he can barely move and he's in constant pain. The more I can do for him the easier it is for Maureen. But, one day, I really would like to have a restaurant of my own,' she told him with absolute certainty.

'Have you somewhere in mind?' he asked enthusiastically only to be halted by her impatient, 'Slow down, Callum. I have to get some savings behind me first. In any case I could never leave my aunt and uncle now, not while he's so poorly. Any hopes I have of getting a place of my own are years and years away.'

'It depends on the type of premises you're after. There's nothing to stop you looking at some. It might be easier than you think.'

She sighed. 'I know it sounds straightforward to you, Callum, but not for me. I don't have a wealthy family to fall back on. All I have is what I can save from my earnings. Uncle Maurice is generous with my salary but I've a long way to go yet.'

'I apologise,' he said, looking chastened. 'I do tend to get a bit carried away with myself sometimes. Tell me what sort of place you want,' he encouraged her, genuinely interested in her plans.

'I haven't even got that far. Something I could build up gradually I suppose. Something with potential.'

'Why a restaurant? Wouldn't you need some sort of formal training for that?'

'Because I love cooking. It's about the only thing I'm good at. And I am formally trained. I have a diploma.'

'Yes, of course! I remember you telling me that when we first met. I wondered what you were doing in Kilweem. It's not the most obvious place for someone with your ambitions, is it? I would have thought Edinburgh was more likely to offer you the kind of experience you're after.'

Her heart almost stopped. Now was her chance to be at least partially honest with him. 'I came to Kilweem when I left my husband. I had absolutely nothing. No job, nowhere to live and hardly any money. I was hurt, angry and frightened. All I was sure of was that I didn't want to live in a big city. Places like Edinburgh scare me. I wanted a new home, a place where I could start again and where I could actually enjoy living. Somewhere beautiful. I chose Kilweem because of Maurice and Maureen. Not to come and sponge off them, you understand, but just so I'd know someone.'

'That sounds like Kilweem,' he said softly, then waited for her to go on.

'When I got here I realised how stupid I'd been. Uncle Maurice and Aunt Maureen were away on holiday. There were no jobs, the locals weren't inclined to be friendly and I couldn't even find anywhere to stay. That's why I was so grateful to Rosie, at the shows. She gave me a bed that first night, offered me a job and told me about Mrs Dalgleish. If it hadn't been for her I would have ended up sleeping on the beach. Anyway, then Uncle Maurice offered me a job. That was the best thing that's ever happened to me . . . I really love working there. They're a marvellous couple and it's great to be with my family . . . I'm very close to them . . . especially Maureen, she's a wonderful friend . . .' She couldn't look at him.

'I didn't know you'd been married,' he said quietly, when she ran out of things to say.

She nodded, wary now, sure it was all over before it had had a chance to begin. 'It didn't work out. I had to leave . . . Look, Callum, I think I had better tell you everything but it's not a pretty story.'

It wasn't. She could see that even he, trained to hide his feelings, was having trouble keeping the shock off his face. And she spared him nothing, wanting him to know the whole, sordid truth, understanding that any future she and Callum might have depended on her absolute honesty.

Then there was a long, painful silence. Callum, who had paled, sat with his head cradled in one hand, staring at his empty plate.

'I'm sorry, Maxine,' he said eventually, still looking at his plate. 'Your husband sounds like the worst kind of human being. You must have been dreadfully unhappy.'

'I was. I had to get away. I'm not proud of my past, Callum, and I'll understand if you would rather take me home now.'

At last he raised his head and looked at her. 'No, Maxine, I don't want to take you home. I can't pretend I'm not shocked. I had no idea . . . I sensed there was something . . . that you were unhappy, but this . . .'

'I know I should have told you before, Callum, but it's not an easy thing to talk about, even now. My stomach goes into cramp every time I think about Archie Cree.' She was very close to tears, believing she had lost him, forfeited even his friendship. 'I know what you must think of me.'

'Do you?' he challenged, anger in the deep, blue eyes, giving his face added strength. Then he sighed and said, 'What right have I got to judge you, Maxine? I have never experienced any of the things you've told me about. What I am sure about is that it must have taken a lot of courage to be so honest with me.'

She watched him closely, still unsure, but saw no condemnation in his face.

'I was so afraid you'd be disgusted with me . . . by me. You are a priest after all. I've done so much that must shock you. I thought you wouldn't even want to speak to me again.'

'Don't be stupid, Maxine. Surely, if I was as narrow-minded as that, then I shouldn't be calling myself a clergyman.'

'You can't approve,' she whispered, knowing she had to be sure of him.

'No! How could I? Everything you've told me is against all that I believe in. It seems to me that everything happened because a man, a much older and more experienced man, took advantage of you, exploited your innocence. What happened after that, happened because you tried to save the situation. How can I condemn you for that? All you did was make the mistake of trusting two people who didn't deserve your love.'

'A lot of it was my own fault, Callum. Paul used me, yes, but he didn't rape me.' It was deliberately brutal. He didn't flinch.

'Do you think about it a lot?' he asked, gently. 'Because you really shouldn't let it eat at you. You can't change what's happened, so put it behind you.'

'I do try,' she admitted. 'And you really don't want to take me home?' she asked, teasing him gently now, trying to lighten the atmosphere before she really did let herself down in front of him by bursting into tears.

'Definitely not,' he assured her softly. 'It's early days for us yet, Maxine. Let's just eat our meal and enjoy ourselves.'

*

'I have enjoyed tonight, Maxine,' he said later, when he left her at her front door.

'So have I. Thank you, Callum.'

She was aware of him standing disturbingly close to her, looking down on her for what seemed like a very long time. At last he brought his face down to hers and she closed her eyes when he brushed her lips very lightly with his. And then he was gone.

Maxine stood for seconds longer, her emotions a mass of confusion. The attraction she felt for Callum Mackie was incredibly strong, far greater than anything she had experienced before but, even at this early stage, it was tempered by fear. Fear of exposing herself to be hurt again. Callum had been charming and good-humoured throughout the evening, making no further reference to her disclosures, but she had seen how shocked he had been, had even sensed a slight withdrawal. And surely that was a perfectly natural reaction for a clergyman? No matter how much he might try to reassure her to the contrary, there was simply too much in her past that he must instinctively despise. That brief, almost dutiful kiss had said it all. She climbed the cold, deserted stairs to her flat and let herself in with tears brimming in her eyes.

Callum was equally disturbed. It had demanded every ounce of his excellent self-control to disguise his reaction when Maxine had told him, so casually, that she was already married. The rest, the lover, the pregnancy, the violence, was nothing. She had been innocent, trapped by the worst kind of man, he genuinely believed that. But marriage. He had never guessed she might be married and that was the disclosure which had overshadowed the whole evening.

Deeply troubled he parked his car and climbed slowly to his self-contained flat on the upper floor of the rectory. Without bothering to switch on the lights he found his way across the living room and sank into a soft, old armchair in the window, looking out over the calm waters of the estuary.

He spent many hours here in times of difficulty. Sometimes merely struggling with the wording of a sermon, at others debating with himself on some theological point – and there was much he was unsure of. Frequently he sat here burdened with the troubles of a parishioner, sometimes finding a solution, more often not, and then feeling a complete and total failure. How strange it was that they brought their troubles to him, a twenty-six-year-old, raw and inexperienced curate, expecting him to dispense solutions like some kind of clerical chemist and worse, accepting his opinions as if he was infallible. But nothing had tested him as much as this.

In the months it had taken him to persuade Maxine to go out with him he had gradually fallen in love with her, had revelled in it, looking forward to the life they would build together, feeling sure of himself, and of her. Never had he imagined that a barrier of this magnitude would be placed in front of them.

Callum wasn't even sure what the church's official attitude would be to one of their curates marrying a divorcee. Certainly it would be frowned upon and he could expect no further preferment. It was entirely possible that the marriage would not be permitted at all, and definitely not in a church.

And that was the crux of his dilemma. Unless a marriage could be sanctified in church it had little real meaning for him. And those vows, once made before God, could never be broken. Even without the probability of official objections to their marriage, in his own mind Callum believed that Maxine had already made her vows before God and nothing but death could release her from them, no matter what the law courts might say.

Callum stood and gazed sadly out over the Firth, stretching his cramped limbs. Sometimes it was possible to see boats making their way towards the upper reaches of the river, spots of light on a featureless night sea. Tonight there was nothing, not even a glimmer from the moon, to lighten the darkness. It was absolute, like the despair in his heart. Callum sank back into his chair and closed his eyes. He was facing an impossible choice. How could a mere mortal be expected to make it?

Callum settled himself at a table in the café minutes after they opened their doors on Monday morning. Smiling, Maureen called Maxine who was in the bakery.

'I don't think it's me he's here to see, do you?' she asked. 'You see, I told you he'd be back. You forget, I've been watching the way that young man has been looking at you for months now.' Maureen had been anxious to know how Maxine's date with Callum had proceeded and dismayed to learn her young friend's fears. 'Go and speak to him, Maxine,' she encouraged the girl. 'You've got nothing to worry about now. You've been absolutely honest with him, you can't do any more than that.'

'He probably only wants a cup of tea,' Maxine said. How could she believe anything else after Saturday night?

'Rubbish!' Maureen gave her a none too gentle shove which propelled her into the café with a distinct lack of grace.

Callum didn't appear to notice anything amiss but looked up and smiled. 'I wasn't sure if you'd be here at this time of the morning. I'm busy all day and this is the only chance I had to pop in,' he explained.

'Can I get you something?' she asked, making a face at Maureen who was loitering rather obviously behind the counter.

'No thanks. I've only just had breakfast,' he admitted. 'I don't want anything to eat or drink, Maxine. I want to talk to you, if you've got time.'

The café was empty. Maxine glanced questioningly at Maureen who nodded her grey head then beat a tactful retreat. 'Just for a minute or two then,' Maxine said, slipping into the chair opposite him, expecting him to tell her that he couldn't see her again.

'I just wanted to ask if you'd like to go to a concert on Saturday. At the Usher Hall. Vivaldi . . .'

She stared at him. '. . . I . . . Yes, thanks, I'd like that,' she stammered.

'Why so surprised?' he asked, disconcerted by her obvious astonishment. 'Clergymen are allowed to appreciate other types of music. It's not all hymns and organ recitals you know.'

'Yes. Sorry.'

'Maxine? Have I said something stupid . . . ?'

She sighed. 'No. It's me that's being stupid,' she admitted, candidly.

'Well, not stupid . . . A little strange perhaps,' he teased. 'Want to tell me why?'

'Not really . . . och, I just thought you wouldn't want to go out with me again, that's all,' she said, blushing.

'That's all!' he teased but didn't ask why she had thought that. He already knew.

'You know what I mean . . . after what I told you . . . about me being married.' She couldn't look at him now.

'Maxine,' he leaned across the table, put a finger under her chin and tilted her face gently up, making her look into his eyes. 'I tried to be honest with you. I told you I was shocked, how couldn't I be? But I also told you I understood.'

'Yes. But that didn't mean you'd want to see me again.

I thought, when you left me . . . I mean . . . You hardly even bothered to kiss me!'

He smiled, lighting up his whole face then, very slowly leaned towards her and brushed her lips with his. Tantalisingly he drew back a little almost as soon as they made contact but then slipped a hand round the back of her neck and held her face still while he brought his lips down on to hers for the second time. It was as if someone had injected brandy and lemonade into her bloodstream. Her whole body fizzed. Heat raced through her veins, pulsed urgently in her head, then tingled down into her breasts, her groin, the top of her legs. His lips were firm and suddenly demanding. His tongue was hard, probing and flagrantly sensual. Too soon they drew apart, his hand lingering at her neck.

'Is that better, Maxine Lennox?' he asked quietly, his intense, blue eyes searching her deep grey ones.

'Much better,' she answered, gravely, a slight tremor to her voice.

The café door opened, they sprang apart like guilty children.

'The window of a café is not the most private place for a first kiss, is it?' he laughed.

'I'm sure we'll find somewhere better than this on Saturday,' she promised as he turned to leave.

'I'll keep you to that,' he smiled, touching her face lightly with a finger.

Outside he had to button his coat quickly. The physical effect she had had on him was rather embarrassingly obvious.

After that they simply couldn't get enough of one another. Every free minute was spent together. Callum took Maxine to restaurants, to concerts, to plays. Afterwards

316

they walked, talked and kissed. For Callum this was a self-imposed torture. He ached for Maxine, could hardly be in the same room as her without suffering an acute, physical reaction.

The beach was an obvious place for two young lovers to walk. Callum and Maxine spent many hours there, sheltered from inquisitive eyes by the compliant dunes. But when, six weeks into their affair, Callum attempted to make love to Maxine it was very nearly a disaster.

'I love you, Maxine,' he murmured, the words coming from his very soul.

In answer she covered his mouth with her lips, twining her tongue round his, groaning as his hands caressed her body, writhing with unfulfilled longing. Never had a man roused such passion in her. But suddenly, as he eased her hand down to grasp him, she felt the coarseness of the sand beneath her, the ruffle of the breeze on her skin and memories of other occasions, on another beach, flooded her.

'NO!' She shoved him aside and struggled into a sitting position. Almost angrily she turned away and stared out to sea.

Callum took some time to recover his composure then tidied himself to a degree of decency before going to her side.

'Maxine? Max . . . Are you OK?' he asked, gently.

'Yes . . . I'm all right.' But she wouldn't look at him.

'No you're not . . . What did I do?' he asked, anger, frustration and guilt all vying for first place in his emotions. His heart was still hammering and even now, rigid and angry-looking, she inflamed him. As a priest he knew he should restrain himself. The place for sex was inside a secure, loving marriage. But with a warm, sensuous woman like Maxine, such a suggestion was fatuous. And then it occurred to him that perhaps she had expected him to be less ardent, more controlled. After all that had happened to her, had she expected to be safe, sexually, with a priest? But no, that couldn't be the case. Her response to him had been unmistakable, or so he had thought.

'Nothing. You didn't do anything,' she answered.

'I thought you wanted . . .'

'It's not that,' she interrupted his halting apology.

'Then what is it, Maxine?'

She shrugged awkwardly. This wasn't easy to talk about but honesty had been the hallmark of their relationship so far. 'It's just that this isn't the right place.'

He slipped an arm round her and was relieved to feel her relax against him. 'We can't go to my flat. The Rector would hardly approve.'

'I know.'

'This beach is as private as the world gets, Maxine. Look, there's not a soul in sight.'

'Callum . . . I can't. Not on a beach. Not with you . . . Don't you see . . . With Paul . . . The beach was where we always went. But not with you, Callum. It wouldn't be right.' There, she had said it.

'I see. OK. Come on then. I'll take you home. It's getting cold anyway.' He was hurt, she could hear it in his voice.

It took them nearly half an hour to walk back to her flat.

'It's early yet,' she said, casually.

'Yes,' he agreed. 'Do you want to do something else? We could go for a drink if you like.' But he sounded far from enthusiastic.

'No . . .'

'What do you want to do then?' he asked, glancing at his watch.

'I want you to take me to bed, Callum,' she said, facing

318

him, reaching up to brush a wayward strand of hair from his face and kissing him lightly on the lips.

For a moment he looked at her as if he didn't believe what he'd heard.

'I want you, Callum,' she said softly. 'Just not on the beach. Not the first time. The first time has to be special.'

Letting out a long sigh, his ardour instantly reviving, he pushed her back against the wall and kissed her deeply, pressing his body into hers so she could be in no doubt of his urgent desire.

'People will talk if they see me sneaking out of your place with the milkman,' he said.

'To hell with people, Callum,' she laughed, leading him upstairs.

Then they were in her flat, shutting the world out. Touching her softly on the side of her face with gentle fingers he said, 'Smile at me, Maxine. You look so serious.'

It was easy to smile back and admit, 'I'm nervous, Callum.'

'Are you sure you want me to be here?' One last chance for her to change her mind.

'Yes,' she whispered, very softly. This was right, unavoidable, almost pre-ordained.

With infinite tenderness he touched his lips to her eyelids, her neck, her mouth. He made no attempt, yet, to touch her body but the feel of him, the taste of him, made her ache so badly that she pressed herself against him, her breathing as ragged as his.

Quickly he pulled the curtains and switched on her bedside light, casting a warm, golden glow in a circle at the side of the bed, leaving the rest of the room in shadow.

He came to her from behind, reaching his hands round on to her breasts, kissing her neck, breathing in the smell of her. Lifting her head she leaned back and covered his hands with her own. How she wanted him!

'No, let me do it,' he whispered when she started to struggle out of her clothes.

Then she was naked. His eyes travelled over her body, absorbing the details of her firm breasts, her soft skin, the fine hair. No one had ever looked at her with such frank admiration. It had never occurred to her that her body might be worthy of such display. She stepped back a pace, into the shadows but he pulled her forward again and into his arms.

It was her turn now and she fumbled a little. Then, as she ran her hands over his chest, through the fine cluster of hair there, he sank his head between her breasts with a groan before lifting her and carrying her to the bed.

He set her down gently then leaned over her, searching her face. 'It's all right. I'll be gentle,' he promised.

'I don't want you to be gentle, Callum. I want you to make love to me,' she whispered, her voice heavy with longing.

Groaning he lowered himself on to her and she clasped him urgently, drawing him into the heat of her. They moved together hurriedly, greedily, their passion bringing them both to rapid, violent climaxes which left them spent and languorous.

Afterwards, their sweat mingling, they lay together teasing, feeling, exploring until they were ready to love again. This time they were less selfish, more sensitive to each other's needs, slower, taking time and pleasure in one another, the culmination, less violent but infinitely more intense, leading them into entwined, sated sleep.

He woke suddenly, cold where the blankets had slipped away. Four a.m. He should get home. Shivering he slipped out of bed.

'Where are you going? she asked, reaching out to touch his naked skin.

'I should go home. I can't be seen leaving here in the morning.' His voice was gravelly with sleep.

'No. Stay. Please.' She pulled his arm. 'Come on . . .' She threw the cover back, inviting him, tempting him again.

'Oh God . . .' The sight of her creamy, naked body was too much. The morning could take care of itself.

Callum thought God had set him a test. If that was the case then he had failed, miserably. For the first time in his life he had an inkling of what life must be like for those wretched creatures who depended upon alcoholic or chemical stimulus to get them through each day. For him the addiction was Maxine. Three months into their relationship and he was hopelessly, completely in love. Aware of the possible consequences to his career, his conscience and, possibly, his soul, he still couldn't face losing her.

After a week of agonising, a week in which he abandoned his parishioners and spent countless hours on his knees in the darkened church, Callum knew he wasn't strong enough to make the sacrifice God seemed to be demanding of him. He emerged shattered, wondering whether he was truly fit to be a clergyman and despising himself for his own weakness. And still he knew he could not live without Maxine.

'Do nothing hasty, Callum,' advised the Rector when Callum, red-eyed and exhausted, finally sought his advice. 'She's a fine young woman but perhaps she's not for you. If you truly feel you are unable to live without her then you must be prepared to consider your future in the Church. I do sympathise, Callum, but apart from begging you to wait, I cannot advise you. Pray and perhaps God will guide you.'

Maxine's feelings for Callum were still confused. There was no doubt that she was strongly attracted to him but, she asked herself, what woman wouldn't be? His strong good looks and charming manner would be more than enough for most women. The evidence of moderate family wealth in the form of a most uncurate-like preference for fast, sporty cars and an extensive wardrobe of smart clothes, elevated him to the status of eligible bachelor.

Nor could she doubt that Callum loved her. He told her so often enough. But it was the very intensity of his feelings which scared her, especially when seen against the conflict her marriage had raised in his conscience. It terrified her to know how torn he was between his beliefs and her and it awed her to understand just how deeply he must care about her to contemplate compromising his faith for her sake.

Her own emotions were much more deeply engaged than she dared to let him see, more than she would even admit to herself. He was exciting, infinitely disturbing and sexually desirable. Their snatched, shared nights together, made all the more exciting because of the risk of discovery, left her astonished at her response, at the appetite of her own body, yet still she held something back from him because, deep in her mind, there lurked the fear of losing him. For all Callum's apparent modern thinking and his unfeigned understanding of the circumstances of her marriage, he was still a clergyman and she believed that the deep core of faith which ruled his life must, ultimately, lead him to reject her. Faced with the final choice between her and his Church, she was convinced the Church would claim him.

To shield herself from further hurt, she deliberately centred her ambition, not round Callum, but on the business she was still determined to build for herself. A business she saved every single penny for. In a couple of years, when Maureen and Maurice retired, she should have enough to buy herself a modest lease. And this time she would make something of herself without relying on anyone else, not even Callum. Independence was something she craved but in her more honest moments she knew that it wasn't so much a case of wanting independence but of fearing marriage. To make that commitment again, to put herself into someone else's power, even someone as fine as Callum, was a thought that put a film of fear on her lip and sent her stomach into painful cramps.

And marriage was a subject which inserted itself into their conversation with increasing obstinacy.

'Don't do anything until you're quite sure, Maxine,' Maureen advised, 'but for goodness sake don't take that poor boy lightly. He's suffering agonies over you. You can see that just by looking at him.'

'But I'm so confused,' Maxine pleaded.

'I can see that, too. Perhaps you both need a little time to think things through. But why you think an old spinster like me can give you advice of this sort I don't know.'

'Because you are the sanest person I know,' her niece smiled, fondly.

'Och, Maxine, I wish I could help you but the truth is, nobody else can make the decision for you. Only . . .'

'Only what, Maureen? Come on, I need you to tell me what you really think.'

'Only . . . Maxine I have never, in all my life, seen two people more suited to one another than you and Callum. Don't throw it away, Lass. Love like this is far too precious to waste.'

*

323

'I want to marry you, Maxine. More than anything I want us to be married. But . . .' Callum was pacing the floor of his flat and now swivelled to stare out over the North Sea, the turmoil of the waves reflected in his own face. '. . . I just feel it's so important to be married in church, to make our vows before God. How can we do that when you have already made those vows to another man? Even if the Church agreed to marry us, I would still feel it was wrong.'

Slowly she walked to his side and slipped an arm though his, feeling his agony. 'I do understand, Callum, honestly I do. How could you feel any other way? But what are we going to do?'

'I don't know. I wish I did.' He turned suddenly and took her into his strong arms. 'I should say we have to stop seeing one another but I've not got the guts to do that. But what does that say about me as a minister of the Church?' he sighed and pulled away from her.

Maxine was aware of the dark shadows under his eyes, testimony to his state of mind, and felt her heart go out to him, felt, too, her growing resentment of the Church which seemed to demand so much from him and give back so little. But the one thing she must never do was criticise his other love in front of him.

'This is all my fault,' she said, bitterly.

'NO!' He roared it, making her jump. 'How could it be? Did you know, when you married Archie Cree, that you would one day want to marry a curate?'

'I don't want to lose you, Callum,' she whispered. But neither was she ready for marriage yet, would never be ready while Callum still agonised over his choices. If he took her for his wife she needed him to do so with a clear conscience and a peaceful mind so there could be no chance of bitter recriminations later.

'We can't get married, we have to face that,' he said,

angrily. 'I'm sorry, Maxine. I know this is unfair to you but I can't help the way I feel. If I marry a divorcee it makes a mockery of everything I believe in.'

'Callum, please . . . I accept that, but couldn't we just live together?'

Unexpectedly he laughed then took her into his arms again. 'Oh, Max, I do love you but you must see that I can't do that. In a place like this it would be all over Strathannan in a week and in the national papers before the month was out. I can see the headlines now. "Curate Lives in Sin." The Rector would have a heart attack, half the parishioners would defect and I'd be drummed out of the choir. It'd be bad enough if they realised we were making love right over their heads, but actually living together . . .' He chuckled to himself quietly before kissing her gently and adding, 'There's no way out of this, Maxine.'

'Are you saying we should split up?' she asked, in a barely audible whisper.

'I don't know. I just don't know,' he admitted, bleakly. 'Perhaps I should leave the Church.'

'Would that change your beliefs? Would that suddenly make you able to marry a divorcee with a clear conscience?' she demanded.

'Of course not.' He sounded defeated.

'Callum, I think we're way ahead of ourselves,' she suggested gently, looking for some way to take the pressure off them both. 'We've not been seeing each other for very long and I'm not ready for marriage yet. I haven't even done anything about a divorce. It's too soon for us to be making such important decisions.'

'What are you trying to say, Maxine?' he asked, looking drained and exhausted. 'Do you mean you don't want to marry me?'

'No, Callum, that's not what I mean! All I am saying

is I need more time. We both need more time. We have to be very sure before we commit ourselves, to anything. And anyway,' she went on in a deliberately happy tone, 'you know I'm determined to have my own business. And that is something I have to do before I settle down.'

'Why?'

She shrugged and struggled to put her feelings into words which wouldn't hurt Callum. 'I need to prove to myself that I can make a success of something on my own. Everything I've done so far in life has ended in disaster. I have to achieve something for myself, Callum, so I never have to turn to anyone for the wrong reasons again.'

'I still don't know what you're trying to say,' he muttered, uncertainty clouding his eyes.

'Only that we don't have to make any choices yet. Neither of us is ready to make them. You never know, in another year or two we might feel quite differently about each other. You might have changed your mind about the Church and what it means to you. Perhaps you'll feel able to compromise. Or maybe we'll meet other people,' she added with deceptive lightness. 'If that happens we'll part as friends. I would never try to hold you, Callum, knowing you can't marry me. But, until that happens, if it happens, can't we just be together?'

'That will never happen. I promise,' he replied, without a trace of humour then sank his face greedily to hers.

NINETEEN

It was as if the elements had conspired to present Craigie at its very worst. Bowing to pressure from Callum's parents who were anxious to meet the girl who featured so heavily in their son's conversation, Maxine and Callum had agreed to meet one another's families. Maxine had fervently hoped for good weather to soften Craigie's harshness but rain fell in continual, soaking sheets from a sky which promised plenty more of the same for the rest of the day.

From the comfort of Callum's car the pall of smoke which hung over the village was visible from over a mile away. The dampness had brought down smells which reminded her of her childhood, acrid, thick and cloying, seeping even into the car. The houses looked uniformly drab and uncared for. Rows of dark, closely-built, ugly buildings which depressed Maxine even to look at them. The uncultivated gardens, boarded windows and generally unkempt air proclaimed this to be a poor area; the vandalised phone boxes, the shop windows, covered in heavy, protective mesh, warned that it was a rough one. The few people on the streets were poorly dressed, dirty looking and sullen. Maxine felt embarrassed then ashamed of herself for feeling such antipathy towards her own people.

'This is it,' she told Callum, watching his face carefully. If he was shocked he certainly wasn't showing it.

Maxine stepped out of Callum's brand new Triumph, uncomfortably aware of how out of place the two-seater sports car was beside the rusting, ancient models which stood outside the other houses in the street. The prefab, still there despite having exceeded its expected life span, was as unprepossessing as ever. The tiny patch of front garden made her wince. Empty beer cans nestled comfortably in the long grass where skeletally thin dogs scavenged for scraps in an old chip paper. The gate hung drunkenly on one rusty hinge, as it had miraculously managed to do for the last ten years and the concreted path to the front door was broken and uneven with grass and weeds flourishing in the cracks. She led him to the grime-streaked front door, her head held high with defiance, preparing herself for the comment he must surely make. But Callum was perfectly calm and contained.

The doorbell wouldn't work so she rapped hard with her knuckles.

Her father's voice came clearly from within the house. 'Is that you, Hen? Come along in.'

But he didn't bother to come to the door himself.

Inside the place hadn't changed at all. The same furniture, even more shabby now, the same scuffed linoleum in the same minute hallway, the same bit of carpet, now with holes in it, in the living room. She doubted if her father even noticed how scruffy it all was and knew he wouldn't care anyway.

George was in his old chair, ostensibly watching Playschool on television but looking very much as if he had just woken up. When Maxine and Callum crowded into the tiny living room he pulled himself out of his customary slouching position and grinned toothlessly at them.

'So, you've brought your young man to see your old father, have you?' he asked, bringing the colour flooding to his daughter's cheeks.

'This is my friend, Callum Mackie, Father. Callum is the curate at St Peters in Kilweem, Dad. I've told you about him. Callum, this is my father, George Innes.'

'I am very pleased to meet you, Mr Innes,' Callum shook the older man's hand with enthusiasm.

'Och, call me George, er . . . Reverend, and sit yourselves down.' He eyed the stark, white, clerical collar uncertainly.

Callum laughed. 'Callum will do for me, George.'

'Aye. Right.' George looked and sounded relieved. He sank back into his seat leaving his daughter to clear enough old papers off the settee to make room for her and Callum.

'Export?' George handed a four-pack to Callum then took a long draught from his own can, wiping the froth from his mouth with the back of his hand and belching loudly when he had finished. Maxine groaned to herself and glared at her father who ignored her.

'Not for me, George,' Callum laughed, 'I've got to drive back to Kilweem later.'

'Och well, suit yourself. Stick the kettle on will you, Hen? There's a good lass.'

Maxine escaped to the kitchen where she rinsed her hot face with cold water. A minute later the door opened and two arms crept round her waist as Callum planted a soft kiss on the side of her face.

'Calm down,' he chuckled.

'Oh, Callum,' she sighed. 'Look at the state of this place.' She waved a hand round the disordered kitchen at the unwashed dishes, the filthy cooker, at the grubby washing – including some very holey underwear – on the airer over their heads.

'Do you think it bothers me?' he asked, forcing her to meet those keen, blue eyes.

'It bothers me,' she retorted, more sharply than she should have done.

'Your father is a man living on his own. If it wasn't for the Rector's wife seeing to my place, it wouldn't be much better. Men aren't worried about something as minor as a few unwashed pots. Anyway, it's none of your business any more. If your father's content here, then that's all that matters. It is his home.'

She broke away from him, resenting the lecture, and fiercely scoured three grubby cups with salt and water before pouring the tea. 'Don't preach at me, Reverend Mackie,' she retorted. 'I think he might have made the effort to tidy up a bit when he knew I was bringing you home with me.'

'Pour his tea and stop worrying,' he laughed. 'The object of this visit is for him and me to meet, not for you to nag him about the way he chooses to live. Get back in there and try to enjoy yourself. You don't see him very often so make the most of it.'

'OK,' she agreed, somewhat reluctantly.

Back in the living room, George had his nose deep in a newspaper, trying to decide which brace of horses to put his money on that afternoon.

'What about "Edinburgh Lad"?' suggested Callum. 'He won last time out.'

Maxine gasped and stared at him. 'How do you know that?' she asked but Callum was afflicted by temporary deafness.

George peered over the rim of the paper and said, 'Did he now? Well, I'll just take a wee walk over to the bookies. Why don't you come with me, Callum? We'll listen to the race over there and stay to collect our winnies if he comes in,' he chuckled and slapped Callum on the back. 'Aye, that'll give them something to talk about, a man of the cloth in the bookies. Especially if that horse of yours does come in . . .'

Vastly amused he led the way out of the house. Callum winked wickedly at Maxine and followed him.

They were gone for well over an hour. Maxine didn't know whether to be relieved or furious but it did give her the chance to do a superficial job of trying to restore the living room to order. When she had accomplished as much as she could without resorting to a wet scrubbing brush she surveyed the results without pleasure. On the whole, she thought, it had been better before she started. The bare patches on the carpet had been less noticeable under all the abandoned cups, papers and jackets.

Callum and George were laughing when they finally got back.

'Well, Lass, this vicar of yours is a right good 'un,' George said, slurring his words slightly. 'Old "Edinburgh Lad" romped in. I made more than six pounds on him.'

'Beginner's luck.' Callum glanced at Maxine and shrugged sheepishly. 'Though I hate to think what the Rector might say.'

'Well,' Maxine sighed, when they were driving back up the coast. 'You certainly made a hit with Dad, but I'm glad it's over. I was dreading that almost as much as I'm dreading meeting your parents.'

'That'll be easy. They're bound to love you. Just be yourself.'

'Myself? Wee Mary Cree with the Craigie accent and the poor crippled husband?' she whined in an accent so thick it was barely comprehensible.

Callum winced. 'But that's not you any more, is it? You don't need to be ashamed of your background, Maxine, you should be proud of it for making you what you are. Anyway,' he added. 'My mother won't understand a word if you talk like that. And neither will I.'

Maxine took a great deal of care over dressing for her first meeting with Mr and Mrs Mackie, aiming to strike a balance somewhere between false sophistication and outgrown innocence. In the end she opted for a plain, cream dress with a hemline at least two inches lower than she usually wore. It looked much too severe she thought, disappointedly, as she surveyed herself in the mirror, two minutes before Callum was due to collect her. A striking necklace or brooch was desperately needed to relieve the faintly insipid effect the neutral colour had on her pale skin and blonde hair.

Hauling her drawers open she hunted frantically until she found a brightly patterned scarf. It improved the plain neckline but the dress needed something more. The only thing she had which was even remotely suitable was the jewellery her Aunt Minnie had given her as a wedding present. The ear-rings and necklace were unwearable but the brooch might just do. It was old and hugely ugly but big enough to break the daunting expanse of drab colour. The clasp was stiff with disuse but eventually she got it pinned just below her left shoulder. The metal was tarnished and dull but the stones, imitation rubies, sapphires and diamonds, with a large, black bead in the centre, went well enough with the scarf.

She grimaced at herself. The brooch was too heavy for the fabric of the dress and more suitable for someone much older than she was. In fact, it was without doubt the most ugly piece of jewellery she had ever seen, but it would have to do. From the road below a horn sounded. She glanced out to see Callum's car pulling to a halt. There was no time to change now.

The Mackies lived in Coustrie, a smart village on the northern edge of Strathannan, well away from the sea. The house was impressive, like a small manor, set back from the road and surrounded by well-manicured, lawned gardens.

The door was opened as they mounted the front steps

by a middle-aged, homely looking woman with rather wayward hair and a plain, serviceable dress. She welcomed them with a beaming smile. Maxine relaxed at once. If Callum's father was as pleasant as his mother appeared to be the weekend should pass off easily enough.

'Thank you,' Callum said, handing his coat over.

Maxine smiled, determined to make a good impression. 'Thank you for inviting me, Mrs Mackie,' she said quietly and was startled to see the woman's eyebrows fly up in disapproval then blanched in dismay when she simply ignored her and turned to Callum.

'Your parents are in their sitting room, Mr Mackie.'

Aware that she had made a dreadful blunder and thankful that Callum didn't appear to have heard, she followed him across a spacious hall and through wide, double doors, her face still flushed with the bloom of humiliation.

It was the sort of room she had sometimes seen featured in magazines. Maxine's overwhelming impression was of rich, golden colours from the deep, glowing wood of the escritoire just inside the door and the dull mustard of the heavy, velvet curtains, to the pale sunshine colours of the upholstery. To her untutored eyes the whole room shouted wealth, luxury and impeccable taste. Her unease increased to the point where she wanted to run away.

A large sofa and several easy chairs, all covered in pale yellow, regency-striped silk which was echoed in the pattern of the wallpaper, filled the centre of the room. A middle-aged man rose from the depths of one of the chairs and waited for them to reach him.

'Father, I want you to meet Maxine Lennox,' Callum shouted. 'Maxine, this is my father, James Mackie.'

Maxine looked into a lined and slightly ruddy face which bore the faintly drooping expression of an elderly Bassett hound. But his eyes were the same startling blue as Callum's.

'Miss Lennox. I am glad to meet you at last,' he boomed, enthusiastically. 'Callum has done nothing but talk about you for the past three months.' A smile twitched the corners of his mouth.

'I'm pleased to meet you, too, Mr Mackie,' she answered.

'Sorry? What did you say?' he asked, leaning towards her.

'You'll have to speak up, Maxine. Father's a little bit deaf,' said Callum in a stage whisper. 'And this is my mother.' Callum steered her on and Maxine found herself facing a diminutive but severe woman who remained firmly seated in a chair which dwarfed her. Everything about this woman was rigid, her pewter-grey hair, solidly fixed in a stiff, outdated style, her lips, drawn in two unerringly straight lines of disapproval while her back would have made a sergeant major weep with pleasure. Cold blue eyes scanned Maxine from head to foot before finally settling on her face. The expression in them was critical and unfriendly.

'I am very pleased to meet you, Mrs Mackie,' Maxine said, wondering whether to offer her hand. The other woman merely nodded slightly and turned to her son.

'Callum, how nice of you to make the effort to come home. Perhaps you would show your guest to her room. I am sure she needs to rest and tidy herself after your journey. And while she's doing that you can bring me up to date with all your news.'

'We have only come from Kilweem, Mother. Twenty minutes by car is hardly a journey.' Callum laughed but Maxine could already hear the note of tension in his voice.

'Nevertheless . . .' Mrs Mackie insisted.

'It's all right, Callum,' Maxine intervened hastily. 'Your mother is right. I would like to see my room.'

'Forgive Mother,' Callum pleaded as he showed Maxine

334

to a beautifully decorated and furnished guest room. From the way he spoke, in short, uncharacteristically terse sentences, she knew he was very angry. 'She is very highly strung. It makes her appear brusque. It can be unsettling at first.'

'I don't think she approves of me,' Maxine suggested.

'Don't be silly! It'll be fine, you'll see,' and with that he left her to her own devices until dinner time, more than two hours later.

Dinner was served, in some style, at an enormous table, capable of seating ten in comfort. Mrs Mackie sat at one end, her husband at the other. Callum and Maxine found themselves marooned on opposite sides, hidden from each other by a huge, floral centrepiece.

The meal might have been deliberately composed of all Maxine's most hated foods. She forced prawns and avocado down her reluctant throat then found herself grappling with a chicken leg, smothered in lemon and very strong garlic sauce. She knew she would carry the smell on her breath for the rest of the weekend. Frantically trying to wash the unpleasant aftertaste away she emptied her third glass of wine, shuddering at the sourness of it, and knew she had already had too much to drink. The unsubtle sherry trifle which followed almost made her stomach rebel publicly. It was all made so much worse because she felt as though she was eating alone. No one spoke to her. Every time Callum attempted to draw her into the conversation his mother interrupted in an insistent voice which could not be ignored. Mr Mackie was too far away to talk to without shouting and even then Maxine couldn't make herself understood. After a couple of unsatisfactory attempts which were further hampered by his wife's loud voice he shrugged apologetically, and concentrated on his food. At last the table was cleared, the irritating centrepiece removed and the coffee served. Callum caught her eye and winked but by now Maxine was far too angry to respond. The prawns, wine and sherry fought their own noisy battle in her protesting stomach and her head was aching abominably, made worse by the noxious cigar smoke wafting at her in great blue streams from Callum's father.

The coffee, poured by Mrs Mackie, was thick, black and bitter.

'Now, Miss Lennox.' When Callum's mother finally spoke to her guest, her smile was sweet as hemlock but Maxine was ready for her. 'My son tells me you work in a shop.'

'I am deputy manager of the local bakery and tea shop, yes,' Maxine responded, keeping her tone fairly pleasant for Callum's sake.

'Cups of tea and sandwiches I suppose. I shouldn't think that calls for any special skill. That sort of work suits you does it?' the older woman sneered.

'Maxine is saving to buy her own business. She already holds a diploma in catering and is only working in the bakery to gain experience. In fact she is a marvellous cook,' Callum interposed loudly, rage making his voice tremble. 'And the business is owned by her great uncle and aunt.'

Maxine flashed him a quiet look of searing resentment. She was more than capable of speaking out on her own behalf.

'Much the best way to approach anything.' Unexpectedly Callum's father joined the conversation. 'Better to work in the business first. Find out all you can and save making expensive mistakes with your own money later,' he said approvingly. 'You be sure and come to me when you do decide to take the plunge on your own, my dear. I'll make sure you get the best deal.'

She smiled at him gratefully. 'Thank you. I will.'

'I can't pretend to be an expert on cooking. I can hardly scramble an egg.' Mrs Mackie ignored the interchange and managed to make her own lack of domestic skill sound like a worthy attribute.

'I get a great deal of pleasure out of cooking good quality, nourishing food, Mrs Mackie. To be honest I would be ashamed to admit I couldn't cook,' Maxine retorted.

'Of course, but then your circumstances are quite different to mine. I can assure you that in my case domestic skills are not necessary,' she said loudly.

Mr Mackie coughed his embarrassment but would never dream of taking issue with his wife in public. Callum seemed edgy and angry.

Maxine flushed, knowing she had been put in her place and unable to find any reply which wasn't downright rude. She stared into the tarry depths of her cup and fumed inwardly. To listen to this woman talk you could be forgiven for thinking she was nobility. Callum's father, like his father before him, was a successful, country solicitor. He and his wife were respected members of their community but that hardly merited the airs Mrs Mackie wore so blatantly.

'You should have warned Maxine that we dress for dinner, Callum,' was Mrs Mackie's next remark.

'Maxine is dressed,' Callum shot back.

'Hardly, Callum, she was wearing that dress when you arrived.'

Maxine's temper flared then boiled over. They were talking about her as if she wasn't even there. 'I'm sorry if you don't like my dress, Mrs Mackie,' she said icily. 'It's one of my favourites.'

'It is a very practical little dress, my dear, but not quite right for dinner.' Now the woman was patronising her. 'I only mention it because we have been invited to the Morrisons' for dinner tomorrow and you will, of course, have to dress for the occasion. I do hope you have something suitable.'

'Maxine and I have to be back in Kilweem tomorrow, Mother,' Callum snapped, scarlet with anger. 'I have to prepare for services on Sunday. I should have thought you would have realised that much by now.'

'Oh, I see.' She was not to be bettered. 'Well, under the circumstances, perhaps that is for the best.'

When the vile coffee was finally finished they returned to the sitting room for the remainder of the evening. Mrs Mackie immediately suggested they play bridge.

'I'm sorry, I've never played,' Maxine admitted, wondering whether she could plead illness and escape to bed.

'It's very simple. I'll try to teach you if you think you can understand it,' Mrs Mackie offered maliciously.

'Mother! Bridge is not a simple game. It takes months to master it, as well you know. Besides, I hate it. We'll play canasta. Is that all right, Maxine?'

She nodded curtly, having no wish to play anything. Her head throbbed and her stomach felt definitely queasy.

Canasta was a game with which she was perfectly familiar, she and Callum having played with the Rector and his wife several times. However, in this guise it was far less a game than a battle for supremacy. Paired with a resigned Mr Mackie, Maxine soon saw that she and her partner were about to be thoroughly trounced. Callum's mother played with grim concentration which forbade conversation but, apparently, made cheating perfectly acceptable. Several times Maxine caught her peering at the cards her husband held so carelessly in his hands and couldn't make up her mind whether he was actively co-operating or not. On balance she decided he was simply bored stiff.

'I think we can safely say that Callum and I have won,' Mrs Mackie announced with an air of smug satisfaction.

'Yes. Five thousand to our fifteen hundred is convincing enough.' For the sake of Callum who was looking decidedly strained, Maxine did her level best to be gracious.

'Sorry, my dear. To be honest I detest card games. I haven't my wife's capacity for remembering what cards have already come out. I'm afraid I let you down rather badly.' It was such a charming apology that Maxine couldn't be angry with Callum's father.

'I don't think either of us can match Mrs Mackie's skills,' she said, pleasantly.

'What does your father do, Miss Lennox?' Game over Mrs Mackie reverted to the satisfying sport of baiting her guest.

'He's retired.'

'And what did he do before he retired? Was he in business?'

Maxine looked frantically for Callum but he and his father were deep in what appeared to be a very serious discussion and were paying no attention to the two women.

'In the business of hewing coal,' she said, bluntly. 'Didn't Callum tell you, Mrs Mackie?' She was sure he had. 'My father was a miner. Craigie, where I come from, is a mining village. All my family were colliers. And proud of it,' she added with her head up, challenge glinting dangerously in her steely-grey eyes. 'My grandfather was killed in the Craigie disaster of '38.'

'How very unfortunate,' the older woman sniffed.

'It was for my grandmother! She was left with five children to bring up in a two-roomed hovel with no sanitation, no electricity and no running water.' Maxine spoke out fiercely, revealing her own background with stubborn determination to make the differences between them all the more apparent. 'I was raised in a two-bedroomed prefab, sharing a room with my three sisters and brother. When my mother walked out on us I got the job of running the house and looking after the children. We wore second-hand clothes and were glad of them. And that, Mrs Mackie, is why I am determined to set up in business on my own, so that I never have to go back to living like that.' She was aware of Callum and his father staring at her.

'And the easiest way to do that is to net yourself a wealthy husband?' Mrs Mackie asked, a stiff smile disfiguring her face.

'No,' Maxine said distinctly. 'The only way to do that, Mrs Mackie, is to work for it and that is what I intend to do. Marriage is not a part of my business plan at all.' Just in time she stopped herself from going on to say things which would hurt Callum. Instead she got to her feet, ready to excuse herself for the night. She kissed Callum coldly on his cheek, murmured goodnight to his father who was looking increasingly uncomfortable and turned to bid a terse goodnight to Mrs Mackie. Maxine was astonished when the older woman suddenly leaned forward and with bony fingers, examined the brooch which was pinned to Maxine's dress.

'Forgive me for saying this but considering what you have just been telling me I am surprised to see you wearing such a fine brooch. Have you borrowed it for the weekend?'

'Mother!' Callum was horrified but Maxine was so startled that she forgot to be angry.

'Borrowed? No, it's mine. My father's sister gave it to me as a wedding present. I think it's extremely ugly but it's the only thing I could find to go with this dress. I have ear-rings and a necklace to match but they are too big for me to wear.'

'Really?' For the first time the sneering, derogatory tone disappeared. 'Have you ever had them valued?'

'Good heavens, no! They're not worth anything. Just costume jewellery.'

'Are you sure? I have several valuable pieces. Jewellery is a hobby of mine and I think this looks real enough.' Her voice changed abruptly, reverting to the highly rancorous manner she had used all night. 'You are probably right. I would be amazed if you owned such a thing.'

It was a long, uncomfortable night. Though she knew it was unreasonable to expect Callum to come to her room Maxine still resented the fact that he didn't. Her head ached abysmally and her stomach churned so violently that she thought she was going to be sick. By the time she heard sounds of morning activity in the house she had had less than two hours' sleep but at least her stomach was recovering, though her head still ached dully. Groaning she dragged herself out of bed and prepared to face Callum's mother again.

Breakfast was eaten in what was called the morning room. Maxine had no idea which one that was so made her way along the lower hall until the sound of voices attracted her to what she assumed was the right room. She hesitated for a second, steeling herself for what she suspected would be another ordeal then heard Mrs Mackie's strident voice through the half-open door.

'Really, Callum,' she was saying. 'How could you let yourself become involved with a girl like that? She is as common as it is possible to be.'

'Please, Mother! Don't talk about Maxine like that! You

know I'm very fond of her.' White with rage, Callum rounded on his mother, his words emerging as an angry hiss.

'Callum, calm down,' she ordered. 'You are my only child. I have your very best interests at heart. I want you to be happy, you know I do. That is why I have to speak out. You must know that if you wish to advance in the Church you have to choose a wife who will be a credit to you. Someone who knows how to conduct herself in society. That young woman doesn't even know when she's expected to dress for dinner. And that accent! It must be obvious to any fool what sort of background she comes from and she hasn't even got the sense to keep quiet about it! I'm warning you, Callum, you are making a very grave mistake in letting yourself become infatuated with someone like her.'

'It is not an infatuation,' Callum stormed.

'You are letting yourself down. For goodness sake! Think about what you are doing. A woman with a failed marriage already behind her. Second-hand goods! What will people think?'

'I don't care what people think!' he exploded.

'This will finish you in the Church. You will never even have a parish of your own. She's ignorant, ill-mannered and common. You will regret this affair for the rest of your life if you don't put a stop to it now.'

'How dare you . . . !' Callum raged, more angry than he had ever been. 'I . . . I . . .'

Fury got the better of him and he failed to form the words he needed. For a few seconds he forced himself to take deep, calming breaths then faced his mother again. 'I can assure you, Mother, that I have thought through all the implications. I am very well aware of what Maxine will mean to my future in the Church . . .'

'Callum,' she interrupted him ruthlessly, not allowing

him to finish. 'Listen to me. You know I am only thinking of you. My greatest wish is to see you happily settled and I am telling you, you cannot possibly be happy with that young woman.'

'You are judging her too harshly, Mother, jumping to conclusions. It is quite possible that Maxine and I will never marry. We both need time to make up our minds. Our relationship is complicated enough as it is without you opposing it. Maxine is a wonderful person . . . I was hoping that you and she could be friends . . . that you could take her under your wing, help her . . .'

In fact Callum loved Maxine just the way she was and didn't want to change a single thing about her but neither did he wish to alienate his family who, despite their natural disappointment when he told them he did not intend to follow his father into the family firm, had stood solidly behind his decision to go into the Church. His sense of loyalty was deep and this was simply a ploy to try and prevent a rift by appealing to his mother's considerable pride.

Outside the door, Maxine listened in absolute horror until she could contain herself no longer. Shoving the door wide she stormed into the room and confronted them.

'Help me?' she hissed at Callum, her anger dominating the room despite her diminutive size. 'You want your mother to help me? Why? Am I such a hopeless embarrassment to you?'

He stared at her, absolutely appalled to realise she had overheard any part of his conversation with his mother but unable to defend himself in the face of such consuming fury.

'This is me, Callum, look.' She stood a bare six inches from him, grey eyes blazing into his blue ones. 'This is me and I will not be changed, especially by someone with such superficial values as your mother. If you can't accept

343

me the way I am, forget me. Find someone who won't be such a hindrance to your career!'

With that she strode from the room, ran back up the stairs and flung everything untidily back into her overnight bag. She had known this would be the test of their relationship. Well, it had failed. It was over.

Five minutes later she was stalking out of the house, anger driving her forward at a gallop.

Callum threw one dreadful look at his mother then charged after her.

'It was a mistake,' she told him bitterly when she had finally been persuaded to accept a lift back to Kilweem. 'Your mother is right. I'm nothing but a common little upstart from a rough mining village. I could only ever be an embarrassment to you.'

'Stop it!' Callum was reaching the limits of his patience. 'You know that isn't true.'

'Do I?' she asked, sharply. 'You want your mother to take me under her wing. To help me! I heard you say it, Callum.'

'I know you did. But try to look at it from my point of view. I love you, Maxine and I love my parents too. I suppose you'd laugh if I said I feel I have a duty towards them, but it's true. I have. I don't want to lose any of you. I was trying to manipulate you both, attempting to appeal to my mother's vanity. She loves to feel important, needed. I know I used the wrong words but if you hadn't come into the room when you did, I'd have told you all about it later and we'd have laughed together.'

'Would you?' she sneered, still too angry to care if she was hurting him. 'I doubt it, Callum.'

'Yes,' he snapped, very close to losing his temper now. 'I would have told you. And whatever else you think of me, Maxine, never accuse me of lying because that is something I do not do.'

344

'No, Callum, of course you wouldn't lie. That would be too much like a human failing, wouldn't it?' she sneered.

But suddenly all the fight went out of her. Callum was right. He never lied, she knew that, but it still hurt. 'I'm sorry. I shouldn't have said that,' she offered, after a minute of throbbing silence.

'No, you shouldn't,' he agreed. 'Look, can we just forget this weekend ever happened? It doesn't really matter. All that matters is us.'

'That's not true, Callum and you know it. You're not facing facts. You know what the real problem is as well as I do. You don't know what you want. Is it me or is it the Church? Because I don't think you can have both and it's no good pretending you can. I was wrong, I thought if we left things alone they'd sort themselves out in the end, but we'll never solve anything that way. Your mother saw that. That's why she behaved the way she did. Even the Rector knows it. And you have got to face it, too, Callum. You have got to make a choice and I can't help you do it.'

'I want you, Maxine,' he whispered, hoarsely.

'Are you sure, Callum? Because I seriously doubt that, and until you can make up your mind, decide where your true loyalties are, I think we should see less of each other.'

'Just because you and my mother didn't get on?' he asked, incredulously.

'No, Callum. But it's the same thing, isn't it? You couldn't bring yourself to stand up for me against your mother because – you said it – you don't want to lose either of us. It's the same with the Church. You can't make a decision because, like a little boy, you want both. Well, life's not like that, Callum. Sometimes you have to compromise, settle for the best you can get. That's what you've got to do now. I'm a married woman, someday I might be a divorced woman. Either way, the Church does not approve. And even if the Church was prepared to turn a blind eye and let us get married, your conscience wouldn't let you do it, would it?' she challenged him, sounding infinitely sad now. 'So, you have to make a choice. And until you do . . .'

'I see,' he spluttered, furiously. 'You were determined that this weekend would be awful, weren't you? This is exactly what you wanted to happen. It's a perfect way to break it off and blame someone else. It's all this talk about being independent that's behind this, isn't it? You don't want me, Maxine. All you want is that business you're so busy dreaming about. You just didn't have the guts to say so. Well, don't worry. I've got the message. Huh,' he snorted. 'The Rector was right. He told me not to make any hasty decisions. He said God would help me, show me what to do. Well He has, hasn't He?'

'I can't argue with God, Callum,' she said, letting herself out of the car and walking slowly up to her flat without looking back at him.

In his car Callum sat on for a full fifteen minutes, a picture of dejection. How could he have been so foolish as to think someone as lively and attractive as Maxine could really care for someone as boring as him? But what was it about her that drew him, making him take risks which could damage his career, bringing such confusion, such conflict to his mind? Or was the risk part of her appeal? Did the knowledge that she was totally unsuitable, that the Church could never approve of their union, make her even more attractive? How many nights had they sneaked up to his rooms, knowing full well that the Rector, tucked into his own bed on the floor below them, would heartily disapprove, the subterfuge bringing added excitement for both of them? But on how many Sunday mornings had he been shamed by the necessity of Maxine having to linger until everyone else in the Rectory had gone to church before sneaking off to her own flat? And how many times had he been in church, assisting with the service, even preaching to the congregation about the importance of moral standards, while all the time his lover was still warm in the bed where they had thrashed around in unbridled passion less than an hour before? Even in Maxine's flat there was danger. If word ever got back to Mrs Dalgleish that he was a regular overnight visitor, she was certain to tell the Rector. Not that their relationship was a secret. The villagers had got used to seeing them together now. It was the extent of that relationship which was dangerous. But he could no more resist the temptation to spend as many nights as he could with her than he could deny his faith in God.

With a despairing sigh he straightened and crashed the car into gear, his head thumping so badly that he could hardly think straight. Not caring, not even wanting to think, he drove home, opened a bottle of gin and drank until he could drink no more.

From her attic window, Maxine watched him drive away, a lump of pain congealing behind her breastbone. Wretchedly she emptied her bag and packed her things away. That done she wandered into her kitchen and put the kettle on, then unplugged it again and went to stand aimlessly by the window. The day stretched before her empty and uninviting, like her life would be without Callum. She prowled her flat, unable to settle to anything, then suddenly shoved her feet into her outdoor shoes again and grabbed her handbag. She would go across to the bakery and talk all this through with Maureen who was a reliable source of sympathy and common sense. At the front door of her building Maxine stopped, remembering that this was Saturday, the bakery's busiest day. Maureen would be extra busy without Maxine there to help out and certainly would have no time to listen to her niece's

TWENTY

Having finally accepted that there could be no future for her and Callum, Maxine threw herself, heart and soul, into the bakery and tea shop. She had grown so close to Maurice and Maureen, from whom she had no secrets, that it was not difficult. Maureen, whose warm heart ached for her niece, believed that hard work would help Maxine cope with her heartbreak and encouraged her to take on new responsibilities in the bakery while always providing a ready, sympathetic ear. Without their support Maxine would have found it impossible to cope with the strain of breaking up with Callum. Especially now that Janette's letters had become so infrequent. When they did arrive they were disappointingly short, almost dutiful, with barely a page or two of the most mundane news. Maxine always wrote back promptly, with her own, more personal, news which she longed to share with her friend but always got the same sort of unsatisfying reply. She missed the emotional release those letters had given her and recognised, sadly, that their close friendship was not going to survive the separation.

When the summer brought a fresh invasion of tourists to the area, Maxine applied all her energies into making the shop capitalise from them. The first thing she did was to persuade Maurice to let her widen the café's menu and then, with the help of some extra staff, to stay open in the evenings. The increase in profits was instantaneous and limited only by the size of the café itself. By the end of the season they were calling the newly-decorated café a

349

restaurant and taking advance bookings for evening tables. Most nights found them healthily busy.

Desperate to keep herself fully occupied, Maxine planned the menus, costed them, cooked, ordered and supervised the staff and knew it was almost entirely due to her that the business was thriving. The price she paid for this involvement was a gradual loosening of her ties with her father and sisters who were growing tired of Maxine's preoccupation with the bakery. Too many times she made work the excuse for not going home to see them all and more than once they arrived to spend the day with her in Kilweem and found instead that she was working while Maurice and Maureen had been delegated to entertain them. Glad though the whole family was to have this warm relationship with their elderly aunt and uncle, their attitude to their sister was tinged with resentment. The invitations became noticeably fewer and the visits rare. Maxine hardly noticed.

The bakery had a permanent staff of fifteen. Maureen, over seventy now, found she was able to take a less active role in the day-to-day running of the business which, for all practical purposes, was in Maxine's more than capable hands, and devoted her time to her ailing brother.

Maxine, who had been given the title of manager and an increase in salary as a measure of appreciation, revelled in the responsibility and challenge of it all and watched her savings grow with a feeling of deep satisfaction. The day was not far away when her dream of running her own small restaurant would become a reality. But not just yet, she still hadn't amassed enough money to make her ambition possible and loyalty to her great aunt and uncle made it easy for her to shelve her own plans until such time as they decided to retire.

Then, at the height of the season, Maurice suffered a stroke. The results of that, combined with worsening arthritis, confined him to bed. Overweight, in pain and frustrated by his inability to communicate clearly, he was a far from easy patient. Caring for him placed an almost intolerable burden on Maureen who was losing weight, tired easily and was constantly worried. Concerned for her ageing relatives, Maxine did as much as she could but felt that Maureen should have some professional help. Her elderly aunt wouldn't even consider it.

'Think of it like this,' she told Maxine as they sat together, as they often did, in the Archibolds' upstairs sitting room. 'If you were your Uncle Maurice, in pain and ashamed of the things your body did without you being able to control it, would you want to be messed about by people who don't know you and don't really care?'

Maxine then went to see Ina. Although her grandmother still obstinately refused to come to Kilweem, even for a few days, Maxine did return with a generous invitation for Maurice and Maureen to go to stay with their sister, where the whole family would play their part in caring for Maurice. Maxine went back to Kilweem much relieved that she had found a way to give her aunt a desperately needed rest. To her dismay Maureen reacted with rare anger.

'What made you think you could bundle us away, out of sight?' she demanded.

'No! That's not what I meant . . .' Maxine defended herself.

'Why else would you want us to go to Craigie, away from everything we know?'

'Maureen!' Maxine was close to tears to think that this woman, of whom she was so very fond, could have misjudged her so badly. 'All I was trying to do was give you a wee rest. I could stay here and look after the business so you wouldn't have to bother about that. And in Craigie—'

'Disgusting place!' Maureen interjected. 'Who in their right mind would want to live in a hell-hole like that?'

'In Craigie,' Maxine raised her voice and carried on. 'There's Linda, Catherine, Dad and Gran. They could help with Uncle Maurice so you wouldn't have to worry about him.'

'I want to worry about Maurice! How could you be so cold? I will not take my brother to live in Craigie. Is that quite clear?' Maureen stormed.

'I don't want you to go there to live! Why won't you listen to what I'm trying to say instead of imagining I'm trying to get rid of you?' Maxine retorted, equally angry now. 'I wanted you to go to Gran's, yes, but only for a week . . . two at the most . . . Good God! I want you to have a rest, Maureen, that's all. Get some sleep, let other people help out.' She sighed and reached out to take her aunt's shaking hand. 'Look at you! You would never have blown up like that at me a month ago. You're exhausted. I'm doing as much as I can but what with the shop and restaurant I can't help you as much as I would like to. Can't you see, I was just trying to make you have a break, before you get ill, too?' she pleaded, tears hot in her eyes.

Maureen looked at the girl she had come to love and felt ashamed of her outburst. Suddenly the anger fled and she held Maxine to her in a trembling embrace. 'Och, Lass, I'm sorry. Of course I know what you were trying to do. You're right I'm tired. But that changes nothing.' She held Maxine away from her and looked into her eyes. 'This is my home, Maurice's home. I know you meant well, Lass, but if I dragged him to Craigie do you really think I'd ever be able to bring him home again? No, Maurice and I will stay here, where we belong.'

After that Maxine knew there was nothing she could say to make Maureen change her mind.

As she was the only other person Maurice would allow

to do anything for him, Maxine compromised by staying with him herself as often as she could, freeing Maureen to get some much-needed rest. She read to him, played cards, gossiped shamelessly and argued vigorously, never failing to rouse him. His niece's cheerful presence brightened his otherwise dull existence and he looked forward avidly to the hours she spent with him. Even after she left, the echoes of her personality bounced round the room, making him feel less helpless and more optimistic.

But, inevitably, Maurice's condition continued to worsen and Maureen was fast approaching total exhaustion. As a last-ditch attempt to lighten her aunt's load, Maxine delegated the running of the bakery and restaurant to her trusted senior staff and practically moved into her aunt and uncle's spare bedroom, taking her turn at Maurice's bedside for much of the morning and evening. That way she was on hand if Maurice needed anything during the night, which he usually did.

Despite all the care and attention the two women gave so selflessly, Maurice slipped further and further away from them. With a sad heart Maxine knew it was just a matter of time before they must lose him.

The crisis came on one of the increasingly rare occasions when Maxine had spent the night at her own flat. Alerted by the doctor's car parked outside, she knew there was something wrong as soon as she arrived at the bakery, early the next morning. Fully expecting the worst she flew up the private stairs and knocked softly on Maurice's bedroom door. As she opened it she was hit by a wall of stifling heat and the terrible, cloying smell of sickness. Her head reeled and she gagged slightly but, catching a glimpse of Maureen at her brother's bedside, she took a deep breath and steeled herself to go inside.

Maurice was propped up on his pillows, his face tinged

with yellow, his lips an ominous blue. His breathing was laboured and noisy.

'Maurice had a second stroke during the night. I didn't realise until this morning.' Maureen was sad but out-wardly calm.

'I have been trying to persuade Miss Archibold that her brother would be better off in hospital. But . . .' the doctor, who had been on the point of leaving, appealed to Maxine for support.

'Doctor Cunningham has explained that Maurice cannot last very long like this.' Maureen took her brother's waxen hand. 'But however long he lasts, he will stay here. I will not send him to die among strangers.'

Maxine looked at the two people she had come to love so dearly and knew Maureen was right. 'I agree with my aunt, Doctor. This is what they both want. I'll be here to help. We'll manage.'

Maureen threw her a look of deep gratitude and Maxine caught the glint of tears in the elderly woman's eyes before she settled determinedly back at Maurice's side.

The next week was entirely taken up with caring for Maurice who clung to his slender thread of life with great tenacity. Maureen hardly left his bedside and then only when bullied away by Maxine who took her place while her aunt slept.

The old man just gradually slipped away. When the end came he stopped breathing so gently that neither of the two watching women knew it had happened, though both understood the end was imminent. Then Maureen touched her brother's relaxed features and sighed softly.

'You know,' she said, reaching for Maxine's hand. 'You may think this is a callous thing for me to say, but I'm glad he's gone. Maurice wouldn't have wanted to go on like that. There was nothing left for him after that second stroke. He didn't know me, his own sister. And think of all those visitors he had, people he'd known for years, villagers who have been his friends for most of his life, and he didn't recognise one of them. Not even you, Maxine, and he thought of you as his daughter. All he was aware of was the pain in his body. That was no way for a proud man like Maurice to live.' She grasped Maxine's hand tightly, smiled sadly and was lost in memories.

The next few days were a sad blur of visitors. The family, including Ina, all came from Craigie to pay their respects. The villagers came in ones and twos to say goodbye to someone they had known and liked all their lives. The Rector called to offer his condolences and Callum visited every day. Maxine was grateful to him for offering his services as a friend, giving no hint of the relationship they had once shared but was distressed that, in the midst of her grief, she was still aware only of him whenever they were in the same room. The spear of sexual longing which shot through her every time she looked at him both shocked and shamed her. What would he think of her if he knew what she was thinking? Fortunately for her composure his attention was almost exclusively for Maureen. The only time he spoke directly to her was after the funeral when he took her elbow and led her back to the waiting car, talking softly about Maurice while the Rector performed the same courtesy for Maureen. Under the circumstances her sudden pallor caused no comment.

It was a full two weeks before Maxine could put her mind back to the bakery and restaurant but, less than a fortnight after that, the two women were sitting together in Maureen's office, going over the books.

'Well,' Maureen said, linking her hands together in front

of her and assuming her most businesslike manner. 'I have a proposition for you.'

'Proposition?' Suspecting nothing, Maxine settled back in her chair, ready to listen.

'Yes.' There was no mistaking the smile of satisfaction which lit her aunt's face. 'I have decided to let you have the flat over the shop,' she smiled. 'You are the manager after all and it will be more convenient for you than that pokey little hole you like to call home.'

'But what about you? Where are you going to live?' Maxine's face was a portrait of confusion.

'I am going to move away. I'm too old to work any more, Maxine, and now that Maurice has gone I really don't want to stay here. There are too many memories. I'm over seventy. I've worked in the bakery since I was ten years old. First with my father, then with Maurice. I think I've earned my retirement, don't you?'

Maxine laughed her agreement. 'More than earned it.'

'I have the notion to move to a comfortable little house somewhere on the coast, where I can look out over the sea, perhaps with a small garden,' she laughed gustily. 'Maurice and I have lived in Kilweem for all our days. Always in this house and always tied to the business. Considering what a beautiful place Kilweem is and how lovely the beach can be, I've seen precious little of either. And you certainly can't appreciate the village from here, can you?'

Maxine had to agree. The bakery was housed in an ancient building which was a point of interest in itself but was hemmed in on all sides. None of the windows looked out on anything more inspiring than harled walls or, from upstairs, crow-stepped gable ends and tiled roofs. The front opened on to the busy, setted main street of Market-gate while the back yard, entered from a narrow side wynd, faced the back yards of a row of old fishermen's cottages which dated back almost two hundred years.

'I understand,' Maxine said at length. 'You're probably doing the right thing and you'll still be able to keep an eye on us.'

'You do not understand!' Maureen rapped her fingers on the table in a tattoo of impatience. 'I have absolutely no desire to keep an eye on you, Maxine. You have proved that you are more than capable of running this place without any interference from me. I want to get away from it! The bakery has dominated my life and I'm sick of it! You forget, I'm an old woman now. I do not want to be like Maurice. He worked so hard all his life, and what for? No, I want some time to myself. To do the things I always wanted to do. Sssssshhhh!' She silenced Maxine when she tried to interrupt. 'Hear me out, please.

'I don't have a great deal of money. It's all tied up in this place and it's mortgaged – we had to raise a lot of money for repairs a few years back. But this is what I intend to do.' She lit a cigarette and waved it at Maxine. 'No interruptions until I'm finished.'

'OK,' Maxine agreed, intrigued.

Businesslike and efficient, this was the Maureen of three years ago. 'Right then, I need money to live on and you need a job. So, I am going to sell you my half of the business and keep the half that Maurice left me. You will have to raise a bank loan so you can pay me in cash. Wait,' she shook her head vehemently when Maxine tried to butt in. 'The mortgage is small so you can lease the building from me for just enough to cover the repayments. That will be considerably cheaper for you than trying to set up on your own and, in any case, the mortgage has only two more years to run. We'll be equal partners so we share the profits and, of course, since you'll still be working here and I won't be, you will be able to draw a salary, just as you do now. I've got Maurice's insurance money and, with what you will pay me for your share of the business, I'll have enough to buy myself a comfortable house. My pension and the income from the profits should be more than enough to live nicely on. Of course, any extra profits will be reflected in what you can draw and, when the mortgage is paid up, there will be more money to play with. You'll have a completely free hand, naturally. We'll be partners on paper but, in fact the business will be yours to run as you see fit.' Pausing she stubbed out her cigarette and lit another one immediately. 'I've been into it all with my accountant and he assures me the idea is feasible. Och, I know it's not a great scheme as it stands. You'll have big repayments on the loan as well as paying me enough rent to cover the mortgage so you'll have to work hard at keeping the place profitable, for me as well as for yourself. But your personal income should stay much the same as it is now and you'll have a rent-free home thrown in. In the end you could make this do very nicely for yourself, Maxine. Of course, when I die, you can have the bally lot.' She said it so casually. 'I have already changed my will. You will be the main beneficiary, though, of course, I should like your sisters and David to have something to help them along.' She rubbed her hands together in satisfaction. 'Well, what's wrong with you, Lass? Tell me what you think.'

But Maxine was beyond words.

Leaning across the desk, Maureen put a wrinkled hand to the younger woman's face. Her voice was gentle, filled with emotion. 'This was Maurice's wish, as well as my own, Maxine. The restaurant is thriving and it is you who did it. You deserve to get some reward for all you've put into it. But it's not just that . . . Maurice and I, neither of us were lucky enough to have children but I can't imagine I'd feel closer to anyone than I do to you. You really are the daughter I never had, Maxine. I would hate to think of all this ending up with strangers.'

Maxine still couldn't force words past the enormous lump in her throat.

Smiling now Maureen adopted a brisker tone. 'Tomorrow you have an appointment at the bank. For now, all you have to do is say yes.'

She laughed outright when Maxine was still too overcome to do more than nod her golden head.

'There is just one possible snag,' Maureen said. 'I don't want to pressure you but you should know everything.'

'What?' Maxine asked, softly.

'Well, you have to understand that I must sell, Maxine. There is nothing I want more than for you to stay on here but . . . well you're still young and perhaps you won't be able to raise the money. In that case,' she stopped, genuinely distressed. 'In that case I have already had an offer. The solicitor will tell you the details tomorrow. I should have to sell, Maxine.'

Maxine smiled and caught the other woman's hands. 'It'll be all right. But I would understand, Maureen, of course I would.' But she wouldn't let it happen. The village restaurant and bakery were going to be hers. The place she had always dreamed of.

TWENTY-ONE

'I am sorry, Miss Lennox, but the bank is unable to help you.' The bank manager, a pompous barrel of a man, peered at her over the top of his horn-rimmed spectacles. All through the interview she had felt his attitude towards her to be condescending, but she hadn't expected this instant rejection. The delight of yesterday gave way to abject misery but she wasn't going to give this self-important little man the satisfaction of seeing that.

'Why, Mr Fairbairn? I have had an account with this bank for several years and you must be able to see how the sum has increased steadily. Surely that proves I can manage my money?'

He laughed, a portly, dismissive, rumbling noise. 'My dear Miss Lennox, saving a little bit each week from your wages is not quite the same as entering into a sizeable loan agreement for a business such as this. You have no collateral and it is not as if the business would be yours, you would still have large payments to make to Miss Archibold for her share of the profits.'

'You've seen the accounts. You know I could meet those payments, Mr Fairbairn. The business is doing very well. If I put in all my savings I only need another two thousand pounds. Is there no way I could borrow that amount?'

'Not from this bank, Miss Lennox. Perhaps your father could be persuaded to buy into the business . . . ?' He glanced at her hands. 'Are you by any chance engaged to be married?'

'Why?' she demanded, anger surging through her.

'In such a case I am sure I could consider an application from your future husband, assuming he had a regular income . . .'

Maxine took back the account books. 'Good morning, Mr Fairbairn. I am obviously wasting your time,' she said, coldly.

Unhappily she walked back along the High Street in Cupar, where she banked, towards Callum's father's office. Messrs Mackie and Malcolm looked after Maureen's legal affairs. Despite the disastrous weekend she had spent at his home, Maxine liked and trusted Mr Mackie who was sympathetic but unable to help.

'Oh dear, Miss Archibold does so want you to be able to buy into the business, and it would be a wonderful investment for you, but I can only recommend that you approach another bank. A different, perhaps a younger manager, might have a more modern approach. Or perhaps you could borrow the money from a relative?'

She laughed. 'My relatives don't have that sort of money, Mr Mackie.'

'I'm sorry, my dear, but I don't know what else to suggest. You see, most lending houses are likely to take the same view as the bank. They all want collateral and you have nothing to offer them as security.'

'How long do I have?'

'Your aunt is anxious to settle this as quickly as possible, though I am sure she didn't seriously expect this difficulty. I do know she has seen a house she wants to buy and I can also tell you that she's had a very fair offer from Angelou's who are pressing for a decision.'

'Angelou's?' Maxine repeated. 'Who or what are Angelou's?'

The solicitor shrugged dismissively. 'It's an Edinburgh company. Ice-creams, hamburgers, that sort of thing. I believe they're very popular with the youngsters and of course, it's just what the tourists are looking for.'

Maxine made a disgusted face. 'Not in Kilweem! We're an old-fashioned village, that's what makes us so special. I'm sure no one would welcome a place like that.'

'I know your aunt doesn't want them to buy the bakery,' James Mackie agreed. 'This is the second offer they've made. The first time was a couple of years ago. Mr Archibold wouldn't even consider it. Of course, now he's dead, they probably think they have a better chance of persuading his sister.'

'And they might succeed if I can't raise this money,' Maxine sighed.

'You have until the end of the month, Miss Lennox. And I for one wish you every success.'

Intrigued by conflicting impressions of fragility, determination and shrewd business sense, tempered by areas of disarming naivety, and charmed by her uncomplicated beauty, Mr Mackie escorted Maxine to the door, exercising all his slightly old-fashioned gallantry on her. It really was a pity, he thought, watching her walk away, that his son's romance with that young woman had failed to blossom.

Maxine wandered back on to the street, lost in thought as she frantically sought ways to raise the extra cash. It was an impossible task.

'Hello, Maxine. Are you all right?' a deeply concerned voice asked.

She jumped like a frightened kitten then looked up to find herself staring into Callum's serious face. His habitually worried expression reminded her of the first time they had met.

'Callum! You startled me. I was miles away,' she said.

'Sorry! I'm on my way to see Father,' he explained easily, chuckling at her and banishing the worried look. 'How are you and Maureen coping now, Maxine?'

It irritated her to hear him sounding like a concerned curate, just as if she was nothing more than another troubled parishioner. Instantly she knew she was being unreasonable.

'Oh, we're OK. Maureen still misses Uncle Maurice of course. We both do but it's harder for her.'

He nodded his head. 'Of course . . . You were pretty deep in thought there?'

'Yes . . . I've just lost the opportunity of a lifetime, that's all,' she smiled, wryly. 'I've been to see your father about buying a share in the bakery but it looks as if I won't be able to do it.'

Callum frowned again. 'What's the problem?'

She shrugged, not wanting to discuss this with him, especially in the middle of the street.

'Look, I've got to return this book I borrowed from Father. Do you think you could wait for me? I'll not be more than five minutes and then I'll give you a lift home.'

He was off along the road before she could think of a suitable excuse. He really was the last person she wanted to see right now. Her life was complicated enough without Callum reappearing to confuse her just when she needed to be extra clear-headed. He really was far too attractive to be a curate, she thought as she watched him striding along the pavement.

True to his word he was back in five minutes, slightly breathless, but smiling brightly.

'The car's this way,' he said, leading her across the road as if, she thought, she was a geriatric and he was doing his good turn for the day. For the second time in ten minutes she knew she was being grossly unfair.

Anxious to keep their conversation flowing on the drive

back to Kilweem and so avoid any possible reference to their past relationship, she told him about Maureen's offer.

'So, it looks very much as if I won't be able to raise the money. It really is a pity though. I'll never get another chance like this.'

'And Kilweem will be stuck with an Angelou's on its main street. Yes, it is a pity,' he agreed, pulling up outside her home. 'Wait a minute, Maxine.' He stopped her as she started to get out of the car. 'Perhaps there is a way for you to raise the money.'

'How?' She turned back to him, hope alive in her face.

'You could let me lend it to you,' he suggested, wondering what on earth had made him make such a rash offer.

'NO!' she cried, too quickly and too loudly, then tried to make a joke of it. 'I think that's carrying Christian charity a bit too far, Callum, even for a curate.' She saw the warning flash of anger in his blue eyes. Callum's sensitivity about his calling was his weak spot. 'Thank you, Callum. I appreciate the offer but I really couldn't take money from you,' she said quickly.

'Why not?' he persisted, seeing again the dainty features, the soft, blonde hair, the perfect figure, the challenging, determined eyes and remembering the touch of her body beneath his as if it had been only yesterday. He could feel the heat in his groin already.

'We could make it a business arrangement,' he explained hastily to take his mind off physical things. 'Pay me back as if I was the bank.'

'No.' It was a stubborn refusal. Here was the path to her goal. Pride made her refuse him. Pride and an unwillingness to be obligated to him.

'We could have it done legally . . .'

'Are clergymen allowed to do that . . . money lending I mean?' she teased, unable to take her eyes off him now, feeling flutters of excitement in her stomach.

364

But that was the way to misery. She had been there with him once before and had no intention of repeating the experience. Callum Mackie had made his choice, had put the Church solidly before her. It had hurt so much that she had wondered if she might actually fade away and die for him, like a spineless heroine in some old novel but now, strangely, she reviewed his decision with a kind of angry pride in his integrity.

'I think so . . .' He seemed momentarily lost.

'No, Callum. Thanks again, but absolutely not. This is something I have to do for myself.'

He turned away and shrugged. God knows why he had even made the offer. Maxine Lennox was obviously the same ambitious, stubborn, deliciously entrancing temptress she had been two years ago. The sooner he got away from her the better.

'Thanks for the lift,' she called after him, trying to make it sound as casually friendly as possible.

He managed to smile but he felt as though he had a dose of 'flu coming on, so badly was he shaking.

It was a week later and a little after nine in the evening when there was an unexpected knock at Maxine's door.

'Who is it?' she called out.

'Me,' came the voice she recognised instantly. 'Callum.'

She opened the door a few inches and peered at him. 'What do you want?' she asked, ungraciously.

'I need to talk to you. Can I come in or not?'

'Can't you come back in the morning? I'm tired.' She tried to close the door but he had jammed his foot in the gap.

'So am I!' he roared in a manner which would have astonished his older parishioners. 'I have been sick visiting at the hospital all morning. I've had the woman's group this afternoon, confirmation class when everyone else was having their tea and then Brownies this evening, because Mrs Scott isn't well. I've had nothing to eat since breakfast and now I've got the grandmother of headaches and still I was stupid enough to think that you would at least be polite enough to listen to what I have to say to you, so I walked down here too. Still, if you're too tired, forget it.'

He made a big issue out of taking his foot from the door and making for the stairs. It had been that final hour with the Brownies which had destroyed what was left of his usual good humour and caused his head to start thumping. Callum liked children, singly or even in groups of two or three. Twenty shrieking eight-year-old girls was more than even he could stand.

Maxine recognised the fatigue in his face and regretted her coldness instantly. 'Callum, come back,' she shouted, with no regard for her neighbours. 'I'm sorry. I shouldn't have been so rude. I've been in a foul mood all week. Come in and I'll make us a drink.'

He turned and grinned sheepishly. 'Thanks, I could do with something.'

He collapsed on to her settee, his long legs stretched out in front of him and relaxed while she produced tea with sausage rolls and cakes – brought home from the bakery – and aspirins.

By the time she came back he was almost asleep. He sat up with a start and rubbed at his eyes.

'You do look tired,' she said softly. 'Here, you'll feel better if you have something to eat. There's some aspirin for your head, too.'

'Thanks.' He helped himself to a hearty plateful. 'I just don't seem to have had time to eat. The Rector's away, talking with the Bishop all week. I have been rather busy.'

'What did you want to see me for?'

'That money you were trying to raise . . .'

'I've already told you, Callum. No.' She wouldn't let him finish.

He sighed and raised his hand. 'Permission to speak?'

She shrugged. 'You're wasting your time if you're here to offer to lend it to me.'

'I am not here to offer to lend you anything. You know, you can be really aggravating when you want to be, Maxine.'

She had the grace to smile at him and he grinned back, clearing the air again. 'I know. I'm sorry. Go on.'

'I've had an idea about how you might be able to raise some of it.'

'How?'

There was a bright gleam of interest in her eyes now and a flush of colour on her cheeks that had nothing at all to do with money and everything to do with finding herself alone with this man. A man, she realised now, for whom she still had uncomfortably strong feelings. Her mind strayed back to the occasions when they had made love on the settee where he was now sitting. The memory of his strong, hard body made her flush deepen to scarlet.

'Well,' he began, unable to take his eyes off her, even though he could see from the angry flush on her face that she didn't appreciate him watching her so closely. 'I was telling Mother about your plans the other night and she suggested . . .'

'Your mother!' All the old resentment and anger ignited so fast that she was on her feet and screaming at him before she knew she was doing it. 'What the hell were you doing discussing me with your mother?'

'I merely mentioned your plans to buy into the bakery,' he replied honestly, realising what a lucky escape he had had in avoiding marriage to this harridan.

'It's none of your business,' she spat, making for the door. 'Goodnight, Callum.'

'For goodness sake,' he spluttered. 'Get off that pedestal of virtue you've got yourself stuck on and listen to me. You might even gain something from it.' Something made him resist the impulse to fling out of the room and leave her to simmer in her own pride. And she really was magnificent when she was angry.

'I doubt it,' she retorted.

'When you came to my parents' place that weekend, do you remember my mother saying something about a brooch you were wearing?' he asked, getting the words out in a fast stream before she could shout him down again.

'Brooch?' she asked. The incident had completely slipped her mind. 'I can't remember . . . everything was so dire that weekend . . . I can only remember her being so bloody unpleasant.' She swore deliberately, hoping to shock him, and he knew it.

'I heard a lot worse than that from the Brownies this evening so if you want to shock me you'll have to try much harder,' he retorted. 'Just forget about my mother for a minute and think about that brooch. Apparently you said it was a wedding present. She recalls that very clearly because, until that moment she didn't know you had been married. I hadn't told her.'

'Too ashamed . . .' she started, then bit it off guiltily. 'Sorry. And I do remember now. Aunt Minnie's brooch. But it's just a piece of ugly rubbish.'

'And perhaps not. My mother has an eagle eye for anything valuable, especially jewellery. She collects the stuff and she thinks it might be genuine.'

'Callum, people like me don't have valuable bits of jewellery.'

But Aunt Minnie might have done. Her father's older sister had married a Catholic man, a betrayal her staunchly Protestant family had never forgiven her for. From the little Maxine recalled they had lived in a large house, somewhere in the Glasgow area, years and years ago. When her husband died Aunt Minnie had been reduced to a much meaner standard of living and that was why she had only been able to give her niece the old and rather ugly jewellery as a wedding present. She could afford nothing else. Maxine did remember both her father and her aunt telling her to look after the gift. Still, it was hugely unlikely that the whole set was worth more than fifteen or twenty pounds.

'Have you still got the brooch?' Callum broke into her reverie.

'I don't know . . . I suppose I must have. Somewhere.' She looked vaguely round the room. 'I don't think I've seen it since that weekend.'

'See if you can find it,' he ordered.

'Now?'

'Yes, Maxine. Now. I want to have a look at it. If it's what my mother thinks it is, you should at least have it valued.'

'Your mother's an expert I suppose?' she muttered sarcastically, half under her breath as she tore open a cupboard.

He heard her. 'No, but she can spot something valuable a mile off. Especially,' he added with a boyish grin, 'when it belongs to someone else.'

'I don't know where I can have put it,' she admitted, hunting through a set of drawers. 'Ah! Here's the case.' From under a pile of scarves and gloves she produced a red, velvet case. 'See for yourself. Ugly and unwearable,' she said, tossing it across to him.

Callum opened the box and looked thoughtfully at its contents. 'Ear-rings and a splendidly horrible necklace,' he laughed, dangling the offending items from his fingers. 'Where's the brooch?'

'Isn't it there? God, I don't know.'

He coughed uncomfortably at her unthinking blasphemy.

'Sorry, Callum,' she offered, smiling.

'Don't you ever throw anything away?' he teased, as she scrambled in the bottom of her wardrobe, turfing out old handbags, ruined purses and disused make-up.

'It's a good job I don't,' she exclaimed triumphantly. 'Look, here it is. This is the handbag I took with me that weekend. I must have stuffed it in here then tossed the lot in the wardrobe in a fit of temper.'

Callum rotated the articles in his hands, held them under the light then rubbed gently at the tarnished settings with his sleeve.

'Well?' she demanded, impatiently.

'I don't know. I'd agree with you I suppose. They don't look as though they're worth anything. Just glass beads I think but they're so dirty it's hard to tell. It might be as well to get someone to look at them though, just to be sure.' He placed them back in the case and she could tell from his expression that he was disappointed. 'I'm sorry, Maxine, I've got your hopes up for nothing.'

'Never mind. It was a kind thought. I'm no worse off now than I was an hour ago. I am pretty tired though and you look exhausted. Maybe you should go now and we'll both get some sleep.' Suddenly it was very important to get him out of this room. Old emotions were dangerously close to the surface tonight and she didn't want to risk starting anything with him again. So why did she feel so disappointed when he jumped to his feet with almost indecent alacrity and went on his way without so much as a smile?

In the morning light the jewellery looked no more attractive than it had last night and even less likely to be valuable. Over a skimped breakfast Maxine examined the pieces again, wondering what it was that had caught Mrs Mackie's eye. Nothing that she could see. Sadly she rearranged them back in their box and closed the lid. The velvet case with its gold lettering looked more valuable than its contents. She turned it over in her hands, loath to simply store it away again. Maybe, just maybe, she would get it valued. Even if it fetched twenty pounds it would be more useful to her in her bank account than falling to bits in a drawer.

The surge in tourism in Strathannan had yet to spawn the antique and curio shops which were starting to flourish in some other areas. Nor was there a jeweller in the immediate vicinity. To get any reliable idea of her jewellery's value Maxine decided to go to St Andrews where there were several of both.

That afternoon found her hesitating outside the most expensive jewellers in the historic burgh, wondering if she was about to make a complete fool of herself. A man, wearing what appeared to be a morning suit, looked up when she went in.

'Good afternoon, Madam,' he greeted her somewhat profusely. 'It is a beautiful day is it not? How may I help you?'

'I would like someone to have a look at this and tell me what they think it might be worth,' she said, sliding the case over the glass-topped counter towards him.

The smile faded and his manner became distinctly icy. 'We do not buy or sell second-hand items, Madam, unless they are of exceptional quality.' He seemed about to push the case back to her. He certainly made no attempt to open it.

'How will you know whether this is of exceptional quality unless you look at it?' she inquired sweetly, subjecting him to a penetrating stare while resisting the impulse to slap his smug face. 'And I don't recall saying anything about buying or selling.'

She was gratified to see him lose his self-assurance and for a moment he looked very much as if he didn't know what to do.

'Very well,' he agreed at last. 'Fortunately we are quiet at the moment but should a customer come in I shall have to attend to them.'

She nodded, eased the box a fraction closer to him and watched in silence while he first examined the case, then opened it and peered very closely at the jeweller's name, etched in gold inside the lid. His eyebrows shot up in surprise and he snatched a disbelieving look at Maxine. She felt her heart thump in growing excitement. With infinite care he extracted the pieces and laid them on a chamois cloth. Then, with an eye glass screwed firmly into one eye, he subjected them all to a very close scrutiny. After some four or five minutes he replaced them in the box and shut the lid but kept one hand firmly clamped over it when he asked, 'Where did you get these, Madam?'

'Oh, they were honestly come by, if that's what you mean,' she assured him. 'They belonged to my father's sister. She gave them to me for a wedding present.'

'And where did she get them?'

'I really don't know,' Maxine replied frankly. 'I suppose her husband bought them for her. He was fairly well off.' Now her heart was leaping inside her. They were worth something, that was quite obvious from the man's manner.

'I see,' he said thoughtfully, rubbing the point of his chin.

'Can you tell me anything about them?' she asked, impatiently.

'Not without time to examine them properly and – '

372

'How much might they be worth?' she demanded, knowing he would find such a bald question in bad taste.

'That would be very difficult to assess. Without proof of ownership no reputable dealer would agree to handle them for you. I certainly couldn't.'

'I am not asking you to handle them for me. And if you are implying what I think you are . . .'

'Please, Madam . . . If you would care to leave the pieces with your name and address I will have them formally valued. There will be a charge of course.'

'No, I don't think so,' she smiled, whisking the case out from under his hand and stuffing it back into her handbag.

'Wait.' He followed her to the door, suddenly eager. 'Please understand. We have to be careful. Our reputation . . .'

'Good,' she beamed at him and left him holding the door open for her. He had told her just enough to give her confidence.

In a street behind the castle she discovered exactly the sort of small antique shop she now knew she should have come to in the first place. This time, confidence high, she walked straight in.

'Yes?' An elderly man behind the counter stopped cleaning the watch he had in pieces in front of him and beamed at her.

'I've got something here I'd like you to have a look at, tell me anything you can about it and try to give me some idea of its value,' she said, brightly.

'Aye, well, that could be a problem,' he admitted, rubbing a hand over his balding pate. 'I'm your man if it's watches or jewellery but anything else and it's my partner you need. And he's not here.'

'It's jewellery,' she smiled, handing him the case.

'Ah, wonderful,' he enthused as soon as he flipped the lid open.

'Really?' she asked, liking him immensely.

'Too soon to be sure,' he admitted, squinting at the earrings. 'Here, come and have a seat. This might take a little time.'

She squeezed round the wooden counter and perched on a high, old-fashioned chair while he got on with examining Aunt Minnie's gift.

'Well,' he sighed at last. 'The stones are real enough and the setting. They're in the original box and though there are no marks on the pieces they are entirely in keeping with the work of this jeweller. The set was made in London, as you will have seen from the box. Do you know anything about jewellery?' he asked, his eyes twinkling with enjoyment.

'Not a thing,' she admitted.

'Well, this is a very famous jeweller,' he said, pointing to the inscription inside the lid. 'And this is a very good set and in lovely condition. Dirty, mind, but that's easily remedied.'

'How much do you think it could be worth?'

'Now that's a difficult one,' he said, packing them back in the case and handing it to her. 'I'd be a fool to even try to put a price on it. The stones alone, they're sapphires, rubies and diamonds with jet in the middle, all in a gold setting, must be worth a couple of thousand, anyway.'

Her legs went weak and for a second she thought she might faint.

The old man laughed. 'There, that was a pleasant surprise, wasn't it?'

'It certainly was.'

'Are they yours, Lass?' he asked, watching her closely.

'Yes. An aunt of mine gave them to me for a wedding present. I'm not sure how she came by them though. I

374

think her husband must have given them to her as a birth-day present or something. They're both dead now so I'll never know for sure.'

'It was a very generous wedding present.'

'I don't think she can have known what they were worth. I never thought they were anything more than glass until recently and I certainly can't wear them, they're so ugly.'

'Ugly?' he cried in mock outrage. 'They're beautiful. Absolutely wonderful. They knew how to make jewellery then.'

'And they're genuine?' she persisted, hardly able to believe her good fortune.

'They're real stones all right and I'd stake my reputation on them being genuine pieces.'

'Could you sell them for me?'

He appeared to consider this for a moment then shook his head. 'No, Lass. I'd not be doing you any favours if I took them. Most people round here would react in just the way you did. They want something reasonably modern. I might get a thousand for them.'

'I thought you said two!'

'Aye, I did, but not in this shop.'

'I see.' So this wasn't going to be the marvellous wind-fall she had hoped for.

'Don't look so down-hearted. That's here. In St Andrews. But, if I was to take these to Edinburgh, or London, they should sell at auction for a lot more than that. A collector might even be willing to pay three or four thousand pounds.'

'Oh God!'

'Look, Lass, my best advice to you is to take them to Southarts, in Edinburgh. Let them give you an expert valuation. Then, if you still want to sell them, let Southarts auction them for you.'

'I'll do that,' she said. 'Thank you, thank you very much.' She was keenly aware that this old man could easily have taken advantage of her ignorance. 'What do I owe you?'

'No, Lass. It's been a pleasure. A real pleasure,' he chuckled and bent his grey head back to the dismembered watch.

'Southarts,' he called after her as she went through the door. 'No one but Southarts.'

Southarts, better known as a London auction house, had an imposing branch in Edinburgh's George Street. Full of confidence now that she was sure her jewellery was valuable, Maxine went into their impressive foyer feeling she had every right to be there. Five years ago she would have been too intimidated to even stand outside the place.

An hour later she was running for her train back to Strathannan, the velvet case safely in Southarts' safe and the receipt tucked into the back of her purse.

She had to wait less than a week for their formal valuation. But before they could be auctioned, in London, she had to provide proof of ownership.

'That's wonderful, Maxine,' Callum, who had called in for a progress report, resisted the very strong urge to kiss her, suspecting that she just might slap his face if he was rash enough to try anything like that too suddenly.

'So, do you think your father would sort out this ownership thing in a hurry?' she asked

'Of course. I can swear they're yours but it would probably be better to get a statement from your father too. Unless you have the wedding gift tag. I know some people keep things like that.'

She chuckled gleefully. 'I do! All the cards and things are in a box at Dad's. If I remember rightly there's a wee note from Aunt Minnie on the back, something about always keeping the jewellery in the case to stop it from tarnishing.'

'Perfect! We'll run down to Craigie and see your father tonight.'

'We will?'

'Well, you've no car any more so you'll need a lift, won't you? There are no buses that'll get you there and back tonight. You'd have to go into Cupar, then Inverannan . . .'

'OK. You win,' she laughed. 'Thanks, Callum.'

Maurice's old saloon had broken down before he died. The cost of the necessary repairs was far more than the value of the car which lingered in the local garage. So far neither Maureen nor Maxine had had the heart to assign it to the scrap heap.

'That's all right. I feel sort of responsible for this. I want to make sure it all works out without any last-minute hitches.'

'Aye, that's right, Hen. Your Uncle Eddie gave them to our Minnie. It was a wedding anniversary present as far as I mind.' George chuckled and took a noisy gulp from one of the cans of Export that Callum had been thoughtful enough to provide. 'Your Aunty Minnie hated them. She wasn't one for fancy jewellery.'

'Dad,' Maxine asked the question which had been bothering her for some time. 'How could they afford something like this? And why give it to me? Aunty Minnie should have sold them herself.'

'As far as I mind old Eddie picked them up cheap in a second-hand shop, a pawnbroker's I think. They cost him a fair bit, too. Fifteen pounds if I mind right. Our Minnie was black affronted that he could give her second-hand stuff. They had a right set to about it. Aye, but he was an old bugger. He must have had a fair idea of what they were worth. Mind you, I don't think our Minnie could have known. I suppose she just thought they were worth the fifteen pounds Eddie gave for them. And it was a good enough wedding present for you, even at that. All she could afford to give anyway.'

'Better than she knew. It's a shame really, isn't it?'

'Don't worry about it, Hen. That's the way life goes. You sell them and get some good from them.' In his easygoing way George was delighted for his daughter and not the least bit envious of her good fortune.

'We'll have to get going, Dad. I'll let you know what happens at the auction.'

'Right you are, Hen. I'll away to the Greyhound and have a wee advance celebration for you.'

Maxine caught Callum's amused eye and smiled. Her father would never change. It was reassuring somehow.

After he had gone to all the trouble of driving her to Craigie, Maxine knew that it would be good manners to invite Callum up to her flat for coffee. The knowledge that she was still dangerously attracted to him, and didn't want to be, stopped her.

He waited hopefully for a couple of minutes but finally gave up and broached the suggestion he had been playing with all night while they were standing on her doorstep.

'Tomorrow is the last day of the month.'

'I know.'

'I thought you had to have the restaurant sorted out by then?'

'It would have been better if it had worked out that

378

way. Maureen has seen a house she likes in Sauchar. Offers close tomorrow but she won't make a move until she knows whether I'm buying a share in the restaurant. If I can't and Angelou's go ahead it could be two or three months before she settles with them. Thanks to Aunt Minnie it won't come to that.'

'How much do you need to raise?'

'Two thousand. I have the rest in my savings account.'

'Och, you'll make that easily!'

'Maybe. Maybe not,' she said, uncertainly.

'It seems a shame that Miss Archibold should lose the house she's got her heart set on just for the sake of a couple of days. On Friday your jewellery will be sold and you'll be able to go ahead. But it will be too late for Miss Archibold.'

'I know. I feel awful about it. It's a lovely house too, just right for her. Near her friend, Mrs McMurray, and overlooking the golf course . . .'

'Shame.'

'There's nothing I can do about it, Callum. I wish there was. Maureen could have sold out to Angelou's already and had her money by now but she's absolutely determined to give me every chance to raise that money. Anyway, Callum, thanks for cheering me up and making me feel guilty,' she retorted, wondering why her mood seemed so erratic when Callum was around.

'Here,' he reached into his pocket and, grinning widely, slipped a piece of paper into her hand.

'I can't take this,' she whispered, staring at the cheque. 'Oh, Callum, we've been through all this before.'

'And you are going to be just as stubborn as you were the last time I suppose?' he asked, his pleasure rapidly melting away.

'I won't take your money.'

'I know, I know. You want to do it all on your own.

What you really mean is that you're letting that stupid pride of yours get in the way again. Why can't you think of someone else for a change? Your aunt has done her very best for you and here's a way for you to repay that kindness. But you are too . . . too blasted stubborn to put your own fine feelings behind hers, just for a day or two. Why won't you let me help, Maxine? Are you frightened I might want something in return, is that it?'

'No.' She denied it quickly.

'Well, what is it, then?' he persisted. 'Or are you simply stupid?'

'How dare you . . .' she roared, then stopped, horrified by the laughter she saw in his face.

'You really are amazing when you're angry,' he spluttered.

'Callum!' Why was she always so confused when she was with this man?

'Please, Maxine, take it. In a week or two you'll have the money from the sale but it will be too late for Miss Archibold then. Take this and buy your share of the business. Pay me back when your money comes through and that'll be the end of it. I promise.'

'But what if I don't get two thousand?'

'You'll get two thousand. If, by some strange quirk, you don't, then you can pay me back at so much a month. But don't worry about that. It will never happen. I shouldn't tell you this but I know my mother would be prepared to pay that much for it. She thinks it would be an excellent investment.'

'She's going to the sale?'

'No,' he laughed at the aghast expression on her face. 'My father is. He asked me not to tell Mother, but he's going to try and get it for her as a birthday present. It's her sixtieth in a few weeks' time. Poor man, he thinks it'll be a tremendous surprise for her but she's done nothing but chuck out brick-sized hints for the past fortnight, ever since she knew you were selling.'

'I hope she doesn't get it.'

Callum looked at her sharply. 'Why not, Maxine? You don't want it. Surely my father's money is the same as any one else's. At least my mother would appreciate it for what it is.'

It was all said with a total absence of anger and she felt terribly ashamed.

'I'm sorry, Callum. That was an awful thing to say,' she admitted.

'Yes, it was.' He forced a smile back on his face. 'Let's not argue. My point is that I can guarantee you will have enough to pay me back. Two thousand is the reserve price and I know my father will willingly pay that. Take the cheque now and let Miss Archibold have the house her heart's set on.'

'I don't know . . .'

'No strings, Maxine. Just borrow this until your money comes through. I won't expect you to treat me any differently because of this.'

'Honestly?' she asked, torn between instinct and common sense.

'Do you really think I would try and buy my way into your good books?' he asked. 'OK, I'll be honest with you, if that's what you want,' he said, shivering in the draughty doorway. 'I would very much like us to get together again, Maxine. Very much. But we both know it wouldn't work. Nothing's changed. You're still married and I'm still a curate. But this cheque has nothing to do with that. We're friends, I hope, and friends do help one another when they can. Or, if you prefer, call it help from one of Miss Archibold's friends. After all, it is for her benefit, not yours.'

'I think you've talked me into it,' she said, softly.

'What? Me or the money?' He couldn't resist teasing.

'The money of course. This is purely business, Callum. Between friends,' she insisted, sounding less convincing with every word. 'Let's get this over with and then, when the sale goes through, you can take me out to dinner, to celebrate,' she conceded.

'Oh no,' he objected, making her head jerk up in shock, wondering if she had, after all, totally misunderstood. 'Oh no! YOU will take ME out to dinner. And to the best restaurant I can find.'

'Deal,' she whispered, smiling softly.

'I hope you don't expect me to shake on it,' he murmured.

Before she could step away he claimed a kiss from lips which were unexpectedly soft and willing. She was still shaking when he jumped back into his car and drove away.

The auction raised more than she had ever, even in her wildest dreams, imagined. Within the week she had a cheque for just under nine thousand pounds, the business was half hers and Maureen had signed the contract for her retirement home in Sauchar.

Before she left to meet Callum, to buy him the meal she had promised, Maxine wrote a cheque of her own and slipped it into her handbag. Full repayment of his loan. She was flushed and excited when she met him and it had very little to do with the sale of her jewellery.

They went to an unpretentious restaurant in St Andrews. Callum, making no concessions over his calling, was every inch the clergyman in a light grey suit, complete with dog collar. Every time Maxine looked at him her stomach contracted painfully.

It was obvious that he was as aware as she was that this evening could lead to the resumption of their affair. Their conversation was stiff, almost formal as they strove to avoid contentious issues. The atmosphere was strained and neither of them enjoyed, or even noticed, what they were eating.

By the time they got to the coffee she was so tense that she almost wished it was over and she was back home again. Almost.

She expected him to drive straight back to Kilweem. To her surprise he took his car down to the harbour.

'Come on, after that meal I could do with a walk,' he said, springing out and opening her door for her.

'Ah-ha! I remember your idea of a walk, Callum, and I'm not dressed for hiking,' she said, looking at her rather uncomfortable high heels.

He laughed. 'I thought you seemed taller than I remembered. We won't walk far, just along the jetty and back.'

The night was perfect, still, calm and mild, the sinking sun reflecting dramatically off the lazy swell of the sea. Lovers sat in their cars, looking out over the water and another couple, arms wrapped round one another, walked round the far side of the harbour, clearly oblivious to everyone else. Maxine watched them for a moment, a lump rising in her throat, then looked away again, feeling she was invading their privacy.

Callum caught her hand as they started to walk then linked his fingers through hers. Already her heart was hammering.

They reached the end of the jetty and stood looking out to sea, the silence broken only by the gentle lapping of the water round the base of the harbour wall, six feet below them.

'It's so beautiful,' she whispered.

He nodded, squeezed her hand but said nothing and she risked a look at him. The breeze caught a wisp of his dark blond hair, rippling it gently before laying it down again.

There was, she decided with a liquid feeling in her chest, an innate strength in Callum. More than his firm jaw, straight nose and clear eyes, or even his athletic build suggested. As she watched him the wind caught at his hair again. He raised a hand and smiled as he flattened the wayward strand. There was nothing vain in the gesture, it had been completely natural and unaffected, an automatic reaction, but the fluid movement of his hand, the slightly impatient toss of his head, seemed to her to be an electric reminder of his sexuality. She longed to touch him, to feel the warmth of him, the strength of him. Unconsciously she moved closer, so her shoulder was touching his. Still he didn't say anything, didn't look at her. She couldn't stand the tension building in her any more. She had to speak, make him look at her.

'If it wasn't for you I'd never even have known about that jewellery.' She said the first thing that came into her head.

'If it wasn't for my mother,' he corrected her with a quiet smile in her direction.

She caught the gleam in his eye and knew he was teasing. 'You couldn't resist that, could you, Reverend Mackie? Are you trying to make me annoyed with you already?' She couldn't hide her own smile.

He laughed openly now. 'I love you when you're angry, Maxine Lennox.'

'Is that the only time you love me?' she asked, quietly.

Now he turned to face her fully, reaching out and pulling her closer to him before he spoke. 'You know damn well it is not the only time,' he said passionately. 'My God, Maxine, have you any idea how awful tonight has been for me? The woman I love is sitting three feet away from me and all I dare do is make stupid conversation about the weather . . .' He was still tense from the effort, still unsure of her, frightened of her reaction to this declaration.

She shivered. 'Callum . . .'

'OK, I know that wasn't fair, Maxine . . . I'm sorry. I can't help how I feel.'

Sick with longing every time he passed her in the street. One glimpse of her was enough to condemn him to nights of fevered frustration. And tonight had pressed him to the very limit of control, and past it. If only he had had the sense to keep his mouth shut.

'Callum, look at me,' she demanded.

He raised his head and looked into her eyes, surprised to see no sign of anger there. 'Guess I'm making a complete fool of myself.'

'Tell me again. Tell me you love me again . . .'

He hesitated, still not sure, then glimpsing the sheen of tears in her eyes, murmured, 'Oh God, Maxine, I love you. I have never stopped loving you. I have never been so miserable as I have been in the last two years.'

Then his face was on hers, his arms imprisoned her, pulling her into the contours of his body as their tongues entwined.

'And I love you, Callum,' she gasped at last, through salty tears, clinging to him as if she was afraid he might walk away and leave her.

'Can I come home with you, Maxine?' he asked, stroking the water from her face with a gentle but unsteady finger.

'Only if you come right now,' she managed to laugh.

'I might just do that if you don't keep still,' he retorted, bringing his mouth down to hers again.

In Craigie George was having a celebration of his own. One of Maxine's first actions on getting her money had been to send some of it to her father, hoping he would spend it on something to make his life more comfortable, but suspecting that a fair proportion of it would find its way into the till behind the bar of the Greyhound.

She was right. By the time she met Callum for dinner that night George was comfortably seated in his favourite corner, telling everyone who cared to listen about his daughter's good fortune and generosity. Open handed by nature he needed no persuasion to buy everyone in the crowded bar a drink.

'Aye, you wouldn't believe it, would you?' he asked his cronie, Jimmy Murie. 'All that money for a bit of old jewellery. Aye, she's a good lassie, my Mary, my Maxine. That's what she calls herself now. Grand name for a grand lassie. Five hundred pounds she gave me.'

'What are you going to do with it, Geordie?' Jimmy asked, waving his empty glass under his friend's nose. 'Another pint would be a good start.'

'Right you are, Jimmy.' George obliged with a beaming smile and extended his generosity to the four men at the next table, bearing no ill-will towards any of them.

'Thanks, Geordie. That's right good of you,' Archie Cree said, edging nearer to the man who was still, unofficially, his father-in-law.

'So your Mary has come into some money, then?' he asked. George was much too drunk to notice the sharp edge in the other man's voice. 'How much, exactly, did she get?'

'Nine thousand pounds,' George supplied the answer in complete innocence. 'Aye, it's a fair wee bit. She'll be nicely set now. You know,' he slurred, leaning towards the other man, 'it's a pity youse couldn't have made a go of it. Then you'd have had a share in the restaurant she's buying.' He reeled back to an upright position and stared happily into his glass, quite content with his world. 'Aye,' he hiccoughed. 'Life's grand, so it is.'

'Aye,' Archie turned and looked significantly at his listening brothers. 'Life's grand.'

TWENTY-TWO

Maxine ran up the stairs to her flat over the restaurant. In one continuous movement she flung the bundle of papers she had brought with her on to the bedside table, stripped off her blouse, pinned her hair on top of her head, started the bathwater running and kicked off her shoes. Callum would be here any minute now and, as usual, she had stayed in the restaurant much longer than she had planned to. The very thought of his name brought a smile to her lips as she sank into the suds of the bath. She lay back and closed her eyes letting the warm water engulf her. She would steal five minutes to unwind, otherwise she would bore him to tears with her constant chatter about the new restaurant.

Callum had been a wonderful support over the past stressful weeks. Always there offering his help and encouragement but never interfering. It was amazing how easily they had fallen back into their old relationship. Or, not quite their old relationship. This time they were much more wary of each other, both avoiding any talk of the future and marriage, both unhappily aware that such a step was still impossible for them. Callum's beliefs, if anything, had strengthened over the past years. Marriage between himself and a divorcee was still out of the question.

Not that Maxine was able to call herself a divorcee. A court action and all the unpleasantness it would inevitably entail was something she always avoided facing up to. The fact that she was, in law, still Archie's wife, didn't

388

disturb her unduly. As far as she was concerned there was only one man she would ever want to marry and that was Callum. He couldn't marry her, so getting a divorce was absolutely pointless.

She pushed those unpleasant thoughts aside and concentrated instead on thinking about the frantic weeks of planning, rebuilding and redecoration which would culminate in the formal opening of Kilweem's first and only 'proper' restaurant – Maxine's.

It had been obvious for some time before Maurice's death that the bakery, popular though it was, was far less profitable than the café. Everything produced there was of the very highest quality but, because of that, also highly priced. Local people only bought their cakes there on special occasions. Some treated themselves to a 'real' loaf at weekends, but, for their everyday items, they turned to the local grocer who had started to buy his bread in bulk from the co-operative bakery in Inverannan for half the price.

Under Maxine's influence the tea shop had turned into a café and then graduated into becoming a modest restaurant. But she wasn't content with that. Maureen wholeheartedly agreed that what the area lacked was a good, but not exclusive, restaurant. One which served a wide menu of well-prepared, familiar dishes and a smaller range of more adventurous ones. Ideally it would be a place where local people could treat themselves to a night out and be impressed but not overawed or uncomfortable; a place which would eventually attract customers from outside the immediate area and, above all, it would be the obvious choice for tourists looking for a satisfying meal.

She and Maureen had spent hours closeted with architects and builders, planning the changes which would transform the old bakery into a fully equipped and modern restaurant while emphasising the original charm and character of the old building so that their clients would have a memorable place in which to dine. At the same time, Maxine, who was financing the whole thing by utilising a large proportion of her remaining capital, had some minor alterations made to the upstairs flat which was now her home.

Most of the work had been managed while the existing restaurant continued to operate, if with great difficulty, but for the final two weeks there had been no option but to close. Tomorrow night was to be their first night in the refurbished premises. The restaurant was due to re-open in less than twenty-four hours.

Maxine roused herself, towelled herself dry with amazing speed and dredged her skin with talcum powder to absorb the excess moisture. Three minutes fixed her hair into her ubiquitous but unfailingly tidy knot and another three minutes added the subtle blusher and eye shadow which were all she wore when she was with Callum who insisted that no amount of make-up could improve on what nature had given her. She adored the compliment but preferred to give nature a discreet helping hand.

She was almost ready when there was a tap on her door. It could only be Callum. He was the only one who came in the outside door, at the back of the restaurant and up her private stairs without first ringing the external bell. Even Maureen rang the bell, insisting that Maxine was entitled to absolute privacy in what was now her home.

'Come in, Callum. I'm almost ready,' she called out, as she pulled light tights on. The door clicked open, then shut again but he didn't bother to call out to her. That was unusual in itself. As a rule Callum was ebullient when he arrived, his pleasure at seeing her translating into a talkative cheerfulness. Unless something had happened to one of his parishioners. A death or illness could depress him for days, even when he barely knew the victim. Pausing briefly to check her appearance in her mirror she went to join him.

'You're quiet tonight,' she said, as she walked into the room, her eyes going to the settee where he normally sat. It was empty, Even as her eyes raked round the room searching for him he spoke.

'You're looking wonderful, Hen. The sea air really agrees with you.'

Archie stepped away from the window where he had been half-hidden by the full-length curtain and smiled at his wife.

'Archie!' She dropped her handbag and ignored the mess of keys, money and various feminine items which spilled over her new carpet.

'Aye. Archie. Were you expecting someone else then?' he asked.

'What . . .' her voice was nothing more than a grating croak. She cleared her throat and tried again. 'What are you doing here?'

'I've come to see you. What else?' he responded, still smiling.

'What about?' she demanded, anger taking over now.

'Och, this and that. It's time we talked, do you not think so?'

'You had no right to barge your way in here, Archie.'

'I did knock on that door downstairs. You didn't answer but I knew you were in. I saw the light on up here, so I didn't think you'd mind if I came on up. And I knocked on this door.'

'So you did . . .' she sighed. 'Sit down, Archie and tell me what you want.'

He limped over to the settee and sat where Callum usually sat. Maxine watched him, privately shocked by his appearance. He seemed shrunken, shrivelled. His red hair was sparse and dry looking, his face was thin and heavily scored with lines and he was bent, much more so than when they had been married. When he eased himself on to the settee he grunted, as if in pain. The instinctive fear she had felt when she had first seen him there faded. This poor, crippled man posed no threat to her.

'I just thought it was time we had a talk, Mary. We are man and wife after all.'

'In name only Archie.'

'Aye. That's true enough . . . You know, I was talking to your father the other night. He's a good man is your father . . .'

'Yes,' she said, wondering what was delaying Callum.

'He was saying what a shame it was that we didn't make a go of it,' he added, cautiously.

'Archie, that was all a very long time ago. There's no point in talking about what might have been.'

'No . . . but we could talk about the future.'

'The future?' she exclaimed, astonishment making her gape at him.

'Aye . . . I'm a changed man, Hen . . .'

'My future does not include you, Archie Cree,' she stormed to her feet and roared at him.

'Mary! Mary! Calm yourself, Hen. I only wanted to talk to you, nothing else. Surely you can spare me half an hour after so long without losing your head in the first minute.'

'Half an hour then. Not a minute more,' she agreed grudgingly, perching herself on the edge of a chair, not too close to him.

'I said I've changed, Mary, and it's true. Och, I was just young when we were married . . . too young. I know I wasn't good to you then but things would be different this time.'

He was a sad, rather pathetic figure and she didn't want to hurt him unnecessarily.

'Archie, I can't come back to Craigie. My life is here.' With Callum, she added silently.

'You don't have to come back to Craigie! I won't ask you to do that. I'll come here, to you. I'll miss my friends mind, but I'll do it for you, Mary.'

Understanding dawned on her. 'For me?' she asked, coldly.

'Aye!' He sat up as straight as his spine would allow, his eyes shining. 'Aye, I was thinking we'll be well set up, what with the money from the jewellery and all.'

'Get out, Archie!' She was on her feet again in an instant. 'That's what this is all about, isn't it? The jewellery! How do you know about that?'

All trace of good humour evaporated. 'Your father! He can't keep his mouth closed when he's got a pint of heavy in his gob,' he said, acidly.

'Oh no . . .' she sighed. 'Archie, just go home. There's nothing for you here . . .'

'No, please, Hen, you don't understand.' Now he was pleading with her. 'Och, things haven't gone right for me, Mary. All I need is a bit of help . . . a wee bit of cash to tide me over . . . you know.'

'No.'

'Don't say that. Listen to me.' He waved his hands wildly. 'Ever since you went, I've not been the same. It ruined me, Mary, you going off like that. Everyone knew . . . They all talked about me. It made me ill. I can't work . . . I'm not fit any more . . . The back . . . Just a wee bit, Mary . . . Just a wee bit. Just a bit of what you owe me.'

'No, Archie. I owe you nothing. Nothing at all, do you understand?'

'Nine thousand. That's what you got. Your father told me. Half of it's mine. That was a wedding present. For both of us.'

'From my aunt!'

'Half of it is mine,' he roared, stumbling to his feet and lunging in her direction.

Downstairs Callum, fresh from choir practice and still wearing his cassock, let himself in and ran lightly up the stairs, humming to himself. He was on the landing when a raised and obviously angry voice halted him. He waited outside the door for a second, trying to make out what was going on then threw it open and ran in.

Maxine was on her feet, face to face with a man who was little taller than she was, screaming at him.

'You are getting nothing from me, Archie Cree. Now get the hell out of my flat.'

The man, badly crippled but murderously angry, raised his arm, as if to hit her but found himself caught from behind and dragged helplessly away. Released he rounded on his assailant, ready to wade in with his fists but stopped, reeling with shock when he saw the long, black cassock and dog collar. Hitting a priest was something even he was not prepared to do.

'Miss Lennox has asked you to leave,' Callum said, staring the man down with frighteningly angry blue eyes.

'Her name's Cree. Mrs Archie Cree,' Archie spat. 'Though she likes to forget that.' He rounded on Maxine again but keeping well back this time, uncomfortably aware of the threatening bulk of the clergyman behind him. 'You owe me . . .' he said, jabbing a finger in her direction. 'You bloody owe me.'

'Out!' Callum had him by the collar and through the door before the words were properly finished. 'Out and don't come back or I will call the police.'

'No . . . No, I'm going.' Archie had no wish to tangle with the law. 'But you'll pay me what you owe me, Mary. I'll make sure of that.'

'OUT!' Callum advanced on him again and Archie

hobbled down the stairs as fast as his disability would allow. Maxine, watching from her window, saw him scurry across the street, clamber into an old mini van and drive away.

'I've locked the door,' Callum said when he came back in. 'Are you OK?'

She nodded. 'A bit shocked I suppose . . . He was the last person I expected to see.'

'What did he want?'

She related the story, almost word for word and felt better for telling him.

'Archie Cree has no claim on you. He's jealous, that's all. Try not to let it worry you,' he said when they had discussed it for a couple of hours.

'I'm not sure he'll leave it there,' she said, unable to dismiss the niggle of doubt from her mind.

'Then I think we should put a stop to this right away. We'll go and see my father, first thing tomorrow morning, ask his advice.'

'Good idea.' She felt easier now she was going to take some positive action. 'You've got your uses after all, Reverend Mackie,' she teased, burrowing under his cassock.

'In more ways than one,' he chuckled, as he pulled her down beside him.

Maxine had been angry even before she went to see Callum that morning. She was tired, too. The restaurant's opening had been a great success but it was hard work and the stress was beginning to tell. She found it difficult to wind down after the place closed, around twelve midnight, and seldom managed to get to sleep before three or four in the morning. The letter which had been waiting for her when she crawled out of bed this morning had sent her temper soaring so much that she was left with a hideous, thumping headache.

Archie's response to the official letter from Callum's father had been to consult a solicitor of his own who was now suggesting settling for a totally outrageous sum. The threat to drag the whole thing through the courts if an amicable solution could not be found had finally ignited Maxine's temper to blistering heat. Furious at the prospect of having to pay Archie for the misery and pain she had endured with him she had stalked over to the church to vent some of her frustration and anger on Callum, confident of finding him there after the twice weekly, mid-morning service.

The small Episcopal church faced directly on to Fishergate, at the northern end of Kilweem. There was only a six foot strip of rough concrete between its heavy main doors and the street. On the eastern side of the building was a rambling graveyard, on to which opened the vestry door. Not wanting to go into the church itself where Callum might well be engaged with a parishioner or even with the Rector, Maxine walked down the narrow alleyway which ran between the side boundary wall of the graveyard and the neighbouring building. Set into this wall, opposite the vestry door, was a low gate into the churchyard. Maxine arrived there, still in a filthy temper, to be confronted by the unwelcome sight of the man she loved paying uncomfortably close attention to a disturbingly attractive young woman in the shelter of the vestry porch.

Stunned, Maxine slipped quickly back behind the wall and watched, feeling that her whole world was crumbling.

The two were in an undeniably close conversation and it was perfectly obvious that they knew each other very well indeed. Callum, fresh from the service and fully attired in cassock and surplice, was laughing. The girl was standing so close that the fresh wind, whipping unchecked from the sea, caught his cassock and seemed to enfold her in it for a few seconds. Smiling, the girl put a hand up to Callum's face and then kissed him. He responded, hugging her closer to him so that now, she was completely lost in the flapping, black and white fabrics. Obviously enjoying himself, Callum only pulled away very slowly then led the girl, one arm draped round her shapely shoulders, along the side of the church, towards the front of the building. Unable to stop herself, Maxine followed at a distance, keeping well into the shelter of the outer wall. The couple were now standing on the narrow public foot-path, talking animatedly. At last they separated and Callum opened the door of the car parked there. The girl got in but not before kissing him again. And again he returned it, clasping her to him for so long that Maxine was forced to let out the breath she had been holding so painfully.

Callum waved as the car drove off then, hands shoved into the pockets of his trousers, through his cassock, strode jauntily back into the church, through the main doors, with the air of a man on top of his world.

Aware only of the indisputable fact that Callum had kissed this very smart and attractive young woman, and in full public view, Maxine was very close to tears.

She knew her relationship with Callum was fraught with danger. He would not, could not, bring himself to marry her, but equally, he could not stop seeing her. His innate honesty made him tell her, very early in their renewed affair, that it could never lead to marriage. There had been sadness in his eyes when he said it and pain in his voice. She had believed him absolutely when he told her he loved her, that he despised himself for not having the strength to let her go, to put her out of his mind forever. But she had not wanted him to set her free. Her love for him was all-consuming. If they couldn't have marriage then she was more than prepared to settle for friendship, to be covert lovers in the full knowledge that their love could take them nowhere.

In some ways their situation suited her very well. She had the business to think about and she still wasn't ready for the greater commitment of marriage. Too late she realised that she had never really considered Callum's position in all this and had merely assumed he was ready to compromise forever if necessary. But unlike her he was ready to settle down, although he had told her again and again that she was the only one he wanted to spend the rest of his life with. Now it occurred to her that he could be tired of living a perpetual lie and had decided to seek solace with someone his conscience wouldn't reject.

But, she thought bitterly, he should have warned her. They had always been honest with each other. It wasn't fair to let her find out like this. In a flash Maxine decided to face him about it, there and then. Angrily she rushed after him, catching up with him in the church porch where he was talking with the Rector's wife.

'Callum!' Maxine shouted, ignoring the other woman's startled interest. 'Who was that?'

'Who was who?' he asked innocently, startled by her unexpected appearance.

'That woman you were wrapped around not more than two minutes ago,' she yelled, almost crying in anger, as the pressures of the last months pushed her beyond the bounds of common sense or reason. 'Don't tell me you've already forgotten.'

'Excuse me, Callum. We'll finish our discussion this evening.' The Rector's wife fled from the scene as quickly as she could.

'Maxine!' Callum flushed to the roots of his fair hair and hauled her out of the church. 'What do you think you are doing, Maxine? I was talking to Mrs Drabble, in case you hadn't noticed. Couldn't you have waited for five minutes?'

'What the hell do you think you were doing kissing another woman?' she screamed, beside herself with anger.

'I wasn't . . .'

'You were! I saw you! Don't bother lying about it.'

'Don't you ever call me a liar!' he bridled at once. 'And be very careful before you go jumping to conclusions,' he warned.

'There is only one conclusion. You're seeing someone else. How could you, Callum? After all the things you've said to me?'

'I am not seeing anyone else,' he hissed.

'Oh, I see, you just make a habit of kissing every good-looking woman who steps into the church?'

'She came to see me in my official capacity . . .'

'Oh, yes, Callum. Of course she did. Any fool could see that what you two were doing was official business.'

'Will you listen to me?' he roared, broadcasting their dispute to anyone within five hundred yards of them.

'I am listening, Callum and it had better be good.' She folded her arms and stared angrily at the cloudy sky, tapping one foot impatiently.

'Don't stand on the graves.' He hauled her away, thoroughly angered by now.

'Don't push me around.' She shook him off making more of it than she should have done.

'Then show some respect. This is consecrated ground,' he snapped, gesticulating violently.

As they stood there, facing each other aggressively, the wind blustered round them sending Callum's cassock flying out round him and tangling her long, loose hair about her head. They looked wild, out of control and in the grip of some terrible, destructive emotion.

Abruptly Callum turned away, keenly aware that this

was not the place to lose his temper. When he faced her again his face was expressionless, his voice was even and his body still. Only his eyes betrayed the fact that he was very, very angry indeed.

'Firstly, Maxine, you had no right to come into the church like that. St Peters is a place of peace, not a battle-ground for our personal disputes, under any circumstances. Secondly, if you had had the good sense to wait I would have told you all about it this evening.'

'Who is she, Callum?' she asked, coldly.

'Eileen Williams is an old friend of the family. We have known each other for years, since we were children. In fact,' he added rashly, wanting to hurt her now, 'she is an ex-girlfriend of mine.'

'Ex? You could have fooled me.'

'Do you want to hear this or not?' he growled.

'Go on.'

'Eileen has just become engaged. She is getting married next year and came to ask if I could perform the ceremony.'

'Very original, Callum.' She actually applauded him.

He ignored it, valiantly trying to hang on to some of his self-control. 'You are not even trying to understand, Maxine. Eileen Williams is a nice girl.'

'I could see you certainly think so. An ex-girlfriend . . .'

'Well,' he challenged. 'Do you think I spent my whole life just waiting for you to turn up? You're a fine one to talk. Just look at your own past before you dare to criticise me. At least I've never done anything to be ashamed of.' Until now, he thought, even as he said it, bitterly regretting the unforgivable words.

She stared at him, stunned into momentary silence, pain already welling inside her. 'At least I told you the truth,' she stammered at last. 'And I'm not hiding behind my religion, using God as a convenient excuse. You won't marry me, Callum because your holy conscience won't let you marry unless it's in church and we both know we can never marry in church. Even if we could, you say I've already taken my marriage vows and they can't be broken, by anyone. You hypocrite!' she spat the words at him. 'That's all an excuse. It doesn't stop you from sleeping with me, does it? Your conscience isn't so fussy when it comes to your own pleasure. And it doesn't seem to stop you from enjoying other women.'

'We were saying goodbye,' he said dully, sickened by the venom in her voice.

'It didn't look like it to me,' she whispered, exhausted by her own jealousy.

'It was. Though after what you've just said, I wish it hadn't been.' More rash words he would regret later.

'You bastard, Callum!' Her hand caught him sharply across the cheek, injuring his pride at least as much as his face. 'Find yourself someone who isn't such an affront to your conscience. And get out of my life!'

'It'll be a bloody pleasure,' he bellowed at her retreating back.

Maxine cooled her temper by taking herself off for a very long walk along the beach. Would Callum always hold her past against her? she wondered, kicking at the fine sand and reliving again and again the pain of his words. Every time they argued would he throw her past in her face? Was it truly more than the impossible question of being able to pledge themselves before God which stood in their way? Was it deeper, blacker even than that? Was it, in fact, that in his heart, Callum was unable to forgive her for things which had happened when she was very young and inexperienced?

She trailed to the edge of the dunes and sat down to

watch the sea rolling in softly-breaking waves, then closed her eyes and let the sound engulf her, searching for the peace of mind the unstoppable rhythm of the sea invariably brought her. Today it failed.

Callum had been kissing that woman, she had seen that much with her own eyes, had seen the way he clasped her to him so that her slender body disappeared into the folds of his cassock. Maxine choked on a stifled sob and opened her eyes again, trying to banish the unhappy image from her stubborn mind. She knew she had over-reacted, that she had been wrong to confront him in the church but she wouldn't apologise. His behaviour had been the cause of the argument and he should be the one to apologise to her. If he couldn't, well, that would prove how shallow his feelings for her really were. Better to find out now than later. It was, after all, what she had come to expect from men. Paul, Archie, even the disgusting Douglas, they had all used her for their own ends. Broodingly she looked back and saw the same traits in her own father. He had been so absolutely selfish that her mother had been left with no option but to leave her young family and everything she knew and loved.

Yes, she decided miserably, this had been a lucky escape. Men had been nothing but trouble for her. From now on they would have no place in her life. Especially not Callum Mackie who could never offer more than a hole-in-the-corner relationship he was ashamed of. Why did she even think she needed a man? She was strong, capable, intelligent. More than able to live her life without relying on anyone else for support. If she needed someone to talk to she had Maureen who had been a much better friend than any man could ever hope to be.

A grim, determined look on her face she retraced her steps and strode purposefully home to the restaurant and her flat above it. Without even bothering to take off her coat she wrote out a cheque for two thousand pounds and placed it, with a scribbled note, in an envelope to Archie's solicitor. It left her with almost nothing to fall back on but if that was what it took to get Archie Cree out of her life forever, then so be it. It was probably cheap at that, she thought bitterly as she shoved it into the letterbox.

TWENTY-THREE

Callum had filled a gap in Maxine's life that she hadn't even known was there until she lost him again. She compensated by filling every waking moment with work, watching the restaurant grow and prosper with pride, knowing it was all due to her own efforts and skill.

Maxine's was now open a full seven days a week. Apart from herself, Maxine employed three chefs, ten kitchen assistants, fifteen waitresses and a head waiter. Her success was, she knew, because she placed a strict emphasis on service, high-quality food and reasonable prices.

Her insistence on pleasing her customers, on refusing to serve anything that was less than perfectly prepared and presented, gained her an enviable reputation, both with her staff, who regarded her with awed respect, and with her clients, who showed their appreciation by returning again and again.

It was already obvious that her first season in the newly-furbished restaurant would show a healthy profit, largely thanks to the tourists. Now her aim was to establish a wider reputation.

Sheer drive and determination, coupled with an unexpectedly acute business sense led her to market the place aggressively. Leaflets were printed and placed in the tourist information centres both locally and in Edinburgh. A regular advertisement feature was taken with the local press and a tasteful sign attracted casual diners. Before the end of her first year, Maxine's was one of the most popular restaurants in Strathannan.

But, throughout all this, Maxine had gradually lost contact with her family. There was simply never time to go and see them all for more than a couple of hours every two or three months. It took Maureen to point it out to her.

'You know, Maxine, this restaurant isn't the only thing worth thinking about,' she said suddenly, after sharing a meal with her niece during which Maxine had seemed unable, or unwilling, to talk about anything other than Maxine's.

Maxine stopped in the middle of describing a new dish she wanted to try and stared at her ageing aunt. 'It's important to get things right, Maureen. And that takes time and attention. I thought you would understand that.'

'This is your canny old aunt you're talking to, Lass, and you cannot fool me. This . . . this obsession, started when you and Callum broke up the first time. You got over it when you and he got back together again but now you're worse than ever . . . Shhussh. Please. Let me have my say.' She silenced Maxine's objection imperiously. 'I understand. It was a good thing then, to get your mind on something productive, but don't you see, you've let it get out of hand. You eat, sleep and dream this place. It's all you can talk about.'

'It's all I need. This place and you of course.'

'Aye, well, you can hardly ignore me when I turn up on your doorstep, can you?'

'Maureen! You know that's not fair. I come to see you as often as you come to see me.'

'Och, I know that, Lass. And I'm glad of it too. But what about the rest of your family? When was the last time you saw your gran? She's not getting any younger herself you know. And what about those sisters of yours? I'll swear I see more of them than you do.'

Maxine sighed, unable to deny the truth when it was so baldly stated. And Maureen's reprimand had made her realise that it was more than a year since she had last heard from Janette. And until now she hadn't even noticed. Perhaps Maureen had a point. 'I guess you're right.'

'I know I am. You get off to Craigie for a week or so. Your father'll be that pleased to see you and the break will do you good.'

'What about the restaurant?'

'You think it's going to fall down without you there to prop it up? Good God, Lass, you've a first-class staff there. Young Martin's worth his weight in gold, thanks to your training. You can trust him to run the place while you're away. It'll give him the extra bit of confidence he needs. And I'll be around to keep an eye on things,' she promised.

'OK. I give up,' Maxine laughed.

Maxine steered her new car off the main road and into Craigie. The village never seemed to change. Unlike Kilweem, which was still growing, no new houses had been built in Craigie for more than fifteen years. It was a community of drab council houses occupied mainly by successive generations of the same families. No one from outside ever came to live in a place as grim as this from choice. Only one private developer had been brave enough to risk offering houses for sale in such a depressing area and those houses were so far to the edge of Craigie that their owners liked to pretend they lived in a different village. The few incomers tended to be desperate people, glad to have a roof anywhere, or miners transferring from communities in the west when their own collieries were forced into closure, doomed by faults which rendered their seams uneconomic to work. The houses themselves were well below average standards, cold, damp and badly maintained by a council who considered Craigie and her sister villages to be a never-ending source of complaint, a dumping ground for problem families. Coal fires still predominated, belching their smoke out as heavily as ever, turning the buildings from grey to black. What warm air these inefficient fires did generate escaped through warped window frames and thin walls. Walls which leaked sound as readily as warmth, ensuring that only the dumb could hope to maintain any degree of privacy.

She turned in by the shops where a dozen miners waited on the coal board bus to pick them up for work. Looking at them was like looking at a scene from ten, twenty, thirty or even forty years ago. Their clothes were the same, the voices were the same, the coughs were the same and the stooped stance of permanent weariness was the same. She knew from her father, who kept in touch through the Greyhound, that conditions underground were vastly improved, that pay was more in line with outside industry, but understood, too, that the work was still dangerous and exhausting. She would never allow any husband or child of hers to contemplate going underground.

The clutch of prefabs remained, defying the council to pull them down. Maxine parked and hurried inside, trying to ignore the ribald comments from the small crowd of miners who had been attracted by the shiny car and her own smart clothes and well-groomed appearance. The front door, recently renewed by the council after years of complaint, was stiff and she had to knock.

'Mary, Lass! Come along in . . .' Undemonstrative by nature it was, nevertheless, quite obvious that George was delighted to see his daughter. 'Come on through, Lass. Sit yourself down and I'll get the kettle on.'

Expecting the place to be in the same sorry, worn condition Mary followed her father to the living room.

'Good heavens, Dad. What have you been doing to the place?' she exclaimed.

He grinned, looking suddenly boyish. 'Och, I thought it was time to tidy up a bit.'

He left her to look round while he made the tea, the first time she could ever recall him doing such a thing when there was someone else available to do it for him. The room had been transformed. A new, plain beige carpet covered the floor and was a vast improvement on the old, flowered design atop checked linoleum which had been down for as long as she could remember and which had shrunk the minute room even further. Gone, too, was the old, lumpy settee and two mismatched chairs. Now there was a compact, cottage-style, three piece suite. New curtains graced the windows and the whole room shone, as if newly and lovingly polished. Even the newspapers which had always littered the floor had disappeared and there wasn't a pair of discarded shoes in sight. Smiling to herself Maxine settled in a chair. Whichever one of her sisters had taken him in hand she had done a first class job.

'What do you think of the place?' George asked, handing her an unchipped mug of tea.

'It's wonderful, Dad . . .'

'Just wait till you see the rest of it.' He was jigging in the doorway, obviously wanting her to let him show her round instantly.

The kitchen was spotless, even the cupboards were tidy, the dishes all washed and dried, the underwear on the overhead drier neatly folded and so white that they could not possibly be the product of George's rather casual approach to hand washing.

The bedroom which had once been shared by all four

children now sported just two single beds, neatly made with colourful covers thrown over them. George's own room was neat, the bed made and the surfaces all clean and dust free.

'You've certainly made a difference to the place,' she laughed at him. 'Who does the housework? I know it's not you.'

George avoided the question by looking at the old clock, still ticking away on the mantelpiece. 'It's time I was away to my work. I'll be back round six. Make yourself at home, Lass.'

'Work?' Maxine almost choked on her tea.

'Aye. I'm caretaker at St Michaels. The Episcopal church. The job was advertised in the *Inverannan Press*. Our Linda wrote off for me. Then I had a wee word with your Reverend Mackie. Aye, Callum put in a good word for me.'

'He didn't say anything to me.' But how could he when they went out of their way to avoid one another? 'You didn't say anything either,' she accused her father.

'Well, Hen,' he said reasonably. 'We never see you to tell you anything. If you'd come home to see your old father more often you'd know I've been working for a year.' With that mild rebuke he grabbed his jacket from the hook behind the front door and was off, hurrying up the street as if there was a rabid dog on his tail. Maxine could only stare after him.

'Well. And about time too,' was Ina's fine welcome an hour later. 'I was starting to think you had turned your back on us altogether.'

'I've been busy, Gran . . .'

'Busy! Too busy to drive fifteen miles to see your family . . . It isn't good enough, Lass. You saw what

409

happened with me and my family. Your family is the most precious thing you've got. It's too easy to lose touch and almost impossible to mend things when they go wrong.'

'Don't start, Gran. I've already had all this from Maureen.'

'I daresay,' Ina laughed. Age was mellowing her and despite her hard-edged manner she was very fond of this girl, and proud of her too. 'Aye, Maureen was always a blunt talker.'

'Anyway, why blame me? Why can't you come to Kilweem for a change? You never do that anymore. Any of you!'

Ina raised a cryptic eyebrow. 'Think hard, Lass and you'll know why.'

'Just tell me, Gran. I haven't got time to play games if I'm to go and see Linda and Catherine before Dad gets home,' she sighed. Why did her grandmother always end up nagging her?

'You haven't got time!' Ina's voice was scornful. 'Don't you understand yet?'

'Understand what, for God's sake?' Maxine was thoroughly irritated now.

'For someone who's supposed to be so clever, so successful, you're being as thick as a haggis. Time! That's why no one will come to see you, Mary. Think on it, Lass. The number of times we've all clambered on the bus, your sisters with the weans in tow, your father, me . . . And what happens when we get to Kilweem? Eh?' she demanded, banging her fist on the table.

'I give you all a bloody good meal, that's what happens,' Maxine retorted, fiercely.

'Aye. You do that right enough. And then you send us off to the beach, or rope poor old Maureen into looking after us while you go back to running your precious

410

restaurant. It takes an hour and a half for us to get there, an hour and a half to get back, costs good money too, and then you have a job to spend more than an hour with us. And you wonder why we don't come back!'

Maxine blanched but she was never one to sidestep the truth. 'My God! Is that how you see it?'

'Aye. What other way is there?' her grandmother asked.

Maxine sighed. 'When I was a kid we went to Kilweem and spent the day on the beach. It was wonderful . . . ! I just thought you would all rather do that than hang around in the restaurant. I wanted you all to enjoy your day! Not feel you had to waste it. And I do have responsibilities. I can't just take a day off whenever I feel like it.' There was a tremor in her voice now.

'Och, Lass. It's you we come to see. Not the bloody beach,' Ina said, softly. 'Just remember that in future.' She put a dry, bony hand over Maxine's smoother, younger one and squeezed it gently. 'Now, dry your eyes and let's see if we can't enjoy one another's company for a change.'

They shared a reasonably companionable half hour before Ina asked, 'How do you find your father, then?'

'I can hardly believe the change in him. I didn't know he was working but it's certainly done him good.'

'Something's done him good,' Ina agreed cryptically.

'If you came home more often you'd have seen him changing,' Linda accused later, rescuing her second child from her sister's incompetent arms where she was squirming and screaming. 'You couldn't even come to the wean's christening.'

'I know. I'm sorry but I was really busy just then. I sent a card and a gift . . .'

'A baby doesn't care about gifts, Mary. It would rather have its family round it.'

'I'm sorry.'

'Huh.'

'I'm really glad you've come for a wee while, Mary.' Catherine, lacking the Lennox love of confrontation, greeted her sister more warmly.

'Thank goodness you're not going to lecture me about staying away,' Maxine sighed, sinking into a chair.

But even the good-natured Catherine wouldn't let her off that lightly.

'No. But I do think it's a pity we don't see so much of you,' she sighed and sat down next to her eldest sister.

'You look tired, Cath. Is the baby keeping you awake at nights?' Her sister's energetic two-year-old was like a tornado in the room.

'Him? No. He exhausts himself by bedtime, thank God . . . No, it's just I'm a bit under the weather still, that's all.'

'Still? Why? Have you not been well?' This was the first she had heard of it but the coughs and colds of the entire clan could not be her concern.

'I lost my baby, Mary,' Catherine said quietly, hurt and reproach in her voice.

Maxine felt sick. 'Oh God,' she croaked, appalled. 'I didn't even know you were pregnant again.'

Catherine tried to smile. 'One of us would have told you when we saw you.'

'You could have phoned!'

'It's not the sort of news to give on the phone . . . Oh, Mary, I do wish you'd been here. We'd been trying for so long for another baby and then this . . .' Catherine was crying now.

'I'm sorry, Cath . . .' Maxine reached for her sister's hands. They were icy cold.

Catherine wiped her eyes. 'Sorry. I shouldn't make you miserable with my problems.'

It was almost as if Catherine saw her as a stranger, Maxine thought bitterly.

'I'm your sister, Cath, even if we don't see as much of each other as we should. I wish I'd known . . .' Memories of her own lost children brought a catch to her voice.

'So do I, Mary. It's happened to you and you were the only one who might have understood.' She sighed. 'Still, it's all over and done with now.'

'Can I do anything? Do you want to talk about it?'

'No.' Catherine smiled sadly and shook her head. 'It's too late.'

By the time Maxine went back to the prefab she was much subdued and deeply regretting the overwhelming immersion in the business which had led her to ignore her family for so long. Yet, though each of them had made their opinion of her plain, not one of them had sounded resentful or envious, merely hurt.

Lost in thought she let herself in to the small house and collapsed on to one of the new armchairs feeling very close to tears.

A noise from the kitchen disturbed her. She sat up, listening. It sounded as if saucepans and plates were being moved around. Her father wasn't home yet, she was sure of that, so it was probably one of her sisters, come to make their father his evening meal. One of them was obviously keeping the house in order.

The kitchen door was shut. Maxine opened it, fully expecting to see Linda or Catherine but found a comfortably built, middle-aged woman who was inspecting whatever it was she had in the oven. She looked momentarily startled but recovered long before Maxine did.

'Ah, you must be Maxine. George told me you'd likely be here the day.' She straightened, smiling broadly. 'I was just about to make a cup of tea. You look as if you could use one, too.' She offered the national panacea cheerfully.

'Thanks.'

Maxine watched while she gathered cups, saucers, spoons, tea, milk and all the rest with the surety of a woman on home ground. 'I'm sorry,' she ventured at last. 'Dad didn't tell me you'd be here.'

'No?' The homely face creased in surprise. 'I thought . . . Och well, I daresay he'll tell you tonight . . . I'm Annie Minto . . . from Ochil Wynd . . .' She laughed, a pleasant, rich sound. 'Och, I see you don't remember me and that's no wonder. But I can mind of you as a wee bairn. Here's your tea, Lass. I've finished here so I'll be off home. All you have to do is turn the tatties on.'

'Right.' Maxine felt as though her brain was mired with glue. 'You come in to see to my father do you?' she asked, as the woman let herself out.

Annie Minto looked back at her and laughed. 'Aye. I suppose you could say that, Hen.'

'Why didn't you tell me?' Too late she realised just how often she had said those, or very similar, words that day.

George shrugged. 'Didn't get the chance, Lass. We've not seen much of each other, have we?'

'So everyone keeps telling me. I am sorry, Dad.'

'Nae, Lass. It's my fault. If I had kept my big mouth closed about that money you gave me, Archie Cree would never have got wind of it. I let you down there, Lass and I'm right sorry for it.'

She was horrified. 'Is that why you think I've not been home?'

'Well . . . I can't say I blame you. Your grandmother was spitting bricks when she found out what I'd done.'

'Dad, the only reason I didn't come home was because I've been too involved in the business. Nothing else. Archie Cree had nothing to do with it. Honestly . . . But how . . . I mean, I never told anyone Archie had been to see me.'

'Och, it was all over the village how he'd been to see you and got you to give him some money . . . he couldn't resist bragging about how much he'd got from you . . . Your gran went off to see old Mrs Cree and got the full story . . .'

'She would!'

'Aye,' he chuckled, relieved to know she didn't hold him responsible. 'That's your gran all over.'

'And what about Annie Minto?' she asked, determined not to be side-tracked.

He looked sheepish. 'She's a braw woman. Good-hearted . . .'

'Dad, are you telling me you're winching?' she asked, laughing.

Now he actually blushed, colour rising to his sandy hair. 'Aye. I suppose I am.'

'That's wonderful!' She was genuinely delighted for her father. And no wonder he looked so well, actually appearing younger now than he had five years ago.

He let out the tense breath he had been holding and visibly relaxed. 'You don't mind, then?'

'Mind? Why should I mind, Dad? I'm really happy for you.' And she was.

'That's a relief, Hen. I was wondering how you'd take it. You see, we're to be married.'

'Already?'

'I've been keeping company with her for nearly two years!' he retorted.

'Two years . . .' Something else she hadn't known.

Something else they hadn't told her. She tried desperately to hide her hurt feelings for his sake.

'Och,' he chuckled. 'I asked her to wed me after just three months. And she said no. Just like that.'

'But she went on seeing you?' she asked, intrigued.

'Aye, but on condition that I got myself organised. Found a job, sorted the house out . . . I can tell you, getting a job after all these years was the hard part.' The fact the he had been prepared to work for a living again was, in itself, a measure of his feeling for Mrs Minto. 'I thought it was all going to fall through for want of a regular job. Then your Callum helped me out and here we are.'

The front door opened, interrupting them.

'That'll be Annie now. I asked her to drop in. Meet you properly.' He drew his lady into the room, pride bringing a beaming smile to his face. 'Here, Annie, love, this is my oldest daughter, Mary, or Maxine as she likes to be called.'

Maxine stepped forward and took the older woman's hand in hers. 'Dad's told me you're getting married,' she said, real warmth in her voice.

'Aye,' the other woman laughed, warm brown eyes twinkling back at Maxine. 'You understand I couldn't say anything to you earlier, Lass? It wasn't really my place. That sort of news had to come from your dad.'

George looked from one to the other and when he was sure they would get along happily, announced, 'I'm off to the Greyhound. Leave you two to have a cosy chat.'

'Right you are, George. No more than two, mind,' Annie Minto warned him as he hurried off. Then she turned to Maxine. 'Come on, Lass, let's sit down and get to know each other. I'm sure there's a lot you want to know about me and I'm longing to hear all about this restaurant of yours . . . Och, your father's so proud of you,' she beamed.

'I've just one thing to ask you, Mrs Minto.'

'Annie, Lass. Everyone calls me Annie.'

'OK. But tell me . . . what on earth has my gran said about you and Dad?'

Annie chortled in delight. 'Don't you worry that pretty head about Ina. She and I had a sort out right at the start. She told me what she thought and I told her to mind her own business and that was that. We get along just fine now, Lass. Just fine.'

Already Maxine had warmed to her, feeling that this big-hearted, strong-willed woman was precisely what her father needed. What an enjoyable week this promised to be after all.

George and Annie were married with the minimum of fuss two months later. Only the immediate families were asked to the reception which was thrown in the house Annie was leaving to her married daughter while she moved in with George. A week later, when the newly-weds came back from a week in Blackpool, Maxine treated her family to a celebratory meal at Maxine's, reserving a quiet corner so they could enjoy themselves in relative privacy. She took the precaution of entrusting the running of the restaurant to Marty, her head waiter, so that she was free to spend the whole evening with them. She could see the pride on her father's face as he ate cod stuffed with salmon and prawns, all encased in a feather-light pastry, though he did confide in her later that he would have preferred plain cod and chips. That, however, didn't stop him boasting loudly to everyone within earshot in the Greyhound the following day about his daughter's posh restaurant.

It was a wonderful, heart-warming evening. One that made Maxine very aware of the priceless love of her family, love she had been so close to losing. Genuine, forgiving affection was too rare, too precious to throw away. Realising that her family weren't the only ones who had been overlooked recently, Maxine sat down the very next day and started to write a long epistle to Janette. It took almost a fortnight to complete and cost a fortune and a half to post but at least she had brought her friend up to date with all her news. But as she came away from the post office she couldn't help wondering if she would ever receive a reply.

TWENTY-FOUR

Maxine would have recognised Paul Kinsail easily had she seen him that night. Even though his dark hair was cut shorter than it had been when she had known him in St Andrews, his rather rugged face with its prominent nose and heavy brow were unaltered. Nor had his manner which, when he first stepped into Maxine's was haughty and impatient, changed. For his part Paul Kinsail had been astonished to recognise Mary Innes in the popular restaurant where he had taken his latest lady-friend to dine. Still with a slight, girlish figure and wearing her golden hair in that same, smooth knot he would have known her anywhere. But, as he watched her, admiring both her poise and the elegance of her figure, he understood instantly that she was a long way from being the raw girl he had known in St Andrews. This Mary Innes, who seemed to be perfectly relaxed making conversation with the restaurant's customers and at ease when instructing her staff, was a beautiful, sophisticated and confident young woman. Everything in her manner as she moved among the diners suggested quiet, composed authority, in vivid contrast to the self-effacing young lass who had provided a summer of such heady sport during his final term at St Andrews. Even before the waiter confirmed it for him, Kinsail knew this had to be her restaurant. The knowledge both impressed and excited him.

Fortunately there had been no tables available. The waiter advised him to book in advance before coming again and Kinsail managed to get off the premises before

Maxine, as she was apparently calling herself these days, recognised him.

If his unfortunate companion that night found him more than usually dour and uncommunicative that was because he was allowing all the resentment he had felt for Mary Innes to fester anew. Thanks to her, he had been forced to resign from his well-paid and undemanding post at the university and even, in a bid to escape the gossip, to move from the burgh itself. It had been a pointless exercise. His wife, driven beyond all reasonable patience by this final insult to their marriage, had left. A ruinously expensive divorce had been followed by the blow of seeing his wife remarry and take their children to live with her new husband in Surrey. That left him with absolutely nothing. His present job, with the county council, was boring and unfulfilling, without even the compensation of a decent salary. His home was a cramped and dingy terrace and his social life was frustrating and expensive. Above all he missed his children. And all because of Mary Innes.

Whatever it was that had attracted him to her and led him to take such foolhardy risks with his marriage was still there. Paul Kinsail's initial reaction to seeing Mary Innes again had not been tinged with the bitterness of those memories nor by any immediate remembrance of the traumatic results their affair had had for her. Instead, there had been sensuous appreciation of this infinitely more attractive, mature woman. It was only later, as he pondered the change in her, the obvious success of her restaurant, that a thin, ugly smile stretched his lips. To think that he had once had an affair with this obviously successful and, presumably, wealthy woman. Perhaps his luck was changing at last. Maybe the time was ripe to turn that former relationship to his advantage.

Two nights later, Maxine, casting her usual critical eye over the restaurant, was faintly surprised to see a lone gentleman at a window table. More normally the restaurant attracted couples, families and occasionally, a group of businessmen. A lone diner, especially in the evening, was a rarity. Busy with the demands of what promised to be a hectic evening she merely glanced at his back with passing interest before carrying on with her tasks. Much later, after ten o'clock, she was startled to see he was still there, apparently lingering over coffee.

'Is that the same man?' she asked Marty, her young but impressively efficient head waiter.

'Which man?' he asked.

'The one at the window. Table seven. Is he the one who came in around seven?'

'Yes. I know how you feel about not rushing people through their meals so I let him be. Sure took his time though. Do you want me to drop a gentle hint that it's time he was leaving?'

'No. It's OK. You did the right thing. No one must ever get the idea that we want them to gobble down their food and get out fast to make room for more paying customers. It's important that anyone who comes in here can feel at ease. Even a single man who takes up one of our best tables for three and a half hours,' she added wryly. 'You finish up here and I'll deal with him.'

Plastering her most professional smile on her tired face, Maxine made her way to table seven. 'Is everything all right, Sir?' she asked, her attention partially distracted by a customer who paused on his way out to compliment her on the meal he had just eaten.

Kinsail looked up, watching her as she acknowledged the praise graciously. 'Everything is fine, thank you. The meal was excellent,' he said, when the other diner had moved away.

Maxine shivered at the sound of his voice then looked

at him properly for the first time, meeting that enigmatic, superior smile full on.

'Why don't you sit down and talk to me for a little while,' he went on, in that gravelly voice she knew so well.

Without making the conscious effort, Maxine found herself in the chair next to his. 'Paul?' she asked, discovering she was suddenly hoarse.

'You do remember me! Well, that's a relief,' he laughed, sounding relaxed and friendly, as if they had never been anything but the best of friends.

'Of course I remember you.' Resentment got her back on her feet. 'I'll get your bill,' she said coldly, anxious only to be rid of him. At the till she fiddled with the pen, dropped the pad of receipts then simply couldn't bring herself to face him again.

'Marty!' she called. 'Will you give this to the gentleman at table seven, please.'

'No need.' Paul's voice made her jump and she turned to find him standing behind her, smiling slightly as if he knew she wouldn't go back to his table.

Unable to bring herself to look at him she thrust the flimsy sheet in his general direction, took his money, struggled to calculate his change and then handed it to him, all with her face averted. To her horror he clasped his hand round hers as she held out his change and she was unable to tear it away without attracting attention.

'Look at me, Mary,' Paul ordered, in a low whisper.

'Let go of my hand,' she hissed.

'Look at me first,' he demanded, tightening his grip a fraction.

She glared up at his face and found herself meeting the warm, brown eyes which had melted her heart so completely almost seven years ago now.

'That's better,' he grinned, instantly changing his face

from something dark and vaguely sinister to that of a warm-hearted friend. 'Please, Mary, can't we talk?'

'Talk!' She was amazed. 'Oh, I don't think so, Paul.'

A small voice inside her head warned her to stay icily cool, but the old attraction was still there. What was it about this man, she asked herself? Another seven years had aged him. Grey strands ran through his dark hair and his face was marked by lines and shadows which hadn't been there before, but it was as if he held some sort of magnetic attraction for her.

'We have nothing to talk about, Paul.'

'I think we have,' he insisted. 'The least you can do is allow me to apologise.'

She hadn't been expecting that but even so it angered her. 'Apologise, Paul? It's too late for that. Seven years too late.'

'It's never too late, Mary. We were both young and foolish. I know I treated you badly. If only you knew how often I think about you, how much I regret . . . I even tried to find you, but you just disappeared. I thought I would never see you again,' he lied blandly, carefully keeping his eyes fixed on her lovely, flushed face and resisting the urge to appraise her slender body.

'Please, Paul. This isn't the place. And I'm closing for the evening.'

'Come and sit with me and have some coffee. That's not asking too much is it?' he begged, still smiling.

Frantically Maxine looked round, hoping Marty would come to her rescue but, sensing that something intensely personal was going on the young head waiter had tactfully busied himself elsewhere. Maxine shrugged, knowing she was beaten. 'Just for a few minutes,' she conceded.

She poured coffee quickly and took it to a table in the very centre of the dining room. Paul smiled to himself then slid into the seat facing hers and leaned across the table.

'I know what you must think of me, Mary,' he began. 'My behaviour was inexcusable and, believe me, I have often regretted it.'

'Not as much as I have,' she answered, bitterly.

'I was spoiled,' he said, with what he hoped was disarming frankness. 'In a place like that a professor is open to all kinds of temptation. I could have had my pick of any one of ten different girls. It's quite an occupational hazard. I was stupid enough to think I was something special. You weren't the only one I took advantage of. Does that shock you?'

'No.' She stirred her coffee and refused to look at him.

'And then you came along. To be honest I was out of my depth, I never intended it to be anything but . . . well, I found myself falling in love with you.'

'You had a very strange way of showing it,' she snorted, disbelievingly.

'I know. What use is it for me to say I'm truly, deeply sorry? I know it's much too late for that now.'

'If you felt so strongly about me why didn't you help me at the time?' she challenged, her eyes blazing with remembered anger. 'You ruined my life and when I turned to you for help you didn't want to know me.'

He shrugged. 'I wish I could explain. But I can't. I only know that I've regretted it ever since. If only you hadn't gone off like that . . . I would have been able to see you, to make things right. As it is you must have hated me for the last seven years.'

His voice was low and intense, so plausible, she thought, glancing up and finding herself under close scrutiny from his pale, unblinking eyes then unable to look away again. She shook her head, confused, not knowing what to think any more.

'Mary . . . I was married. I already had a wife and family. When I realised how complicated things were getting with you I think I panicked. I took the easy way out. Even when you told me you were pregnant there was nothing I could do. My wife had just had another child. I couldn't leave them. I didn't know what to do. It was easier for me to pretend nothing had happened, to go home to my wife . . .'

'Is that what you're going to do tonight?' Maxine interrupted.

'No. Not this time, Mary. I wouldn't have come here to talk to you if that was the case. No. My wife and I are divorced. You see, nothing was the same for me after you . . . I did try to find you.'

He sounded so sincere and she had left St Andrews very quickly. She watched his face closely but could see nothing to doubt in it.

'I'm sorry,' she said at last. 'I guess we both lost out.'

'Yes,' he admitted. 'And I know it was my fault.' He took her hand over the table. She made no attempt to remove it. 'I know there's nothing I can say to make you think any better of me, but I do want you to know that I've changed. I was younger then, Mary. Arrogant. But I've learned my lesson. I'll never make that mistake again.'

'No,' she said, returning the pressure of his hand then hating herself when she realised she had done it and adding quickly, 'Not with me you won't, Paul.'

He was there every single night, sitting alone at his table, waiting for her to finish. Each evening she spent five or ten public minutes with him, telling herself she was in control, that Paul Kinsail was having no effect on her and knowing, all the time, that she was lying to herself.

'Let me take you out to dinner,' he pleaded.

425

She laughed. 'I go out to dinner every night.'

'Then let's just walk, try to get to know one another properly. I don't think we did that last time, did we?'

'All right,' she conceded. 'Tomorrow.' After all, Paul had been coming here for a week now and it was clear that he was a changed man. She believed him when he said he regretted the past and he had been very courageous to seek her out after so long. But, above all, Maxine was lonely. Despite all she had said to herself when she and Callum had parted, she desperately needed someone to share at least a part of her life with. She had loved Paul Kinsail once, perhaps she could learn to love him again.

This late in the year the evenings were cool, often made cooler by the sharp breeze which whipped in off the North Sea. After a drink at the Lobster, still the only public house in the village, and one which retained its local clientele and customs, Maxine and Paul wandered down to Kilweem's small harbour.

Only two fishing boats remained to bob on the swell now. The crates and nets which were draped against the wall of the old gutting shed were but a fraction of what would have been there twenty years before. But still, though the catch was small these days, the whole area was redolent of fish.

It was, Maxine thought, like stepping back in time to come down here. The narrow wynds were still cobbled with square setts, making it almost impossible to walk on heeled shoes. The houses which clustered round the harbour and straggled up the steep wynds were narrow-fronted and either grey harled or painted white, with their windows framed in black, just as they always had been with their red pantiles and crow-stepped gables.

This part of the village had changed little over the years.

From down here none of the newer houses were visible, adding to the illusion that this was another, former decade. As she looked out over the small quayside to the far wall which protected it from the sea, Maxine was sure that Kilweem would have looked very much the same on any other September night for the past fifty years or more.

She loved it, appreciated the quaint beauty of the village and the steady, reassuring pound of the sea. But it was the very beauty of the village which was threatening to ruin it. Kilweem, like the other charming villages dotted along the Strathannan coast, had long been popular with visitors, but only in the last two years had they begun to edge towards becoming tourist resorts. Tourism had replaced fishing as the main industry in many places, encouraging scores of people to tramp through the narrow streets, depositing litter, noise and confusion along with their money. Only at this time of the year did the villages revert to their true character, peaceful, solid and invincible, protecting their tight knit communities as fiercely as the sea wall guarded this harbour.

It was, she had soon discovered, as if there were two villages here. The older, established village, people whose families had lived here for generations past, still stayed in the tangle of wynds round the harbour and Marketgate. The newcomers, people who had bought the new houses, lived to the north of the village in the skein of streets which had spread along the main road out of the village. Each of these two communities stayed within itself to the exclusion of the other. Maxine knew she had never been accepted as belonging to the old village, and never would be. Kilweem was proud of its heritage, and too closely knit to admit newcomers. By now she knew most of the villagers by sight and name, and was herself recognised and greeted, not with real warmth, but with the restrained cordiality which was the very most any outsider could

427

hope for. She understood that this small concession to her presence in the village was due at least as much to her relationship with Maurice and Maureen as to her friendly personality and genuine love of Kilweem. She also knew that there were some villagers who actively objected to what she had done to the bakery. But she felt no resentment towards any of them but rather admired their independence, their dogged refusal to be swallowed up by larger communities or the commercialism of the tourist trade.

Tonight, as she and Paul meandered through the narrow wynds, making their way towards the beach, the beauty and character of the place struck her anew. She turned and looked back at the old village, loving it.

'Isn't Kilweem a wonderful place?' she whispered to Paul.

'Kilweem!' He snorted his derision. 'It's a hundred years behind the times. There's nothing here. I can't understand what you see in the place. What on earth do you find to do here?' He scowled round him, seeing nothing of the quaint, old-fashioned beauty which so captivated her. 'Come on. Are we going for a walk along the beach or not?'

In a few tense words he destroyed the lovely, warm feeling which had been growing inside her. As they walked down the Butts and on to the beach she knew they had nothing in common.

Once on the beach he ploughed through the fine, golden sand, forcing her to trot to try and keep up with him. Shivering in the freshening breeze, he turned and waited impatiently. 'Let's get out of this bloody wind. It'll be more sheltered in the dunes.'

She shrugged and caught at the hand he offered, allowing him to help her negotiate the sliding sand hills. As soon as he found a sheltered hollow he threw himself into it and pulled her down beside him.

He was on her before she had time to get herself comfortably settled, pushing her back, trying to kiss her, his hands already working their way under her coat. Furiously she jerked away.

'Stop it,' she yelled, sitting up.

He sighed. 'Oh God! Are you going to play stupid games with me, Mary? I thought there was no need. After all, we've done all this before.'

'That was a long time ago, Paul.'

He retreated into moody silence, lit a cigarette and stared out over the sea, ignoring her. Her enjoyment of the evening was shattered. She stayed as stubbornly mute as him until, at last, he seemed driven to break the impasse.

'OK. I'm sorry.'

'It's all right. I'm cold. I'd really like to go home now.' She started to get to her feet.

'Tell me about the baby. What was it, a boy or a girl?'

Dumbfounded she sagged back into the sand and he moved closer to her, his mood and character seeming to change with disturbing ease as he slid a gentle arm round her shoulders and pulled her into the warmth of his body.

'I didn't like to ask you before in case you thought I was more interested in the child than I am in you. I was hoping you might tell me without my having to ask.'

Still she couldn't say anything, silenced by the torrent of conflicting emotions rushing through her mind.

'He's my child too, Mary.' How he missed his children, more, much more than he missed his wife. Perhaps, through this other child, he might find something worthwhile in his life again.

'There is no child,' she whispered, not daring to look at his face.

His arm fell from her shoulders and he jerked her round

to face him. 'No child? But you told me you were pregnant. That's why you left St Andrews.'

'I was . . .'

'You didn't have it!' he interrupted her angrily now. 'Are you telling me you didn't go through with it?'

'I lost it.'

'Lost it or had an abortion?' he demanded. 'Do you know what you did, taking an innocent life?'

Maxine surged to her feet, driven by blind, blood-red fury. 'You bastard,' she screamed. 'No. I did not have an abortion. I lost the child. How could you ever understand what I went through then? And why are you suddenly so concerned? You didn't care at the time and I don't believe you really made any attempt to find me – I wouldn't have been that difficult to trace if you had really wanted to get in touch. Now, seven years later you turn up out of nowhere and start accusing me of murdering my own child! Go to hell!'

She stormed away from him, slipping and slithering down the dunes and on to the beach, almost falling in her rush to get away from him.

He caught up with her before she was more than fifty yards along the shoreline. 'Wait, Mary. Why didn't you tell me before?' he panted.

'You didn't ask,' she spat.

'I was waiting for you to say something first,' he said, holding on to her, trying to stop her from running off again. 'I thought it would be hard for you to talk about. I didn't want you to think I was going to try and interfere with the way you were bringing the child up . . . that I was suddenly going to ask for my paternal rights . . . Can't you see how difficult it was for me? For God's sake, Mary, how was I supposed to know?'

Tears streamed down her face and she shivered in the wind, cold with shock and pain. Paul opened his arms and dragged her into them, holding her tightly against his warm chest, murmuring endearments into her ear while he waited for her convulsive sobbing to die away.

'Come on, I'll take you home. You need a drink.'

Unable to face the restaurant, which would still be busy, she allowed him to lead her through the back entrance and up to her private flat. He held her, reassured her, wiped her tears, listened to an abbreviated story of her life, kissed away fresh tears and finally led her to the bedroom.

When he took her she lost herself in him completely, deliberately allowing her mind to go blank so there could be no comparison between him and Callum. If he was rough with her she encouraged him, almost as if she wanted to be punished. When it was over she turned away and wept bitterly into her pillow while Paul slept like a child, a contented smile curving his lips.

'Why don't I stay here with you?' he suggested in the morning when she was barely awake.

'Stay with me?' she repeated, staring at him through gritty lids.

'I could help you,' he insisted. 'You told me you were lonely, that you could do with some support.' Already he could visualise the lucrative future this business could give him.

How she regretted those unguarded, emotional outbursts last night. 'It's much too soon to be talking about anything permanent, Paul.' All she wanted to do was get him out of here, to leave her in peace.'

'Of course it's not. I'm lonely too, Mary. We need one another so why not share our lives? And this is a wonderful business you've got here. With me to help you, we could really pull in the customers. We need to update it a bit, offer a smaller menu, put in a few more tables, be a little less generous with the portions, maybe put the prices up a bit . . . We could double the takings.'

Anger collided violently with the shame which was already making her face burn. Each time she looked at him she saw Callum's face. Good, honest Callum whose calm, easygoing manner disguised such high moral principles. Callum who was trustworthy and generous, gentle and passionate and who had never, ever taken her in anything other than love.

'This is my business, Paul. I have made it what it is and I have no intention of changing it,' she said flatly, clambering out of bed and dragging herself into some clothes, wanting to do this with some dignity. 'I don't want to share anything with you, Paul, not my life, not my business. Nothing.'

'After last night? I thought you were pretty keen to share yourself with me then,' he sneered, without any hint of tenderness.

'Are you asking me to marry you?' she challenged, seeing him for exactly what he was for the second time in her life.

'Of course not,' he answered lightly. 'It's much too early for that. Perhaps later.'

'Too soon to marry but not too soon to muscle in on a share of the business?' She threw it at him and was gratified to see him pale slightly. 'Just get your things and go, Paul. Last night . . . last night was a terrible mistake. This whole thing has been a mistake.'

'I see,' he snarled. 'You were just using me.'

'No!'

'Then why can't I stay? You're over-reacting, Mary. If last night meant anything to you at all, let me stay. It'll work out perfectly, you'll see.' Chameleon-like he changed again, seeming soft and tender as he came towards her, holding his arms open. 'I've got it all worked out. I'll give up my job, sell my house and invest the money in this place. We'd be partners,' he ended triumphantly.

After all, what were a couple of years of living with her compared to the rewards he would reap? If their relationship survived, so much the better, if not he would claim half the business and still be considerably better off than he was now.

She backed away. 'I already have a partner. Now go, Paul. Please go.'

'You owe me more than this, Mary.' His face was cold and hostile. Ugly.

'I owe you?' She couldn't believe this. 'You were the one who turned your back on me, remember? And you were the one who wheedled your way in here last night.'

'You were glad enough to have me. You've learned a lot since St Andrews, Mary. Then you were a naive little girl. Last night you behaved like a prostitute. You were begging for it.'

She slapped him so hard that she thought, for a second, she had broken her fingers with the force of that one, concentrated blow.

He reeled back against the wall, growling in anger. He took a single step towards her, raised his hand but then thought better of it.

'You'll be sorry you did that,' he promised, snatching up his jacket.

'Get out,' she screamed.

'Don't worry, I'm going. I wouldn't stay here if you got down on those skinny little knees and begged me. But don't think you've heard the last of me, Mary Innes. You ruined my life. You and your tales. I lost my home, my family, my career and my wife, all because of you. I'll get even with you if it's the last thing I do.'

The door banged behind him and she heard his car fire up and race off along the road. For many minutes she simply stood and stared after him, unable to move. Then, walking slowly she sank on to the bed, covered her head with her pillows and began to sob softly. It was hours later before she was able to rouse herself and take her place in the restaurant.

It was there that she received the dreadful news which made her fall to the floor in a dead faint.

Almost two years to the day after her brother's death, Maureen Archibold followed him to the grave. Grieving deeply Maxine sat through the funeral in a daze. It was all too unreal. Only two days before her death Maureen had been chatting on the phone to Maxine. She had sounded so lively, just like her normal, healthy, happy self and was even considering taking herself off to Spain for a few months to escape the cold and damp of another Scottish winter.

She had been felled by a massive heart attack while playing golf on her favourite course with three of her many friends. Overcome by a crushing sense of loss Maxine could hardly bear to listen as the Rector intoned the service but leaned against her sisters for support. Maureen had been her understanding aunt, her mother and a wonderful friend, all rolled into one unique and generous person. Nothing would ever be the same without her.

Although Maxine was well known in Kilweem, without Maureen, and now that she had lost contact with Janette who still hadn't written, she had no close friend, no one in whom she could confide her hopes and fears, no one to share the worries and successes of the business with.

Most of the young people of her own age, like her own sisters, were married now and busily raising families, giving them little in common with Maxine. Many villagers, like Eileen Crombie who had been her friend when she first arrived in Kilweem, had left the village for the better employment and housing prospects of the towns. It hadn't worried her at the time because she had had Callum, and Janette, who had been the best friend anyone could hope for, was still writing to her. Even when Janette's letters stopped and she and Callum split up Maxine had been confident that she needed nothing more than the challenge of the restaurant and her aunt's friendship and support. But now the unthinkable had happened. Maureen was dead leaving Maxine absolutely bereft.

Callum, assisting the Rector, watched as Maxine fought to control her emotions and wished there was something he could do to ease her pain but she was surrounded by her family and he felt it wiser to let the Rector take the role of comforter at the end of the service.

The will was read at the office of Maureen's solicitors, Mackie and Malcolm. Maxine presented herself wearing her black funeral suit, her long, blonde hair bundled under a hat which hid her eyes and drained her face of all colour. It reflected her mood.

The will itself was just as Maureen had said it would be. Her house in Sauchar, her personal possessions and a surprisingly large number of shares and other financial assets were to be divided among Maxine and her brother and sisters with small bequests for both George and Ina. On top of that Maxine had inherited the building which housed the restaurant – the mortgage now fully paid. But she knew that the most valuable part of the legacy was the other half share in the business which made her the sole owner of Maxine's. But it gave her no pleasure at all. Willingly, gratefully, she would have gone back to being a humble bakery assistant if only she could have had her dear aunt back.

TWENTY-FIVE

It was a quieter, less cheerful and much more subdued Maxine who turned her full attention back to the restaurant. In the past she had made a point of circulating round the dining room, stopping for a friendly word with her customers, taking their few criticisms seriously, making a careful note of any suggestions and generally ensuring that every diner felt welcome and comfortable. The Maxine of three weeks ago had responded to the mild flirting and general flattery from some of her male clients with sparkling good humour, but now, still grieving for Maureen and upset by the dreadful memory of what had happened between her and Paul Kinsail, she felt unequal to the effort of sustained smiles and petty banter. Relying on Marty to fill the role of host she limited herself to the kitchen.

For that reason she didn't see the four men who took a table on Saturday evening when the restaurant was at its most crowded. The sounds which filtered through to the kitchen were usually ones of quiet chat, muted laughter and the satisfying chink of cutlery on china, punctuated by the occasional pop of a champagne cork. Tonight, though, as Maxine coaxed an unco-operative sauce in the kitchen, she was aware of unpleasantly coarse laughter and raised voices.

Janice, one of her waitresses, hurried in, loaded with dirty plates. Maxine looked at her and frowned. 'Everything all right out there?' she asked uneasily.

'I think so,' the girl answered, carefully depositing her burden by the sink before gathering her next order.

'It sounds a bit lively.'

'There are four men on table three. They've all had a lot to drink and they're making a bit of noise but they're OK.' Janice rushed away, anxious to serve the next course before it had a chance to cool.

Reassured, Maxine returned her attention to her sauce, checking the saucepans of freshly cooked vegetables in a never-ending round of activity.

Minutes later her head shot up again when she caught the unmistakable sound of voices raised in anger. Hurriedly wiping her hands and tearing off her protective apron, she went into the dining room, checking herself just outside the door so that her entrance would not appear flurried.

Quickly she cast a practised eye over the diners who all seemed to have stopped eating. Some looked embarrassed, others stared openly at the source of the disturbance. Marty, who was doing his best to pacify a customer who was swearing at him in a voice loud enough to be heard outside, looked flustered.

'This fish is off! Bloody hell, I can smell it from here,' her irate customer roared. 'Here,' he shoved the plate under Marty's unhappy nose. 'Smell it for yourself.'

The man was about Marty's own height but barrel-chested and powerful looking. His tweed jacket was limp and shabby looking, and too tight under the armpits while the collar ends of his washed-out, checked shirt curled untidily. His tie was loosened, the top two buttons of the shirt undone, adding to his untidy appearance. Maxine caught the strong odour of sweat from him and saw that the fingers which grasped his plate were ragged and black-rimmed. His three companions, similarly unkempt, grinned their encouragement. She recognised the drunken slur in the man's voice and knew, at once, that this could mean serious trouble. As she glided smoothly towards the centre of the commotion she saw with dismay that several of her clients who had chosen fish were laying their cutlery down and sniffing suspiciously at their plates.

'I am telling you,' he bellowed. 'This fish is off. I'm not eating this. Do you want to poison me? Bloody cheek. At the prices you charge.'

Maxine purposefully removed the plate from his hand, sniffed it, tasted it, then, fixing her brightest smile on her trembling lips said, 'I can assure you, Sir, that this fish was landed at Anstruther this morning. It is as fresh as a fish can possibly be. I wouldn't serve anything less. However, if you would prefer something else from the menu I would be happy to cook it for you.'

'Not bloody likely. Keep your fucking fish. I wouldn't eat anything from here after this. And I'm going to make an official complaint, to the health inspector.'

Kicking his chair back violently enough to make it fall with a clatter, he motioned to his companions and led them from the restaurant, still complaining loudly. Behind her, Maxine noticed a couple who had ordered but were not yet eating, hastily gather their things and leave. Another couple, waiting in the small bar for their table, rapidly followed suit.

'I am very sorry, ladies and gentlemen,' she turned to face her clients. 'I can assure you that there is absolutely nothing wrong with the fish which is freshly caught, as always. I can only assume that the sauce wasn't to the gentleman's liking. Please, continue with your meals. I hope the evening hasn't been spoiled for you and, naturally, there will be no charge for your main course.'

Back in the kitchen every member of staff was forced to sample the suspect meal. They all agreed that it was perfectly good. Frowning, Maxine scraped the remains

438

into the waste bin. The incident had left a very unpleasant sensation in her mind, made no easier by the niggling suspicion that the whole thing had been stage-managed. But why? Surely there was no reason for anyone to want to damage her business.

What was certain was the almost non-existent demand for her excellent puddings and the fact that the restaurant emptied a full forty-five minutes earlier than it usually did, her customers seeming reluctant to linger, even over coffee.

The following evening passed uneventfully, as did the whole of the next week. There was no visit from the health inspector and trade was as brisk as ever. Maxine thanked God that any customers lost through Saturday's unpleasantness would be limited to those who had actually been in the dining room at the time, and none of them had been regulars.

The incident had been relegated to the back of her mind when, again on a Saturday night, she heard the sounds of disturbance in the restaurant.

Not waiting to remove her apron this time she hurried into the dining room. Stunned she actually came to a confused stop just inside the door when she recognised the source of the upset.

Swaying drunkenly, red-faced and angry looking, Samuel Cree, Archie's older brother, surveyed the room, making sure of his audience.

'There's a bloody rusty nail in my pie,' he bellowed. 'I could have choked to death. I want the police to see this. Do you hear me?' He grabbed the sweating Marty by the throat and hauled him to within six inches of his face. 'Call the police.'

'What do you think you are doing, Samuel Cree?' Maxine yelled, anger making her forget the other diners who were all agog at the scene, meals forgotten.

'What am I doing?' Sam growled, beside himself with assumed anger. 'I am trying to buy my missus a meal, is what I'm doing. It's our anniversary.' He stared round, making sure he held the attention of the entire room. 'So, I thought, where better to go than wee Maxine's place? After all, we're family. No favours asked, mind. I expected to pay the full price for a decent meal, just like anyone else. And what do I get? A rusty bloody nail! It shouldn't be allowed. I'll sue. I've got witnesses,' he bellowed.

As the truth dawned on Maxine her stomach contracted with anger but, aware of her other customers, she did her best to smooth things over without losing her temper.

'There cannot have been a nail in that steak pie, Sam. I made it myself, this morning.'

'Aye, well, you never were much of a cook, Mary Cree. It's a wonder you've not poisoned someone before now,' he replied, loudly.

'Look, Sam, I don't know what all this is about but . . .'

'Look at the state of it,' he yelled, holding a very long, extremely rusty nail aloft for the other customers to appreciate.

Already people who were half-way through a perfectly satisfactory meal were shoving their plates away. A table of four left, muttering angrily about hygiene standards.

'Come on,' Sam jerked his head at his wife who had been quite unable to meet Maxine's eyes. 'I am not staying here another minute.' With that he stomped theatrically from the restaurant, leaving Maxine to try and apologise to her unsettled diners, again.

From then on Maxine tried to keep a careful watch on the customers arriving at the restaurant, suspecting that she hadn't heard the last of this. She was right.

Try as she might she simply couldn't be in the dining room all the time. It was inevitable that some customers were seated before she had the chance to see who they were. Marty did his best, drawing Maxine's attention to anyone who looked remotely suspicious, but it was an impossible task.

It was the following Friday before the now dreaded sound of argument brought her running to investigate. Seated at a central table was Archie himself, his mother, Arthur – his other brother – and Arthur's wife. Both men appeared to be exceedingly drunk and were doing their utmost to disrupt the calm atmosphere Maxine prided herself on.

Already the other diners were fidgeting uncomfortably.

'This is not what we ordered,' Archie slurred, appearing to accidentally knock his plate to the floor.

'This steak is like rubber,' his mother whined, pushing her plate away in feigned disgust.

'I want to see the manager,' Archie demanded, lurching to his feet and facing his wife who was watching the performance from the doorway.

'Certainly, Sir. If you and your party would like to follow me.' Marty grabbed the opportunity to remove this latest band of trouble-makers from the dining room and steered them towards Maxine.

Unexpectedly Archie complied, tottering belligerently towards the door with his family trailing after him. To Maxine's fury he stopped at every table he passed to drunkenly prod meals and pass derogatory comments on the food so that a good third of her guests found themselves quite unable to finish their course.

'What the hell do you think you're doing, Archie?' Maxine stormed as soon as he was out of the dining room.

'What do you think?' he asked, suddenly absolutely sober.

'You're ruining me!'

'Like you ruined me!'

'I did not . . .' she stopped, suddenly aware of the futility of argument. 'What do you want from me, Archie?'

'A fair share of the profits. You are still my wife, Mary, and I am entitled to a share of anything you earn.'

'Never.'

'I'm only asking for what's right.'

Behind him she saw her in-laws leaving the restaurant, apparently content to leave this to him.

'You have no rights over me, Archie.' She practically spat it at him. 'It's over, finished, and has been for years. Why can't you get that through your head? I gave you a share of the money from the jewellery. You're getting nothing else.'

'You gave me two thousand pounds! It should have been twice that. You still owe me, Mary. That wedding present was for both of us.'

'It was from my aunt! You're lucky I gave you that much.'

'You still owe me, Mary,' he repeated, a thinly-veiled menace in his voice which made her shiver.

'I owe you nothing. Now get out of here before I call the police,' she hissed, belatedly aware of the stares of her customers who could both see and hear the argument through the glass-panelled door. Turning her back on her husband she started for the relative safety of the kitchen. He stopped her with a hard grab for her arm.

'Don't you walk away from me. We have things to discuss, you and me.'

She snorted. 'You and I have nothing to say to each other.'

'If you want this business of yours to survive you had better think hard, Hen. I want a share of the profits.'

'Never.'

'How many complaints do you think this place can take,

Mary? How many rusty nails and how much rotten fish before you have to close down?'

'I can't afford to pay you anything, Archie. I'm barely in profit as it is.'

'Don't give me that. What do you think I am? I can see for myself, can't I? All I want is my fair share. If you don't pay up, I'll ruin you,' he threatened, anger turning his face a stiff, mottled red.

'That's blackmail!'

'Aye, Miss, that's what it sounded like to me.'

They both span round at the sound of the unfamiliar voice and were confronted by a uniformed policeman.

'Sorry, Maxine,' Marty shrugged. 'I thought it was about time someone put a stop to this. I called the police even before I went to try and deal with it.'

'Your head waiter has been telling me there have been several similar incidents?' the policeman said, thumbing through his notebook.

'Yes. That's right,' she agreed.

Archie, she recalled, had an almost pathological fear of the police. She had no intention of making any complaint which might result in damaging publicity for the restaurant but, judging by the sudden pallor of Archie's face the very presence of the law might be enough to deter him from organising any further episodes like this one.

'Blackmail is a very serious offence,' the officer said, looking pointedly at Archie.

'Can you not use your common sense and see this for what it is, Officer?' Archie said in a placatory tone. 'This is my wife. She walked out on me, ruined my business, took things that weren't hers and sold them.'

'I took nothing of yours, Archie and well you know it.'

'My pride doesn't count, I suppose,' he snarled, bitterly. 'Officer, just look at me. I'm a cripple. Life is hard enough for someone like me without your wife lousing it up for you. I'm only trying to get what's mine.'

'Do I take it then that this is a domestic argument?' the policeman asked, sounding suddenly bored.

'Yes,' Archie answered quickly. 'An argument between a man and his wife and nothing to do with anyone else.'

'I'll be the judge of that, Sir,' the officer responded, obviously irritated by Archie's whining manner. 'Whatever happened between you and your wife doesn't give you the right to disturb the peace and issue threats.' He turned to Maxine. 'Do you wish to take this any further, Miss?'

Maxine pretended to consider her choices. 'No,' she said, sounding reluctant. 'Not this time.'

The policeman nodded slowly, watching them both closely. 'All right, but I should warn you, Sir, that if there are any further disturbances, you will be arrested and charged. Now, let me have your name and address for the record.'

Archie grudgingly supplied the details and Maxine could see he was shaken. As soon as the policeman was satisfied with the information, Archie took himself off, but not before he had given her a look of such deep hatred that she felt nauseated.

'Are you all right, Miss?' the officer asked.

'Yes, thanks. I'm sure it will be OK now.'

'Be sure and call us back if you get any more bother,' he instructed, replacing his cap and retracing his steps to the back door.

Maxine sagged back against the wall, the colour draining from her face in a sudden reaction to the night's events.

'Here, Maxine, drink this and sit down.' Marty pushed a glass of neat brandy into her hands. She swallowed it in one gulp.

'Let's hope that's an end to it,' she said, trying to sound positive.

'Let's hope so. But this evening isn't over yet. There are still twenty hungry people in there, wondering what's happened to their meals. Best get back to the kitchen.' Firmly he pulled her to her feet and guided her back to the stove. 'We'll lose the customers we've still got if we don't feed them soon,' he laughed.

'OK,' she said. 'And Marty . . .'

'Yes?'

'Thanks for calling the police. It was the right thing to do. Let's just hope all this doesn't have an adverse effect on the business. The last thing we want now is for trade to drop off.'

'It won't,' he assured her. 'I think we stopped it just in time. This restaurant's damned good, Maxine, everyone who's eaten here knows that. We'll survive.'

Somehow his certainty was infectious. They would survive. Archie Cree and his awful family would never get the better of Maxine Lennox.

TWENTY-SIX

Tragic though Maureen's death had been, it did have the effect of bringing about an appreciable improvement in Maxine's finances. The half share of the profits which had been payable to Maureen was now hers and there was also a sizeable cash sum from her share of the sale of Maureen's house. Together they led Maxine to seriously consider an issue she had been toying with for some time.

Although she lived above the restaurant and made a point of being there nearly every night, taking her share of the cooking, which was what she loved to do, as well as making sure everything was precisely as she expected it to be, Maxine knew that under Marty's capable management Maxine's would operate just as effectively without her. Her staff were all well-trained, efficient and loyal enough – both because she paid them well and because every single one of them knew she simply would not tolerate slackness – to keep to her high standards, even when she wasn't there to oversee them personally. It was, she realised, only the need to fill her life that kept her tied to the restaurant night after night. The challenge had faded with success. But her ambition hadn't and what she needed now was something else to engage her lively mind.

Maureen's money gave her the chance to find it.

The more she thought about it the more Maxine saw that she could now afford to open a second Maxine's. One which would be hers, right from the very start.

Brimming with enthusiasm for her new project she set

off on a tour of Strathannan, seeking out suitable premises. Because she loved the seaside villages she visited them first, but found nothing. In any case, she realised, another Maxine's so close to the original one would probably not increase her total custom but merely split it. Perhaps a town site would be better this time, one which didn't rely on the tourist industry quite so heavily and was less affected by the seasons.

Weeks passed. To Maxine's intense disappointment she didn't see a single property which was even remotely suitable. Then she heard about an old farmhouse which was being offered for rent and went to look at it with keen interest but immediately saw that turning it into a restaurant would be an impossible undertaking. Netherdrum House itself was marvellous, old and full of character, but it was in a fairly remote location, well inland from the regular tourist routes along the coast and in a place which had very little passing traffic. As a country hotel it would have been ideal but as a restaurant it was much too grand. Half the rooms would have had to be left unused while the others would have to be completely stripped and refurbished, all at huge expense. It was such a lovely, mellow old house that Maxine even considered selling the old bakery in Kilweem and sinking everything into making Netherdrum House into a small hotel. She retained her hold on common sense for long enough to know that she had neither the expertise nor the capital for such a venture.

It was three months before her solicitor, Callum's father, called her with details of a property in Inverannan. As always she was obliged to speak much more loudly than normal because of his deafness.

'I hadn't seriously thought about Inverannan,' she told him.

'Say that again, my dear, and talk up,' he laughed.

'Is it within my price range?'

'Yes. But remember you will need to do a lot of work to it and because of the town centre location the price might seem high compared to more rural sites.'

'Yes, I understand that,' she shouted down the phone. 'Have you got any details?'

'Not yet. It's new on the market. Reeves and Murchieson of Inverannan are handling the sale. I'll arrange for one of their people to show you round if you like.'

'I suppose I really should look at it. It's the first place I've heard of that's already operating as a café. It would be much easier for me to get something like that than start converting a house or a hairdresser's,' she laughed.

'I'll make the arrangements, then.'

'Yes, please.'

A week later Maxine parked her car and walked through Inverannan town centre towards the property she wanted to view. When she had been given this address by the solicitor she had been momentarily stunned. Cross Wynd was where Alessandro's had been, the shop where her mother had worked before finally running off with the owner. It was some time since she had last been in Inverannan town centre but as far as she could recall there wasn't another café on that particular street. It had to be the same place. At first she had been reluctant even to go and look at it but she could hardly back out now, not with the solicitor's clerk waiting to show her round. Anyway, it wasn't as if it was Alessandro's any longer. Now it was a branch of Angelou's, the company which had been interested in buying the old bakery at the time of Maurice's death. At least this café was ideally situated, right in the heart of the small town on a steep, setted wynd which led from the High Street to the bus stance, and always busy with people.

The town of Inverannan itself, though small compared to places like Dundee and Edinburgh, was the largest town in Strathannan. It was a quaint and faintly old-fashioned place, proud and more than averagely prosperous. Although the town relied on its four mills which produced high-class linen goods, and had several clothing factories, it had neither the appearance nor the feel of an industrialised town. The county council itself liked to stress the burgh's importance as the administrative centre of Strathannan, a white-collar image strengthened by the immaculately maintained grey stone, turreted and towered town hall which dominated one side of the High Street.

Built on the eastern side of the river which gave the area its name only five miles before it lost itself in the mightier Forth, the town boasted modern amenities in the form of two cinemas, several respectable pubs, a good hotel, a splendid park, a musty library, a masonic hall and solid representation of all the mainstream religious denominations. It did not have a football team, a bingo hall or traffic wardens. All in all, Inverannan had managed to retain the essentially restrained and refined character which had tempted the wealthy folk to build their solid houses there.

Maxine knew there was only one other restaurant in the town, although the hotel had an enviable reputation for food, and there were several café-type establishments. It was obvious that Inverannan would be the perfect place for a second Maxine's and it would be nice too, she thought, to have a reason to be in Inverannan more often and the chance of seeing her family.

She was outside the café now, looking up at a brightly-lit sign. Angelou's, which had once been Alessandro's. Really it was nothing more than a glorified snack bar selling coffee, soft drinks, ice-cream and burgers. The flashing neon sign and the garish colours on the shop frontage looked oddly out of place on this narrow, cobbled road, she thought, and she wouldn't have permitted the filthy litter of discarded paper bags and drinks containers which turned the whole area into something of an eyesore. Inside the tables were all taken, mostly by youngsters and behind the counter the waitresses seemed busy enough. Maxine watched it all closely for a minute or two, wondering why such an apparently thriving business should be up for sale.

When she finally went inside she easily identified the solicitor's clerk whose pin-striped suit looked conspicuously out of place among the anoraks and duffle coats preferred by the teenagers who occupied most of the other tables.

'Miss Lennox?'

'Yes,' she smiled as she shook his hand, attracted by his dark good looks.

'I'm David Morrison. Would you like some coffee?'

'Please.' She settled into the seat opposite him.

'I hope you didn't have any trouble finding the place?' he said, conversationally.

'Actually I knew where it was. I used to live in the area.'

'I thought you came from Kilweem?' he said, sipping his coffee and watching her appreciatively over the rim of his cup. He wasn't often fortunate enough to have such a beautiful client and she was no empty-headed blonde either, judging by her assured manner and direct, grey eyes.

Maxine knew he was watching her and enjoyed it. It was a long time since she had attracted that sort of attention or, if she had attracted it, she hadn't had time to notice. 'I live on the coast now but I was raised in this area,' she confided.

450

'Well, if you've finished I'll show you what's what,' he offered.

In his late twenties, well-dressed, confident and good-looking, David Morrison attempted to charm her into ignoring the delapidated state of the seats, the old-fashioned kitchen, the flaking paintwork and the disused upper floor.

Maxine deliberately shut her mind to him and concentrated on looking at the areas which were important to her. Very quickly she saw that the proportions were almost ideal. A large dining room and a generous kitchen could easily be adapted from the existing layout. There was a small, dry cellar which could be used for wine and ample storage space. Disadvantages included the lack of adequate toilet facilities and the unsuitable façade, nor was there adjacent parking which might be a problem though there was plenty of space nearby.

Suppressing the determined bubble of excitement which was gurgling round her stomach, Maxine cast an appraising glance round her again, allowing none of her pleasure to show on her face. If the entrance door was moved over there, there would be room for a small bar where customers could have a drink while waiting for their tables. Even the cobwebby first floor could make a very convenient flat, either as an incentive for a first-class chef or restaurant manager, or to be rented out to provide extra income.

On the whole she thought there was less work to be done here than there had been at the old bakery when it had first been converted and much of what had to be done was cosmetic. Yes, the place had very definite possibilities but, keen as she was to expand her business, Maxine felt the asking price was excessive and said as much to David Morrison.

'The price is realistic for the area, Miss Lennox,' he

smiled, at his charming best. 'It includes all the furniture and fittings.'

'Which I will have to pay to have someone remove!' she retorted quickly. 'They're useless, Mr Morrison. Don't think I walked round with my eyes closed. The paint's peeling, the furniture is disgraceful and, as for the kitchen equipment, none of it is of any use to me. It's hopelessly outdated and in very poor condition. Any offer I make will reflect that.'

'That is your decision.' He was unruffled. 'I have already shown two potential buyers round and we have had several other enquiries. Personally I don't think price will be a problem.'

She shrugged and turned her beaming smile on him. 'Oh well, shame. I must admit I could probably have done something with this place and Inverannan is such a sweet little town. But, in view of what you've just told me, it's hardly worth me putting in an offer. And really, it is a bit too far from Kilweem. I had hoped for something closer. There is one place I've seen which would suit me better. It needs more work doing on it but in the long run it will be a lot less expensive than this place. I'm sorry, but thank you for showing me around.' She acted her role perfectly, convincing him that he had lost a potential buyer.

'Tell me,' she asked casually as they walked to the door. 'Why are Angelou's selling? It looks viable enough.'

'I'm not in a position to discuss the details, Miss Lennox, but I understand that Mr Angelou died. The sale is his wife's decision.'

'Oh . . . I see . . . Poor lady.'

'Yes. She comes from Inverannan originally, though I believe she's lived in Edinburgh for several years. I have heard that she wants to sell the café and buy herself a house back in the town.'

It was a sad story and Maxine didn't really want to

think about anything as depressing as a grieving widow now that she thought she had found the perfect site for the new Maxine's. To change the subject she said, 'I remember this place when I was a kid. It was called Alessandro's then. When did it change hands?'

'It didn't. Only the name changed. I don't know why. Mr Angelou's full name was Alessandro Angelou,' he said, dropping the devastating information casually into their conversation as he wondered whether it was worth asking her out to dinner. 'Miss Lennox, I hope you don't think I'm being presumptuous but I was wondering if you would have dinner with me?' he asked, imagining where dinner might lead and finding his hands sweating with anticipation.

To his horror her face drained of colour and her mouth gaped open. 'I'm sorry,' he mumbled. 'Maybe I could phone you instead.'

'What is her name?' Maxine whispered, oblivious to his agony.

'I'm sorry . . . ?'

'Mrs Angelou,' she snapped it at him, making him take a sharp step back. 'What is her first name?'

'I . . . I can't remember,' he stammered, racking his brain.

'Evelyn. It's Evelyn, isn't it?' she demanded.

'Yes . . . Yes, that's right! How did you know that?'

'I knew her once,' she said, stepping out of the shop into the setted wynd, and running blindly away from him, back towards her car.

If only Maureen was still alive. Maureen would have been able to help her, would have listened and then given her an honest, straightforward opinion. But Maureen was no longer available a quick phone call or a ten-minute drive away and there was no one else she could talk to about this. Her father and Annie were comfortably settled into their own routine and to remind him of the past would be unnecessarily cruel now. Neither did she want to talk to her sisters or brother. They, like her, would be too emotionally involved to be of any help. Never had Maxine felt the need for a close, trustworthy friend as she did now.

As always when she needed to think, she walked down to the Butts and on to the beach. It was October and blustery so she knew that, apart from a stalwart local or two exercising their dogs, the beach would be deserted. Wrapped up well in a thick jacket, scarf and gloves, she strode along the beach on the line of the receding tide, deep in thought.

Only rarely did she think about her mother and never with affection. The bitterness and anger had faded long ago, but there had been nothing at all to replace it. Or so she had thought.

But now her mother was suddenly a real person again, a person it was possible to contact, something she had never even considered doing before. From what little David Morrison had told her, her mother's circumstances must be difficult. It could well be that she desperately needed to sell Angelou's. Well, she wasn't going to buy it, Maxine told herself, astounded at the depth of vitriol which prompted that decision. Nothing would induce her to part with her own hard-earned money to make her mother's life more comfortable, even if it meant throwing away her chance of the best site yet for the new Maxine's. Evelyn Innes, or Angelou, had been responsible for the whole family living in misery for years and if it was now her turn to sample poverty and unhappiness, well that was simply natural justice.

Maxine trembled and shoved her hands deeper into her

pockets but knew it was shock which was shaking her, not cold. Shock and anger, with her mother for turning up again so unexpectedly and with herself for that poisonously bitter reaction. It was a terrible self-revelation to discover she could feel like this. Surely her years with Archie Cree should have made her more sympathetic to her mother's plight? Really, apart from the fact that they had had no children to be hurt by such a defection, what she had done to Archie had been little different to what her mother had done to her father. Why, then, did she hate her so much?

She braced herself against the wind and looked out over the choppy water. Caught by a violent gust, flecks of spray splattered her face, making it sting with cold. It was more like December than October, she thought dismally. The sky was an unrelenting grey, promising even worse weather overnight. Maxine shivered again, thinking about the small boats which might be trying to run for home before the storm broke. It would be a quiet night at the restaurant too. Few sane people would choose to leave the warmth of their own homes for a wind-lashed village on the edge of the North Sea on a night like this one was promising to be. A drop of rain settled on the end of her nose, warning of what was to come. She sighed. There was nothing more beautiful than the Strathannan coast on a fine day and, in this type of weather, nowhere more inhospitable. Maxine had been caught in the rain on the beach before and knew she would be drenched long before she reached home. Pulling her collar up she sprinted along the shore line and, with more difficulty, across the looser stuff and on to the ancient setts of the Butts. Keeping her face down she started the long climb up the hill to Marketgate.

'Maxine . . .' The cry was lost in the fury of the rain as it started to squall down in earnest. She ran, her hair already soaked, then jumped aside violently when a car, right behind her, blew its horn.

From the safety of the roadside she turned to glare at the bad-mannered driver.

'Get in. You're going to be soaked.' Fully attired in clerical garb, Callum gestured like a deranged bat.

'Oh, am I glad to see you,' she panted wetly as she threw herself on to his passenger seat.

'I was visiting Mrs Storey,' he explained. 'I thought it was you I saw on the beach.'

'I went for a walk.'

'What on earth for with this storm brewing? Surely you knew you'd get caught in it?' He was teasing but so intent on peering into the rain that he frowned while he spoke, giving the entirely wrong impression.

'Well, I'm sorry, Callum but unlike you I don't have a direct line to God so he couldn't tell me what he was going to do with the weather.' She was angry with him, angry with everything.

Callum darted one startled look at her then returned his concentration to the road.

Maxine felt that look, knew he hadn't deserved her sharp reply and apologised. 'Sorry, Callum. Something's happened . . . something awful. The rain just capped it all.' She managed a wry smile.

'S'OK. Well here we are. To make up for your appalling rudeness you will have to offer me some coffee.' He was already out of the car and sheltering in her doorway, grinning.

'A gentleman would have opened a lady's door for her,' she accused as she scrambled for her key.

'A lady's door, yes,' he agreed happily, following her inside.

The restaurant was deserted but as she fiddled with the coffee maker, choosing to entertain him here rather than

456

upstairs, Marty hurried in, dripping water all over the immaculate floor. Maxine took the opportunity to talk to him about the level of business she expected that evening.

'The way the weather is I think you'll be polishing cutlery all night. I can't see many people risking this.'

'No, not even for your excellent food,' Callum smiled at Marty and accepted his coffee gratefully.

'Brr,' she shivered. 'Don't sit there in the window, Callum, it's far too miserable. Come over here by the fire.' She called him back from his chosen seat where he had been watching the downpour pensively and sank into a comfortable chair in the bar area. 'It's gas but cleaner than the real thing and almost as comforting. Real fires always remind me of when I was a kid,' she smiled, dreamily.

'That's better,' he observed, watching her closely. 'At least you've managed to summon a smile for an old friend. I thought you were going to scowl at me all evening.'

She grimaced. 'I did warn you I was in a bad mood.'

'What's happened?' he asked, quietly.

'Who wants to know?' she retorted. 'The friend or the professional agony uncle?'

'Neither if you're going to be like that.' He drained his cup, walked calmly over to the coffee maker where he poured himself another and chatted comfortably to Marty for a few minutes before strolling back to Maxine. 'Want to talk about it or not?'

She sighed. 'I don't know, Callum. I'm missing Maureen. I used to talk about everything with her. Even you,' she laughed softly. 'Strange wasn't it? There was such a huge age gap but I was so close to her.'

'I know you were. She was an extraordinary woman, wasn't she? So full of energy.'

'She was much more than just an aunt to me, Callum. She was my friend.'

457

She stared into the flickering flame of the fire, remembering the woman who had made it possible for her to own this restaurant. Inevitably her thoughts wandered back to her own mother. Maxine tried to recall her face, the line of her mouth, the shape of her eyes or even the sound of her voice, but couldn't. All she could see was Maureen's much-loved face.

'She left me very well off. Did you know that?' she asked.

'I guessed,' he admitted.

'It's so unfair!' she burst out suddenly. 'She worked so hard all her life but I'm the one who's getting the benefit of it all.'

'It's what she would have wanted.'

'No! At least, not so soon. She wanted time to do all the things she never had the opportunity to do before. But she never got the chance.'

Callum heard the intense sadness in Maxine's voice. 'That's true but it's not your fault, Maxine, so don't feel guilty about all this.' He waved a hand round the room. 'Perhaps you should come to church? Say a prayer or two for her. It might help,' he suggested, expecting her to ridicule the idea. 'Maureen found a great deal of comfort at St Peters after Maurice's death.'

'I know she did . . . I'll see,' was all she would say.

'I'll have to be g – '

'Callum,' she interrupted, just as he was preparing to brave the weather again.

He smiled. 'What?'

'Could I tell you something, as a friend, or even as a curate, and would you tell me what you think? What you honestly think?'

'If you're sure it's something you want me to know and if you feel I can help,' he said, gently.

'I need to tell someone.'

'I'm not always right. I can only give you my opinion.'

'That's what I want. You always seemed to talk good sense to me, before . . .' she blushed now, remembering what had been between them.

'You didn't always think so at the time,' he reminded her. 'So, go on.' He sat back seeming alert but perfectly at ease.

'The money from Maureen's estate has just come through. Added to what I've managed to save over the last couple of years it gives me quite a nice sum in the bank. I have Maureen's share of the business now, too. The restaurant is all mine, the building's paid for, so that means my income is quite healthy too.' She glanced at him but he only nodded slightly to show he was listening. 'So, I'm thinking about buying another restaurant.'

His heart sank. So that was it. As ambitious as ever. Well, he deserved that for being arrogant enough to hope he could turn this to his own advantage.

She waited now, obviously expecting some sort of sensible response from him.

'It sounds like an obvious move, Maxine, if that's what you really want to do. It'll take up all your time and attention, I suppose, so you will have to be quite certain about it. The rest just depends on money, doesn't it? It's not the sort of thing to go into if you're under-funded I should think. But I'm not qualified to give advice on that sort of thing.'

'I'm bored, Callum,' she said, forcefully. 'This place runs itself. I'm superfluous. I need something else in my life. Starting up a new place, from scratch, would be quite a challenge. But that's not the problem.'

He laughed. 'You always were determined to make your mark, weren't you? I'm sure you'll make a success of whatever you do. Good luck to you.' He managed to

459

say it all with absolute sincerity, giving no hint of the sadness welling inside him.

'And perhaps not,' she sighed. 'I went to look at a place this afternoon. I thought it sounded just about ideal.'

'Really? Where?'

'Inverannan. It's a café. It's been there since I was a child. A bit tatty but I could have it converted fairly easily. It's a fair-sized building, plenty of potential and the location's perfect.'

'But?'

'But . . . but it's called Angelou's. They're an Edinburgh company with quite a few branches, I think. Anyway, apparently the owner died and his wife is selling the one in Inverannan. I don't really know the details . . .'

'Is price a problem?' he asked.

'No.' She swallowed hard and went on. 'No, the problem is that Angelou's used to be called Alessandro's. Mr Angelou's full name was Alessandro Angelou, so you see, the café's never really changed hands since I was a child. It just changed its name. It's the same place . . . the same place.'

Outside the wind sent a sheet of rain clattering against the window. The lights flickered briefly. Callum left his seat to come and crouch at Maxine's side, taking one of her cold hands in his strong, warm ones.

'The same place? What happened there, Maxine?'

The wind seemed to whip under the door and curl icily round her legs. She shivered.

'Callum, do you remember me telling you that my mother walked out when I was fifteen?'

'I remember,' he nodded.

'Before she left she had a job. In Alessandro's café.'

'Ah . . . I see . . . But that was a long time ago now, Maxine. Any bad memories the place has for you will soon disappear when you've altered it to suit your own needs,' he reassured her, surprised that this loose connection could disturb her so much.

'NO! Callum, just listen . . . My mother left us to go and live with this Alessandro. Mr Alessandro, that's what my father always called him. But David Morrison, he's from the solicitors dealing with the sale, he told me that Alessandro was only his first name. His full name was Alessandro Angelou. It was still his café, right up until he died, a few months ago. And now his wife is selling it. And I want to buy it from her. Or I did.'

'Oh!' Callum finally understood. 'Maxine, are you sure this Mrs Angelou is your mother? Did they actually get married?'

'Yes. My mother wrote and told my grandmother.'

'She didn't tell your father?'

'No. The only contact they had was through solicitors when they divorced. My mother just walked out one day and pretended we'd never been born. She never even sent us a Christmas card. Dad said it was better that way.'

'Are you quite sure? If you've had no contact it's possible your mother and this Mr Angelou never even got married . . .'

'Mrs Angelou's name is Evelyn. She's my mother all right.'

'OK . . . But presumably she's got no way of knowing who she's selling to, if you decide to go ahead. That is what's worrying you, isn't it?'

'Partly . . . It's so complicated, Callum. Part of me hates her. It sounds as if she needs to sell. She's lost her husband so she must be going through an unhappy time . . . And I'm glad! I don't want to use my money to help her. It's Maureen's money and she was a better mother to me than this Mrs Angelou ever was.' She sighed and wiped a tear from the side of her nose. 'I know what you must be thinking, Callum,' she accused. 'I'm ashamed

461

of myself for feeling like this. I know it's wrong, but I can't help it.'

'I'm not thinking anything except I wish I could help you, Maxine. I'm not in a position to judge you or your mother. Though I think I can understand why you feel the way you do.'

'Can you?' she asked, doubtfully. 'One part of me knows I'd be stupid to miss out on a good deal just because of her. After all, if I don't buy it, someone else will. And like you say, she doesn't have to know it's me, does she?'

'I wouldn't rely on that, Maxine. In a small town like Inverannan it's quite possible . . .'

'There's so much, so much I want to know. And what about Dad and my brother and sisters? Surely I should tell them?'

She lapsed into agitated silence.

'Do you still want my honest opinion?'

'Yes, Callum. Please. If only to help me sort it out in my own head.'

'Well, I think, if you really want this place you should go ahead. As you say, why throw away a chance like that? If you do let it go, it'll just be something else to blame your mother for. That wouldn't be right.'

'Don't sympathise with her, Callum. She turned her back on four kids just when they needed her most. She expected me to take over the house, and I did. I'd been doing it for years anyway. She treated me like a drudge. If it hadn't been for that, maybe I wouldn't have been so keen to get away from it all. Perhaps I wouldn't have gone to St Andrews and met Paul Kinsail . . .' She was sobbing openly now.

Callum was finding it almost impossible to maintain a professional detachment. He slipped an arm round her shoulders and held her until she stopped sobbing.

'And perhaps you'd be married to some loser with five

kids in tow by now,' he said gravely. 'Look at me, Maxine. Stop crying and think about what you have got. You're an attractive, successful woman. You have your own business, financial security and . . .' He had been going to add friends to the list but suddenly realised that friends were something she did not have. It was the price of ambition.

'And?' she had noticed the pause.

'And I think you should try to contact your mother.' It was suggested without any deep consideration, just the instinctive belief that Maxine needed to face this woman who was affecting her so badly.

'Contact her? Meet her, is that what you mean? I couldn't. I don't want to meet her, ever.'

'I think you do.' He held her eyes and saw he was right. 'You don't have to make friends with her. You don't even have to like her. Maybe she won't want to meet you. But you should take this chance to try and sort things out with her, to understand her a little. Even if you don't stay in touch it'll help to put your mind at rest. And what about your brother and sisters? Don't you think she'd like to know about her grandchildren?'

'She knows where to find them if she's interested.'

'I suspect she's frightened after all this time. She probably thinks you all hate her.'

'She's probably right.'

For what seemed a very long time Maxine stared into the flames of the hissing fire. Finally she lifted her tear-stained face and smiled at him. 'Thanks, Callum. You are right. I think I do want to see her. I'll probably be very nervous and try to pull out at the last minute but I think I'll feel better if I speak to her. I'd never rest, knowing I'd got so close but done nothing about it.'

'And what about the new restaurant?'

'I'll wait. I'll try and see her before I do anything about that.'

All Callum was aware of was the tantalising closeness of her, the silky softness of her hair, the deceptive fragility of her slender body. Understanding he was dangerously close to betraying her trust in him he tried to get up unobtrusively but got his feet caught in his cassock and grunted impatiently.

'I'd better be getting back,' he said eventually.

'Yes . . .' She went with him to the door. Rain drummed depressingly on to the pavement, collecting in dark puddles. 'Callum.' She called him back before he could dash to his car.

'Yes?' he turned, his face alight.

'Thanks.' She reached up and kissed his cheek, catching her breath at the familiar smell of him, the feel of his soft bristles. 'Thank you for listening. It really helped. You must be a very good clergyman, Callum.'

Disappointed somehow he ran for his car and she closed the door before he could turn and wave at her.

TWENTY-SEVEN

Rather than contacting her mother herself and running the risk of getting involved in premature explanations, Maxine asked her solicitor to make an appointment for her, saying only that there were some aspects of the business she wanted to discuss before she could make an offer. She half-expected that there would be some difficulty but a day later she was informed that Mrs Angelou would see her on the Friday afternoon.

Maxine was so nervous that from Thursday onwards she could eat nothing. Even the weak tea she drank gurgled uncomfortably round her stomach. During the drive to Inverannan she rehearsed time and time again what she was going to say to this woman, letting it fill her mind to such an extent that she took a wrong turning and travelled three or four miles in the wrong direction before realising it. Then, in Inverannan's largest car-park she let her car run forward into a low wall, damaging the bumper. Half-way up the High Street she realised she was running and forced herself to slow down, taking deep breaths in an effort to calm herself. Her appointment was for two o'clock and it was still only one-thirty. With nothing better to do she spent a long, restless half-hour staring into shop windows but, when the town clock finally struck the hour, she walked into Angelou's looking pale but perfectly composed.

The café was absolutely packed, mostly with women shoppers taking a break over a cup of tea and a light lunch. The air reeked of cigarette smoke. All the assistants were busy and it was a minute or two before she managed to tell one of them who she was.

'Och, aye, that's right,' the cheerful but rushed woman smiled. 'She did say she was expecting someone. I'll show you to her office.'

It was more a cupboard than an office. When David Morrison had shown her round it had been littered with papers but now someone had obviously made an attempt to tidy up. The cabinet tops were relatively clear and the floor was uncluttered. With her back to the door, leaning over a desk, as if she was working, was a woman. She turned quickly when the waitress announced Maxine.

Maxine stared at the woman she knew must be her mother, stared so hard that Mrs Angelou's welcoming smile faded a little. Try as she might Maxine could see nothing familiar in the face which was now looking back at her in open puzzlement.

'Miss Lennox?' the woman asked.

Maxine had gathered her wits sufficiently to be polite. 'Yes. Are you Mrs Angelou?' It was clear that this woman had no idea who she was speaking to.

'That's right. Please, sit down there, Miss Lennox. Would you like some coffee?' The accent was local but refined and soft.

'No thanks.' Maxine perched on the edge of the chair, unsure of how to start, all the rehearsed words flown from her mind.

'My solicitor tells me you are interested in buying this place but there are some things you need to know about it first?' Mrs Angelou seemed a little stiff and formal in her manner but was almost certainly not suspicious.

'Yes, that's right,' Maxine knew she was hardly giving the impression of a serious businesswoman.

'The accounts are available but I understand you were thinking more of a restaurant than a café so they're not

466

strictly relevant. Still, you're welcome to see them. These are the main account books, audited, as you can see.' She chatted on, explaining the figures in a calm, unemotional voice. Maxine watched, nodded where necessary but heard nothing.

This woman was different from anything she remembered. In her mind was a lank-haired, thin-faced woman with a sharp tongue and impatient manner. A woman it was impossible to please. Last night Maxine had spent hours peering at old photos, the most recent taken only two years before her mother had left, trying to refresh a memory which was one of images rather than detail. It had been a fading picture of a grey woman and greyer children. They all looked so dirty, so untidy, so poor, even in what must have been their best clothes. Surely the thin, sunken-eyed creature with bowed shoulders and straggly hair wasn't the same person as this neat, well-preserved woman? Mrs Angelou was of medium height and not thin at all but generously built, curvaceous and feminine. Her dress black, out of respect to her dead husband Maxine supposed, was decorous enough but was made of soft material which clung to her, emphasising the voluptuousness of her breasts. A gold cross nestled in a cleavage which betrayed its age in a slightly crepey appearance. Her hair was a glossy, well-managed chestnut. Maxine looked hard but couldn't see a single strand of grey. Her face was skilfully if heavily made up in bright colours and seemed to defy her years. Only faint lines around her eyes and a puffy, double chin couldn't be disguised. And the hands were a real give-away, but more an indication of her background than her age. They were wrinkled, heavily lined and dry looking. The short fingernails were ragged and unpainted, the stubby fingers devoid of any ornament except a slim, gold wedding band.

When Mrs Angelou raised her face and looked at her,

Maxine noticed deep, blue shadows under her eyes which were faded, lost in deeply shadowed sockets giving her a tired and strained appearance. She saw, too, that the smile was an effort, that in its unguarded state this woman's mouth was down-turned and unhappy. Suddenly Maxine understood that Mrs Angelou was deeply troubled and making a great effort to appear businesslike. Which was only natural, she thought with cool detachment, if her husband had just died.

'That's all I can tell you, really. You see, this was my husband's business. I wasn't involved with it myself.'

Mrs Angelou closed the books and waited for her visitor to say something but now she was peering at Maxine, as if she was unsure of her. 'Is there anything else I can show you?' she asked when the younger woman made no immediate comment.

Maxine's strangely abstracted manner was unsettling and Mrs Angelou had been uncomfortably aware of the close scrutiny she had been subjected to while going over the figures. She sensed that, for some reason, the younger woman's manner was hostile. Eventually, still getting no response, she stood up, hoping to bring this to a rapid close.

'Perhaps you could tell me why you are selling, Mrs Angelou? The business appears to be thriving,' Maxine asked. She had to be quite sure this woman was her mother before she said anything foolish.

Evelyn Angelou relaxed a little. Maybe this woman was simply suspicious of her motives for selling. That could account for the unfriendly manner, though, for a moment, she had wondered if they had met before, the younger woman seemed vaguely familiar.

'My husband died two months ago.'

'I'm sorry,' was the automatic response.

'So am I . . . I'll tell you the full story then you'll understand. This was my husband's very first shop. He bought it just after the war. When his younger brother grew up a bit and saw how well it was doing he decided to open a similar one in Edinburgh, where the family lives. My husband took him, and his father into partnership. In the end, they had half a dozen Angelou's in the Edinburgh area. They did think about opening more over here but there was a lot of opposition from the locals so they decided to stay in Edinburgh. When my husband died his brother took over the business. All except this place. Alessandro left it to me.' She smiled softly. 'It never made any sense for him to keep hold of this place for so long, so far from the others, but it was a sentimental thing with him. We met here. That's why he left it to me. But what good is a café to me? I don't intend to run it.'

'No. I can see you wouldn't want to do that,' Maxine said.

Evelyn Angelou caught the coldness in Maxine's voice and turned away quickly, regretting the confidence.

Maxine stared at her mother's back, her mind a seething mass of jumbled emotions. The woman she had loved, then hated, then understood, only to hate again was nothing more than a sad, disappointed woman who, in the flesh, struck no particular chord with her at all. On impulse she dragged the clasps from her hair and shook it so that it hung straight over her face, as it had done years before.

'You don't even recognise me, do you?'

Evelyn span round, a chill of horror making her heart thump. She knew, even before she looked at her daughter's face and understood now why this young woman had unsettled her so much.

'Yes, I do recognise you,' she answered coldly, sitting stiffly in her chair. 'I didn't, not at first, but I do now.'

469

After that first spasm of shock it was as if a shutter had drawn down over her face.

'I wouldn't have known you either,' Maxine offered in a conciliatory tone.

'Why didn't you tell me who you were right away? Why call yourself something different?' Evelyn demanded, angrily.

'I have been calling myself Maxine Lennox for years. Ever since my marriage broke up.'

'How could you just turn up here, without any warning? It's been so long . . .'

'So long and not even a birthday card. For all I knew you could have been dead!' Responding to the animosity she felt from her mother, Maxine put all the bitterness she had ever felt into those words.

Evelyn made no attempt to reply so Maxine sat down and seemed lost in the heavy silence. Eventually she looked up and attempted a smile.

'All these years and we can't find anything to say to one another.'

'What do you want me to say?' was the immediate challenge. 'Do you expect me to apologise for leaving you all? Is that why you've come here? Because if it is you might as well go now. I did what I did because I had to.'

'Did you ever think about us?' Maxine had to ask. 'Did you think about us at all?'

'Of course I did! Do you think it was easy?' Evelyn spluttered. 'What right have you got, turning up here and interrogating me about something that happened years and years ago?'

'The right of a daughter,' Maxine said, softly. 'The daughter who got left to bring up the other kids and run round after Dad because you walked out on us.'

Even that didn't seem to touch her mother. 'Why did

you come here? What do you want?' Evelyn demanded, angrily.

What did she want? Maxine stared at her mother and couldn't answer. 'I don't think I want anything,' she muttered at last. 'Just to see you, that's all.'

'To make me feel guilty? Well, if it makes you happy, I've felt nothing but guilt because of you. Does that satisfy you?'

'It never made you come back though, did it?'

'No.' Evelyn straightened and looked at her daughter with hard, brown eyes. 'No, I never went back. I wasn't that brave.' She sighed. 'Dear God! I had such plans when your father and I married. I was going to be somebody. I was going to be the one they all envied. Huh . . . I ended up at the bottom of the heap. Even the people I despised looked down on me because my man couldn't keep me and my kids decently fed and dressed.'

'Is that why you left?'

'Yes. And don't even try to understand, Mary. You have to live like that even to begin to know what it's like to be constantly disappointed, degraded, to grow old and shrivel . . . Your father was a lazy, idle good-for-nothing. He stopped working for a living before you were born. I doubt if he changed after I left.'

'NO!' Maxine denied it angrily.

'Oh, you've come here to see me, God knows why, and now you're here you can't even tell the truth,' Evelyn sneered.

'Don't tell me I can't understand,' Maxine flared. 'And at least Dad never hit you.'

'Is that what Archie Cree did to you?' Evelyn asked, quietly.

Maxine nodded, feeling ashamed. 'How do you know?'

Evelyn smiled, a strange self-satisfied grimace. 'Then

we're not so different after all, you and I. We both ran away. Your grandmother kept me in touch for a while.'

'I didn't leave four kids behind.'

'Then you'll know how much harder it was for me! How much longer it took me to make up my mind.'

'You ran off with another man. All I did was escape from a brutal, twisted husband.'

'That makes a difference, does it? The fact that I was lucky enough to find a gentle, caring man, and you didn't?' Evelyn's eyes flashed dark with temper.

There was no answer to that. Both women retreated into silence, searching for composure.

'Why did you really come here today, Mary? It certainly wasn't to buy this business, was it?'

'As a matter of fact it was . . . well partly. But I don't know why I wanted to see you, if that's what you mean. Maybe I hoped we could go back . . . be friends or something.'

'Friends!' The idea seemed ridiculous. '. . . We might keep in touch I suppose . . .'

'Do you want to?' Maxine challenged.

'I don't know, Mary. You're not being very fair about this. I need time to think. This has been one hell of a shock, you waltzing in here.' She coughed, uncomfortably. 'Are you serious about this place?'

'Yes. Didn't Gran tell you?'

'Your grandmother and I don't keep in touch any more.'

'Oh . . . Well. I have my own restaurant. In Kilweem. It's doing very well and I'm hoping to open another one soon. This place would have been ideal. I didn't even realise it was yours until I came to view it. The solicitor's clerk told me your name and that Alessandro's and Angelou's were the same place. I put two and two together then asked him for Mrs Angelou's first name. That settled it! After that I wasn't at all sure I still wanted to buy the place,' she shrugged. 'A friend of mine said I would be stupid to let it go just to spite you,' she admitted candidly, still hoping to strike some chord of friendship.

'So that's all it was – coincidence? You hadn't been trying to find me?' Evelyn asked, feeling irrationally saddened.

'No. To be honest I never think about you,' her daughter responded, with unnecessary cruelty.

'I suppose I should be grateful. What about the others . . . your sisters and David? Do they know you're here?' Was the whole family going to start making demands on her?

'No, not yet. I wasn't sure you'd want to see them.' Now Maxine voiced the question which had been on her mind since she had first considered contacting her mother. 'Did you . . . I mean have I . . . Have you got any more children?' she stammered.

Evelyn had been expecting it, she didn't flinch and answered immediately. The sudden warmth in her voice was a vivid expression of the love she had for her sons. 'You have two half brothers. Pierro is eleven and Marco is nine. They are good boys but they miss their father dreadfully.'

With a stab of guilt Maxine remembered that her mother was very recently widowed. 'I am really sorry about your husband,' she offered. 'I suppose you'll go on living in Edinburgh?'

'No, I don't think so.' For the first time Evelyn's manner towards her daughter softened a little. 'You see, no matter what you might think, Alessandro and I really did love one another, but his family never accepted me. He divorced his first wife because of me. A real Italian she was and well liked by the family. They blamed me. And it wasn't as if we had a home of our own. We always lived with his parents. That's the way his family was, staying together. I never fitted in. Alessandro knew that. That's why he made sure I would have something of my own if he died. He left me this place as a sort of insurance for the future. For the boys.'

Her eyes were luminous, filled with deep, aching sadness. Maxine felt a lump of sympathy rise in her own throat.

'So, where will you live?' she asked, already knowing the answer.

'Strathannan somewhere. It's strange. I couldn't wait to get away from the place but now, well, I'd like to come back to somewhere familiar.'

'Perhaps it would help your boys if they got to know their aunts, uncles and cousins,' Maxine suggested. 'Make them feel they're part of a family here, too.'

Evelyn looked up sharply, then away again, already resenting the pressure this young woman was putting on her. She got to her feet and went to open the door. 'I've got a lot to do. I'm sure you understand.' It was so coldly said.

Maxine blanched but collected herself rapidly. 'Of course.'

'And what about this place? Will you be making me an offer?' Evelyn asked as she stepped past her.

Maxine gaped at her mother in disbelief. 'Is that all you're concerned about? Don't you want to know about your grandchildren? Do you want our addresses? And what about you and I? Can we meet again? How can you be like this . . . so, so cold? I'm your daughter for God's sake!'

Evelyn shook her head. 'It's too late. Much too late. You get on with your life and leave me to get on with mine. We've managed perfectly well without one another so far. Let's just leave things as they are.'

Evelyn had always known what she wanted. Once

before she had made the mistake of saddling herself with a clinging, demanding family. To resurrect all that now, just as she was free to take her beloved sons and start a truly independent life, away from her Italian in-laws, would be to change one set of gaolers for another, would be to throw away her last chance of real contentment. She knew what it would be like. They would expect her to play the loving mother, the doting grandmother, to make up for all those missing years, to atone for her sin again and again. Well, she wouldn't. She couldn't. She would come back to Strathannan, preferably to Inverannan, where she would meet people she used to know, people who would appreciate how far she had come and envy her smart house and fine sons. The last thing she wanted was for herself, or her boys, to be dragged back to Craigie, to have her sons influenced by the sort of rough, working-class people Catherine and Linda undoubtedly were, married to miners and stuck in the same dreary existence which had so nearly choked the life out of her.

'Goodbye, Mary.' The look she fastened on her daughter was emotionless, hard and absolutely determined. 'I don't think we should meet again.'

Maxine slipped into St Peters as unobtrusively as possible, feeling more than a little out of place. By denomination she was Church of Scotland and the only time she had been inside the Episcopal church had been for funerals. On both occasions she had been too upset to notice its beauty.

Unlike the church she had attended in Craigie, which was plain to the point of austerity, this was a light and welcoming place. Set at the very edge of the high point at the north end of the village, before the ground tumbled away towards the rocky headland which divided the harbour from the beach, the church pointed out over the sea. When Maxine walked through the old, oak doors she was met by a glimmering flood of warm, dappling light which filtered through the huge stained-glass window over the altar. Outside the day was fresh and clear, here, softened and coloured by the glass it could have been a mellow summer's day.

The warm, golden wood of the polished pews seemed inviting, welcoming. At the altar a middle-aged woman was arranging flowers while another dusted and polished the ornately carved pulpit, sending the sweet smell of lavender back to Maxine. Near the front, a lone woman knelt in a pew, her head bent in prayer. As Maxine lingered, not sure of what she should do, she stood up and walked quickly down the aisle, smiling and nodding at Maxine when she passed.

There was no sign of Callum, she wasn't even sure that he would be here at this time of the morning. Quietly she crept towards the woman who was still shining the pulpit with such loving care.

'Excuse me,' she whispered, much as she would have done had she been in a library.

'Hello, Hen,' Mrs Montgomery greeted her cheerfully. 'Are you looking for the Rector?'

'No. I was hoping to find Callum . . . Reverend Mackie,' she explained.

'As far as I know the curate's in the vestry, setting out mouse traps.'

'Mouse traps?' Maxine laughed.

'Och, it's the choir boys. They bring crisps and biscuits and goodness knows all what, and stuff them into their cupboard. It stinks and no wonder the mice think they've found an easy living,' she chuckled. 'Mind you, when the Rector tried to set the traps he caught his finger in one. I hope Reverend Mackie doesn't do the same or they'll neither of them be able to turn the pages of their prayer books.'

Maxine chuckled. 'Can I go in?' she asked.

'Best not to. Have yourself a seat, Lass, and I'll see if I can find him for you.'

Mrs Montgomery bustled off, humming to herself, leaving Maxine to wait on the hard pews. The lady who had been placing flowers round the altar put on her coat and called a friendly goodbye as she left, leaving Maxine quite alone.

It was absolutely and totally silent. Maxine gazed at the sunlit window and felt the deep, embracing peace of the church envelop her, giving her the first glimmering understanding of the comfort some people found here. She looked at the shelf in front of her, at the hassock at her feet. Perhaps a moment or two on her knees would help her to come to terms with her mother's harsh rejection. But she had never prayed like this before, only at Sunday school services where she and all the other kids had been packed off to give their long suffering parents an hour of peace every Sunday morning. Half-embarrassed by this sudden compulsion she looked round furtively to be sure there was no one else in the small church before sliding to her knees and resting her head on her linked hands.

The only prayer she could recall was the Lord's Prayer. She said it slowly, then stayed where she was, letting her mind range freely over what had happened between her and her mother, absorbed and unaware of the passing minutes.

Callum, who had been in the Rectory until summoned by Mrs Montgomery, slipped through the main doors and saw her at once. There could be no mistaking the purity of that hair colour, made almost ethereal by the light shining through it. Silently he sat in a back pew and watched, content to wait until she was ready, astonished and incredibly happy to have found her praying with such relaxed, unconscious sincerity.

Unaware that she was being observed, Maxine's mind felt easier, clearer and some of her anger had faded. At last she opened her eyes again and looked towards the altar, feeling faintly awed but perfectly happy to remain on her knees as she pondered what had happened to her. Three or four minutes passed before she suddenly remembered Callum was probably on his way and slid slowly back into a sitting position, feeling much more relaxed.

As soon as he saw her move Callum stepped into the aisle and started to hurry towards her, as if he had just walked through the door.

'Maxine! I hope you haven't had to wait too long.' He greeted her with a light kiss on her cheek. 'I was in the Rectory.'

'How long were you watching me?' she asked with a smile, realising she should have heard his footsteps approaching long before she actually had done.

He shrugged. 'I didn't want to disturb you.'

'I was just thinking really. Not praying,' she chuckled. 'I only know one real prayer. Does that shock you, Reverend?'

'That's what most people do when they're on their knees. Just think. Most of us like to feel that God is listening, helping us along.' He made it sound so absolutely natural, so matter of fact, that she lost her self-consciousness.

'It's such a strange feeling. Perhaps it's this place. St Peters is a lovely church, isn't it? That window is magnificent. I didn't know it would be possible to find such peace inside a building. Usually, when I want to do some serious thinking, I take off for the beach. Perhaps I'll come here in future.'

'The door is always open during the day, Maxine,' he said gently. 'Now, what did you want to see me about?

478

Is it something to do with what we were discussing the other day?'

'Yes. I took your advice and went to see my mother. It wasn't a success.'

He saw the worried expression which crossed her face as she spoke and slipped into the pew beside her, so close that a fold of his cassock fell over her leg. 'Want to tell me what happened? Would it help?'

'Have you got time?' she asked guiltily, thinking she was rather taking advantage of his good nature.

'Of course I've got time. I hope we're friends, Maxine. As a friend I want to help. But, if you'd rather have me in a professional role, that's fine too. Either way you've got as much time as you need.'

Telling him about it made the pain of rejection seem more acute, made her understand that her mother's determination was absolute. Her voice shook. Seeing her agitation Callum was tempted to put a consoling arm round her shoulders but knew this wasn't the place for such a move.

'Do you think I should contact her again? Try to explain how I feel? I'm sure I gave her the impression that I'm very bitter.'

'Aren't you?' Callum asked, sharply. 'And isn't that a fairly natural reaction?'

'But I never used to be. At least, I was to start with but after a while I really thought I understood why she left.'

'And then?'

'Then? Then I suppose I didn't think about her at all. Until now.'

'Because you have your own life to lead. What happened in the past simply isn't important any more. And you certainly can't change it.'

'What do you think I should do, Callum?'

479

He laughed. 'You know I can't tell you what to do, Maxine. You have to make up your own mind.'

'She sounded so certain. I really believe she doesn't want to see us.'

'Maybe she's right. It would be very painful for you all. You know, not everyone can be a good or caring parent.'

'She's got two sons . . . she's a good mother to them. I could hear it in the way she spoke about them.'

'Children from a happier marriage, that's why she feels differently about them. It's probably more a reflection of your father versus her second husband than the way she feels about you as a person.'

'That's not how it felt yesterday!'

'Maxine, from what you've told me, your mother had a pretty hard time when she married your father. Think about it. Four children. No money coming in, a husband who wouldn't work, a critical mother. It was so bad she felt she had to get away. She was lucky enough to meet a man who loved her, who was reasonably well-off and who treated her well. Now he's dead she's determined to hang on to what she's got, no matter what. She's probably scared stiff that without her husband she'll end up back where she started, especially when you turn up out of the blue and remind her of everything that drove her away in the first place.'

'So, you think she's right?'

'No. I'm just trying to make you see that it's not your fault.'

'She's evil, selfish, cruel . . . I didn't think a mother could react so coldly to her own child.'

'You are not a child any more, Maxine,' he said sternly. 'You are a grown woman. Perhaps your mother is selfish and cold, I don't know. Maybe she's shocked and depressed by her husband's death. In a year or two she might change her mind. Who knows. The thing is, you can't let yourself get bitter over this. You told me just now that you weren't bitter before, that you didn't even think about her, so you're no worse off now than you were before you went to see her. Just don't close your heart to her, make allowances, but don't hope for too much.'

'I suppose you're right, you usually are, but I'm so angry.'

'That's natural, too. Anyway, have you decided to buy the place or not?' he asked, trying to distract her a little.

She looked at him blankly. 'Oh God!' She covered her mouth quickly. 'Sorry, I'd forgotten where I was. I haven't given it a single thought since yesterday.'

'You'll have to make a decision soon, won't you?'

'By noon on Monday,' she sighed. 'I want that place, Callum. It's perfect. But why should I give my money to her?'

'That's a sensible reaction, Maxine. Turn down something you really want just to spite her.'

'I don't want to do her any favours.'

'It sounded like a straightforward business transaction to me. Not a favour. Still, if you want bitterness to get in the way, who am I to criticise? Even if it does make you as bad as her?'

'That's not fair,' she shouted in exactly the reaction he had hoped to provoke.

'Don't yell, Maxine. This is a church.' He got up and glanced at his watch. 'There's nothing else I can say. You're the one with the decision to make but, whatever you do, try to make sure you don't regret it later.'

He started to walk away, leaving her fuming and confused then turned to offer one last piece of advice. 'Perhaps you should try the hassocks for size again, Maxine?' He looked at her in irritation then relented and smiled.

TWENTY-EIGHT

It had been a hectic few months. Now, with the purchase of Angelou's complete and plans well under way for the opening at Easter, Maxine was exhausted and longing for a few days of rest. But, before she could do that there was Christmas to be got through.

Missing the steady stream of day trippers and tourists who filled her dining room to capacity until late September, Maxine knew Christmas was her chance to make a solid profit in an otherwise lean season, as well as further enhancing the restaurant's reputation. Much to her delight the place was fully booked for the whole of December and much of January. Out of consideration for her hard-working staff she was closing for Christmas Day itself but tomorrow, Christmas Eve, promised to be their busiest night yet. The freezers and fridges were full to bursting point while the cold store and larders held more food than she normally got through in a complete week.

After her staff had left for the night, considerably cheered by her generous bonus payments, Maxine checked round the kitchen. Her body ached with fatigue. If anything she worked even harder than her staff but she knew it would be impossible to relax until she had gone over everything once more, trying to foresee possible pitfalls in her arrangements. Had she overbooked the dining room? Were her staff, good though they were, going to be able to cope smoothly with yet another pressurised day? Had she ordered enough of the right wines; prepared a wide enough range of sweets? Would any of the parties get out of hand and spoil the evening for the other diners? Sighing she ran a hand over her aching head, longing for the comfort of warm sheets and soft pillows, but she knew she wouldn't be able to sleep yet. She was still far too tense for there to be any hope of sleep and now her head was starting to pound.

Sparing one last look at the cookers, making sure everything was quite safe, she threw her coat on and let herself out of the front door, closing it quietly behind her. The Tollbooth clock struck the half-hour. Half an hour into Christmas Eve.

Even though it was dark, the moon hidden behind scudding clouds, Maxine had no fear of being out so late. Confidently she made her way along Marketgate, glimpsing the comforting bulk of St Peters through a gap in the buildings, then almost ran down the Butts and on to the beach. If anyone happened to be looking out they would think she was quite mad, she thought wryly.

She walked about a hundred yards, until she was clear of the buildings then stood there, her feet buried in soft sand, letting the chill breeze buffet her face, feeling the tension already starting to drain from her in the sure rhythm of the waves pounding the beach. She loved it here, especially at this late hour and at this time of the year. So close to Christmas everything was utterly peaceful and the beach just here was particularly beautiful, wonderfully isolated and wild, despite the houses, less than a quarter of a mile away. Wide and sandy with high dunes protecting it from the road, it was her refuge. She had lost count of the number of times she had come here when she was tired or worried, revelling in the splendid power of the sea and the calming solitude which could be found here. There were times, when the place was teeming with tourists, when it seemed to her that the village was being spoiled, that they took its character from it, burying it under broken bottles and blowing litter. But Maxine also realised that without the tourists she would never have found success so quickly.

Sometimes, like tonight, she caught herself wondering if she hadn't been too successful. The restaurant had taken over her whole life but already it wasn't enough for her and she had embarked on another challenge starting from scratch with a new restaurant. But what then? Why was she constantly pushing herself on to more success which, in material terms, meant very little to her? There were times when she had nothing to go back to, night after night, but her smart and lonely flat over the restaurant, when it all seemed so pointless.

Standing there, gazing out over the choppy water, she was overcome by crushing loneliness. This time of year emphasised the unpalatable fact that there was no one she could share the festivities with. Her father and Annie were spending the day with her daughter. Ina had her own group of cronies and had casually dismissed her well-meant invitation to spend the day with her. Her sisters were fully occupied with their own families and assumed she had made arrangements of her own. Maxine seriously doubted if they even spared her a single thought after they had opened her gifts. Her brother, David, still in the navy, was at sea.

Even Callum would have a full and satisfying Christmas, assisting at services, sharing the Rector's Christmas dinner, and his family would undoubtedly expect him at some point. Unlike her, he wouldn't be spending his time isolated in his flat, watching television just for the company it offered. Tears of self-pity overspilled her eyes and splashed on to her cheeks. She brushed them aside impatiently. Wallowing in misery wouldn't help. If she expected to feel better then she was the one who had to make the effort.

Sucking in a huge lungful of cold sea air, she straightened her shoulders and disciplined her mind, pulling it back from the brink of the overwhelming depression which had dogged her recently. She made a decision. On Christmas day she would go to church. It was a place she had come to feel secure in and there would be other people there, singing carols and celebrating. It would be good for her, better than skulking around on her own all day. And, of course, Callum would be there too.

Her fair hair, ruffled by the wind and dragged from its neat knot, flew wildly round her head as she hurried home. Feeling much more ready to sleep she went straight upstairs, washed down two of the sleeping tablets which had been so necessary for the last couple of months and fell into bed. Within minutes she was asleep.

Crouching in a narrow alleyway, opposite Maxine's, Archie Cree waited until he saw the bedroom light go off. Blowing on his frozen hands and stamping his feet softly he peered cautiously into the broad expanse of Marketgate to check there was no one else around. Then, keeping well into the shelter of the buildings, he scurried round the edge of the square, crossing to the Tollbooth in the middle before hurrying on to Maxine's. A bulky package shoved inside his anorak made his curiously rolling gait even more ungainly than usual. Constantly looking round, ready to bolt if there was any sign of life, he peered through the restaurant windows to make sure the place was deserted.

After his abortive attempts to discredit Maxine's, Archie had spent long months planning complicated, impossible ways of getting even with his wife but knew they were all beyond him. Inside he was eaten with bitterness, blaming her for the misfortune which seemed to shadow him. After Mary had left him his mother had badgered him into making an effort to pull himself back from the brink of alcoholism which had been yawning in front of him. Bullied by his brothers and nagged at by his mother, he had worked hard, rising at dawn and rarely coming home until after eight or nine o'clock, as he struggled to make a decent living from the butchery round. But no matter how strictly he pared his prices, he simply couldn't compete with the supermarkets. After six days of hard graft he was lucky to make any sort of profit and then had to endure the scorn of his family when he was unable to make a fair contribution to the household finances. Most of the money Maxine had sent him had been spent on a second-hand bus to replace the old van which he had been forced to sell to meet debts. But the bus was even more ancient than the van had been and broke down so often that even his most loyal customers got fed up with his unreliability and took their custom elsewhere, adding to his problems. In his mind he blamed all this on Maxine. All he needed was enough cash to pay off his outstanding debts and to buy a decent van. Money like that would be nothing to her now and he was still married to her and entitled to his share of her profits. Anyway, she owed him at least that much for all the trouble she'd caused him. If it wasn't for her the business wouldn't have collapsed the first time. As the months passed and the business finally folded, his attitude became more bitter and twisted until, at last, he conceived a simple, foolproof way of getting his hands on at least some of what Mary owed him. Which was why he was in Kilweem tonight.

Any fool could see that, at this time of year, the restaurant takings would be enormous and, with no bank in the village, all that money must be kept in the restaurant overnight. What's more, there was a stock of whisky and cigarettes which would make sure that he and his family had a very lively New Year. If he could just get his hands on them it would make the point to his brothers that Archie Cree was still capable of making a worthwhile contribution. Oh yes, he would show them all that he was still a man to be reckoned with. For all their fine talk, neither of his brothers would have the guts to do what he was planning here tonight.

Saying only that he was going to see Mary and promising to make it worth their while, Archie persuaded his brothers to drive up here and collect him, around three o'clock. Unable to resist the lure of being paid for their trouble they had agreed. Archie couldn't wait to see the expressions on their faces when he showed them what he'd got.

Before leaving Inverannan, Archie had treated himself to a half bottle of Bells and had sipped at it surreptitiously on the bus ride to Kilweem. By the time he stepped off the bus at the Tollbooth he was cheerfully, carelessly drunk. With hours to waste before he could put his plan into operation, he took himself off to the Lobster until closing time. The long, uncomfortable wait in the close opposite the restaurant had sobered him a little but his walk was still erratic and meandering as he found his way to the narrow lane which ran past the back of the restaurant. Pausing again to make sure there was no one about he crept unobserved into Maxine's back yard. It was the work of minutes to force a window at the extreme end of the building, where the damage was less likely to be noticed, and clamber clumsily inside. He took a couple more minutes to get his bearings then padded silently towards the front door and the bottom of Maxine's private stairs and paused, listening for signs of movement. There was nothing but deep, satisfying silence.

Even in his intoxicated state Archie knew precisely what

he wanted to achieve here tonight and the most important thing was the money. He already knew where the till was and it didn't take him long to find the big bunch of keys that Maxine kept so carelessly on the kitchen wall. Chuckling to himself he tried two small keys before he found the right one and opened the cash drawer. As he suspected the night's takings were bundled neatly at the back. Gleefully he pocketed the lot.

Happy and dangerously relaxed now, the best part of a pint of whisky still coursing through his bloodstream, he ambled into the kitchen and began a systematic appraisal of the cupboards and refrigerators, gasping at the amount of food stored there. Business, he thought sourly, must be very good indeed. A cupboard under the sinks revealed a generous supply of cleaning materials, disinfectants, bleaches and detergents. For many long seconds he peered at them, an idea slowly forming in his addled brain. Then he looked again at the huge refrigerators and freezers, his face splitting into an ugly grin as the perfect revenge dawned on him.

Scurrying lopsidedly he grabbed a gallon container of disinfectant, hauled open the door of the nearest fridge and doused everything inside in strong, pine liquid. The exercise was repeated at the two other fridges, thoroughly contaminating meat, desserts, fruit and cheeses. Into the deep chest freezers he splashed neat bleach, closing the lids down quickly to trap the fumes inside. Then, content that he had inflicted enough damage to put her out of business over Christmas, at least, he replaced the empty containers and returned to his original plan of action, feeling well satisfied with himself.

One of the doors by the back passageway led, he knew from what he had seen on his earlier visit, to the cellar. That was where the drinks would be stored. Only one door was locked, common sense told him it was the one he needed. It took him several minutes to remember what he had done with the keys and five more to find the right ones to operate the two stout locks.

Stuffing the keys into his anorak pocket he slipped inside and found himself at the top of a steep flight of stone steps which descended into complete blackness. He flailed around with one hand until he located the light switch then pulled the door closed behind him, to keep the light from seeping into the deserted restaurant.

At the bottom of the stairs a huge, cold cellar was revealed, stacked full of stores for the restaurant. At the far end, against a cool wall, stood a long wine rack and, next to it, several crates of beers and spirits. He almost missed the cartons of cigarettes stacked in the corner. Grinning hugely, convinced that he was perfectly safe here for hours yet, he casually tore open a packet of Number Six and lit one. Sighing his content he settled on a crate to enjoy a quiet smoke before embarking on the hardest work of the evening.

Sheer malice drove him to smash as many bottles of wine as he could, confident the noise would be shielded by the thick, stone walls. That done he turned his attention to the spirits. First he selected what he wanted to take back to Craigie with him. The strong carrier bag he had stuffed up his anorak would only hold six bottles of whisky and one of gin – for his mother. He shoved two more inside his jacket and wedged two hundred Number Six in after them, hauling up the zip to hold them in place. The rest he destroyed, breaking the seals and upending bottle after bottle. The liquid ran across the floor, seeping under the cardboard cigarette cartons, soaking them in alcohol. Satisfied he glanced at his wrist watch and saw there was still more than an hour to go before he could venture out to meet his brothers at the Tollbooth. He grinned drunkenly again, envisaging their amazement when they saw his haul. After this they would never be able to accuse him of sponging off them again. In the meantime he had better stay right here. It was cold outside and, even at this late hour, there was the possibility of being seen. Leaning back against the wall, careless of the wines and spirits dripping and puddling around him, on to his jacket and into his shoes, he knocked the top off one of the few remaining whisky bottles, lit another cigarette and settled back to wait.

In Marketgate, a car without lights coasted silently to a halt a few yards past the door of Maxine's. A tall figure, dressed entirely in black and carrying two, obviously full, canisters, got out and crept furtively round the side of the building and into the back yard.

Going straight for the nearest window, this latest intruder forced it open with speedy ease and jumped neatly into the kitchen. Once inside he placed the two canisters against a wall then waited a moment, checking the house was still, before moving purposefully to the front door, releasing the catches, pulling back the bolts and leaving it very slightly ajar. It would be vital for him to get away fast.

That done he hurried back to the kitchen, wrinkling his nose at the overpowering smell of disinfectant, and picked up his cans. Working quietly but swiftly he spilled dark, pungent liquid in a steady stream from the back door, along the rear passage, past the cellar doorway, round the kitchen and into the dining room. Here he discarded the first can and started on the second, making sure everything was doused in petrol, working methodically from the back to the front of the old building, leaving the entrance hall until last. He would throw a lighted match through the front door, into the hall, and be in his car and out of the village before anyone knew what was happening.

Several feet below him, Archie Cree stared drunkenly at his watch and decided the time had come to go in search of his brothers. He lit one last cigarette from the carton at his side and struggled to his feet. Dangerously unsteady now, he clawed his way up the stairs, one hand supporting the precious cargo inside his jacket, the other carrying the heavy shopping bag, filled with bottles. A few steps from the top he slipped on the bare stone, and toppled heavily on to his stomach, crushing the bottles inside his jacket. The glass cut his chest quite badly but he wasn't aware of the pain because of his overwhelming anger at the loss of the bottles.

Awkwardly he pulled himself upright, unaware of the stream of liquid running down his jacket and pouring down his trousers, adding to the alcohol which had soaked up from the floor. When he reached the cellar door he opened it confidently, knowing all he had to do now was walk away with his plunder. Grinning he took the half-smoked cigarette which had dangled from his lips all the way up the stairs and tossed it carelessly on to the floor in front of him.

A blinding, blue flash of flame roared up to meet him, sucking the air from his lungs, releasing his grip on his bottles and sending them crashing to the floor. The blast unbalanced him again, sending him sideways then down on to his hands and knees, into a pool of petrol. Shocked into momentary paralysis he stayed there, gasping desperately for breath, watching as the flames licked at his hands and only lurched back into life when he felt the skin on his palms starting to singe. On his feet now, with flames licking up his legs to his petrol-soaked knees, with fire consuming the passageway behind him, there was only one thing he could do. Archie plunged back down the stairs, his lower limbs ablaze, and retreated instinctively to the farthest reaches of the cellar, splashing unheedingly through puddles of spilled spirits. In less than five seconds he was engulfed in blue flame. When he fell he collapsed over the cardboard cartons of cigarettes which ignited rapidly, spreading the greedy flames to the wooden wine racks which lined the walls. Smoke drifted back up the stairs to mingle with the fumes from the greater conflagration which was racing towards the dining room.

Out on the main road Callum couldn't resist peering into Maxine's as he drove home after the customary, rather boring, pre-Christmas party at his parents' house. He had been poor company, uncommunicative and dour at a time when his religious responsibilities, emphasising as they did the joy of the season, normally revitalised him. But, having felt conspicuously partnerless he was now more morose than ever as he wondered what the woman he still loved was doing over Christmas.

At this time of night he expected the restaurant to be in complete darkness. To his horror he caught the unmistakable flicker of orange flame through the glass of the front door. Standing on his brakes he abandoned his car in the middle of the road and leapt towards the building. As he ran he saw, outlined in the dining room window, the silhouette of a man.

Unaware of Callum, Paul Kinsail had been alerted to trouble by the sound of breaking glass when Archie lost his grip on the bag full of bottles, which was followed by an ominous, deep, booming noise. He wasted vital seconds listening, assuming the sound had come from upstairs, then watched in horror as a voracious pillar of flame spurted into the dining room, following the trail he himself had laid and trapping him there.

Throwing the partially emptied can he was using forward into the already burning room, Kinsail backed up to the window and grappled frantically with the stiff casement.

Callum hesitated only long enough to roar 'FIRE' at the top of his lungs, hoping to wake some of the neighbours, before diving into the building and running up the stairs, screaming Maxine's name. Mercifully Paul Kinail had not had the opportunity to soak the hall carpet so the area at the bottom of the stairs was, as yet untouched, although half-way up the stairway, opposite the dining room door, the banister was already smouldering.

Dense smoke filled the upper landing. Choking, Callum sank on to his knees, frantically trying all the doors until, at last, he found the one to Maxine's room. Slamming the door behind him in a bid to keep the worst of the smoke at bay he grabbed her sleeping form and shook her violently.

'Wake up!' he roared. 'For God's sake, Maxine, wake up.' He shook her again and was rewarded by the heavy flickering of her eyes.

'Callum . . .' she mumbled, confused and disorientated by the sleeping tablets.

'Get up, Maxine. Come on. Move,' he yelled, hauling her roughly out of bed.

'Get away from me,' she shrieked, frightened by this Callum she didn't know and trying to fend him off. Something caught in her throat and she coughed until tears ran down her face.

'It's smoke, Maxine. The whole building is on fire. Come on. We've got to get out of here. Take my hand and don't let go.' He dragged her towards the door knowing they would be lucky to get to the hallway ahead of the flames.

'Fire?' She sniffed, coughed then blanched in terror as she finally understood what he was trying to say.

'Hold this over your face.' He grabbed something soft from her bedside chair and forced it over her nose and mouth. 'Take a deep breath and follow me. Keep hold of my hand.'

A dense cloud of billowing smoke met them at the door.

'Now!' he roared, dragging her on to the landing.

The stairs were dark, filled with choking smoke. Flames licked the banister from the hall but, at the bottom, as he peered through the thickening smoke, Callum could just make out a patch of light. Under them the carpet smoked and smouldered scorching her bare feet.

'My feet!' she screamed as he tried to pull her on. 'They're burning.' He turned, threw her over his back and half fell down the stairs with her, throwing them both through the front door milliseconds before the staircase erupted into flames behind them.

'Call the fire brigade,' Callum coughed and panted at the small crowd which had materialised.

'They're on their way,' someone reassured him as willing hands helped them to safety on the far side of the street.

'Are you all right?' Callum asked Maxine, anxiously.

'Yes,' she nodded, shocked and shaking then sinking to the ground as her legs gave way beneath her. 'What about you?'

'I'm fine. Stay here.'

'Where are you going, Callum?' she yelled after him. Then, realising he was attempting to get back into the restaurant, struggled back to her blistered feet and hobbled after him, oblivious to her painful burns.

By now the flames were licking avidly round the front door. Through the dining room windows they could see the whole interior was ablaze.

'You can't go back in there,' she screamed, terrified for him.

He shook her off roughly and ran to the windows, feeling the heat through the glass.

'Callum . . . ' she begged. 'There's no one in there. I was on my own. Come away. Please.' She dragged at his arm.

'I saw someone . . . In the dining room. I saw the flames and then I saw someone . . . ' He turned, desperately searching for something to break the window with.

'No!' Still she tried to stop him.

'Yes!' He faced her now. 'Don't you see? Whoever it was that I saw in there started this fire.'

She gaped at him, too terrified to assimilate the information. By the time the full import of it had begun to strike her Callum had grabbed a milk crate from the pavement and was using it to shatter the glass. As soon as he had cleared enough space he levered himself into the swirling smoke.

From where she stood, restrained by her neighbours, Maxine could see flames licking at the walls not ten feet from him.

In the distance came the sounds of rapidly approaching fire engines.

As Maxine watched, Callum sank to his knees. To her it seemed that he had collapsed. She screamed hysterically and tried to clamber through the window after him. Strong arms pulled her back.

Behind them the first fire engines screeched to a halt and the area filled with helmeted figures.

'Come away, Miss. There's nothing you can do.' An officer attempted to drag her away.

She fought him. 'He's in there. You've got to help him, please.'

'Who's in there?' he demanded, appalled but ready for instant action.

'Callum,' she sobbed. 'He thought he saw someone else

inside. He got me out then went back in. Please, help him.'

The officer turned away, issuing a string of rapid orders to his men.

'Hurry. Please hurry.' She danced on her injured feet, not caring about anything but Callum.

At that moment a shadowy figure appeared at the window.

'Help me,' Callum spluttered as he struggled to haul something limp and bulky over the smoking sill.

Strong hands dragged him out as water started to play on the front of the building, sizzling and spitting as it met hot wood and stone. Two firemen, fully kitted out in protective clothing, clambered through the window. Seconds later they carried an unconscious body into the night air.

Beside Maxine, Callum coughed, struggled for breath and gulped gratefully at the oxygen offered by a fireman. Maxine watched helplessly, sure he was dying, then dissolved into shocked tears when he finally shoved the mask away, rather impatiently, and struggled to her side. When his arm circled her it was reassuringly firm.

'Do you know the identity of this man, Sir?' one of the policemen who had joined the fire fighters, asked.

Callum looked at the blackened figure, labouring to breathe on the ground close to him and shook his head.

'He's in a bad way. Best get him into the ambulance,' a fireman said, just as the stretcher arrived.

The figure coughed again and stirred.

'Paul!' Maxine stared at the charred figure, illuminated by the flashing lights round them then collapsed into a crumpled heap as the implications hit her.

Callum was instantly on his knees beside her but was eased away by one of the ambulance crew. 'Just shock I think. Feet look a bit sore though. Best get her to hospital.

You too, Sir. Just to be on the safe side. You've one or two burns on your hands and face.' Callum hadn't noticed.

Paul Kinsail was already on a stretcher and in the process of being wheeled to the ambulance. Callum shoved the startled crew aside and bawled at the semi-conscious man. 'Open your eyes, Kinsail.'

Kinsail obliged, staring with startlingly clear eyes into the angry face of the man who had saved him from certain death.

'You bastard,' Callum roared. 'You tried to kill her.' The policeman moved closer.

'What did you say, Sir?'

'This man started the fire. I saw him in there.'

'We'll take a statement later, Sir. Let's get this man into the ambulance first. He's going to be all right but he needs to see a doctor.'

Callum paused, his anger under control again but still white hot. 'Take him then and make sure he recovers.'

Kinsail groaned and covered his face with his hands.

'It's all right, Mate, we'll soon have you comfortable.' One of the ambulancemen misinterpreted the groan for one of physical pain.

'Wait!' The voice was weak and ended on a rasping cough. 'There's someone else in there,' Kinsail wheezed.

'What?' Everyone stopped and stared at the blazing building. Driven back by the intense heat the firemen were playing their hoses on to the flames from yards back. 'Are you certain?'

'In the kitchen or back hall, I think. He started the fire. I put down the petrol but someone else started it before I was ready . . . I'm sure there's someone else in there.' The one agonised scream which had been audible even over the crackle and roar of the fire still rang in his head.

'Archie! Jesus, Archie!' A large, rough-looking man detached himself from the crowd and staggered towards the building where he was forcibly restrained by two policemen.

Maxine, just conscious again, stared at him in disbelief and breathed, 'Sam?'

As she spoke he turned, saw her and lumbered to her side. 'Is he in there? Was our Archie with you tonight?'

'Archie?' She shook her head feeling confused and ill. 'I haven't seen him since . . . since you tried . . .'

'But he came to see you the night. He asked us to pick him up.'

'Oh no . . .' Maxine stared at the blazing ruin of everything she had worked for and knew, in her heart, that Archie Cree was in there somewhere.

It was the next day before Archie's charred remains could be recovered from the basement. Mercifully, Maxine was spared having to see the awful results of his night's work because she was confined to a hospital bed while the burns on her feet were treated. There was plenty of time to think.

Callum suffered nothing more than a very sore throat and some superficial burns to his face and hands. For a few days he was restricted to a ward on the other side of the hospital where he, too, spent long hours lost in thought.

Paul Kinsail recovered within forty-eight hours and was released to police custody to face charges which carried a long prison sentence.

'Well, at least it looks as if the insurance company are going to pay up,' Callum said cheerfully as they sat in his living room more than six weeks later.

She nodded absently.

'Aren't you pleased? It's a very quick settlement. With any luck you'll soon be back in business.'

He deliberately injected enthusiasm he did not feel into his voice. Callum had learnt his lesson the hard way. If what Maxine wanted was independence and her own business then that was what she could have. Anything, so long as they didn't lose one another again. If necessary he was even prepared to give up the career he loved, to leave the Church, for her. But, after the events of the last six weeks, that might not be necessary. It was something he hadn't yet discussed with Maxine, because he wanted her to be fully recovered first.

'What do you think?' he asked, sliding an arm round her. 'Do you want to open Maxine's again?'

'I don't know. It doesn't seem important any more.'

'Not important?' He was amazed.

She smiled back softly. Nothing mattered. The damage to her property, the ruin of her business, the loss of income. It was all totally and absolutely unimportant. The consuming fear she had felt when Callum had gone back into that burning building had been more than enough to make her understand that none of it meant anything to her. Only Callum mattered. How could she ever have been foolish enough to think that her own pride, or even her stubborn need to prove she was capable and independent, that she had risen above her humble origins, were of more consequence than being with him?

'I love you, Callum,' she admitted softly. 'And nothing else matters anymore.'

'And I love you, Maxine Mary,' he answered, stroking her face gently. 'I want to marry you, Maxine. If you'll have me.'

She hadn't been expecting this, had been more than willing to settle for the usual covert relationship to protect his position in the Church. 'We can't, Callum. I could never ask you to do that. Not now. The Church . . . '

' . . . has no objection to widows. It's an entirely different situation. Archie's death has left you free to marry again without the risk of breaking your original vows. "Till death us do part"?'

Now that Maxine was a widow, no longer married and without the stigma of a divorce, there was no impediment to their marriage, even to his exacting conscience.

'I never thought,' she laughed through unexpected tears. 'Can we really be married, Callum?'

'Yes. If that's what you want. Do you think you'll be able to stand being a vicar's wife?'

'I can put up with anything, as long as you're with me,' she answered from her heart.

'Even Craigie?'

'Craigie?'

'From the first of next month I'm to be the vicar of St Michaels, in Craigie.'

Maxine tried to speak, failed, then turned to look out over the sea, watching it sparkle in the bright winter sunshine, imagining how damp and dismal Craigie would look by comparison. The depressing streets of run-down council houses, the gangs of cheeky, dirty kids, the drunks on Saturday night, the smell of the pits.

'Oh, Callum,' she smiled, facing him again. 'That's wonderful. Congratulations.'

She flew at him in genuine delight and he caught her, swinging her round in the air before lowering her gently to the softness of the sofa.

TWENTY-NINE

Even with the furniture shoved back against the walls, there wasn't a spare inch of space in the living room of the prefab. It was jam-packed with people, all fussing round Maxine. Her long, pale peach dress was smoothed and tugged then smoothed again by Linda who was crawling round on her hands and knees, her bottom in the air, seeking out imperfections in the lie of her sister's skirt, determined that everything should be absolutely right for Maxine's wedding. Above her, Catherine did her best to readjust Maxine's head dress, frightened it might slip off the shining fall of golden hair which Maxine had insisted on wearing down, knowing full well that Callum liked it that way. Behind them Annie fussed and fiddled with the bouquets, distributed on various chairs, worrying that they might wilt, get sat upon or even be forgotten at the last minute. Every thirty seconds she put a hand to her own head where a wide-brimmed hat persisted in tilting over one eye.

The remaining floor space was fully occupied by Carole, Maxine's niece, Linda and Mick's daughter. The four-year-old stood as still as a statue, frightened to rumple her beautiful bridesmaid's dress but wondering how she would manage to go to the toilet with all these layers of frothing net and silk which would surely fall down the pan. She crossed her legs and clenched her muscles but it was no good, she was desperate. Annie caught the child's worried expression and smiled.

'Come on, Lass,' she whispered mindful of the youngster's pride. 'We'll be a while in the church. Best have a wee before we go, eh? How about if I come in with you and hold your dress up?' The little girl nodded, relief flooding her chubby face and held out a dimpled hand. Her cousin, Robbie, Cath and Bobby's son, stuck his tongue out at her as she rustled out of the room. He was bored and perched self-consciously on the edge of a chair, wishing this was all over with. His biggest fear was that one of his pals would see him dressed like this in kilt and sporran, a carnation in his buttonhole, making him look like a great big pansy. He sighed enormously and went back to twisting the leather buttons on his green, tweed jacket until his great-grandmother hissed at him angrily then rattled his knuckles with her prayer book. Ina, kitted out in her Sunday best with an astounding concoction of feathers and net skewered to her thinning hair, was seated firmly on an upright chair where she could keep her stern eye on the children and was watching it all with a smile of wry amusement,

'Well,' she said to no one in particular. 'I would never have thought I'd be seeing our Mary in a white wedding dress.'

'It isn't white, it's peach,' Linda and Maxine chorused in unison, then giggled together.

'Looks white to me,' Ina insisted. The girls exchanged knowing looks but made no comment. 'Still,' Ina went on. 'Whatever colour it is I have never seen a bonnier bride. You look beautiful, Mary.' In a rush of emotion she folded her granddaughter in her arms and held her tightly.

Astounded by the glaze of tears in the old woman's eyes Catherine and Linda froze in mid-action.

'Right, Lass. The cars are here.' George, unable to squeeze into the room, had to shout from the hall.

Annie, back from her errand with Carole, kissed Maxine

503

on the cheek. 'Aye, for once Ina and I have something to agree on,' she laughed. 'You look marvellous, Lass . . .'

Linda and Catherine were next, both tending towards tears as they kissed their sister and hastened to the waiting cars, steering their children before them.

Suddenly alone in the little living room after all the commotion and fuss of the last three hours Maxine could feel her heart thumping wildly. After so long, after so much disappointment and unhappiness, was she finally going to find the happiness she craved with Callum? Just as importantly, would she be able to make him happy? A swirling feeling attacked her head. Maybe this was a mistake . . .

She began to pace round the little room, trying to take the edge from what she knew to be nothing more than an attack of pre-wedding nerves. Of all the things in her life her love for Callum was the most certain.

Still looking for something to distract her for a minute or two she took the list of guests from behind the clock on the mantelpiece.

As the replies had come in Annie had put a tick or cross beside the name. Even her brother David and his wife, Sally, had come all the way from Gibraltar for the wedding, making the whole thing into a double celebration.

Only two invitations had been declined. Janette, who Maxine would dearly have liked to have had with her on that day, had at least replied to the invitation, giving a new address in Montreal where Maxine would be now able to write to her. How excited she had been when she had seen that letter with the familiar handwriting and Canadian stamps after such a long time. And how deeply disappointed she had been to find only a single page of writing. A brief, undetailed block of impersonal news followed by a long, emotional wish for Maxine's happiness.

An invitation had also been sent to her mother. In the wake of Maxine's unsuccessful attempt to re-establish contact, both of her sisters had written, via Evelyn's solicitor, enclosing photographs of themselves and their children. Both had hoped for some response, despite Maxine's pessimistic report of her own failed attempt at reconciliation. The family had been horrified to receive a solicitor's letter which in effect, instructed them to stop pestering their mother. After a lengthy discussion which had ended with Ina walking off in disgust, the family, including Annie, had agreed that it would be wrong not to send Evelyn an invite and one had been despatched, through the solicitor. It had been ignored. And maybe that was for the best, Maxine thought. They all had their own lives to lead, even her father, and none of them needed their mother any more.

Behind her George coughed nervously, breaking into her thoughts. She jumped and replaced the list carefully.

'You look as nervous as I feel,' she smiled, feeling a surge of affection for him.

'Whatever you feel like, Lass, you look fabulous.' He stared at her shaking his head as if he couldn't believe it. 'Aye, you're just beautiful, Mary. You're making your father very proud today, Lass. It'll be just grand having you and Callum back in Craigie with the family.'

'Thanks, Dad,' she whispered. 'I'm really glad to be coming home again.'

'We'd best go. The car's waiting,' he said, feeling choked with emotion.

She took a final look round then preceded him out of the house, laughing as he scattered pennies round him and the local children scuffled on the pavement to pick them up.

It took them less than five minutes to reach St Michaels where the retiring vicar had been delighted to be asked to perform the ceremony as one of his last duties before officially handing over his parish to Callum.

Maxine stepped out of the car and into the church porch where she was immediately engulfed by her sisters who rearranged her dress and shooed the bridesmaid and page boy into position with a mixture of pleas and dire threats. The strains of the Wedding March sent Linda and Catherine scurrying for their own seats.

'Are you ready?' Maxine turned and smiled at her niece and nephew who both smiled and nodded back. Taking a final second to compose herself Maxine turned to her father who stepped forward and offered his arm. Maxine caught the sheen of emotional tears in his eyes, found her own throat too tight to speak so kissed him gently on the cheek instead as they moved off down the aisle.

She had eyes only for Callum who had stepped into the aisle and turned to watch her, admiration and love plain on his face. Their eyes locked and her emotions boiled inside her, making her catch her breath in a little sob. She knew that this was an image of Callum she would carry in her mind for the rest of her life, that she would always picture him as he was now, waiting for her to join him. So tall, so straight and still with that subtle impression of strength which was heightened somehow by the plainness of his suit and the dog collar, crisp and white at his throat. As she reached him, Callum stepped forward and held out his hand. George took his daughter's arm from the crook of his elbow and handed her to her fiancé, linking their hands and giving them both a slight squeeze before stepping back to his own place.

From then on Maxine's recollections of the day, which sped by in a haze of happiness, were like a series of short videos. Callum, always Callum. Herself, almost dumb with nerves, terrified she would muff the words or speak too quietly, until she looked at Callum, saw the gravity, the love in his eyes. Then, knowing exactly what these sacred words meant to him, she repeated her vows steadily, keeping her eyes on his, pledging herself to him with every fibre of her being, hearing him return the words in a voice which was clear and vibrant with emotion.

Outside the church they posed for photographs which captured forever the unlikely sight of Ina and Annie sharing a joke together. And then, at the hotel, when she and Callum welcomed their guests, Mr Mackie hugged her, claimed a kiss and welcomed her to his family with such obvious sincerity that she felt a lump rise in her throat. But now it was the turn of Callum's mother. She clasped her son, kissed him then offered her congratulations while Maxine waited uneasily. She and Callum had been reunited and arranged their wedding so quickly that Mrs Mackie had had little time to get accustomed to the idea. The open hostility which had marked their first meeting had been replaced by exaggerated politeness and Maxine had been too busy with her wedding arrangements to spend too much time trying to establish a rapport with the woman. When Mrs Mackie turned to her, Maxine smiled warmly but tensed, half-expecting some bitter comment which would ruin the day for Callum. To her amazement Mrs Mackie kissed her quite naturally then held on to her hand while she spoke.

'I don't often admit to being wrong, Maxine, but I know I was terribly wrong about you. I said things to you, and about you, that I bitterly regret. Not just for Callum's sake but because I would like you and I to be friends, if you can find it in your heart to forgive me.'

Maxine saw her mother-in-law's eyes were swimming with tears, felt them wash at the corners of her own eyes and was glad to be able to press her face into the other woman's shoulder for a second.

THIRTY

Maxine slipped out of her pew at the back of the small church and was back outside in the fresh air before the rest of the congregation was properly off its knees. Holding her flowered skirt closely round her thighs in a manner most unbefitting a vicar's wife, especially on a Sunday, she hared round the side of the rather unattractive church and through the low gate which led into the vicarage garden.

Safely through her own back door she kicked off her shoes and switched on the kettle before checking the progress of the roast and setting the potatoes to brown. Satisfied, she gathered the Sunday papers from behind the front door and spread them over the broad, wooden expanse of her immaculately scrubbed kitchen table. There was ample time for a cup of coffee and a quick scan through the headlines before Callum had any hope of getting home. Sunny Sundays were the worst. Half the congregation seemed to want to linger for a chat with their vicar – and with his wife, too, if she didn't manage to escape quickly enough.

It was almost an hour before he came in, still wearing his cassock.

'Something smells good,' he smiled, grabbing her and kissing her deeply while running a hand over her backside, pressing her to him before releasing her with a sigh and collapsing into the opposite chair and claiming a colour supplement.

'Roast beef and the usual trimmings,' she laughed,

509

glancing at the wall clock. 'I told them one o'clock. They'll be here at any minute.'

Even as she spoke there was the sound of crunching footsteps on the gravelled driveway accompanied by chattering, laughing voices. She opened the front door before they could ring the bell and was almost bowled over by her own two offspring, five-year-old Rachel and six-year-old David, who flung themselves at their mother, both talking at the tops of their voices.

'Slow down,' she laughed, ruffling their hair and returning their kisses. 'Dad's in the kitchen.'

They rushed off to greet their father with equal enthusiasm and she turned to welcome her two sisters, then their husbands and their assorted children. Behind them George and Annie helped Ina who, despite increasing age and a definite but unadmitted unsteadiness, insisted on making the short walk through the village every Sunday.

The large old vicarage, always a warm and welcoming place, bubbled with happiness and affection as they all helped to serve the meal then settled informally round the huge kitchen table to eat. It was a ritual and one they all cherished. Sunday being the vicar's busiest day the children, who were considered to be too young for the prolonged services, spent the morning with their grandparents until the whole family then assembled for lunch at the vicarage. It was a time to catch up on news and gossip, to make plans and share confidences. Callum, who had been an only child, revelled in it, this certainty of belonging, of being accepted without question. How right they had been to come here and how generously they had been welcomed back into the comfort of the family.

By five o'clock everyone had left. The children played contentedly in the garden while Callum settled comfortably in the homely sitting room and scanned through his sermon for the evening service. He looked up when his wife came into the room casually dressed in slacks and a roomy jumper.

'Going somewhere?' he asked, amiably.

'Only for a walk. Are you coming?'

'No. I've eaten too much to think about walking.'

'Lazybones,' she accused, good-humouredly.

'I know,' he admitted readily enough. 'But I really should read through this again.' And anyway he knew how she loved to get away on her own once in a while.

'OK. I'll only be about an hour. I thought I'd walk up Tower Hill. I'll be back in time for Evensong,' she assured him as she claimed a farewell kiss.

The bottom of the vicarage garden started to slope up gently into the hill which rose steeply behind the village and protected it from the worst of the biting north winds which blasted across the countryside during the winter.

Once out of the garden she climbed quickly, following the footpath worn down by generations of villagers making for the tower which gave the hill its rather unimaginative name. Local legend insisted that it had been built by Robert the Bruce but she had been unable to find even a thread of evidence to support this theory. It took her a full twenty minutes of energetic effort to reach it. For a moment she just stood there, her eyes closed until she got her breath back, not wanting to open them until she could fully appreciate the view.

It was the view that brought Maxine back here time and time again. Today the weather was so perfect, still and clear, that she knew she would be able to see for miles.

And she could. Sighing with pleasure she gazed south-wards first, over the Forth, about a mile away, to Edinburgh and the hills beyond. West of that she could just glimpse a section of the famous, red-painted railway bridge. To the east a cluster of orange roofs nestling in a niche of the coast was the first of the picturesque fishing villages which gave the Strathannan coast such character. Screwing up her eyes she peered into the distance, squinting for a glimpse of Kilweem, one of the prettiest of them and a village where so much of importance had happened to shape her own life, but it was too far up the coast to be visible from here, even on such a perfect day.

Behind Craigie, to the north, lay grander hills, rising away to the real highlands, blue and distant, hinting of romance and mystery. And, at her feet, Craigie itself, even now, at the height of summer, with a faint, grey pall of smoke hanging over it.

From up here it was possible to see all four mining villages, strung out along the main road which disappeared among trees in the far distance. Behind the villages crouched the pits themselves. From this height the winding gear and clusters of low, brick buildings seemed like toy layouts, the dirt and grime indiscernible.

There was beauty in every acre of her beloved Strathannan, even in the pits. They had been the life-blood of this part of the country, of her own family, breeding strong, resilient people, proud of their heritage, like their cousins from the charming coastal villages who wrested a living from the unforgiving North Sea or the farm workers, battling a harsh climate year in, year out. All natives of Strathannan and proud of it. Like her. Absorbed by all she saw she stood for a few minutes more before turning to make her way home, a mature, married woman, wife of the vicar, mother of two fine children, teacher in the Sunday school and owner of two highly successful restaurants, running and skipping with the joy and abandonment of a five-year-old.

She arrived at the vicarage quite breathless. 'I'm back,' she called out, knowing Callum would be getting ready to go back to the church.

'Maxine . . . Come here a minute,' he called from the living room. 'We've got a visitor.'

'Damn,' she thought, rinsing her hands and face under the cold tap. There were times when the demands of the parishioners could be intrusive. Tonight she had wanted to scan through the applications for the post of manager for the Inverannan restaurant, a position she had filled herself until recently. The acquisition of an old country house which she planned to convert into her third and most prestigious restaurant had left her with too little time to do the job properly.

Callum met her outside the door to their living room, pulling it closed behind him so that their unexpected caller wouldn't hear what he was saying.

'It's a woman,' he smiled, trying to keep the excitement from his face. 'She's come about the job, saw the advertisement in the *Evening News*, recognised your name on it. Says she knows you.'

He opened the door again and steered Maxine inside. 'My wife is here now. I'll leave you ladies to talk.' With a smile for their guest who was seated, deliberately, with her back to the door, he was gone.

'Callum has to take Evensong,' Maxine explained as she crossed the room, intrigued by his odd behaviour. 'You've come about the job?' It was a strange way to make an application but then, if they had met somewhere . . .

'Yes . . . I've been living abroad but I am a fully-qualified cook . . . ' the woman said, still with her back to Maxine.

Maxine stared, her heart hammering.

'Hello, Mary.' The woman rose and, smiling broadly, opened her arms in greeting.

It couldn't be . . . It was . . . Oh God . . .

'Janette?'

The woman nodded.

513

'Janette!' Maxine launched herself into her friend's arms. 'Oh God,' she laughed and cried together. 'I've missed you so much.'

Behind the door where he had been indulging in a little shameless eavesdropping, Callum grinned to himself. Then, satisfied that the reunion was going as it should, he set off for church, humming contentedly to himself.

'So, there was nothing to keep me in Canada after the divorce.' An hour later Janette was reaching the end of her story. 'I always knew it wouldn't work, me and Jamie being separated. We were like strangers in the end. He loved Canada, wanted to stay. I hated it. Right from the start really. I should have had the guts to come home after the first year but . . . well, I thought I should stay, make more of an effort, for his sake.'

'I'm sorry. Sounds like you've had a terrible time,' Maxine sympathised.

'I think we both have.' Janette smiled. 'Still, at least you've got Callum, and he's lovely. And so are the kids.'

'I've been very lucky,' Maxine said, softly. 'I'm so happy it scares me sometimes.'

'Well,' Janette rose, ready to go. 'What about the job?'

Maxine laughed. 'I thought that was a joke. Do you really want it?'

'Yes . . . very much. I'm living with my mum and dad but it's not easy . . . A job with a flat thrown in would be a life-saver. And I did the same sort of job in Montreal. For three years. I've got references. I'm asking you for a favour, I know, but you won't regret it, I promise. I really am good at what I do.'

'You're going to come and live in Inverannan?' Maxine could hardly believe this was true.

'If I get this job,' Janette smiled.

'It's yours. It's yours. Of course it's yours.' Maxine was as excited as a child.

'Thanks. I won't let you down, I promise,' Janette said, softly.

'I know you won't,' Maxine sobbed, completely overcome now. 'Welcome home, Janette. Welcome home.'